Gracielis and Thiercelin were no longer alone in the aisle. Silent over the hard road, a horseman came cantering. His head was high. His cloak stirred with a wind that was not blowing. He was hatless; the hair that streamed behind him was longer than fashion required. His clothing was dark; he had neither braid nor bright buttons. The faint moons' light glinted off the pommel of his sword. His face was in shadow. There was a careless defiance to him, lined in posture, in the very angle of that bare head.

Into the silence, Gracielis heard Thiercelin whisper, "Oh, Valdin."

Gracielis leaned forward in the gloom. He said, "I see him."

"What do we do?"

"We wait."

Mothmoon broke through the clouds, illuminating the road. The rider cast no shadow.

He was closer now. In a few moments he would pass by them or perhaps through them, as though they were the creatures of mist and memory.

His face was unmistakable. A little drawn, a little malcontent. High cheekbones, dark brows. He was bearded, like the most typical street bravo. The hooves of his mount did not quite touch the ground.

There was no more time. Gracielis opened the carriage door and stepped down into the road. He was straight in the path of the rider.

He looked into the eyes of the late Valdarrien of the Far Blays, and spoke the word which compelled a halt . . .

"... Look ..."

LIVING WITH GHOSTS

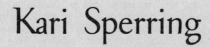

Kari Sperring

DAW BOOKS, INC.

DONALD A. WOLLHEIM, FOUNDER

375 Hudson Street, New York, NY 10014

ELIZABETH R. WOLLHEIM
SHEILA E. GILBERT
PUBLISHERS

www.dawbooks.com

First printing, March 2009
1 2 3 4 5 6 7 8 9

DAW TRADEMARK REGISTERED
U.S. PAT. AND TM. OFF. AND FOREIGN COUNTRIES
—MARCA REGISTRADA
HECHO EN U.S.A.

PRINTED IN THE U.S.A.

To Phil,
who has always wanted to patronize the arts,
with love.

ACKNOWLEDGMENTS

I have been living with this book for a very long time. It has gone through many revisions and rewrites, and many people have helped, encouraged, and supported me along the way. I could probably write another chapter just listing their names. The members of the Apple Writers' Workshop worked their way patiently through the first version; the members of the Milford UK 2007 and Friday the Thirteenth Writers' Workshops read chunks of my most recent revisions. Intermediate versions were painstakingly beta-read by Austin Benson, Nik Ravenscroft, and Jaine Fenn. Storm Constantine and the Immanion Press were kind and generous: thank you. Ian Watson not only copyedited the penultimate version but was hugely supportive. Lisanne Norman has been an inspiration, an ally, a champion, and a dear friend. I also owe huge thanks to my editor at DAW, Sheila Gilbert, for her support and faith and to Chris McGrath for a wonderful cover picture. Finally, my partner Phil Nanson has not simply had to read almost every new draft, but has put up with all the tribulations of living with a writer (and her cats) with patience, fortitude, and immense tolerance.

1

EVEN THE LIEUTENANT'S GHOST looked star-tled as the door slammed shut.

Across the Lower Gold Street coffeehouse, other heads turned to stare. The nobleman who had caused the disruption gazed about him, looking straight through the ghost, then began to make his way toward an alcove at the rear of the salon. Worthy merchants glared at him. Rain dripped off his wide-brimmed hat and splashed on the floor. He wore a rapier under his fine woolen cloak; the end kept catching in the chair backs. He was tall and pleasant-faced, but for all that he did not look to be in the best of tempers.

Seated in the alcove, Gracielis de Varnaq, gigolo and spy, exchanged glances with the ghost. He recognized the nobleman, but he had no desire to talk with him. The circumstances of their first meeting had not been auspicious.

The man halted in front of Gracielis, overlapping the ghost. Gracielis looked up inquiringly.

"I want," said the nobleman, "one hour." Coins dropped one by one from his hand onto the table. Across the coffeehouse, other patrons again turned. "Is that enough?"

Gracielis took hold of himself and smiled. "Perhaps." Pitched soft, his voice carried no further than the table's edge. A faint accent clung to it, alluring as the memory of a perfume. "It would depend on how you wanted to fill the hour."

"Six days," the nobleman said. Gracielis let one brow rise. "Six days it's taken me to find you. I've made an exhibition of myself in half the public salons in the city." Gracielis shrugged, beautiful, apologetic. "Six days. And you say it depends."

"My regrets." Gracielis held out a hand. "Will you sit down?"

The nobleman swore. Gracielis lowered his painted eyes.

"To the river's bed with your airs! Don't you remember me, Gracielis?"

Gracielis looked up. "Do you want me to?"

"Yes!" The nobleman's hand slammed down upon the table. The coins bounced and rolled. One fell. The lieutenant's ghost extended impotent fingers to catch it. Around them the other clients gaped and stared.

"I remember you," Gracielis said. "Lord Thiercelin duLaurier of Sannazar and the Far Blays." Thiercelin sat. The interest from the rest of the coffeehouse began to subside. "I am at your service, monseigneur," Gracielis said.

"One hour," Thiercelin repeated. Gracielis twined his rose-colored lovelock around a finger. Thiercelin continued, "I want to talk to you. That's all."

Looking over the coins, Gracielis selected two, pushed the rest back. He was careful to hide his relief. "You may also," he said, "buy me a drink. Chocolate. I seldom drink wine." At his back, the lieutenant's ghost sneered.

Thiercelin made a sign to a waiter. Then, leaning back in his chair, he said, "You've done well. My wife said you would."

"I'm honored." Gracielis looked down at himself, appraising without vanity. "I wouldn't like to give the lie to a lady." The lieutenant's ghost spat, silent, insubstantial.

"Quite." Thiercelin's tone was dry. "My wife said another thing also."

Here it came. "I don't fight duels."

"Nor I, save with gentlemen."

Gracielis' eyes widened and he bowed. "Forgive me." The ghost laughed soundlessly.

"She said you see ghosts."

Gracielis had been toying with his two coins. Now he stacked them and pushed them back across the table. He said, "I think, monseigneur, you've mistaken my trade."

"No mistake," Thiercelin said. Gracielis shrugged, picking up his cloak. Thiercelin continued, "Six years ago we witnessed a duel, you and I. Both combatants were killed. One of them was my best friend. Valdin." Gracielis reached for the two-colored gloves that signaled his public profession. Thiercelin put a hand on them. The lieutenant's ghost grinned, exposing decaying, phantom teeth.

Thiercelin said, "Eight nights ago I saw him again."

Gracielis let his hand drop back to his side. The ghost was still laughing. "As you said, both men died. How could you see one of them?"

"The watch-captain wanted you flogged for collusion in those deaths. My wife bought your pardon," Thiercelin said. "Don't you think you owe me a hearing?"

Gracielis drew in a breath. His eyes flickered sideways to look at the lieutenant's ghost.

Leaning across the table, Thiercelin's face was strangely defenseless. "Six years ago. I held Valdin's hands as he lay dying. I saw him buried. Eight nights ago, I saw him again, in the royal aisle. He hadn't aged a day."

"Ghosts don't," Gracielis said. "So they say."

Thiercelin looked at his hands. "It was Valdin. He smiled at me . . . I thought I was seeing things. The next night . . ," He shrugged. "Nothing."

"You have your answer, then." Gracielis said. "You don't need me."

The waiter arrived with the chocolate, put it down on the table. He glanced at Gracielis curiously. Thiercelin said, "You could sit down and drink it, at least."

Gracielis hesitated.

"Please."

It was not a lord's place to plead. Gracielis sat, the motion oddly graceless. Thiercelin said, "I need your help. My wife wouldn't lie to me."

"I can't help you."

"You're the only other witness to that death. I'm willing to pay you. I . . ."

"I can't help you." Gracielis repeated. He reached across the table, took one of Thiercelin's hands in his. "Forgive me. I can't."

"Why not?"

"It's forbidden."

"Forbidden? But . . ."

Gracielis squeezed his hand. "Yes. Try to forget this. It was a trick of the shadows, nothing more."

Thiercelin took his hand away. "You're wrong."

Gracielis rose, shaking his head. "Forget," he repeated, turning to go.

Alongside him, the lieutenant's ghost made an obscene gesture of triumph.

In the street outside it was raining. Gracielis held one hand out, and the corners of his mouth twitched very slightly. He pulled his hat down over his eyes and wrapped his cloak about himself. The lieutenant's ghost sneered. He looked at it in momentary thought, then shook his head and turned away down the street.

It was not given to every man to see ghosts. More annoyingly, it was given to even fewer to choose not to see them. Walking, he remembered every necessary bow and smile to passing acquaintances, but inside, he turned Thiercelin's words over and over. He had lived with his gifts all his life, but he had always taken care to hide them from others. To do otherwise courted danger; especially here, especially for a foreigner and an exile. Even in his native Tarnaroq, his abilities could arouse suspicion. Here in Merafi, exposure could mean death. And besides, he was bound. The terms of his exile allowed him little freedom. He was permitted only the lesser arts, of seduction, of allure.

This was the quality of Gracielis de Varnaq; with him all things were a matter of grace. His manner was chosen to disarm, his words to please. His charm was beyond dispute. He was very expensive. Living off the finite fruits of his beauty, he had made sure of that early. He was twenty-six years old.

He had refused to help Thiercelin. In the doorway of a fashionable confectioner, he paused and looked back over his shoulder. His gaze passed through the lieutenant's ghost, dodging disquiet. Some streets away, a guild clock struck a quarter to five. He owed nothing to Thiercelin. The ghost watched him with spiteful eyes, giving no aid. Thiercelin would be gone, and Gracielis had an appointment to keep. He took one halfhearted step back the way he had come and stopped. It was no concern of his. It was, anyway, forbidden.

Forbidden. He looked at the ghost and spoke a soft word. The insubstantial form wavered, clutched, faded. Gracielis put out a hand to the doorjamb, face paler than before. The post was damp, leaving a dark stain on his white lace cuff. He brushed at it, absently. Then he straightened and turned his back to the street. To the side of the confectioner's ran a short passage. Halfway along it was a green-painted door. He knocked twice and waited.

The old woman who opened it did not look pleased to see him. "You're late."

"I'm desolated."

"You're to wait."

She made no move to take his cloak or hat. As he turned toward a door off the hall, she said sharply, "Not there. Upstairs." And then, as she locked the front door, "The small room. You know the way."

"Of course." His foot on the stair, he stopped and bowed to her. "Thank you for your kindness." She scowled. He lowered his gaze and headed up the stairs.

There was a room at the end of the short corridor. It was simply furnished: a high-post bed, chairs, a long dresser. Entering, he took off his hat and dropped it on the washstand. He folded his cloak over a chair. The casement was half-closed. Opening it, he looked down into the yard. It was still raining. The light was beginning to fade. Somewhere, a dog barked. A woman's voice rose to scold it. He could see shadowy forms beyond the windows of the house opposite. There were no sounds from the rooms below him.

He sat on the window ledge and drew a small comb from his pocket. There were no candles. He could just about make out his reflection in the pane. His hair was damp. He set himself to groom it, neatly methodical.

He heard no footfalls on the stairs. He did hear the door open, but by then he was standing, hand white on the comb, as the air brought him the whisper of a name. Sweet musk—and amber and bitter orange. He controlled a shiver as memory supplied him with a face. Without turning, he said, "I was expecting a minion. This is an honor. *Chai ela,* Quenfrida."

Quenfrida did not smile. She said, "Are you disappointed?" He could see her reflection in the window. He watched as she set a candlestick on a chest and lit it with a word.

Her perfume was making him dizzy. There had to be a reason for her presence. The Tarnaroqui spy-mistress here in Merafi seldom troubled herself with him. He said, "Of course not."

They were not speaking the local tongue, Merafien, but their native Tarnaroqui. She lifted the jug from the washstand and poured water into the ewer. There was no towel. Turning, he offered her his handkerchief. The offer was made just a little before she realized the need.

She took it, drying her hands. "I wish you wouldn't do that."

"I beg your pardon. But it costs me nothing to help."

"Indeed." She leaned against the dresser. "But it costs me something to accept it. You overextend yourself."

"I ask your forgiveness."

"Do you?" Her voice smiled. "Have it, then."

"Thank you."

"It costs me nothing."

There was a small moment of silence. He played with his lace, still trying not to look at her. She said, "You have something for me?" And then, "Gracielis? You must have something to report." She had crossed the room toward him. Now she placed a hand upon his breast. She said, "You were late today."

"I was delayed."

"Really?" It was hard not to look at her. The bodice of her plain gown was fastened at the front. Almost casually, she began to loosen it, so that the sleeve tops slid away from her shoulders. He followed the motion, a faint flush heating his skin. She smiled and reached up to unpin her hair. He looked away. Her laugh was deep and not entirely kind. He was her creature utterly, and she knew it. "Sit down," she said, softly.

He sat on the bed, looking at his feet. Cloth rustled as she let her gown drop to her ankles. She said, "You haven't told me your news."

"I have none," he said to the floor.

"None? I'd heard otherwise."

"Then you heard wrongly."

"I did? My sources are usually reliable." She was brushing her hair, heavy and scented across her white shoulders. "You'd do well to remember that."

"I do."

"Of course." There was another silence, as she worked the brush through a knot. He kept his eyes downcast, feeling the pulse beat rapidly through his blood. He had not anticipated her presence. He had not had time to raise his defenses. From outside no sounds were audible.

She laid the brush down. "You're getting careless. One might suspect that your loyalty was failing. That's not healthy."

"I do what I may."

"Do you?" The bedsprings creaked as she sat down beside him. "You erred today, in banishing your shadow."

"It was annoying me."

"You had not the right. You know the limits of your bond." One of her hands tangled in his hair. He shivered. She said, "However, I'm disposed to be lenient."

He closed his eyes. The fingers strayed beneath the neck of his shirt. He said, "You are too kind." It should have been sarcasm. The last word betrayed him, blurring almost to a gasp as she traced the top of his spine.

"You have a new patron, I hear."

"I have several."

She gave one long lock a sharp tug, and he winced. "Look at me."

He drew in a deep breath, turned. She was clad only in her fine shift, cut low over her breasts. "That's better," she said. Her hand left his back, and moved to caress a cheekbone. Her perfume drowned him. One of his hands rose to imprison hers. She twined her fingers about it, stroking his palm.

"I don't want . . ." he began.

She shook her head at him. "Thiercelin duLaurier of Sannazar and the Far Blays has been seen looking for you. Has he found you?" She leaned toward him, and her hair brushed his face.

"It wasn't important," Gracielis said. He was trembling.

"You have seen him, then. What did he want?" She leaned even closer, sky-blue eyes looking straight into his.

"It was nothing. A mistake."

She kissed him. He groaned, resentful, as his arms slid round her. Her hands explored him, unbuttoning his doublet. He pulled free and buried his face in her hair. She pushed the doublet aside and began to undo his shirt. "You're sure of that?"

He closed his eyes, inhaling her perfume. Her skin was smooth beneath his touch. She finished with his shirt and moved onto his breeches. Hands clenching, he said, "I'm sure."

She pushed him away. "Don't waste my time. What did he want?"

He rubbed a hand across his face. "Nothing useful. Truly."

"What did he want?"

Thiercelin's face, curiously bereft . . . An old memory of cold and gunshot and blood. An older one, from the days before his exile, when she had loved him. Her hands caressed his chest, gentle, tormenting. "Nothing I could give him." He bit down on his lip, hard. Her hands strayed lower and he gasped in unwilling pleasure. "A ghostseer. He wanted a ghostseer." Shame was a dark flood within him. Thiercelin's image eddied and faded.

Quenfrida took his face in her hands. Fighting her perfume, her presence, he said, "I can do nothing. You know that."

"Bonds may be loosened for certain purposes."

"I can't." His breathing was quick and shallow, his skin slick with sweat. "It's a private matter to him."

"I'm not asking you to hurt him." She recommenced her caresses. "I'm only asking you to do what you're trained to do. What you've vowed to do. Help him. Renew your acquaintance with his wife. Serve Tarnaroq." She pushed him back against the thin pillows, curled herself against him. His hands somehow found their way to the lacing on her shift.

She was pliant, making no resistance. He let himself be drawn closer, then kissed her as though it could hurt. She smiled as she pulled free. "Well?" Her tone suggested that all things were possible. Her hands reinforced the suggestion.

He shivered. Her perfume was a cloud around him. "Go to him," she said, "Go, and tell him you've changed your mind. Help him a little."

"Why?" Her arms twined about him. He was forgetting to breathe.

Her smile became languid. "We'll see." Her hands ceased teasing and grew urgent. He rolled over, trapping them.

There was no choice. Nevertheless, "I hate you," he said, as he succumbed to her.

She spoke the word that caused the candle to go out, and then, "I know."

He woke alone. His clothing had been folded and placed on the chest. The memory of Quenfrida's perfume clung to his skin and hair. The lieutenant's ghost watched him from the end of the bed. Rising, Gracielis washed and dressed mechanically. The water in the jug was warm and herb-scented. The small wall-mounted mirror showed clear eyes, fresh skin. Recollections of pleasure still shivered through his veins. He felt wonderful.

He hated himself.

Quenfrida had left a small purse atop the pile of his clothing. His pride wanted desperately to leave it. He owed his landlord a half-month's rent. He had to eat, to clothe himself, to buy the necessities of his life. He counted the coins out onto the chest, took enough for his immediate needs. The remainder he left lying, whore's price, on the rumpled bed.

He was alone in the house. He shut the main door behind him and made his way out into the street. It was perhaps an hour after dawn. The rain had stopped some time in the night, though the air was still damp. A faint mist, child of the river, hung over Merafi, deepest in the harbor quarter and the old city island, light as a veil over the aristocratic houses on the high eastern edge.

The cobbled streets were already full. Shop wares obstructed the dry places beneath the houses, and carts made a chaos of the wider thoroughfares. Dodging across the gallows-square, he took a sharp side turn under the Farriers' Guildhall and emerged from the concealed passageway, the traboule opposite the Dancing Bridge. From there, he climbed the lesser stairs to the side of the Island Temple and paid the two sous to use the Priests' Bridge over the river's northern arm. On the opposite bank, he could see the thick walls and low towers of the Old Palace. The toll keeper smiled at him knowingly. "You're early. Client lost interest, Gracieux?"

Gracielis shrugged, graceful as his street name. "She's exhausted."

The toll keeper laughed. "Well, your lies are pretty enough, anyway."

The lieutenant's ghost grinned in sour agreement. Gracielis bowed and passed on over the bridge and out into the wider streets of northwest Merafi. Day came later here, amidst the half-timbered houses of this residential quarter. It was only on the quayside that there was much activity. Walking upriver toward the Gran' Théâtre, his pace slowed somewhat. Almost, he frowned.

A few of his fellow professionals were still working along Silk Street. As he crossed, one of them hailed him, waving her yellow scarf. He smiled at her on reflex and bowed without halting. The lieutenant's ghost leered. She hesitated, then raised her voice and called after him. "Gracieux!"

He stopped and looked back. "Sylvine?" She was young, but her figure tended to the plump. She panted a little as she caught up with him. She looked faintly harassed. Hovering, the ghost leaned toward her, face unkind. "Is something wrong?"

It seemed unlikely. His fellow professionals did not turn to him in need. His reputation for polite disinterest discouraged this. And then, he was not native. He considered her. She returned his gaze with some irritation. She said, "It's too sticky for running. Why didn't you wait?"

"Forgive me. I'm remiss."

"Evidently." She did not sound mollified. He sighed, and looked away with a pretty air of contrition. She added, "Oh, don't play off on me. I know how much you mean it. You're in trouble."

He looked up. "What?"

"There's someone looking for you."

He relaxed. "Indeed. Thiercelin of Sannazar and the Far Blays. I met him yesterday."

"Oh." She pouted, put out.

"But it's good of you to tell me."

"I suppose."

He bowed to her and began to walk away. He had barely taken two steps before she ran after him and shoved him, hard, against the wall. From a window above, someone emptied the contents of a chamber pot into the street below.

Gracielis swallowed. Then he said, "Thank you."

"Wouldn't want to to spoil that finery, would we?"

He kissed her fingers, and she pulled her hand away. She added, "You owe me. See you remember it."

He said, "I will." Her only reply was a shrug. He bowed a second time and turned. His lodgings lay a few streets away, across the Chandlers' Square and into the merchants' quarter. As he reached the corner of Silk Street, Sylvine started to wave, thought better of it. The lieutenant's ghost made a valedictory, obscene gesture in her direction.

Gracielis shook his head at it. "No manners," he said, gentle, reproving. It sneered.

Not all women were Quenfrida. Perhaps.

Across the city, the mist was starting to lift.

*   *   *

Thiercelin of Sannazar woke late, with a hangover, and found his household proceeding quite comfortably without him. He felt too ill to ride or practice fencing, but left to his own devices could find nothing else to do. His sister-in-law was entertaining a particularly rowdy group of friends in the green salon. His wife was deep in governmental paperwork in her study. There were bags under his eyes, and, dressing, he had found three gray strands in his untidy hair.

It was not a satisfactory start to the day.

He prowled the corridors, glowering at passing servants and chewing the ends of his mustache. His wife, encountering him in the long gallery, smiled and asked, "When does the ax fall, Thierry?"

He turned the glower on her. "Yesterday. At least my head thinks so."

Yvelliane d'Illandre of the Far Blays gave his cheek an affectionate pat. "Poor love. Take a powder and consult me in the morning."

He snarled. She reached up to kiss his cheek and made to pass on. He caught her arm. "Yviane, wait."

"Yes?" Her face was quizzical. He slid his hand down to take hers. He wished he knew what she was thinking. He wished he knew what to say to her. *I saw Valdin. I saw your brother, who is dead.* He had no idea at all how she might react to such a statement. Perhaps she would be angry. Perhaps she would think he had taken to deep drinking. Perhaps, if he was lucky, she would worry about him.

Beside him, she was restless. Her hand wriggled within his. "What is it? I have work."

There was always work. He looked down at her hem. "It's just . . . You look nice."

She snorted. "In this dress? You're tired. Go back to bed." And pulling her hand free, she kissed him and went on down the hall. He watched her go with a wistful expression. She was right, of course. Her medium-gray dress drained the color from her skin and did no favors for her dark hair and eyes. He was, as ever, a fool.

Their marriage had been a court wonder, coming as it had only a handful of weeks after Valdarrien's death. *Confused by grief*, said the gossips, for why else would the Queen's First Councillor marry a penniless younger son whose only claim to status was his friendship with her late brother? Thiercelin himself had never been sure if that was true: he had taken care not to ask. He knew only that he had loved Yvelliane for all his adult life, and he would accept whatever fragments of her attention she could spare for him.

The portraits in the gallery regarded him with inscrutable gazes. He resumed pacing. At the gallery end, he stopped, and looked back.

Gray eyes met his. A figure stood partway up the main stair, posed before a mirror . . . *ghosts can't possibly have reflections* . . . Thiercelin, held in the reflected gaze, took a step forward, put a hand out in greeting . . . *Valdin was always vain, I never saw him pass that way without looking in that mirror* . . . Another step. Gray eyes flickered, and were gone.

There was a settle close to where Thiercelin stood. Breathing hard, he sank down upon it, put his head in his hands. Valdin, his ten-year friend and ally, rakehell, troublemaker, and duelist. Living perpetually on the edge of exile and disgrace, his very name a byword for scandal, much feared, much loved, and dead at the age of twenty-five. Six years dead. Memories chased one another. Two youths, still almost boys, racing, fighting, playing. Older, promenading arm in arm, courting the same ladies, espousing the same violent causes. Older yet, and play grown serious, Valdin stocking-footed in the chill dawn, infuriating his cautious sister Yvelliane, and smiling as he killed . . . Valdin, Valdin, Valdin . . .

The family pictures included one of the late Valdarrien d'Illandre of the Far Blays—Valdin to his family and intimates. Raising his head, Thiercelin stared at it, and sighed. Dark hair and cynical gray eyes, smile polite in boredom—Valdin, caught by some fashionable artist a year or two before his death. Before a stranger broke his heart and left him to find his cheap death in an inn yard. Thiercelin's throat contracted. He swallowed. "You fool," he said to the portrait, "you thrice-damned bloody fool."

There was no reply, now as ever. He rubbed a hand over his eyes. They were brown, perhaps two shades darker than his collar-length hair. He was a slender man and tall with it, and not quite handsome. He was not given to superstition. Yet he could not come to terms with the impossible evidence of his eyes. "I saw him die," he whispered, now, into his hands. A trick of the light, Gracielis had said, and part of Thiercelin wanted to believe him. A trick of the light, or a trick of the tongue . . . Perhaps he could have believed that explanation, if it were not for that sudden discomfort in the man whose aid he had sought. Gracielis de Varnaq saw ghosts. Yvelliane would think Thiercelin mad, if he told her that, suddenly, he also saw them. Yvelliane could not be told. She was far too busy. He could not disturb her with something as unlikely as this. It would, in all probability, only make her think less of him.

Gracielis had known that Thiercelin spoke the truth and refused him aid. Thiercelin looked again at Valdarrien's picture, and this time his fist slammed into his opposite hand.

"Thierry?" The touch on his shoulder made him jump. His sister-in-law Miraude stood at his elbow, regarding him quizzically. "Is something wrong?"

Briefly, he considered confiding in her, Valdarrien's widow who had never been a wife. Instead, he smiled and said, "I was counting my blessings. It always depresses me."

"I'm not surprised." She pulled a face and sat down beside him. "It always makes me feel small."

"I think it's supposed to be character-building."

"Hmm. Well, my character must be unusually flimsy."
She looked down at herself, half-mocking, half-admiring.
"I'd stop, if I were you."

"I think I will." He considered her, not without some
amusement. Yvelliane had once remarked that it was a
good thing that Miraude had independent means, for
otherwise it was unlikely that even the Far Blays' revenues could support her. Her present gown was an exotic
confection of embroidery and pearl-strewn lace. She intercepted his gaze and smiled.

"Do you like it?"

"Very smart. New?"

"Yes."

"It's charming."

"It's for the masquerade in the Winter Gardens, the
queen of the peacocks." Her eyes laughed, acknowledg-
ing his amusement at her choice of costume.

"Very appropriate." Thiercelin sobered. "You're going
to that? I'd have thought it would be rather rowdy."

She favored him with a sardonic gaze. "You, of
course, would never have done such a thing in your
youth."

He was thirty-three. Controlling a smile, he said, "In
my youth, I committed all sorts of follies. Of, course,
I'm too incapacitated by age now to do anything at all."

"I didn't mean . . ."

"I know." He let the smile escape. "And I wasn't
criticizing. I was just worrying."

"You could come with me if you like. I'm due to meet
up with friends, but they won't mind."

"Wouldn't I be in the way?"

"I don't see why. And anyway, you look like you need
cheering up. Masquerades are much more cheering
than blessings."

"Valdin would've agreed with you." His eyes flickered
again to Valdarrien's portrait.

She followed the look. Her expression was curious.
She said, "You still miss him." It was not a question.

"He was my best friend."

"Yes." There was a dryness to her voice. "I wonder about him, sometimes. I suppose I didn't know him very well."

Into Thiercelin's mind came again the memory of a narrow, cobbled yard, strewn with straw and blood. Miraude had been barely sixteen. He said, "He was fond of you, I think."

"Yes. But fonder of you."

There was no answer to that.

The lieutenant's ghost sprawled on the daybed, occluding the brocade covers with misty distaste, eyes enviously on a crystal decanter. Drinking water, Gracielis raised his glass to it and turned to look in the mirror. Meeting his gaze, Amalie Viron said, "I shall look ridiculous. I'm too old for masquerades, love."

She was forty-six. Of all his patrons, she was the only one to have told him her true age at once, as if expecting it to be a cause of rejection. It had not been. Her business provided her with funds enough to afford most things she wanted, and he had known it. That in itself was reason enough to become her lover, but her honesty had touched and surprised him. He did not expect to be trusted by his patrons, only paid.

He had been her lover for five years, and of all those who bought and sold his body, she was the only one for whom he felt anything, at least that he admitted to himself. He tried to acknowledge nothing of his feelings where Quenfrida was concerned. Now, he put down his glass and rose. "That's heresy, Ladyheart. I won't hear it."

"Oh, won't you?" She laughed, and, unexpectedly, the ghost laughed with her.

"Indeed not." Coming to stand behind her, he dropped a kiss on her bare shoulder. "And more. I won't let you say it, or feel you have reason to."

"If only. I can give you twenty years."

"The twenty fairest years in Merafi." He took the comb from her, lace cuff trailing across her skin. "Let me do this."

"Not even you can make me young again." She sounded sad. He lifted her hand and kissed it. She squeezed his fingers.

"I wouldn't want to," he said. "For if you were, I'd have to go in fear of your husband. I'd have to duel him for you, and I have the most lowering suspicion that I'd lose."

"Poor love." She turned his hand over and kissed the palm. "Well, then, I'll guard my years." She drew a finger along the vein in his wrist, pushing back the cuff. Beneath the lace was a bruise. Touching it, she said, "You don't look after yourself."

Sometimes, Quenfrida liked to mark her property. He said, "Forgive me."

"I worry about you."

He took his hand away and began to brush her hair. The lieutenant's ghost had moved to stand in the window, back turned. "Do not, I beg you. You mustn't worry."

"Oh, mustn't I?"

"Indeed." He smiled at her in the mirror. "For two reasons." She looked inquiring. "Firstly, because I'm telling you the truth. And secondly, because anxiety makes you frown, and destroys your peace; and if I find myself a cause of distress to you, I'll weep."

"Oh, well, we can't have that," said Amalie. Reflected palely in the glass, the lieutenant's ghost demurred. Even with his hands safe upon Amalie's vital flesh, Gracielis was still chill with this knowledge of his own ill-marked boundaries.

Quenfrida would have him cross them, for the sake of Thiercelin of Sannazar, whom she had no cause to love. For Thiercelin's sake or, more likely, her own.

Gracielis had no desire to obey. He had no choice. On Amalie's rosewood secretaire, beside his gloves and serpent mask, lay a note in his neat hand addressed to Thiercelin. Amalie's housekeeper would see it was delivered.

And he would do as he had been bid. His fingers combed through Amalie's hair, and his reflected eyes caressed hers in the mirror, but he was apart behind his painted face. There was some question of history between Quenfrida and Thiercelin's clever wife Yvelliane, a half-healed wound, rooted in the years that Quenfrida had spent in exile in the northern principality of Lunedith. Quenfrida's presence there had been, he suspected, a punishment for her failure with himself. Yet she had returned from Lunedith creamily satisfied. She would use him for the slow unraveling of Yvelliane d'Illandre, if she could. If he was weak enough.

He didn't want to think about it. Pulling away from his thoughts, he smiled at Amalie. "There," he said, "it's done." She looked at herself, then up at him. "Well?" He made his eyes huge. "You do like it?" She hesitated. His expression played anxiety. "Ladyheart . . ."

"I like it." She shook her head at him. "Perhaps I should employ you full time."

He let his eyes slide sideways to the daybed. "I don't deserve it." The ghost signed scornful agreement.

"You'll do," said Amalie.

"Whoops," said Thiercelin, sidestepping. And then, "Shall I diet, do you think?"

Miraude looked sidelong at him from the almond slits in her mask. "Probably not. Oh, look out behind you!"

"How?" said Thiercelin, twisting. The ground was still damp after a day of intermittent rain. The air showed a tendency to mistiness, not helped by the damply smoking torches. Both moons had risen, but neither provided much light. Clouds hid Handmoon; Mothmoon showed only in crescent. "I'll only knock off somebody's hat," Thiercelin continued, "That was your foot again, wasn't it?"

"I'm not sure." Miraude said, "Oh, Thierry, do give it up!"

"Is my dancing that bad?"

"No. But this crush!"

"I warned you."

"I know, I know. It'll be better in a bit, when they finish erecting the covers."

"Hmm." Leading his partner carefully through the crowd in the dance arena, Thiercelin was unconvinced. He couldn't recall a public masquerade that had not been overpopulated and frantic, but this one was surely worse than average. It was the inclement weather, perhaps, or some obscure side effect of the strike in the docks. Even so, the administration of the event seemed to have dissolved. Too many tickets sold, too many small disasters . . .

Held in the Winter Gardens, the ball was open to anyone who could afford the admission price. Masked in satin, in cotton, in buckram and canvas and figured brocade, the bourgeoisie picked their way through the artisans and laborers, and the nobility flirted with the playful children of innkeepers and shop owners. An insufficient number of pavilions had been pitched, supplying (in theory at least) refreshment and shelter. Torches burned in tree-mounted sconces, smokily lighting the dance floor and the promenades. The music of two orchestras vied for attention with the shrieks of food vendors and the thunderous small talk of the pressing throng.

It was a great pity that it kept raining. The discreet back alleys and bowers were discouragingly damp and the footing uncertain. There was going to be a great deal of work for Merafi's laundries and a great number of body servants honored with gifts of mud-stained finery. Thiercelin, who had never minded sacrificing elegance to comfort, had thoughtfully dressed *en chevalier* and, moreover, rolled his bucket boots up to their highest limit. He had been rather startled when, in the carriage, Miraude had untied the points on her long bodice; but his surprise had turned to amused admiration when she stepped out of her skirt to reveal matching breeches beneath. "In this rain," she had said, laughing, "being my height will be disadvantage enough without having petticoats everywhere." He had conceded the point readily. Her dark head did not quite reach his shoulder: in the milling press of masqueraders, she might easily be trampled.

One arm carefully about her shoulders, he picked out a route to the edge of the dance floor and looked around for seats. The pavilions and covered areas were full, as were most of the nearby tables, but a little judicious use of his elbows secured for them a section of a wide bench built around the bole of a lime tree. "There," he said, and sighed. "I'm exhausted."

"Poor thing." Miraude wrapped her cloak around her and sat hugging her knees. "Sorry you came?"

"Certainly not. Although your friends seem to have thought better of it."

"Hmmm . . ." Miraude looked around her. "I'm sure they'll be here soon. In fact I think I see some of them over by the Wave Fountain." She paused, frowning. Then she said, "Why don't you go and find us some drinks and meet me there?"

"I'm not sure I should leave you."

"I'll be fine. Go on." And she gave him a small push.

"All right, then." He bowed to her and began to try to make his way through to the refreshments. The crowd about the dance arena had not thinned out; his progress was painfully slow, and he began to wonder how exactly he was going to carry back the promised refreshments even remotely intact. He'd need a tray, or a bell, or spiked elbow pads . . .

Someone stumbled into him from behind. Thiercelin cursed as he stepped into a muddy pool of water. Rehearsed in the hazards of these fêtes, he put a hand over his purse and looked around. He had not been robbed; the man behind him was simply off balance. Reassured,

Thiercelin began to move on. Shafts of light from both
moons struck downward from a sudden gap in the clouds.
And then . . . About him, the noise and crowd of the
masquerade dropped away as memory laid hard hands
on him and shook. Underfoot, churned grass and mud
gave way to flagstones.

The air was thick with soot and sour ale. A small
group of soldiers pressed around him, calling insults at
a young man who fought his way toward the narrow
staircase. *This can't be right, this was six years ago.* Despite himself, despite his disbelief, Thiercelin turned and
found himself gazing into the frowning gaze of Valdarrien d'Illandre. The Pineapple. This was the Pineapple,
the cheap inn where Valdarrien had been killed. Thiercelin swallowed, "Valdin?"

"What?" Valdarrien set his beer mug down on the
table with a thump.

"You . . . That is . . ."

"You can't be drunk, not on this stuff." Valdarrien
said.

"No, but . . ." *Not drunk . . . That had to be true, he
hadn't touched anything stronger than watered wine all
day. This could not be happening.* Thiercelin shook his
head to clear it and found himself looking straight at the
young man on the stairs.

Gracielis. Six years younger and a lot less self-
possessed. *This is how it started, with Gracielis and the
soldiers. And with me . . .* One of the soldiers, an infantry
lieutenant, blew a kiss to Gracielis. "New doublet, is it?
Was that a gift from the lovely Yvelliane of the Far
Blays?"

"I bought it myself," Gracielis said.

"But she paid for it, yes?"

"I don't like to discuss ladies in public." Gracielis
bowed and made to continue up the stairs.

The lieutenant laughed. And then, "Yvelliane isn't a
lady, she's a . . ."

No . . . But despite himself, Thiercelin leaped to his feet, fists clenched. *I don't want to go through this, not again.* At his side, Valdarrien laid a hand on his arm. "Don't."

But Thiercelin had paid no attention. He could not change that now. He said coldly, "Apologize for that."

The lieutenant sketched a bow. "My humble apologies, I didn't realize we had gentlemen present." His tone was anything but apologetic.

Valdarrien rose. "Come on, Thierry, let's get out of here."

"Of course," the lieutenant drawled from behind them, "you wouldn't expect much better of a lady whose brother kept a barbarian whore for a mistress."

Valdarrien whirled on his heel and spat in the lieutenant's face. There was a short silence. Then Valdarrien said, "You'll give me satisfaction for that. I'll prove the lie in your blood."

The lieutenant looked him up and down. "I'd be delighted. If you're sure you want a lesson from a real fighter." He fingered the pistol at his belt. "Shall we?"

Valdarrien bowed with exaggerated politeness. "I'd be delighted."

Thiercelin said urgently, "Valdin, don't . . ." But Valdarrien pushed him away and stalked out through the inn's side door.

In the yard ouside, it was cold. The cobbles underfoot were slippery with straw, and the place reeked of urine. One of the lieutenant's friends provided a second pistol; Valdarrien barely looked at it before taking his place in front of the tumbledown stable. *Nothing about this was regular. Why didn't I stop him?* But no one had ever been able to stop Valdarrien in this mood, not Thiercelin, not Yvelliane, not even his beloved Iareth Yscoithi. In the dim light of the inn's windows, the two men took aim. There was a moment's stillness.

"Fire."

Two shots echoed off the walls. For a moment, Valdarrien stood there, smiling faintly, as the lieutenant folded to the ground. Then he swayed, paled, dropped. The front of his shirt was dark with blood.

When Thiercelin reached him, he was already dead.

"Monseigneur." *That happened, too, I remember that voice.* Hands had hold of Thiercelin, shaking him. "Monseigneur de Sannazar." He looked down and found his gaze intercepted by the multifaceted eyes of a snake.

He stepped back, shivering. The glittering eyes watched him dispassionately for a few seconds, then blinked out as their owner swept off his plumed hat and bowed.

"Monseigneur de Sannazar." Heavy auburn curls brushed along the serpent mask, perfumed as the voice which greeted him. Thiercelin swallowed, said nothing. Gracielis continued: "I owe you an apology."

Rather feebly, Thiercelin said, "You do?" None of this made any sense. Gracielis had been there in the inn yard when Valdarrien had been killed. But now . . . He swallowed. "I'm not sure I . . ."

Gracielis looked down. "Indeed. I'm willing to help you."

I don't need your help. I didn't see anything. Only Valdin, at home, and here and now this . . . Gracielis had raised his eyes to watch him: it was impossible to read his expression behind the snake mask. *What would he do, if I told him* . . . Thiercelin could not think. He said stiffly, "I see."

"I sent you a note, but . . ." Gracielis hesitated, looking a little over Thiercelin's shoulder. He seemed to be thinking. Then he drew in a breath and bowed again. "Good night, monseigneur."

"Yes," Thiercelin said. "Good night, then." Gracielis had already turned to go, offering an arm to a trim woman in dark red. Thiercelin straightened, tugged at his collar. He felt light-headed, confused. He should have asked Gracielis, right here, right now. He did not want to think about it, any of it. He wanted to go home and drink and forget everything. The rain was no longer light: he drew his cloak about him, deciding to abandon the quest for refreshments, and take Miraude home. The weather would quench the enthusiasm of the masqueraders. Strange that Gracielis had recognized him, masked . . .

The park was lit up by a sudden lightning flash.

2

IT WAS BEGINNING TO LOOK as though the rain
would never let up. The cobbles were treacherous with
mud; passing carts a hazard to vanity. The rain coated
Merafi in gloom, dripping from carved eaves and roof
posts, collecting in gutters, descending in sudden deluges
from overburdened awnings. Gracielis walked the length
of Silk Street and smiled absently at his fellow whores,
hovering damply in doorways. He did not stop. At the
street's head, he crossed into a congested thoroughfare,
cloak held tight. People pressed close around him: servants, housekeepers with laden baskets, farmers in from
the surrounding countryside to sell vegetables or poultry,
factors and beggars, middle-class ladies and their maids,
apprentices and day laborers. Guild masters or burgesses
strode by, using their elbows and the points of their
canes. Merchants and seafarers from six or seven different countries jostled against egg sellers and flower sellers. The occasional aristocrat passed by in a carriage,
coachmen hollering for the crowd to make way. Street
cries echoed from the sides of temples, rumbled along
the arcades, and rattled through the congested squares.
In the air hung a new tension, an anxiety not wholly
weather-borne.

Changes hung in the rain, nearly visible to Gracielis. It
was a slender thing, fragile as the reflection of a reflection.
The lieutenant's ghost, stalking maliciously through the

fishwives and the carters, was filled with glee, his form
edged with faint, static light. Changes, thought Gracielis,
and could not quite control the shiver that ran through
him. *If I had not failed, if I had been chosen, if I had
been someone else . . .*

It was forbidden. He was Quenfrida's one flaw, her
one mistake. He should not have failed his initiation; he
should not have been able to fail. She had given too
much by the end, so that the gift might not be wholly
withdrawn from him. (Except in death. But her calm,
balancing hands had not seen that route for him, not
then, not yet.) Anomaly, failed priest, flawed lover, reluctant spy—his fault and hers. An obscure comfort,
that. Just as Quenfrida was his one weakness, so was he
hers. For she should have chosen better.

He reached the edge of the road, the dry place under
the overhang of the old buildings, and began to pick his
way through the press of people. The arcades were lined
with stores and workshops: tailors, print shops, spice factors, cloth merchants. It was said you could buy almost
everything somewhere in Merafi. In this district, the
goods being offered were mostly luxuries: fabrics and
trimmings for high-class finery, fine bound books, trin-
kets of silver filigree or ivory or porcelain. In the
squares, stalls sold fresh fruit, vegetables, and flowers.
On the corners, peddlers sold ribbons and needles or
hawked hot chestnuts from their trays. Down the side
streets, he could glimpse small cabarets, some already
open for business, rubbing shoulders with patisseries and
perfumers. When the wind shifted, it brought with it
hints of the fishmarket on the other bank of the river,
or the bloody scent of the shambles. Through open doorways the floors of shops were trampled and muddied,
wares pulled back from the damp, attendants peevish
with chill. Too many people were packed here to avoid
the wet and the mud. There was a smell of stale wine
and soggy wool and worse things. Fastidious, he wove

his way through the unwonted press. The ghost mocked him, smug with his discomfort. He would, at that moment, have greatly enjoyed the indulgence of irritation.

He was silken charm to the bone.

It was a slow progress. Aware of the danger of being late, he began to work his way back to the road and the downpour. Better wet than impolite. Coming to the edge of the shelter, he ducked his head against the rain and pulled his cloak even tighter. His boots were going to require a great deal of work to restore their shine. A man pushing a handcart swerved to a halt in front of him, casting up mud. He looked at the man with mild regret.

At the man, and beyond. All along the length of the street, people were stopping or huddling back against the sides. Turning the corner into the street came a unit of the Queen's Own Cavalry, their horses groomed to a shine, their tabards emblazoned with the flaming eagle of Merafi's d'Illandre kings. The blue and white feathers in their wide-brimmed hats curled lightly in the rain. Neither their boots nor the horses' coats bore more than a light splatter of mud: they had not come far, then. Perhaps someone from the royal household had business with the city aldermen. Along with the rest of the crowd, Gracielis stopped to watch. In the center of the procession rode a smaller group, who had clearly traveled much farther. Their banners hung limp and soggy; their cloaks were rain-dark and bedraggled. Some of these came also from the royal cavalry, but perhaps twenty foreigners rode in their midst, clad in heavy gray cloaks edged in scarlet. Clansmen from the northern Lunedith, the land that had given birth, long ago, to Merafi's royal d'Illandre dynasty. The d'Illandre kings had expanded south and west, carving out the kingdom of Gran' Romagne, with its rolling hills, fertile plains, wide valleys, and rich rivers, and founded their new capital of Merafi, where their widest river met the sea. But Lunedith remained a dependency of its crown, ruled on behalf of

Queen Firomelle by her ally, Prince Keris Orcandros, from the ancient city of Skarholm. The Lunedithin traded in sulfur and timber and pelts; a handful of merchants had settled in Merafi, but most chose to remain in their cold homeland, cleaving to customs and beliefs from before the birth of Gran' Romagne and holding themselves aloof from their neighbors. Strange stories were told of the clans, that they were shapeshifters and hedge witches, though here in Merafi only children chose to believe them. Children, and a handful of scholars and priests, and those who had time for history. And Gracielis. In his Tarnaroqi homeland, legends were treated with caution. It was not unknown for them to have consequences that could, even now, harm you.

Dead Valdarrien of the Far Blays had loved a Lunedithin woman and lost her. Somewhere in the back of Gracielis' mind was a thundering, like the sound of water falling. He took an almost unconscious step forward. There in the party's center rode a woman with level green eyes and braided hair that, when dry, would be a dusty ash blonde. Her strong archer's wrists held her mount in check; her head turned toward the sharp-featured man beside her. Gracielis could taste lemon and dust. The air was heavy with the memory of falling water, with the crack of a gunshot at midnight.

He had already reached for a sword he did not carry. His lips shaped a name that was not his to use. In the next instant, she would turn to him, see him, and . . .

His fingers closed about his wrist, nails digging in. "I," he said, aloud for the neighbor man to hear, "am myself and no other. I am Gracielis de Varnaq, and I hold to my own past." The riders passed, vanishing toward the aristocrats' quarter in the high city. His breathing was his own again, yet he remained motionless gazing after them, while the crowds began once again to move, until a street vendor cursed him for being in the way.

Faces were his stock in trade. He knew that woman. Iareth Yscoithi, Valdarrien's lover, who had left Merafi

six long years before. Gracielis had seen her at the theater, never met her. There had to be some explanation,
some unraveling of what had just passed within him.
Such things should not be possible here in Merafi, where
ghosts seldom walked. He was hedged in by the memory
of Valdarrien d'Illandre, right down to the malicious
spirit that haunted him. The lieutenant's last act in life
had been to kill Valdarrien. Gracielis had mourned neither of them. The lieutenant had been a bully and an
abuser. He had no idea why the man's ghost had
attached itself to him. And as to Valdarrien . . . He had
not known the late lord of the Far Blays, although he
had seen him from a distance a time or two and had
been a witness to his death. His connection to that family had always been through Yvelliane, who had been
swift to see in him a useful source of information. And
now . . . Valdarrien's ghost walked and shadowed the
footsteps of Thiercelin. Two days ago, at the masquerade, moonlight and water had disturbed the echo of
Valdarrien's death. A past that was not his own was
reaching for Gracielis, in the quiet need of Thiercelin of
Sannazar, and the commandments of Quenfrida.

In the cool gaze of Iareth Yscoithi, who had returned
to Merafi. He fought a sudden urge to hide. Instead,
he passed a hand over his eyes and turned away into
the city.

Somewhere, he could hear a sound like river water
falling.

"No, monseigneur, the Rose Palace is relatively new.
I think the present queen's grandfather built it or possibly his father. It takes its name from the color of the
walls. Something to do with the brickwork." First Lieutenant Joyain Lievrier pushed his damp fringe out of his
face yet again, and tried to maintain a smile. Why did
his luck always seem to land him slap in the middle of
tour parties? Six weeks hanging about in the cold at a
border garrison town and another six escorting the river-

damned Lunedithin heir and his entourage to Merafi. And he wasn't even meant to be in command: he was neither senior enough nor well-born enough to merit that. But two weeks after meeting the Lunedithin party, his commanding officer's horse had shied at a sapling, throwing the captain and breaking his leg in three places. Prince Kenan Orcandros was expected in Merafi at the onset of autumn. The captain had not been fit to travel. And that had left Joyain. The captain was the cadet son of a high aristocratic family and a fluent Lunedithin speaker to boot. It was true that Joyain had been assigned to this detail because he, too, spoke some Lunedithin. But while the captain had learned his from scholars and diplomats, Joyain's was considerably less formal. He'd come by it by watching his father haggle with sheep traders, itinerant laborers and petty merchants on his family holding near the western end of the border. The Lievrier family were gentry, nothing more; Joyain was a competent soldier. He had never wanted to be anything more. Now, he suppressed a sigh and continued, "The Old Palace was getting too small. It's part of the justiciary now."

"I see." Kenan Orcandros, the young Lunedithin heir, had red hair and a sour expression. He was the grandson of Lunedith's prince. That did not mean that Joyain had to like him. "We are more attached to our past in Lunedith."

"Yes, monseigneur, I'd heard that." *Inspired,* Joyain admonished himself. *You're really on top form with the small talk today, my friend.* "Is it true that your clan have lived in the same palace for forty generations?"

"Of course." Kenan did not trouble to keep the scorn from his voice.

Joyain sighed.

"We do not believe in abandoning tradition," Kenan said.

"No, monseigneur." Joyain had the liveliest suspicion that Kenan was about as pleased to be here in Merafi as Joyain was to be on escort duty. It was tradition that the heirs to Lunedith came south to Merafi for the winter after their majority at age twenty, to do homage to the queen and to become acquainted with the customs and manners of Gran' Romagne. Joyain rather thought that was one tradition Kenan would have happily have abandoned. It had taken six hours, not six weeks, for it to become apparent that the heir to Lunedith disliked and disapproved of everything and everyone that was not Lunedithin. His companions—all members of Prince Keris' personal household—had done their best to smooth over his antagonism, but it had not been a comfortable journey, even before the captain's accident.

As to himself, Joyain was looking forward to handing Kenan over to the royal household and to the resident ambassador from Lunedith. He wanted a bath and a change of clothing—and some pleasant company, river rot it.

"And your weather!" Kenan shuddered. "I've never seen such rain."

"It's unusual, monseigneur." Joyain tried to sound placatory. He succeeded only in sounding resigned. He suppressed another sigh. "We usually have quite mild autumns."

Kenan looked incredulous. Joyain bit his lip, trying to think of some plausible excuse for the weather. He pushed his hair back yet again. Kenan's temper wasn't the only thing to be suffering from the rain. Joyain's dress uniform wasn't benefiting much, either. Tentatively he said, "Some of the provinces have been quite damp this year, too."

Kenan's expression did not change. Joyain gave up.

From the row behind, Tafarin Morwenedd, the leader of Kenan's Lunedithin bodyguard said, "It has been this wet at home in Skarholm these last several autumns."

Kenan frowned.

Joyain opened his mouth, then shut it again hastily as another of the Lunedithin spoke.

"That is so, Kenan *kai-reth*. Tafarin is right. When I was in Merafi before, the climate seemed temperate." The speaker was another of Kenan's bodyguard, a quiet woman called Iareth. Joyain shot her a grateful glance and could have sworn she answered it with a glimmer of a smile.

Tafarin smiled and said, "You of the otter clan should favor the rain, Kenan *kai-reth*. Especially if our feline Iareth Yscoithi can bring herself to endure it."

Iareth pulled a face. Kenan looked as if he would like to snap, then shook his head and laughed instead. "Very respectful, Tafarin *kai-reth*."

"Indeed. It is one of my virtues."

"Fox's virtue!" Kenan said and made a dismissive gesture. Then he looked at Joyain. "Lieutenant, you have my apologies. I dislike this rain, but my *kai-rethin* are determined that I may not blame that on your city."

"Thank you, monseigneur." Joyain bowed from the saddle and thought longingly of sentry duty. Outside the debtors' prison. In the snow. "Hopefully, the rain will stop soon."

"Hope is a virtue also," said Kenan.

Gracielis found Thiercelin of Sannazar waiting for him in one of the smaller parlors of the fashionable coffee-house called Philosophy. The room was relatively empty; the scowling Thiercelin made an uncomfortable companion for the would-be poets and playwrights who frequented the place. Nevertheless, it took Gracielis several minutes to join him, since he had first to run the gamut of several patrons. When finally he arrived at Thiercelin's table and made his bow, Thiercelin glared at him and said, "Is there no one who doesn't know you?"

He had not issued an invitation to sit. Standing, therefore, Gracielis considered. His hair was beginning to dry, curling from the damp. "That," he said, "depends upon where I am. I never know anyone anywhere that would embarrass them."

"Yes, I suppose you wouldn't," Thiercelin said.

Gracielis smiled.

"Don't hover like that; you're making me nervous."

Gracielis sat, limbs composing themselves into ready elegance. The lieutenant's ghost leaned on the chair back, sardonic.

Thiercelin said, "I have something of yours." He reached under his chair and lifted out a small chocolate pot. He put it onto the table beside him. "I try to honor my bargains."

Gracielis made another small bow.

Thiercelin said, "I wasn't sure you'd come."

Bitter orange and musk . . . Within perfumed memory, Gracielis hesitated. *Chai ela*, Quenfrida. It might not be said, and yet . . . "I try to honor my word."

"Indeed?" For all his indolence, Thiercelin was no fool. Gracielis kept his face candid, watching him. Thiercelin frowned, then turned to pour the chocolate. In profile he looked tired, so that when the cup was passed, Gracielis let his fingers rest against the other's.

It was possible that Thiercelin did not yet know that Iareth Yscoithi was back in Merafi.

I have seen Valdin . . . Gracielis sipped his chocolate, then set it down on the chair arm, through the misty hand of the lieutenant's ghost. "So," he said, "what do you wish?"

Thiercelin did not answer the question. Instead, he said, "He always hated this place. Valdin, I mean. Said the very thought of it made him yawn. That's why I . . ," He sighed. "He wouldn't come here."

"Is that important?"

"He was in my home," Thiercelin said. "His former home, two nights ago. I think . . . And then at the masquerade, it almost seemed like . . ." He paused. "I think I'm afraid." He looked down again, withdrawing from the confidence of the admission. The lieutenant's ghost made a gesture of dismissal.

It was a shadow only, a poor, spiteful thing. Eyes on it, Gracielis said, "That's understandable."

"Two nights ago, at the masquerade . . ." Thiercelin fidgeted with his cup. "That was more than just Valdin, wasn't it?"

Something in the rain, some hint of changes . . . Thiercelin had been standing in water and the light of both moons. Had they both been full, it might have made some sense. Whatever it was that had its hands on him—on them both—was powerful. Gracielis said gently, "Memories can sometimes be stronger than we want." Then he shivered at the memory of a memory that was not his own. "I think you should know," he heard himself say, "that Iareth Yscoithi is back in Merafi."

"Iareth . . . ?" Thiercelin echoed, then stopped. His hand tightened on the chair arm. "Yviane told me that the young heir was due to visit, but she didn't mention Iareth."

"She may not have known," Gracielis said.

There was a silence. Thiercelin seemed to be drawing himself together. Then he said, "I don't go to court often. I don't imagine I'll have to see much of her." He was drinking wine. Refilling his glass, he gestured to the chocolate pot and said, "I commend your moderation."

Gracielis gestured, graceful, dismissive. "Wine is ruinous. And my face and my form are my fortune."

The look Thiercelin gave him was on the very edge of appraising. Gracielis smiled at him. "Very pretty," Thiercelin said, "But it's your mind I need, not your body."

"As it pleases you." Gracielis twined his rose-colored lovelock absently around a finger. "How may I serve?"

"You might," said Thiercelin, "*sit* in that chair, rather than reclining in it."

Gracielis straightened his spine, let his hands fold in his lap, deliciously coy. "Like this?"

Thiercelin growled. "It is," he said, "a great wonder to me that no one has as yet strangled you."

It was restored between them, the ritual bond of patron and servant. The dangerous moment of closeness had fled. Safe from the clutching hands of this man's past, Gracielis relaxed.

Thiercelin said, "Is it true, what Yviane said? Do you see ghosts?"

"Yes."

"Always?" Thiercelin looked about the room, straight through the hovering form of the lieutenant's ghost.

Gracielis arched his brows at the ghost. "Only when there's something to be seen."

"I don't believe in them," Thiercelin said. The lieutenant's ghost laughed. "I mean, I didn't, until . . ."

"They're mostly unreal." Gracielis waved a hand through the ghost. Then he paused, choosing his words. "Their creation is a question of . . . of strength of heart and strength of place. When something or someone, is drawn powerfully by an event or a location, it can happen that a trace lingers. And then sometimes the dead will cling to someone, or be conjured back by a need." Iareth Yscoithi, Valdarrien's Iareth, newly returned to this city, which had seen Valdarrien's death. "They're mostly not harmful. Not very harmful, anyway." The lieutenant's ghost glowered. Gracielis ignored it.

Thiercelin looked at his hands. "I miss Valdin."

"Yes." Again, Gracielis reached out to him in comfort. This time Thiercelin's hand lingered in his.

"If he's really . . . Could you see him?"

"Perhaps. And . . ." *Bonds may be loosened.* Gracielis said, "I may be able to find out what binds him."

"Can you break it?"

There was a cloud about Gracielis, composed of Quenfrida's perfume, and other things. The memory of bruised magnolia and the sound of silver bells in the garden of his Tarnaroqui home. A snatch of his own voice, long ago, and Quenfrida's, sharp with rage. Banishing ghosts lay within the domain of priesthood. Very carefully, he said, "That's harder. I don't know yet."

He drank chocolate to banish the taste of blood from his mouth.

"I see." Thiercelin looked beyond Gracielis and across the room, through the lieutenant's ghost. After a moment he said, "Will you meet me tonight, in the royal aisle?"

"Moon-double is better for seeing ghosts."

"The moons were in separate phases when I saw Valdin two nights ago. And Handmoon was dark the first time I saw him." Thiercelin sounded defensive. He lowered his voice. The lieutenant's ghost stood smirking beside him.

It had been a long time since Gracielis had kept proper account of the moons' positions. Folding his two-colored gloves in his hand, he tried to remember how they had stood the night before. Handmoon had risen early in the east quadrant and shone near full, although he could not remember if it had been waxing or waning. Mothmoon . . . Crescent only, he thought, but he was unsure. Most people—most Merafiens—could not see ghosts at all, or, if they did, saw them only when both moons were aligned and the night clear. That should have been his first question to Thiercelin: how stood the moons when you saw the ghost? He cursed himself inwardly. Quenfrida would have seen this difficulty at once. It was so like her to know more than she told. He would look foolish if he sought her advice now. He raised his eyes. Thiercelin was watching him.

Gracielis said, "Monseigneur, may I ask a question?"

"Probably."

"You speak of Lord Valdarrien. Have you ever seen another ghost?"

Thiercelin frowned. "No. I'd always assumed they were just a story."

Gracielis smiled. Thiercelin looked curious. "Such an attitude is very Merafien. But it's perhaps unwise. Ghosts are no fable."

"I thought you said they were harmless."

"Often." Gracielis took care not to look at the lieutenant's ghost. "But not always. They can be malicious."

"You've seen that happen?"

"No." Thiercelin was beginning to look worried. Gracielis smiled at him and squeezed his hand. "It's rare. It's unlikely you're in danger."

"Unlikely." Thiercelin sounded sceptical. "Valdin wouldn't approve. He liked to consider himself very dangerous."

"So I remember hearing. Tonight, then, if you wish."

"Thank you." Thiercelin hesitated, then added, "How do I pay you?"

Traitor's gold, left by Quenfrida in a rented room. She must have known of the irregularities in this case before giving him her orders, and she would gloat if he came suppliant to her for explanations. Gracielis said, "There will be no charge."

Thiercelin looked surprised.

"You are buying nothing that I sell." Their hands were still joined. "However, should there be anything else . . . ?" The glance with which Gracielis accompanied the words was arch.

"There won't be," Thiercelin said and took his hand away.

Yvelliane placed a brass paperweight on the top of the tall pile of papers that stood at her left elbow and stretched her shoulders. She said, "I have some new information on the illegal imports of steel from the Allied City States. My sister-in-law Miraude attended the public masquerade earlier this week, and she confirms that the Ninth Councillor is meeting with someone from the customs office. I have another agent checking that out now. But it will be at least ten days before I receive the next report from any of our embassies there." She looked across the broad oak table at Laurens of Valeranica, Prince Consort to Queen Firomelle and himself a scion of one of the Allied Cities.

"I'll write to my uncle," Laurens said. "He'll probably deny any official knowledge at his end, but he'll know we're watching. He might decide that makes it too much trouble."

"We can hope." Yvelliane smiled at him. "And meanwhile, I'll make sure that the Ninth Councillor's office is very closely monitored." She stretched again and rubbed the back of her neck.

From her high winged chair beside the fire, Firomelle said, "When did you last sleep, Yviane?"

"Last night."

"At home in your own bed for a sensible number of hours? Or over your papers at your desk for a couple of hours?"

Yvelliane evaded her cousin's gaze. "There's a lot to get through right now, with the formal reception for Prince Kenan tomorrow evening."

It was early evening. The gray autumn light retreated slowly from the tall windows, drawing lines in shadow across the floorboards. Two fires, one at either end of the long room, offered patches of brightness. The table stood in the center, its surface covered with letters, account books, document cases, and papers. Three silver candelabra marched along its spine, none of them lit. In front of Laurens was an impressive array of ink holders, pens, and seals. Three walls were lined with tapestries in yellow and red, depicting the journey of fire from the *Book of Five Domains*. The lower parts of most of them were invisible behind oak bookcases filled with records in red-bound ledgers and roll cases in blue and green. The fourth was set with three tall casement windows. Small carpets stood before both hearths, edged by two winged chairs and a number of stools. Officially, this was the queen's smaller withdrawing room. In practice, it was her day-to-day office, where she met with her closest advisers. Laurens and Yvelliane sat at the east end of the table, close to the queen's chair and the larger of the two fires. Its warm light was kind but could not disguise the hollows in Firomelle's face, the thinness of her hands, or the way she held her heavy shawl wrapped tightly about her. From time to time she coughed, the sound hard and painful. Every time it happened, Yvelliane and Laurens exchanged a glance and said nothing. There was no point. Firomelle had no intention of sacrificing her duties to her health.

Now, she said, "Ah, yes. The heir to Lunedith. You've met him, haven't you, Yviane? Remind me about him."

"That was six years ago." Yvelliane propped her elbows on the table. "He was only fourteen, he may have changed." *A spoiled boy with too much opinion of himself and too little experience to know he could ever be wrong.* She had spent a few handfuls of weeks only in Lunedith, as Firomelle's special envoy, accompanied by restless, troublesome Valdarrien. She remembered the chill of stone walls, rooms that stood half empty, furnished only with benches and chests or an old-fashioned, closed-sided bed and lit only by sparse, thin slits of windows or the gutter of rush torches. Valdarrien had at first pronounced the Lunedithin to be as grim as their granite buildings, but Yvelliane had found Prince Keris, Kenan's grandfather, to be both warm and kind, and Urien Armenwy, his First Councillor, to have a political mind as sharp as her own. Kenan had attended a few of their meetings, thin face set in an expression of disapproval and distrust. He had drawn his circle from the most conservative of the clan-heads and their kin; his comments had hinted at views that were both anti-Merafien and isolationist. She would not have taken him seriously at all had it not been for one anomaly in his behavior. Prejudiced as he was, he had nevertheless shown a surprising friendship for one of the Tarnaroqui envoys also present, the seductive Quenfrida d'Ivrinez. Perhaps it had been no more than a boy's attraction to an older woman. Yvelliane had never gained proof that it was more than that. Yet she and Valdarrien had been ambushed on their way home with the new treaty, and she had long suspected that both Kenan and Quenfrida had had a hand in that.

Six months ago, Quenfrida had arrived in Merafi to become an aide to the ambassador from Tarnaroq. And now Kenan had come. He was twenty: by law, he had to swear allegiance to Firomelle. But that Quenfrida should also be present . . . It was a coincidence that had had Yvelliane concerned for months. She rested her chin on her hands, and said, "He didn't like Merafiens back then. But he's a lot older. He may understand more of the politics." She was not sure she believed it. She had to give him at least the benefit of the doubt. "He aligned himself with the ultra-traditionalists."

"The clans who believe in going back as far as possible to their oldest customs," Firomelle said. "Minimal contact with outsiders and independence from Gran' Romagne."

"Is that technically possible?" Laurens asked. "The Gran' Romagnol dynasty began in Lunedith. They'd have to declare themselves a separate state in law."

"According to our ambassador there, the technicalities don't worry them. They just want to cut themselves off," Yvelliane said.

"In his last few dispatches, he's said very little about Kenan," said Firomelle.

"Dispatches aren't necessarily secure," Laurens said.

"The usual security arrangements are in place," Yvelliane said. "But we have to give him the benefit of the doubt." She glanced over at the queen, who returned the gaze levelly. "We don't want to provoke an incident, I know."

"But you don't trust him." Firomelle paused and coughed. The other two exchanged glances. "Ask that clever sister-in-law of yours to keep an eye on him, Yviane. Six years ago, you suggested he may have a weakness for a pretty woman."

"It troubles me that Quenfrida is here too," Yvelliane admitted.

"So far, she's behaved impeccably."

"I know, but . . ."

Firomelle held up a hand. Blue veins showed in it, as if her flesh grew transparent. "You don't trust the Tarnaroqui, I know. Everyone knows. But we must maintain peace with them. I can't leave a legacy of war to my son when he comes to the throne as a minor."

"It won't come to that," Yvelliane said to the table-top. Laurens reached across and patted her hand. She went on, "You can't say 'when.' "

"I must." There was a silence. About the table, the shadows had lengthened as the sun set outside. Yvelliane stared at her papers. She could hear Firomelle's breathing, rough and uncomfortable. For so many months, she had hoped that this would pass, that her cousin would regain her health and strength. But with each of those months, Firomelle had grown weaker, her body thinning, the cough becoming more frequent, more painful. Last month, she had begun to cough up blood, and the solemn doctors had begun to frown. The crown prince was twelve: Laurens would have to hold the kingdom firm and fast for something on the order of eight years, in the face of an aristocracy always hungry for advancement, and neighbors who were always ready to take advantage. Prince Keris in Lunedith was loyal, but he was an old man and also in poor health. The city states would follow whichever path brought them the greatest advantage. And to the southeast, the vast empire of Tarnaroqui waited and watched, ruled by its cloistered emperor and his network of *undarii*, assassin-priests, who were forbidden by ancient law from setting foot in Gran' Romagne. Yvelliane did not trust the Tarnaroqui, had never been able to trust them, but Firomelle was right: now, above all, they must have peace with Tarnaroq. Laurens had been cultivating the Tarnaroqui ambassador, Sigeris, for most of a year, trying to lay the ground for what must be their future relations. Yvelliane sighed and raised a hand to rub her eyes.

Laurens said, "Sigeris and his entourage will expect to call on Kenan. We'll raise the level of monitoring, but we can't do more. There's no proof that Quenfrida is anything more than she seems. One of my people in their embassy reports on her regularly, and the most he's found is that she's carrying on a flirtation with the Vicomte de Guares." He patted her had again, and Yvelliane looked up. "I'm keeping my eyes on them, Yviane. Stop worrying."

If only she could . . . Yvelliane made herself smile at him. He was a good man, a kind one, and she trusted him. And he was right: there was little they could do at present except keep a careful watch on their troublesome foreign guests. Firomelle coughed again, this time for longer, and Laurens rose and went to her. Firomelle pressed a hand to her side, fighting to regain her breath.

Yvelliane rose also. "Fielle? Shall I call someone?" She made to move toward the bellrope.

"No," Firomelle said through a cough. Laurens poured cordial into a glass from the carafe that stood on a side table and handed it to her. She sipped it slowly while they watched. Yvelliane found her hands clenching and put them behind her back. As far back as she could remember, Firomelle had been her closest friend and comforter, dearer to her than anyone in the world save Valdarrien. When she and Valdarrien had lost their parents, Firomelle had brought them to court and raised them almost as younger siblings. After Valdarrien's death, they had grown even closer. The resemblance between the two women was marked; both were tall and slender and dark-eyed, even though Firomelle's face was hollow these days and there were gray streaks in her soft brown hair. If she were to die . . . Yvelliane did not want to think of that. She made herself unclench her hands and straighten her spine. *Think about the policies, about now, not the future. Think about what we have to do now* . . . She was very tired suddenly. Despite herself, she frowned.

Firomelle said, "Come here, Yviane."

The coughing fit was over: the queen held out a hand. Laurens stood beside her, his hand on the back of her chair. Yvelliane sank to the rug at her feet, and Firomelle stroked her hair. Yvelliane caught the hand. "Fielle . . ."

"Hush."

Yvelliane leaned back. "Listen," Firomelle said, "you're tired. You should go home."

"I still have work . . ."

"You have a husband who wants to see you. He's a good man. Don't neglect him." Yvelliane looked down, hiding her face. Firomelle went on. "He could help you a lot, if you let him. He's intelligent and he adores you."

"Politics don't interest him. He likes to ride and play cards and . . ."

"He's not Valdin," Laurens said. "And he's over thirty."

"I don't . . ." Yvelliane said, and stopped. She liked to think of Thiercelin at home, removed and protected from the grind of government work. Unlike Miraude, he had never shown any interest in it. He had been Valdarrien's friend; he did not belong in her world of papers and gray intrigues. She did not think she wanted him to belong. She had not been able to keep danger away from Valdarrien, and now death reached out for Firomelle. She wanted Thiercelin to be safe. He was her haven: always there, always calm and loving and ready to smile at her. Except that he, too, lately seemed to be hiding something from her . . .

Kenan and Quenfrida in the city. Firomelle dying. Thiercelin perhaps drawing away from her. Yvelliane turned her face into the queen's skirts and tried not to be afraid.

Gracielis was trying to enjoy himself. The rain had finally stopped, and the night's chill had yet to penetrate Thiercelin's carriage. It was drawn up in the shadows at the road's edge, and showing no lights. Clouds covered both moons. Music rang from the bright windows of the nearby Rose Palace. Gracielis could see the shadowy forms of the upper classes at play. It was all most edifying. He said as much to his companion, voice amused in the darkness.

"Watch the road," was all Thiercelin said.

It was Gracielis' private opinion that it mattered little where they kept their vigil. It appeared that Valdarrien's ghost was drawn to Thiercelin in any place. But Thiercelin was set upon waiting here in the royal aisle. He had wanted to do so on foot, unshielded from the damp and cold. Gracielis had objected. He had no wish to risk his livelihood by an untimely bout of pneumonia. Thiercelin had frowned, muttered, and conceded the point. "Although," he said, "I see little point in your presence if you're too wrapped up in blankets to do anything."

"I can see clearly," Gracielis said. "And I'll ensure I have freedom of movement. It will be well."

"I suppose I have to believe that."

Wisely, Gracielis was silent. It was very dark. Little of the moons' light penetrated the cloud cover or filtered through the thick overhang of trees. The lieutenant's ghost was a spiteful blur. The night felt still, as if Merafi, having stirred in its long indolence, had again subsided. He wondered what she made of it, sky-eyed Quenfrida, out somewhere beneath these same clouds. Once he might have dared to ask her and sat at her feet for her reply.

Once is not always.

In self-defense he pulled away from the thought and looked instead at Thiercelin. A man who loved his wife; one might go to the guillotine for that truth. Yet he had chosen not to share this new burden with her. One might wonder why. Yvelliane d'Illandre was not a woman to require protection. Gracielis, who knew her better than he would ever let Thiercelin know, was sure of that. There was some trouble here. It was said on the streets that Prince Laurens was much seen with the Tarnaroqui

ambassador these days. It was also rumored that not all
of the royal council were content with that, readying
themselves for the struggle for influence which must
surely follow the death of the queen. And Quenfrida
had set him this task, which touched upon Yvelliane, the
First Councillor.

He gazed at the shadowy form of Thiercelin, whose
trust was bought and sold, and no longer wanted even
to try to enjoy himself.

Thiercelin was not looking at him, but peering into
the darkness outside. His face was set. Palely, he said,
"Look . . ."

They were no longer alone in the aisle. Silent over the
hard road, a horseman came cantering. His head was
high. His cloak stirred with a wind that was not blowing.
He was hatless; the hair that streamed behind him was
longer than fashion required. His clothing was dark; he
had neither braid nor bright buttons. The faint moons'
light glinted off the pommel of his sword. His face was
in shadow. There was a careless defiance to him, lined
in posture, in the very angle of that bare head.

Into the silence, Gracielis heard Thiercelin whisper,
"Oh, Valdin."

Gracielis leaned forward in the gloom. He said, "I
see him."

"What do we do?"

"We wait."

Mothmoon broke through the clouds, illuminating the
road. The rider cast no shadow. He had more substance
than the lieutenant's ghost, drawn in contrasts rather
than pastels. He was closer now. In a few moments he
would pass by them or perhaps through them, as though
they were the creatures of mist and memory.

His face was unmistakable. A little drawn, a little malcontent. High cheekbones, dark brows. He was bearded,
like the most typical street bravo. The hooves of his
mount did not quite touch the ground.

There was no more time. Gracielis opened the carriage door and stepped down into the road. He was straight in the path of the rider. For once, the lieutenant's ghost did not follow him. He inhaled and sought control. Remembered the words, the ritual from the *Second Book of Marcellan*. There were three chains, three paths which could bind the dead: love and death and the force beneath the world. Three bindings that he must seek, trace, perhaps break. He looked into the eyes of the late Valdarrien of the Far Blays, and spoke the word which compelled a halt.

Valdarrien could see him; that was certain. There was a grimness on his face; a flash of defiance which set the horse to a gallop. Gracielis raised a hand and made himself reach out with his ghost-sight.

There was a roaring in his ears and veins and mind, like thunder, driving out thought. He was falling into it, or through it, soaked in its force. Pain lanced through his right shoulder. Swan wings beat across his vision, through an iron curtain of water. He gasped for breath, fighting to hold his gaze locked onto eyes that were filled with the violence of the water.

It was the key. He fought vertigo and found his voice. Into the thunder, he spoke, softly, carefully. "Water comes to rest. Douses flame, cools heat, lays dust." The language he used was not Merafien, but Valdarrien seemed to understand. Gracielis held on through the words, beneath the insubstantial, flailing hooves of the horse. He was drowning in the fragments of another's memory. Disordered images flapped about him. Swan wings, and the hint of the scent of lemon, and eyes that were green and cool as jade, cool as "The river," said Gracielis and found it there in another man's last, lost hunger. In the memory of a green-eyed stillness that was a woman named Iareth Yscoithi.

All around him the thunder and the violence calmed, slowed, died away. He was Gracielis *arin-shae* Quenfrida, called Gracieux on the streets and in the salons of Merafi. He stood in the aisle that led to Merafi's Rose

Palace and faced down the past. He felt ready to fall. Instead, he looked at Valdarrien and said, as reasonably as he might, "Monseigneur, you must give some explanation for this. You are frightening Lord Thiercelin."

The lieutenant's ghost had never spoken to him, never made any sound of any kind. Valdarrien of the Far Blays looked back at him, then beyond at Thiercelin. His expression was sardonic, a little disdainful. His voice, when finally he spoke, was quite clear, only very remote, as if he must talk from some immense distance. "Tell my Iareth *kai-reth*," he said, "that she was right." And then, more gently, "Thierry, forgive." Raising a hand in valediction, he turned his horse's head about and rode away down the aisle.

Gracielis made it to the edge of the road before he passed out.

"How do you feel?" Thiercelin asked.

Lying on the bed, Gracielis opened one extremely cautious eye and looked at the ceiling. "Mostly dead," he said. "Some small token would be appreciated at the funeral. Flowers. But not yellow. Yellow doesn't suit my coloring at all."

"That," said Thiercelin, "is somewhat debatable."

"Please don't," Gracielis said. And then, "I trust I haven't been too irritating?"

"No."

"Good." Gracielis had closed the eye again. "My sincerest regrets . . . for the trouble."

"It would have made considerably more trouble if I'd left you in the road. Why didn't you tell me it would do this to you?"

"It doesn't, always," Gracielis said. "My apologies."

"Your apologies?" Thiercelin was mildly appalled. "No wonder you refused me."

"It doesn't matter," Gracielis said. "You might consider it a hazard of the job."

"But . . ." Thiercelin said, then shut up. There was a

silence. This had not, after all, been a job, but a favor. Thiercelin had once been taught a little about Tarnaroqui ways, and his mind was busy disinterring those lessons. Gracielis de Varnaq saw ghosts. It was so like Yvelliane to possess herself of such information and to release it in fragments, unexplained. Honesty forced him to admit that it was equally like himself not to have asked.

It was too late to ask now without having to involve himself in turn in explanations.

He did not know. He did not remember. The Tarnaroqui worship their dead, said the voice of one of his brothers, long ago. But no—only death itself, said another voice in answer. They shape themselves to see mysteries, and phantasms, and ghosts. There were tales woven into that drawn from the *Books of Marcellan* and elsewhere, tales of ritual suicide and other darker things. Not the kind of stories to which a sophisticated man, a rational man, should lend credence: tales with no more value than the folklore of men turning into animals, of rocks turning into men.

Yet Gracielis de Varnaq saw ghosts, and so did Thiercelin of Sannazar, who was, after all, a rational man.

He could make no sense of it. He said, "Do you need anything?"

Gracielis managed a faint smile, then winced. "A new head? Don't worry. This will pass. Like hangovers."

"Ah," said Thiercelin, remembering some of his own. "Should I go?"

"Only if you wish to."

"If you want to sleep . . ."

"Not yet." Gracielis hesitated. "I find company . . . comforting."

"I'll stay, then."

"Thank you."

Again, there was a silence. Thiercelin settled himself more comfortably in his chair. After a while, Gracielis said, "It isn't you."

"What?" said Thiercelin.

"It isn't you that binds Lord Valdarrien."

Thiercelin did think to ask how Gracielis knew that. Instead he said, "Who, then?" A name hovered before him, unsaid, expected.

But Gracielis said. "Water." Thiercelin reached for a cup. "Water binds him." Thiercelin sat back, feeling rather foolish. "I don't understand why."

Water. Thiercelin shook his head. "I don't think I know, either. Yviane might know, I suppose, but . . ." He swallowed. "Yviane, or . . ." Another pause as he marshalled himself to say it. "Or Iareth Yscoithi."

"Yes," Gracielis said. "You heard—he spoke of her?"

"Yes."

" 'Tell Iareth she was right.' I've no idea what that means."

"Why should you? None of this is your problem."

To Thiercelin's surprise, Gracielis laughed. His eyes were open, watching some point in the middle distance. He rubbed at his right shoulder, and said, "You might be surprised."

"You were kind to me, the night Valdin died."

"Consider it repaid," Gracielis said, "and more than repaid, tonight."

Impulsively Thiercelin rose and went to the bed. "This—my being here—is very little. After all, I . . ."

Gracielis interrupted him. "Will you do it?" he asked.

"Do what?"

"Will you tell Iareth Yscoithi?"

Tell Iareth kai-reth . . . And then, as ever, *Thierry, forgive.*

Thierry, forgive. "I must," said Thiercelin.

According to the proper procedures, Joyain should have been free of the Lunedithin upon arrival at the Old Justiciary. The commander of the queen's household troop and the Lunedithin ambassador had been there to welcome them and to take charge of Kenan's party, and conduct them to their lodgings. Joyain should have been off duty, at home, or in the mess, looking forward to a well-deserved furlough.

He was beginning to lose his faith in the military "should have." Granted, the disquiet in the dock quarter of Merafi was unlooked for. Granted, too, that pacifying that must take precedence over more formal duties. It was equally true that Joyain had been with the Lunedithin now for some time and was familiar to them. But he had hoped that someone would have been found to replace the captain as their military aide. It appeared that this had not happened. At the Justiciary, they had been given wine and cakes, and Joyain had been handed orders to remain with the delegation for the foreseeable future.

Joyain was beginning to wish that he'd gone into the navy. Or the River Temple. Anything but the army.

At least the quarters for the Lunedithin were properly organized. An entire house in the aristocrats' quarter had been made over for them, and staffed from her majesty's own household, many of whom were probably not spies. A suite for the heir, and luxurious rooms for his escort. Hot food. Hot baths. All the heart might desire, for everyone except Joyain.

And except for His Highness Prince Kenan Orcandros. His complaints had been loud enough to be witnessed by most of the staff. His Highness was displeased by the furnishings; opulence was not gentlemanly. His Highness was surprised that the Allandur—your pardon, the "Queen"— did not intend to greet him until the next day. His Highness' bath was too small, too hot, too scented . . . Trying to get his own men settled in to the quarters allocated to them, Joyain had done his level best to ignore the fuss. It had proved almost impossible. Kenan had changed rooms five times, ending up in a gloomy suite looking out onto a dense line of pines that ran to the west side of the house. Each time he moved, at least half the household had had to move also. By the time he settled, Joyain's soldiers were on their third billet.

Coming back into the main house to locate his own office, Joyain saw several maids struggling upstairs with water for yet another attempt at the royal bath. He was unable to refrain from muttering, "And I hope you drown in it, monseigneur."

"Improbable, I think," came a voice in reply. "Like all of the Orcandrin, Kenan swims rather well."

Joyain jumped, turned, and banged his elbow on the curved newel post of the stair. He said, "Drown it!" And then, "I'm sorry. I shouldn't have been so rude."

It was the fair-haired woman from the bodyguard, Iareth Yscoithi. Even after six weeks, Joyain still had not properly worked out the ranks of most of the Lunedithin. Kenan was the leader, of course; but Tafarin made the military decisions and spoke to Kenan as to an equal. So did all the rest of the escort, come to that. Their habit of referring to one another indiscriminately as *kaireth* (which Joyain had thought was a word meaning a kinsman) set the seal on his confusion. She had not been among the most talkative of Kenan's party on the journey, but she had always been courteous. Now he made her a small bow and looked at his feet with rather poor grace.

She said, "It is Kenan who is impolite. He chooses to forget that to be a guest entails as much duty as pleasure." She sounded amused. Looking up, however, Joyain could see no trace of a smile.

He said, "Can I help you, mademoiselle?"

"Iareth. In Lunedith, only the clan-heads take titles." Her voice was soft, its accent rather less marked than that of some of her companions. "I was wondering, is it permitted for us to leave this building, and go out into the city before our official presentation?"

That would be a serious breach of diplomatic etiquette. The consequences could be disastrous. He did

not know if he had the authority to forbid her. He ran
a hand through his hair and sighed. "I can't recommend
it. There's been some disturbances in some parts of the
city—not near here—but should you become lost or . . ."

There was a curious twist at the corner of her mouth.
"You are kind. But there is no call for you to fear that.
I am not unacquainted with Merafi."

Another thing he could do without was this Lunedithin insistence on using nineteen words where two would
do. It had been too long a day. He had just about
worked his way through the double negative, when she
added, "The night ferry still runs, does it not? And there
is no curfew upon the bridges?"

One of the scraps of news he had garnered at the
Justiciary was that the river was running too high for
the ferry. He said, "The bridges will still be open, I
think, although those which have tolls . . ."

"I am aware that those close at sunset. Apart from
the one owned by the Vintners' Guild, which closes two
hours after." Again, that amused tone. Iareth sat down
on the stairs, hugging her knees, and looked up at him.
"Unless there have been changes?"

"No." Joyain really did not want to go out. "It's raining again."

"It has done so for the past several weeks."

"Yes."

There was a small silence. Joyain wondered just what
it was she wanted to do in the city. He didn't consider
her the type to be interested in taverns, or gambling
dens. . . . River rot it. It was his duty. He said, "I suppose I could arrange an escort for you . . ."

She looked at him. There was something odd in her
face—a kind of recognition. Then she smiled and shook
her head. For a moment, almost, she was pretty. She
said, "I am no better than Kenan. You will wish me
drowned, also. I have no errand that will not keep for
another time."

"Oh, but," Joyain began, mindful still of his orders.

"No." She rose and held out a hand to him. "I thank you. You have been kinder than we have deserved." Joyain looked down. "You must forgive me. It is the rain that makes me restless. It is a part of being Yscoithi."

He made no pretense of understanding that. Instead, he said, "It's nothing."

"I think not."

"No, really, I . . ." It would be graceless to speak of duty. To cover his awkwardness, he said, "You've been here before?"

"In Merafi? Yes."

"With another diplomatic party?"

"No, the circumstances were other. I came hence with Valdin *kai-reth*." That meant nothing to Joyain. Seeing the puzzlement on his face, she added, "That is—to give the titles of your people—Valdarrien d'Illandre of the Far Blays."

He knew that name. He looked at her with some measure of curiosity. "The famous duelist?"

"Even so."

"But . . ." Joyain said. And then, "He's dead."

"Indeed," said Iareth Yscoithi.

Iareth Yscoithi of Alfial to Urien Armenwy, called Swanhame, Councillor and Leader of the Kai-rethin: Greetings.

We are this afternoon arrived in the city of Merafi, having successfully completed our journey hence in the expected time. The roads these last days have been in good repair, and the countryside seems most prosperous. Our welcome at the city was all that Prince Keris would consider appropriate. We are to be presented formally to Her Majesty Firomelle Allandur tomorrow, at which time, Kenan kai-reth will make his homage to her. Our accommodations are comfortable, if a litte too luxurious for some tastes: the Allandur seems to be determined that we shall receive good treatment here.

*We remain accompanied by Lieutenant Lievrier,
of whom I have written before. His Lunedithin is
far below the standard of that of Captain de Meche,
which may be significant. I remain troubled about
the captain's accident; he seemed to me to be an
excellent rider and his fall most uncharacteristic. As
yet, however, I have found no evidence suggesting
any tampering or foul play. I will continue to observe and to watch over Kenan* kai-reth *as you have
instructed me. I will write to you again once the
homage ceremony has occurred.*

I remain your obedient kai-reth,
Iareth Yscoithi.

3

"MIMI, DO YOU HAVE a few minutes?"

Seated at her toilette table, Miraude turned. Her maid, engaged upon dressing her hair in low ringlets, stepped back and waited. Yvelliane stood in the doorway, dressed as ever in a serviceable plain gown. Miraude smiled and held out a hand. "Of course. Come in."

Her rooms occupied the third floor of one wing of the Far Blays townhouse. The building itself dated from the preceding century, but in Miraude's suite, the oak paneling had been painted in eggshell blue and decorated with scrollwork in greens and yellows. Light streamed in from the long windows, artfully augmented by several well-placed mirrors. The wooden floor had been laid with rugs in pale colors, matching the silk curtains. The furnishings, both here in her bedroom and in her salon next door, were all modern, with slim lines and soft cushions. Her bed was hung with bright brocades; at the crown of each post, carved putti held bouquets of ribbons. On the toilette table stood an impressive array of crystal vials, silver-backed brushes, and porcelain boxes. Everything was airy and dainty and fragile. Miraude took great care to ensure that: her intimates expected it. The beautiful Miraude d'Iscoigne l'Aborderie was one of the ornaments of Merafien society; elegance in person, in dress, in surroundings was required of her. Her approval was sought after, her taste everywhere admired, invitations to her monthly salons coveted by friends and enemies alike.

She rose, now, to embrace Yvelliane and bestow a kiss upon her cheek. "You're wearing a horrid dress again. You must let me take you to my *modiste*."

"If I ever have the time." Yvelliane seated herself on a low chair and glanced across at the maid. "I need to talk to you about family business."

"Oh. Oh, of course." Miraude resumed her own seat and smiled at her maid. "Leave me, Coralie. I'll ring when I want you." The maid curtsyed and left. Miraude said, "Well? The Ninth Councillor again?"

"No, although the queen is very pleased with your information on that." Miraude sketched a small bow. Yvelliane continued, "It's a harder one, I'm afraid. Kenan Orcandros."

Miraude half-turned, contemplating her reflection in the mirror. She said. "The heir to Lunedith. The amber and sulfur merchants don't like him. They think, when he's prince, he'll raise export duties and make trouble over imports." She patted a stray curl into place. "He's unmarried, but unlikely to wed outside Lunedith. Old-fashioned—he'd marry his cousin, if he had a female one older than eight."

Yvelliane smiled. "You've done your homework."

"I hear things." Miraude finished with the curl and turned back to face Yvelliane. "And I was rather expecting to be asked, given what's said about him." Her intimates would have been surprised that she could sound so serious. Miraude was very careful as to what she let her intimates know. It did not pay, in matters of intrigue, to be profligate with oneself. There were a hundred people at court who would swear they knew every one of her thoughts and secrets. Outside Yvelliane, the queen, and Prince Laurens, there were perhaps two who knew even a part.

She was Yvelliane's best informer. At sixteen, she had

come to live in the Far Blays household, as wife to Valdarrien. Less than three months later, he was dead, having never consummated the marriage. Beautiful, charming, and rich, Miraude had not lacked for suitors or friends. But it had taken her less than six months to find court life shallow, for all that. Yvelliane had provided her with an endless source of interest and excitement, by offering her the chance to spy for the queen. Now, she said, "Am I looking for anything in particular?"

"No . . ." Yvelliane hesitated. "At least, I'm not sure. Connections to Tarnaroq or to the *undarii* maybe. He used to be friends with Quenfrida d'Ivrinez. There's some suspicion that he'd like to see Lunedith independent of us. I just . . ."

"He smells wrong?" Miraude suggested. "Figuratively speaking."

"Yes. He's unlikely to make it easy for you. He doesn't like Merafiens."

"No. But he likes tradition." Miraude nodded. "I can work with that."

"Thank you." Yvelliane rose and started toward the door.

Miraude said, "We missed you the last couple of days."

"There's so much to do. And Firomelle."

"Yes." Miraude studied her sister-in-law's face. Today, she looked older than her thirty-four years, lines becoming set in her brow. Lately, it seemed, Yvelliane did nothing beside work and fret. "You have to take care of yourself, too."

Yvelliane said, "I do."

Miraude shook her head.

Yvelliane continued, "Laurens was nagging me about that, too. I'll rest soon, I promise." She went to the door. In it, she paused and said, "Mimi?"

"Yes?"

"How's Thierry?"

Miraude rose. There was another piece of information

she had gathered only the day before. She looked at the floor. Yvelliane was tired. Now was not the time. She said, "He's all right, I think."

"His valet tells me he was out late last night," Yvelliane said. "I shouldn't wake him."

"I don't think he'd mind."

But Yvelliane shook her head. "He needs to sleep." And she left, closing the door behind her.

Miraude stood for a moment, gazing after her. Then she sighed and rang the bell for her maid.

It was late in the day when Gracielis awoke. His head and right shoulder ached abominably. The lieutenant's ghost hovered over him in unholy delight. He wished briefly for the strength to banish it, then simply turned his eyes away.

The movement was unpleasant. He set his teeth, let his eyes close again in search of comforting darkness. Somewhere, dimly, in the back of his mind, water was falling.

Something cool was laid over his forehead, easing the pain. A hand stroked his hair back from his face. He relaxed and said, in Merafien, "You should've gone home."

The reply was in another tongue entirely. "All that way? That would be a waste, surely?"

He said a word that, on his lips, would have shocked most of his clients. Then he opened his eyes. "I don't want you, Quena. Go away."

Quenfrida sat on the edge of the bed, watching him. He wanted to lean against her, let her soothe away the pain and discomfort with her clever hands. She said, "That is scarcely graceful, my Gracielis. I've been waiting for you for hours."

He was not a child. He could do without her comfort. She said, "It took you hard, I think. What happened?"

"Nothing." He wanted to pull away from her. "I did as you bade me. Nothing more. Please go."

She took her hands away. The bed rocked as she rose. He listened to her steps as she crossed the room. She poured something into a cup. "Drink this. It may ease you a little."

"I don't want . . ."

"Don't be childish." Her hands slipped under him, lifting. Without thinking, he recoiled from her, setting his head and stomach churning.

He was not going to be sick in front of her. Fighting nausea, he let himself be guided into a sitting position, and opened his eyes.

She said, "Drink."

The glass was at his lips; he drank reflexively. There was a moment's silence as she took the cup away. He watched her covertly, afraid of her presence, afraid of her departure.

She leaned on the table and looked at him. "So. Tell me of this "nothing" that befell you. What did you learn?"

"That other people's ghosts make me sick," he said nastily. The lieutenant's ghost smirked.

She raised her brows. "Very witty."

"Thank you." At another time he might have bowed. "I try to amuse."

"I'm sure you do."

He felt too ill to fence with her. He sighed, watching the lieutenant's ghost hovering at the foot of the bed. He had never been quite sure if she could see it or whether she simply sensed its presence. Resigned, he said, "The moons weren't aligned last night."

"What of it?"

"This is Merafi."

"You astonish me."

"Stop it, Quena. You know what I mean."

"Do I?" She was determined to play games.

"You taught me. Merafi is a null space. Confluence of salt and fresh water. It's harder for ghosts to manifest here, there's no nourishment for them. They need extra force to appear, the combining of the moons." The lieutenant's ghost laughed. Gracielis looked at it and added, "Usually."

"They can be seen at other times if one has the power. Even here."

"Yes, but . . ." His head ached too much for this. "Who is he?"

On another person, her expression would have been shock. It was not possible. She knew him too well to be surprised by him. She stared at him, almost as at a stranger. He heard the catch in her breath.

She said, "Who do you mean?" There was something deadly in her tone. He did not intend to be afraid, but he shivered.

Dry-mouthed, he said, "The moons were wrong . . . He shouldn't have been able to see anything, but he did. Thiercelin duLaurier."

The change in her was like cloud lifting. She smiled and her face was contemptuous. "Thiercelin of Sannazar? He's nobody."

"He saw Valdarrien d'Illandre last night. And at other times, too, when the conditions were wrong for it. At the masquerade . . . When I touched him, I could read his memory—and he experienced it with me."

She shrugged. "Perhaps he simply has a drop of good blood. Forget it. It's unimportant."

If it was unimportant, why had she insisted that he go through with it? It was not in him to ask. She was not going to tell him. She knew something . . . Something to do with a ghost seen untimely by eyes that should have been blind to it.

Eyes without *undarii* training, without *undarii* blood.

Quenfrida was using him. As ever. He said, "That's all, then. I've done as you wanted."

"Have you?" She sounded amused. "You forget yourself. You've grown self-willed."

"I doubt it." He could smell her perfume, like a noose. "Lord Thiercelin has had what he asked for. There will be no further contact between us."

"No?" She came closer. "You're wrong, I think." She ran a finger along his cheekbone. He swallowed. "Your landlord told me he was here into the small hours. That suggests he's concerned about you." She sat down, let her hand stroke his hair. He shuddered. He had no strength for defenses. He doubted he had the strength to do what his body wanted. She continued, "And he's attracted. You'll see him again." She leaned her face against the crown of his head. The softness of her breast pressed against his cheek. She said, "Won't you?"

He bit his lip. "No, Quena. He doesn't deserve it."

She laughed. "He doesn't deserve to be . . . pleased by you? Do you dislike him so much?" Her hands were traveling. "Will you deny him the pleasure of your talents?"

"He doesn't want . . ." Gracielis began and broke off, gasping. "Stop it. This isn't fair." He had opened his eyes again. The lieutenant's ghost watched them avidly.

"To whom?" She took one of his hands and kissed the palm.

To both . . . "To Lord Thiercelin." She licked his wrist. Raising her head, she smiled at him, then kissed his lips. It was hopeless. He could barely move, and she could still do this to him. He said, "Don't."

"My poor Gracielis." She had taken off her shoes. Now she slid to lie beside him. "I don't deal in fairness. Only in truth." Her hands were on him, sweetly tormenting. "Do this for me."

He shivered. "I don't want to." The lieutenant's ghost leaned over him in lubricious spite. "I can't." Even Gracielis was no longer sure to what he was referring.

She kissed him. "Oh, you can," she said, softly. "Let me show you."

*   *   *

Thiercelin missed breakfast, but arrived downstairs in time for lunch to find both his sister-in-law and his wife present. He kissed the latter's hand before taking his place. "This is nice. I didn't know you were home today." A servant placed soup before him.

"I came back midevening yesterday," Yvelliane said. "You were out."

"I wish I'd stayed in, in that case." He raised his wineglass to her. She looked tired. He wished the servants would leave so that he might take her in his arms and kiss her worry lines away.

"You'd have been bored, home with me."

He could never be bored in her company. He said, "Are you here this afternoon? You could bore me then. I'd like it."

For an instant, a smile flickered across her lips. But then, she sighed and looked down. "I have to get back to the palace. I'm sorry."

"I wish you'd woken me."

"Was it fun, your party last night?"

"Not really." Thiercelin stirred his soup. The royal aisle. Valdarrien's ghost and the message he did not understand. *Tell Iareth Yscoithi she was right.* Perhaps Yvelliane would know what that meant. He could not tell her, not now when she was so anxious.

There was a silence. Only Miraude was eating. Thiercelin said, "And tonight?"

"It's the reception for the heir to Lunedith, remember? I told you last week."

He had forgotten, somehow. It would be a chance, perhaps, to speak with Iareth Yscoithi. Did Yvelliane know she was back in Merafi? He did not know if he could risk asking. Yvelliane went on, "You don't have to come, if you like. It'll be very formal."

It would be an evening with Yvelliane. And if she did not know about Iareth, then he would be there to support her. He said, "Of course I'm coming. I want to see you in your party dress. And Mimi, too, of course."

"Yviane's intending to wear that dark gray thing again." Miraude sounded disapproving. "I tried to make her get a new one, but she kept being too busy."

"You have enough new dresses for both of us," Yvelliane said, a smile in her voice. Thiercelin looked up, just to catch it on her lips. She went on, "Besides, I don't want to stand out. Kenan Orcandros and I have met before. He disapproves of me."

"He has bad taste, then." Thiercelin said, hoping to keep her smiling.

He failed. "No, he just has bad politics," Yvelliane said, and sighed. "Firomelle needs me there. She . . ." Her voice died.

He looked at her. "Is she worse?"

Yvelliane looked at Miraude before replying. Then she said, "I can't tell." She rose. "I'm sorry, Thierry; I don't feel like talking. Later, perhaps?"

Later. When she was weary from work and wanted only to sleep. There would be no time at the reception. She looked tired and sad. This was no time to speak to her of her brother or of Iareth Yscoithi. Rising, he held the door open for her. She smiled at him in passing, but her eyes betrayed that her thoughts were elsewhere. He sighed as he sat down again, and Miraude looked at him curiously.

Later. He was losing his faith in later.

Miraude said, "Thierry, is something wrong?"

She was watching him with a certain caution. He said, "No, I don't think so."

"It's just . . ." Her tone was thoughtful.

He put down his spoon and stared at her. "What?"

She evaded his eyes. "It's just something I heard yesterday, from Mal."

"From Mal?" He was baffled. "My so-called friend Mal? As in Maldurel of South Marr? The one with the big mouth and the small brain?"

"You know another one?"

"River forfend! Are you going to tell me what he said?"

"Well . . ." She fidgeted with a knife. "Apparently one of Mal's sisters is supposed to have seen you in a coffeehouse with one of the professional kind. The beautiful Gracieux—Gracielis de Varnaq. And you've been preoccupied lately, and I just wondered . . ."

"If I'd taken a lover?" Thiercelin was torn between outrage and a species of bitter amusement. Dead for six years, Valdarrien, it seemed, was still nevertheless capable of getting him into trouble. He said, "Well, I haven't and so you may tell Mal!"

She considered him. "Mal said he was holding your hand."

"It was nothing like that." For the thousandth time, Thiercelin found himself regretting having ever introduced Miraude to Maldurel. "I love Yviane; you know that." Miraude continued to stare at him. "Do you want me to swear on a holy book or something?"

"No, I don't think so. Men aren't your thing. And I believe you wouldn't hurt Yviane. It's just Mal . . ."

"Mal talks too much.Valdin always said so."

"Oh, Valdin," said Valdarrien's widow dismissively.

Thiercelin was still dealing with his outrage. "If he's going to be telling everyone, I'll . . ."

"Oh, he won't. I convinced him it was nonsense. And anyway, he always said that his sister had too much imagination." Miraude had charming dimples. They appeared now, as she smiled and leaned forward. "So: tell me about Gracieux. You *do* know him? He's supposed to be absolutely fabulous."

"Well, he's fairly unlikely, anyway," Thiercelin said. Miraude pulled a face. "I don't know him well. My connection with him is just . . ." He hesitated, unsure of what to say. "He does translations."

She raised her brows. "You're interested in Tarnaroqi literature?"

"No, but . . . it's for my younger brother." Miraude still looked disbelieving. "I swear it, Mimi, I'm not having an affair with him. Or with anyone else, for that matter. And so you may tell Mal!"

"All right, I'm sorry." She leaned over and kissed his cheek. "I didn't mean anything. I was just worrying."

He looked at her, "You, too? Is something wrong?"

"Not really. I suppose I'm concerned for you and Yviane. And this weather!" She gestured at the window. "All this rain. It makes me restless."

"Like Valdin."

She looked interested. "How?"

"He hated to be bored. Weather like this . . ." He shrugged. "He was always more . . . excitable at such times." Her expression suggested that she had noticed the euphemism. He looked apologetic. "More violent, then. He had an abominable habit of fighting duels in the rain. Very unpleasant for the seconds."

"Poor Thierry."

Thierry, forgive . . . Abruptly, Thiercelin said, "It was worth it. It has to be." He had to face Iareth Yscoithi, tonight, if he got the chance, and without Yvelliane knowing of it. He could hardly burden Yvelliane with his present problems.

"What is it?" Miraude sounded concerned. "Are you sure you're all right?"

I could tell her, Thiercelin thought, looking into her wide eyes. *She was Valdin's wife, she's young, she might understand*. It would be easier, shared. Then he remembered Iareth, who had abandoned Valdarrien when she had learned that he had a wife. Iareth Yscoithi, and a chill autumn night, and slim fingers holding his. He shook his head. "It's nothing, Mimi. I'm just . . . I'm just worried about Yviane."

It appalled him that this was, in the end, a lie.

It was late afternoon before Quenfrida left. Her potions and caresses had eased his discomfort, but Gracielis found no peace. The lieutenant's ghost mocked him, and he flinched from it, afraid of shared comprehension.

She was planning something. She was using him to some purpose that he did not understand. He liked it not at all. Dressing with uncertain fingers, he went over it in his mind. Good blood . . . He had never studied the pedigrees of the lesser nobility of Gran' Romagne. He did not remember hearing that Thiercelin's duLaurier line shared Gracielis' own kind of blood. That was the kind of thing he was schooled to know and to recognize. But his out-of-practice eyes had seen no such traces in Thiercelin.

A ghost out of time. Out of order. (A glance, there, for the lieutenant's ghost, watching him as he drew black lines below his lashes.) In addition, it was raining too much, unseasonally. There was something wrong. Something in Merafi's air bespoke change.

It was not his concern. He was Tarnaroqui, bred to beauty and artifice. There should be no place in him for compassion, for Thiercelin or for dead, murderous Valdarrien. It was nothing to him, what Quenfrida schemed.

Except when she reminded him too sharply of his dependencies. He stroked color along his cheekbones. It was folly, this compassion, in either of his professions. He was merchandise, no more. In him, attacks of conscience tasted only of sophistry. What right had one who lived through the sale of his body to any dominion over his soul? He could not afford the luxury of integrity.

He was, after all, no better than the rest. The lieutenant's ghost watched him, its face expressionless, as if it distrusted this sudden bitterness. Well, and so he did himself. He was better accustomed to fear and dissimulation. They had honed him to be a weapon, the priests of his people, and cast him aside when he failed. Cast aside, but not lost, as long as Quenfrida lived to bind him. The gift and the burden of the *undarii*, the perfumed ones, servants of love and death. They were bearers of the other blood, the true blood that was feared in Merafi, bound together in heritage.

He ran a comb through his disordered hair, and caught the eye of the ghost in the mirror. It took no part in his life, save in its self-appointed role of mockery. Whatever it knew of the changes, it would not share.

No more than Gracielis might share any of his own suspicions with Thiercelin of Sannazar.

And yet . . . There was more to all this than Quenfrida revealed. He did not doubt that she sought to harm Yvelliane, but her course was oblique. There was something else here.

He laid down the comb, and turned to face the ghost. "So," he said to it, to himself, "you have a recommendation?" It made an obscene gesture. "Quite. But that is sadly impossible, given your noncorporeal condition." He spread out his hands. "I must forgo your advice, I think."

He hesitated before opening the chest that stood at the foot of his bed and taking out a small box. It was folly to seek to outguess Quenfrida, especially by these means. And then, his physical condition was weak.

He had no other recourse. The box was not locked. From it, he took a small deck of cards and began to shuffle. Quenfrida had left cups on the table. He had to pause to clear it. Then he looked across at the ghost and began to deal. "I hope you're paying attention. You won't often see me do this." It began to drift nearer, affecting scorn. Gracielis smiled. "So. You never know, you might even learn something."

Privately, he doubted it. He used this method seldom, finding the symbols imprecise. It was too easy to reach generalized conclusions, unless one possessed the necessary mastery, which, frankly, he lacked. He had never been good with cards. As a ghostseer, he was better at reading the past than the future.

Well, it was the present he must try to see now. That was often the hardest of all. It would not stand still.

Inexperienced as he was, the reading was made harder
in that he lacked both Thiercelin's presence and any possession of his to facilitate contact. He laid the cards out
Mothmoonwise, in the spread that divines character, and
stared down at them, frowning. The lieutenant's ghost
peered over his shoulder, disarranging his lace with its
insubstantial breath.

"Opinion?" he said to it. It sneered. "Ah. Too much
privilege, you think? Were you a leveler?" The ghost
made a gesture of distaste. Gracielis shrugged. "Perhaps
not." Anyway, there was little here of privilege, if wealth
was meant by that word. Thiercelin's fortunes had lain
in friendship, and in his own reserves, not so much in
worldly things. The past was clear on that. The future
was confused. Even to himself, Gracielis could admit
that the disarray lay in more than his own shortcomings
as a seer. Change, quadranted in water and earth. No
obvious line of continuity. And as to the present . . .

There was a shadow on that. Too many cards of mixed
meaning. He could make no sense of them. A slow turning, a journey without forward motion. A joining; a
meeting with an enabling stranger . . .

He pulled a face. This was too glib. As ever, he was
blinding himself by viewing only the expected. Shaking
his head, he passed a hand across the cards and jumbled
them. The ghost watched, impassive. He was too remote
from his subject. There were too many variables.

Quenfrida or no Quenfrida, nothing in Thiercelin's
past bespoke good blood. And Gracielis had a talent for
the past, for the dead. It was Quenfrida's mystery, after
all. He had a scarf of hers, kept safe. She would know,
of course, if he meddled.

He needed to know. Fetching the scarf, he spread it
out before him and dealt the cards onto it, one hand
touching it. Not a full reading, she was too well guarded
for that. But a partial one might do; the levin-bolt form
that sometimes—sometimes—struck unaware.

He remembered the warmth of her and the taste of

her skin. Her hands on him, long ago, before he learned to fear her. Long ago, when he had had her approval and her kindness. He should see in his cards her strengths, her ambitions, his own flawed presence. Placing the last card, he looked down at the whole, to read back up to the present moment. Then he froze.

Quenfrida *undaria*. Mistress. Mentor. Under her guidance, it should show only himself, failed acolyte.

The spread was plain, there under his hands. Not one pupil. Not one, but two.

"It's the Duke d'Almeide all over again," Joyain said, dismally. "You can't begin to imagine. And I thought court service would be exciting."

"Poor Jean." Amalie smiled at him. "I suppose another pastry won't help? No, I didn't think so."

"Foreigners," Joyain said, in a tone of the darkest disgust. And then, "I'm sorry, Tante Amalie. It's not really that they're foreign; it's just Prince Kenan. He's enough to drive any man to drink." He sighed again. "And I'm stuck with him for the foreseeable future."

Amalie took a flask from a rosewood corner cabinet and poured a healthy tot from it into a cup. Joyain watched her gratefully. If he had been a gambling man, he would be keeping as far as humanly possible from the tables, the way his luck was running at present. All right, it made sense that the trouble in the new dock should take precedence over the shepherding of a bunch of (supposedly) friendly Northerners around the city, but it still seemed rather hard that the latter duty should have defaulted onto him. He was feeling very put-upon, and rather sorry for himself, and not even the excellence of his aunt's pastries was quite enough to make him let go of his self-pity just yet.

She wasn't really his aunt, of course. She was his mother's first cousin's second husband's sister. However, from their second meeting, they had agreed that aunt was the preferred relationship. "The lax, indulgent kind,"

Amalie had said, mildly horrified to find that her distant kinsman had been expecting her to represent the forces of propriety. An indulgent aunt was, it transpired, exactly the kind of relative that a junior officer from an obscure and impoverished family needed in Merafi. Amalie fed him, listened sympathetically to his exploits, and occasionally lent him money. In return, he escorted her to formal guild functions, helped drive off her more persistent suitors, and maintained an obstinate silence in the face of family queries regarding her personal life.

It was an arrangement that suited both of them. Pouring herself a slighter smaller helping of cordial, Amalie sat down again and said, "It's not all bad, surely? The captain will be pleased with you."

"If I'm lucky." He pulled a face. "It does no good at all being diligent if one—just one—of the Lunedithin decides he doesn't like me." Amalie was giving him a measuring look. "All right. The captain isn't quite that unreasonable. One complaint from a troublemaking guest is survivable. But a guest could make several, or just decide to be the biggest nuisance possible."

"Is that likely?"

Joyain hesitated. It had to be admitted, Kenan Orcandros had so far done nothing worse than be fussy over his choice of room and grumble about the weather. The latter was an activity of which Joyain himself was not wholly guiltless. If he was strictly honest, it was the loss of his free time that galled him most. And if the trouble in the port was as bad as his contact in the city guard made out, chances were he'd be down there up to his knees in mud, if he hadn't been assigned to assist with the Lunedithin. He caught Amalie's eye and smiled. "No."

"Well, then."

"I know." He shrugged. "Most of them are quite decent. Even Kenan isn't too dreadful. He just doesn't like being here." Pausing, he looked at Amalie thoughtfully. Like most of the merchant community, she was not averse to the odd political tidbit. "I'm not certain that his presence is entirely popular with our side, either."

Amalie looked interested. She had already confided to him her anxiety over the current unrest. She was expecting a cargo from the south, and the ship was overdue. Mercantile rumor spoke of interference at sea by Tarnaroqui customs ships. Lunedith, with its sulfur reserves, could seriously upset trade if it elected to deal directly with Tarnaroq, rather than via Merafien middlemen. And, of course, if the arms supply was disrupted, then other commodities were sure to follow. Joyain lacked Amalie's head for figures, but he grasped the broad outlines of the problem. Putting down his cup, he leaned toward her and said, "I'm due to attend the official presentation of the Lunedithin tonight. It'll be a big ceremony. The whole of the royal council will be there."

"Including First Councillor Yvelliane d'Illandre." Amalie was thoughtful. "She went to Lunedith a few years ago when we drew up the most recent trade agreement. I wonder what she thinks of Kenan Orcandros."

If she had any sense, she would dislike him. But Joyain did not say that. Rather, "I'll keep an eye on her and see if she gives anything away."

"Thank you. Word in the guild is that Kenan is anti-Merafien. He's hoping to separate Lunedith from dependency on us when he succeeds as ruler there. . . . Jean?"

"Yes?"

"Have any of the Tarnaroqui faction shown an interest in your Lunedithin, yet?"

"No . . . They've only just arrived, after all."

"Well, yes. All the same . . ." Amalie frowned. "I'm not asking you to spy, but if there is such an interest, do you think you might let me know?"

"Of course," said Joyain, kissing her hand.

Two lines of tall, formal plane trees lined the Grand Aisle through the grounds of the Rose Palace. Torches burned in the scones bound to the trunks of each tree,

lighting their branches with amber light. Leaves—
autumnal brown in daylight—now showed themselves
tinged with warm orange. The aisle was paved in wide
gray stone, spread with fresh straw to muffle hoofbeats
and the rumble of carriage wheels. In front of the north
fascia of the palace, the aisle divided, two sweeping arms
framing an oval of grass and a marble fountain before
coming together to meet at the foot of the stairs to the
Great Entrance. Footmen hovered at its base, to assist
courtiers and visitors to descend from their vehicles.
Most nights, there were no more than four of them. Tonight, there were twelve, all decked out in crisp new
tabards bearing the arms of the queen. Stepping down
from the Far Blays coach, Miraude smiled her thanks to
the man who had helped her, then waited for Thiercelin
to alight. Seven or eight carriages queued behind theirs;
light spilled from every window of the palace. "Well,"
Miraude said, tucking her arm into Thiercelin's, "we
won't be short of company tonight."

"That's something to look forward to." Thiercelin's
hand strayed to the ruffles at his neck. "These things
itch."

"But they look lovely. I'm sure Yviane will agree.
Come on." And she towed her reluctant escort up the
stairs and into the huge first antechamber of the palace
itself.

"I never know what I'm supposed to talk to these
people about." Thiercelin gestured with his chin toward
a knot of finely dressed nobility gathered in the doorway
of one of the long rooms that lined the ground floor.

"Horses," suggested Miraude, before turning to bob
to a passing friend. "Or you could tell them how lovely
they're looking."

"And that's just the men." Thiercelin bowed in his
turn to a distant fourth cousin of his wife's. "I could
almost pity this Kenan Orcandros, having to perform
homage in front of this crowd."

"Nonsense. It's a mark of honor." Miraude had succeeded in leading him through the throng to the bottom of the great staircase which led up to the ceremonial rooms on the first floor. "And besides, this lot down here are mostly the minor nobles. It'll be quieter upstairs."

"That depends on what you mean," Thiercelin said gloomily. "There's going to be chamber music, I daresay. Cremornes, if we're really lucky."

"Don't be awkward. The queen's Master of the Household has impeccable taste. If there are cremornes, they'll be the finest of their kind."

"And they'll still honk."

"That'll be afterward, at the reception. Oh, do come on, Thierry, Yviane will be waiting for us."

It was midevening. After her discussion with Yvelliane that morning, Miraude had canceled her plans for the day and spent the time instead reading history, while her dressmaker made alterations to the gown she had ordered for this ceremony. Kenan Orcandros would not be an easy man to approach, from what she had heard. She would need to proceed carefully. Tonight, she intended to observe. It would not do, in such circumstances, to attract too much attention to her appearance. Her dressmaker had mourned the suppression of silk ruffles and ribbon knots, but tonight the beautiful Miraude d'Iscoigne l'Aborderie chose to seem serious and respectable. Thiercelin had laughed when he saw her. "Goodness, Mimi, are you going into mourning?"

"Only for your wardrobe. I swear, you and Yviane are as bad as each other." And she had eyed his brown coat with disfavor. Now, entering the Grand Audience Chamber on his arm, she was grateful for his sobriety.

The chamber occupied two thirds of the front part of this side of the palace. By day, light streamed into it from the long windows set into two of its sides. At night, it was lit by hundreds of wax candles, set into heavy crystal candelabra suspended from the ceiling or mounted on wall brackets. In the third wall were set the entrance doors, three pairs. The fourth wall was covered, floor to ceiling, with a series of large canvases depicting the triumphs of the Illandre dynasty. Here, a king in old-fashioned armor led his troops into battle against the Tarnaroqui. There, another sat enthroned in judgment. Behind the great chair, used by the queen for high ceremonies, hung a portrait of the first Illandre, Yestinn, in full battle array and holding his own standard in front of the waterfall of Saefoss, where he had defeated his rival, Kenan's ancestor Gaverne Orcandros. Kenan would be unable to forget his status as vassal, standing before that picture. And that, no doubt, was the point. The queen's chair stood on a dais, with slightly smaller ones to either side for her consort and the crown prince. Below the dais to left and right were set a small number of tambour seats, for the senior ladies of the court. Everyone else, from dukes to ambassadors to councillors, was expected to stand.

The dais was still unoccupied, although several servants stood about it; the queen's party would enter from the private door set behind it. Nor had the Lunedithin yet arrived. But most of the great nobility were already present and standing in their allocated places. Miraude and Thiercelin took theirs, close to the dais as befitted the family of the queen's near kin. She would have a clear view of Kenan in profile: that was good. Miraude allowed Thiercelin to hand her onto her tambour and unfurled her fan. The windows were closed and casemented; the brocade curtains had been drawn tight across them. The press of people and the many candles stifled the room. The clash of perfumes and flowers, powders and pomades, served only to thicken the air. She could feel the muslin of her innermost petticoat already beginning to stick to her. This was to be an evening of formal ceremony, not of amusement. Perhaps the heat served as a reminder of that.

The private door opened, and the Second Councillor stepped out onto the dais, flushed and uncomfortable in a coat that was clearly several seasons too tight. He was followed by Yvelliane and then the young crown prince. While the Second Councillor placed himself at the foot of the dais, Yvelliane took a position behind and to the right of the queen's chair. She nodded and the assembled company rose. Prince Laurens entered and stood by the door to offer his arm to his wife. The queen was laden down with brocade and lace and jewelry. The state crown sat heavily on her hair: beneath it, she looked pinched and gray. As Laurens led her to her chair, the court bowed. Watching under her lashes, Miraude noted that Firomelle held tightly onto Laurens, the veins in her hand too pronounced. As the company rose and resumed their places, she risked a quick glance toward the Ninth Councillor, several yards away. There was one, at least, who was already jockeying for position in anticipation of the queen's death. Beyond him, the ambassador from Tarnaroq was smooth-faced and serene. As Miraude began to look away, one of his aides caught her eye and gave a creamy smile. Quenfrida d'Ivrinez was another one upon whom she knew Yvelliane kept a close watch. Miraude patted at the lace on her sleeve and pretended to be scanning the room for *faux pas* in matters of dress. The countess of LaMarche-Retaux was wearing puce with mustard ribbons. Miraude allowed an eyebrow to rise, then turned her attention back to the dais. Yvelliane gazed out over the crowd, frowning. As Miraude watched, she looked briefly at Thiercelin and the frown lifted just slightly. Then the queen coughed, and it returned.

There was a loud knock on the central main door, and all heads turned that way. The chief steward, dressed in full livery and carrying a gilded rod, stood in the doorway and bowed. "Your Majesty, the heir to Lunedith craves admission to your presence."

"Let him enter." Despite her frailty, Firomelle's voice was clear.

The steward bowed again and stood aside. "Your Majesty, Prince Kenan Orcandros of Lunedith. Ambassador

Ceretic of Lunedith. Tafarin Morwenedd, deputy commander of the royal *kai-rethin* of Lunedith." There was a fanfare from the corridor outside, and the Lunedithin party came into the room, Kenan at their head.

He was a slight man, with reddish-brown hair brushed smoothly back from his face and worn in an unfashionable long braid. He wore a simple gray tunic over a pale shirt, and dark trousers; his cloak was likewise gray, but trimmed in scarlet. His sole ornament was the bronze brooch holding the cloak in place. He looked younger than his twenty years: his eyes flickered across the room as though he hunted for someone or something. That was interesting. Miraude followed his glance, again under her lashes. The Tarnaroqui. Very interesting. At his right, Ambassador Ceretic beamed at the company with his usual good humor. The third man, Tafarin, looked awed. Behind her, Thiercelin shuffled his feet, and she gave him a surreptitious poke with her fan.

A handful of soldiers followed Kenan into the room, all from the queen's household troop, their dress uniforms far more eye-catching than the somber clothes of the Lunedithin. Kenan's own guards would be waiting downstairs: they had no place in this ceremony. While Kenan and his flankers advanced through the line of watching aristocracy, the soldiers took up positions by the doors. The room was silent, save for footfalls and the hiss of candles. If Yvelliane had not asked her to be vigilant, Miraude might almost have felt sorry for Kenan, running this gamut of intense scrutiny. He arrived at the foot of the dais and halted. At his side, the ambassador held out a letter to the Second Councillor. It was adorned with a huge seal and tied with cords of scarlet and gray. The councillor took it and brought it up the steps to the queen. Kenan stood firm, face now stern, his eyes on Firomelle. She broke the seal and read the letter once, slowly, before handing it Yvelliane. Then she said, "Prince Kenan, be welcome in our domains. Your grandsire, our ally and vassal Prince Keris, does us honor through you." There was a silence. Kenan looked right and left, then made the smallest of bows. A mutter ran through the lines of nobles, and Ambassador Ceretic began to look worried. Firomelle ignored it. She said, "We will receive your homage. Approach us." There was another silence. Then Kenan climbed the three steps to the top of the dais and knelt, hands together and held out before him.

Firomelle said, "Kenan Orcandros. Your forebears held their lands and title at our good favor and in obedience to us. Do you seek now to be confirmed as heir to those lands?"

"Yes." Kenan's voice was pitched low and hard to hear even this close by. Miraude could sense dissatisfaction forming among the gathering. He would make few friends this way. If, indeed, he wanted to at all.

"And are you now willing to swear to me your loyalty and obedience, as your forebears have done before you?"

"Yes." The second response was pitched even lower than the first.

"Then, Kenan Orcandros, make to me now your oath." Firomelle leaned forward to place her thin hands about his. "Do you swear to hold your lands with justice . . ." She paused for a moment, as if seeking her breath. "With justice and honor?"

"I swear." This time, Kenan's voice was clearer,

There was another pause, this one longer. To Miraude, Firomelle's face seemed flushed. "And will you respect . . . the rights of the crown in peace . . ." Firomelle swayed a little and coughed, once. "In peace and in war?"

"I swear."

Firomelle coughed again, this time for longer. Beside her, Laurens leaned forward, concerned. "And will you . . . render all due services and . . . tributes and . . ." Another cough. There were lines of pain in Firomelle's face. Kenan's eyes were downcast. Miraude found herself gripping tightly onto her fan. She did not believe in omens. But there were too many who did, or would feign to, if it might bring them advantage. Firomelle regained her voice and continued, "And swear obedience . . . to our . . ."

She began to cough again, bending forward with the force of it. Yvelliane reached out toward her. The room echoed back the sound, rough and agonized. Under it, through it, Kenan's voice said, clearly, "I swear."

He lifted his head to stare at his hands. Miraude followed his gaze. His fingers and Firomelle's were coated with blood.

4

*I*ARETH YSCOITHI OF ALFIAL *to Urien Armenwy, called Swanhame, Councillor and Leader of the Kairethin: Greetings.*

Tafarin kai-reth has written to you and to our lord Prince Keris of the incident that disrupted the homage ceremonial: I append this letter for your further information and consideration. I myself was not present at the event and can thus add nothing to Tafarin's account of it directly. Consequent upon Firomelle Allandur being taken ill, the reception was presided over by her consort and her son and passed off well, the prince consort making little of his wife's indisposition. Returning from the palace, Kenan kai-reth seemed more than satisfied with the turn of events, which I will own to finding disquieting. He is due to return to the palace for a private audience with the Allandur in three days' time. In the meantime, I will maintain watch over him as you have directed. Ambassador Ceretic will certainly be writing to the Orcandros about the health of the Allandur and the reactions to it in her court and government.

I have had as yet had scant chance to go about within the city, apart for that small part proximate to our residence and the Rose Palace. Nor have I seen Yviane Allandur save at a distance. I confess myself grateful for this; it seems that my courage in this respect is less than I had believed. But I am well within myself, Father. Do not be concerned upon my behalf. It has been six years since the death of Valdin Allandur. I intend to face such memories as this city contains with firm resolve.

I should report also that this forenoon we received a visit from the resident ambassador from Tarnaroq, accompanied by the Lady Quenfrida, who is known to us . . .

"The Tarnaroqui delegation, monseigneur," Joyain announced. "The honorable Ambassador Lord Sigeris; the Lord Radewund; the Lady Quenfrida." It was not his job to conduct visitors to Kenan, not usually. But they had arrived as he had been about to inform His Highness that the horses were ready for his morning ride, and it had seemed efficient for him to accompany them upstairs. Stepping to his left, he bowed. "I'll send word to the stables that your ride is delayed. Will that be all, monseigneur?"

Kenan Orcandros looked up from the correspondence he had been going over with Iareth Yscoithi. "Thank you, Lieutenant. Do remain." His tone was not quite pleasant. "I'm sure your commanding officer will want to be sure we do not plot treachery under your roof, whatever our various reputations. You, too, Iareth *kaireth.*" Iareth had risen; she nodded and stepped back to stand at a window.

Joyain said nothing. Kenan, it seemed, was still young enough to enjoy rudeness. If Kenan wanted to be insulting—Joyain was pretty sure that the subject of the insult was less himself, than it was his country and the Tarnaroqui delegation—then that was none of Joyain's business. His commanding officer was unlikely to care, and it was up to the Tarnaroqui how they responded. Schooling his face to neutrality, he retired to the door and stood with his back to it.

At least it was dry in here. He had never known rain like it: there was talk in the barracks of sandbagging the old quay, and the floating dock was all but unusable. Ambassador Sigeris had finished making a long—and incomprehensible—speech in Tarnaroqui. Now he bowed, and added in Merafien, "Which is to say, we of Tarnaroq are honored to make the acquaintance of Lunedith's heir." It seemed he, too, chose to ignore Kenan's attempt at insult.

Kenan had not bothered to rise. To Sigeris' speech, he responded only with a curt nod. Sigeris looked momentarily askance, then, recovering himself, asked, "How do you find Merafi?"

"Wet," said Kenan.

There was a pause. The visitors had not been invited to sit. Sigeris stood with his hands behind him, watching Kenan. Radewund was studying his cuffs. To Joyain's experienced eye, he looked hungover. The woman Quenfrida had wandered over to the mantel, and was examining a china figure. Without turning, she said "Would that be slightly, adequately, quite, or very?"

"What?" asked Kenan.

"Wet."

There was another pause. Then Kenan said, "Somewhat. If I may enlarge the parameters."

"Naturally. That's one of rank's privileges." Quenfrida's voice was silken: although he could not see her face, Joyain was willing to swear that she was smiling.

"So it is," Kenan said lazily. "I'd rather forgotten."

"Ah," said Quenfrida. "Forgetfulness."

"Quite. I am, in addition, remiss. I begin to note it." Kenan made a small bow to Sigeris. "Perhaps Your Graces would care to sit and take refreshments with me?"

Sigeris was watching Quenfrida: his expression was curiously thoughtful. As she turned to look at him, it turned into a smile. To Kenan, he said, "That would be welcome."

"So." Kenan gestured to the assortment of chairs. "It's morning. They drink chocolate here at this hour, I think." He glanced at Joyain as he spoke. The latter made a hasty bow. "At home in Lunedith, we drink ale."

So did Joyain, as a rule. Chocolate was for the rich. Iareth left the room; he heard her relaying the order to a footman before returning and resuming her place. The Tarnaroqui delegation seated themselves, and the conversation took a friendlier turn. Kenan had been taken to a performance at the Gran' Théâtre the night before. He had not, it seemed, enjoyed it. (Tafarin Morwenedd had, and the tavern afterward even more so. Joyain's own state of health still bore slight witness to that.) Radewund recommended a different theater company. Sigeris listened. Quenfrida gazed absently into her cup. So far it seemed that from this encounter, at least, the hottest news Joyain would have for Amalie was that there wouldn't be much of a market in Lunedith for either chocolate or theater props. "But," Quenfrida said, looking up, "you will have many demands on your time, I'm sure. Your Highness is the latest novelty. I'm sure you'll be invited everywhere."

"I do not care for frivolity." Kenan spoke in the tone of a septuagenarian. Joyain lowered his gaze.

"Ah, but one finds some splendid hospitality in Merafi," Radewund said.

"And gains the chance to be on good terms with a number of influential people." Quenfrida picked up an invitation card from the table. "The salon of Miraude d'Iscoigne l'Aborderie. She's the First Councillor's sister-in-law, you know, and very charming. You never know what you'll discover at her salons or whom you'll meet. You should go."

"Perhaps I will." Kenan sounded bored, but he reached for the card. "My Iareth *kai-reth*, do you know of this Miraude de Iscoigne? From her name, she might well be distant kin of yours." He turned as he spoke, and on his lips was a cool smile. There was something unkind to it. Joyain glanced across at Iareth.

Calmly, she said, "If so, I know nothing of it. She is, as you say, the sister-in-law of Yviane Allandur. I believe I met her, when I was formerly in Merafi."

"Indeed?" Kenan turned back to his guests. He said, "Iareth is my expert upon matters Merafien."

"A pleasant expertise," Quenfrida said. "Even for a Lunedithin." She smiled at Iareth. "Do you find it so?"

"In parts." Iareth did not return the smile. "Was that your experience, when you came to Skarholm to study matters Lunedithin?"

Kenan looked at her sharply.

"Indeed," Quenfrida said. "It's a fine thing, Lunedithin hospitality." She smiled at Kenan. "I have fond memories of my stay there. And of my hosts. Among others."

Amalie had not mentioned that one of the current Tarnaroqui embassy had formerly held a post in Lunedith. Perhaps she had not known. What Joyain found more interesting was that Kenan and Quenfrida had effected not to know one another. Not for the benefit of Sigeris, surely? The latter would certainly to know the backgrounds of his aides. In which case . . . Trying to unravel the puzzle, Joyain missed Kenan's reply to Quenfrida, and Sigeris was relating some anecdote about a court masque.

The conversation continued for some minutes longer upon desultory matters, before the Tarnaroqui rose and took their leave. Kenan dismissed Joyain and Iareth in their wake. In the hall, he rang the bell for the footman to take a new message to the stables and waited.

After a moment, Iareth said, "Do you know this Tarnaroqui embassy?"

It was an odd question. Joyain said, "Not personally."

She looked briefly surprised. Then she shook her head. "So: I'd forgotten. The guards of your queen are not as our *kai-rethin*." That did not seem to need a reply. She said, "But you know of the embassy?"

It appeared that rather a lot of people were interested in the Tarnaroqui. Somewhat stiffly, Joyain said, "A little, yes."

"Indeed." Again, Iareth paused. "It is only that I wondered, somewhat, concerning this Quenfrida . . . She has been long in Merafi?"

"I'm not sure."

"No." Her tone was absent. Glancing at her, he could read little from her face. Unexpectedly, she looked up and smiled. "Once again, I'm inconveniencing you."

"It doesn't matter."

He did not understand the look she gave him, half-measuring, half, perhaps, regretful. But she said only, "Thank you," and went away down the passage.

Although it was still early autumn, cold shrouded the city. Two chill nights followed two gray days, rain churned the streets to mud, and the river swelled within its banks. A full quarter of the wharves were unusable, not counting those in the disrupted and uneasy new dock. Some of the wells in the low city were beginning to taste salty. The pleasure gardens were waterlogged, and shop awnings hung limp and dulled.

It was a poor season for pleasure, and poorer for those who must live by those means, as the rich withdrew into the warmth of their private houses. In coffeehouses and inns, the landlords muttered; at the Gran' Théâtre, the manager sighed over his receipts. Everywhere, in the mansions of the nobility and the countinghouses of merchants, in guildhalls and temples, in garrets and tenements and shanty-huts, people discussed their queen's health in hushed tones. She had hemorrhaged in full view of the court. It mattered little that the day after she had walked in her gardens with her son and visited the main fire temple with her consort: there was still talk of ill omens. Some of the foreign merchants raised their prices, while native traders looked grim. The number of petitioners outside the houses of certain councillors increased. It was said Yvelliane d'Illandre, who would surely know more than any other how serious matters were, had not left her offices at the Rose Palace since the night of the reception for Prince Kenan.

The night of the reception, Gracielis had awoken chill and disturbed from fitful sleep. Ever since, it seemed to him that a mood drifted over the city, invisible, cold, malevolent. Two days after that evening, he walked one of the paths alongside the northern arm of the river. It was not raining, but he shivered despite his heavy cloak and fur-lined two-colored gloves. Something waited. Something he did not wish to feel. To one side, the lieutenant's ghost paced him, hazy with moisture. To the other, Amalie walked, holding his arm.

He could not imagine why she wanted to promenade here, in this weather. In any weather, for that matter. But it was not for him to question her. There were rules to this, as to any job. Besides, it pleased him to please her. And then, he had to eat.

She said, "You're very quiet."

"Your beauty silences me." She snorted. He said, "I'll talk, then, if it pleases you."

"You know it does. You practice." She squeezed his arm. "Everything about you pleases me, love."

"I'm glad. It's my greatest fear, that I'll cease to please you."

She laughed. "I'll let you know."

"Thank you." The ghost sneered at him. He ignored it. "And are you pleased by this scenery?"

"Do you have that in your power as well?" She shook her head at him. "I don't deserve your talents."

"Not so. My talents are inadequate." He smiled. "Is there something you'd have me change?"

"I wish!"

The river was high, heavy with mud and debris. The towpaths were all but deserted, and they had seen only one barge. The day was very still. He was again aware of a quality of waiting, caught in the air.

Amalie said, "I wanted to look at the river, but . . ."

"I was in the old town last night. The south channel is very high. I believe ships can still pass, though."

"Are you sure?"

"No, but I can ask."

"Thank you." But she sighed.

Gracielis looked at her. "Has your ship arrived?"

"Not yet." She sighed again. Gently, he lifted her hand to his lips.

He said, "It will be well."

"Yes, I suppose so. And I can sustain the loss, if necessary. But with this news of the queen in addition . . . My trading partners in the Allied Cities won't like it. They're sure to want to charge me more and pay less for my goods. My guild is unhappy."

"They say that she appeared quite well at the temple."

"Yes, I know. But all the same . . ."

She was worrying, it was clear. Stopping, he placed his hands on her shoulders and looked down into her eyes. Carefully, kindly, he said, "Ladyheart. Do not."

"Don't what?"

"Frown." He circled her face with a finger. "It makes wrinkles."

"That would be a calamity."

"Assuredly." Over her shoulder, he could see the river, hazy beyond the lieutenant's ghost. It looked as if a mist might be rising. He asked, "Are you cold?"

"Not especially. Are you?"

"A little. Your Merafien climate . . ."

"No resilience." But she slipped her arms around him and rested her cheek on his shoulder. He began to wrap his cloak about them both, then paused as the ghost moved, improving his view of the river. That moved brown and slow, blurred with the mist, which was beginning to seep into the streets and alleys and gardens. There were shapes in the mist, and beneath the surface of the river, moving against the current, adopting forms they should not take. They uncoiled with lazy confidence, less substantial than the lieutenant's malicious ghost. Under them Gracielis could sense something more, a heavy immanence of water, falling in thunder and spray.

He inhaled sharply. Amalie stared up at him in consternation. "What is it, love?"

She was blind to it, he could tell. Blind as Thiercelin had not been . . . Gracielis controlled his breathing and found a smile for her. "Nothing, Ladyheart. Only the cold."

"I knew it. Let's go back."

He wanted nothing more. He drew her against him, and her arm slid around him again as they began to retrace their steps. After a while, she said, "You're too thin, you know."

"That's my nature." The lieutenant's ghost glowered at him. Rain was starting to fall. Gracielis pulled his cloak more securely closed.

He did not look back to where the river bore its cargo of restless changes to breathe across the waiting city.

The same day, Thiercelin presented himself at the Lunedithin residence. It had proved harder than he had anticipated to bring himself to this point. Some part of him shivered from the idea of Yvelliane learning he had had dealings of any kind with Iareth Yscoithi. She had enough troubles. After Firomelle had been taken ill, he had hovered near Yvelliane's offices in the Rose Palace for most of the night, in case she should want him. She had not: Around daybreak, one of her secretaries had come to order him home. Yvelliane herself remained behind and had not responded to his messages. Nor had he been able to see her. He had waited at home until Miraude accused him of moping. He was, and it helped no one. If he saw Iareth, perhaps he might learn something that could be of help to Yvelliane, if he did it properly. He was not sure he could. He was very nervous. When the door was opened by a liveried footman, he drew himself up to his full height and endeavored to look forbidding.

The man bowed, and said, "Good day, monseigneur."

Thiercelin said, "I'm here to see mademoiselle Iareth Yscoithi."

"Very good, monseigneur. Please come in." He ushered Thiercelin into a well-appointed chamber off the hall. "What name am I to announce?"

"I'm an old friend . . ," Thiercelin began. "I'm sure she'll be happy to receive me."

"Of course, monseigneur. However . . ." The footman hesitated. "Perhaps you have an appointment?"

Thiercelin had never been a very good liar. Looking at his feet, he said, "The fact is, I . . . Not precisely, no."

"I see." The footman seemed to be making a mental assessment of him. "I will make inquiries."

"Thank you."

It took less time than he had expected. After about five minutes, the door opened. Thiercelin looked up, hoping to see Iareth.

It was a young officer in the uniform of the Queen's Own Cavalry. He bowed to Thiercelin and shut the door. "Good day, monseigneur. I'm the liaison officer for the heir's party. Perhaps I can assist you?"

"I hope so," Thiercelin said cordially. "I'd like to see Iareth Yscoithi."

"Yes, monseigneur, so the footman tells me." The officer had curiously deep-set eyes, lending a serious cast to his countenance. "However, there seems to be a problem with identification." Thiercelin was silent. "I'm sure, monseigneur, that you can appreciate that it isn't good policy to admit unknown persons."

"It does seem reasonable," Thiercelin admitted. He was beginning to wish he had never tried this. He should have sent a note. "But my situation's rather delicate. I'd rather not have to give my name."

"In that case, monseigneur, I regret that you won't be able to obtain an appointment."

"Evidently," Thiercelin said. And then, "Drown it!" The officer was perfectly pleasant, but he might as well have been a stone wall. Thiercelin sighed. "I don't suppose you could see your way to . . ." The officer made no response. Uncomfortably, Thiercelin continued, "I'm not without resources."

"I'm happy for you."

Thiercelin looked at his feet. Bribery went right against his grain. He said, "Perhaps we could come to some arrangement?"

The officer's eyes narrowed. "I doubt it."

"What I meant was . . ."

"I know what you meant," the officer said. "Attempting to bribe one of Her Majesty's officers is an offense, monseigneur. I suggest you leave."

"I need to see Iareth," Thiercelin said, aware that he had succeeded only in giving offense. "My business is quite important."

"As are my duties," said the officer. "Good day to you . . . monseigneur." The pause was just long enough to be insulting. Valdarrien would have challenged him for that.

Thiercelin was not Valdarrien. Controlling his irritation with himself and the situation, he said, "I'd be very grateful . . ."

"I do not," said the officer, "take bribes." He glared at Thiercelin. "So why don't you just leave?"

Thiercelin's irritation peaked. He said, "Are you dismissing me?"

"Yes," said the officer, and turned his back.

"As a gentleman . . ." Thiercelin began.

"I wasn't aware that I was dealing with one."

Thiercelin forgot himself. He stood up straight, "Enough, monsieur. I am Thiercelin duLaurier of Sannazar and the Far Blays, and I need to see Iareth Yscoithi."

"Really?" The officer looked around.

"Are you calling me a liar?"

"Let's say I find it rather odd that the First Councillor's husband would come here and refuse to identify himself."

"I just did," said Thiercelin, stung. The officer said nothing. "And I'll be quite happy to prove it to you. Shall we say the Winter Gardens?"

"Very good. When?"

"Your discretion. I'll expect your second at the Far Blays townhouse."

"Indeed?" The officer looked incredulous.

This was getting out of control. Thiercelin sighed. It had been years—six years—since he had been involved in any kind of duel. And as for acting as the principal in one . . . Awkwardly, he removed his signet ring and held it out. "Look, I don't think . . ."

"Monsieur is afraid to meet me?"

"No," said Thiercelin, "but . . ."

"I don't see the need for further conversation."

It was hopeless. He was committed to the blasted duel. "River rot it," said Thiercelin. "You insisted on proof of my identity. Here it is. However, monsieur . . ."

"Lieutenant Lievrier."

"If I'm going to have to fight you, you could at least go and announce me to Iareth Yscoithi."

The lieutenant looked him up and down. Then he shrugged. "Very well, monseigneur."

He was shown into a small reception room on the first floor. No pictures relieved the dark paneling; the furnishings and rugs were in muted colors. The fire was unlit. He refused refreshments and waited by the window, unwilling to sit, restless.

It was some fifteen minutes before the door opened to admit Iareth Yscoithi. She was as he recalled her, slight and straight and cold. He bowed to her, and she watched him with dispassionate eyes.

She said, "Thierry."

"Iareth, I . . ." He had expected something, some

reaction, anything but this level composure. He said, "You're well, I hope?"

"I am. And you?"

"Yes."

There was a small pause. She sat on an armchair. "It is a kindness in you to call. You learned of my presence from Yviane Allandur?"

"No. That is, I . . ." He hesitated. "It's good to see you again."

"Indeed?"

"Of course. Valdin . . ." Thiercelin was shaking. She watched him without curiosity. "It's only polite to call."

"I see."

She had no warmth. She was ignorant of the grief she had caused. Looking at his hands, he said, "I was there, you know. When Valdin was killed."

"I had heard so."

He said, "Don't you care?" Stopped, for that had not been at all what he had meant to say. He turned and stared out into the rain, not trusting himself to look at her.

She said, "It's past, Thierry. I have my own life to lead."

His back still to her, he said, "He loved you so much. You didn't see . . . you weren't there. When you left him, it was as if he went away, too. He . . ."

She said, "I did what I had to do. I had duties elsewhere. I've always regretted that I should have caused such pain."

"Pain!" Thiercelin whirled round to face her. "He died, Iareth. He bled his life out in a dirty inn yard." His voice cracked. Looking away, he rubbed a hand across his eyes. "He never stopped thinking about you."

He had not heard her move. He started when she laid her hand on his shoulder. He looked down into her eyes. They were dry. She said, "Nor have I ceased to think of him. But time does not stop."

He said, "I'm sorry. I had no right."

She smiled, a little. "You have every right. You were friends."

"Perhaps," Thiercelin said, "I didn't come here to apportion blame."

"I know."

"I came . . ." He paused then lowered his voice. "I came because I've seen him, here in Merafi, in the last weeks. Seen him and heard him speak."

Something changed, then, beneath her calm. She paled and asked, "What did he say?"

He put his hands on her shoulders. "He said, 'Tell Iareth *kai-reth* she was right.' Whatever that means."

"I had feared it," said Iareth Yscoithi.

From the roof of the tower of Merafi's River Temple, Gracielis gazed north and watched the river flow. His hands, bare, rested on the parapet next to his hat. He could feel the years in the stone he touched. He could sense the movement through it of the dreams of the mason who had shaped it. Beside him, the lieutenant's ghost stood, half-shredded in the breeze. It was very quiet. Apart from the wind, the only clear sound was the occasional singing of the priests in the rooms below. Beneath gray skies, the city rested, waiting only partly aware for the changes that were promised.

It was early evening. Weighted with impending rain, clouds extinguished the sun's color. Handmoon hovered on the horizon, pale and slight. Mothmoon was yet to rise. There was no mist; he could see no weaving of shapes across the surface of the river. It was still asleep, this artery of Merafi's power, and its dreams were veiled.

Only at the deepest level could he sense a faint murmur of a threat. Sighing, he shifted to prop his chin on one hand, and let his gaze turn away over the roofs of the city, across the twilight plains, into the horizon, north, and a little west, to where beneath the horizon Lunedith lay, cold within its forested mountains. When footsteps sounded on the leads behind him, he did not turn, but only said, "You will have a cold winter of it, I think."

The lieutenant's ghost wore a leer. It was, for once, not directed at Gracielis. "You call all our winters cold," the arrival said, coming to stand beside him, leaning on the parapet. "And too long. I'm astonished you've never gotten used to them."

"My bones are too frail for your east wind."

"Yet you're looking north. You'd be even less comfortable in Lunedith. Their capital's snowbound half the year."

He shivered. "They have my sympathies. That's barbarous."

"They like it that way."

He spread a hand out on the parapet, glancing down at his fingers. "Then I'll try not to go there," he said, and turned to look at his companion. "Good evening, madame."

Yvelliane of the Far Blays lifted her veil and regarded him. "I'm late, I think." Behind her, the lieutenant's ghost made a crude gesture.

"A little, perhaps. But your presence is sufficient recompense for the delay; and the delay itself no more than befits your beauty." And Gracielis bowed, elegant, selfmocking.

She smiled a little. "None of that. I need to talk, not flirt."

"I hear and obey." He placed a hand over his heart. The ghost imitated him in large motion.

She looked quizzical. "Do you? What if I were ask to you to sever your connection with my husband? He's been writing to you."

It was like her to know of that. There was no way to tell how much she knew. He said, "It would depend on how much you paid me. Is that your desire?"

"I don't think so. When it ceases to divert him, perhaps, or when it begins to annoy me."

She did not know, then, of clinging, unseasonal Valdarrien, or she would not speak of diversion. Her tone had been flippant, but for all that he looked at her sharply. She was frowning. He said, "I'll remember."

"Please do." She was watching the river. The ghost was pale beside her, working up an irritation she could not sense. She said, "Should I forgive you, I wonder?" Gracielis was silent. "For sleeping with Thierry, I mean."

He never discussed one client with another, whatever they sought, however they were connected. Yvelliane was different. Very gently, he said, "I'm not sleeping with Lord Thiercelin."

"His loss, then," she said and sighed.

She looked tired. Well, she had many reasons for that, lately. The ghost, who disliked her for reasons Gracielis had never discovered, was jubilant. Frowning at it, he said, "You work too hard. It shows on your face."

"Thank you."

"You're unhappy. It's contagious. You make Lord Thiercelin unhappy also."

"Hence his interest in you?"

"There is no interest." Not of the kind she meant, but he could not detail that to her. "He's devoted to you."

She said, "You really think he's unhappy?"

"Just as you are."

"You're so sure about me?"

"I hear things. I see things. That's why you pay me to inform."

"Quite so." Her tone was dry.

"He loves you. He worries about you." He had been her lover, once, long ago. It did not give him the right to interfere, but he might perhaps venture comment.

"Unfortunately, I don't pay you to tell me things I already know."

"It's good that you know it," he said. And then, "Forgive me. This isn't my business."

She sighed again. "Perhaps," she said, but her face was bleak.

She was not a person one might touch casually. He turned to look at her. She caught the look. She said, "Shall I cry on your shoulder?"

"If you wish."

She shook her head. "Another day, perhaps. When there's time."

"I'll remember."

"Thank you."

"I'm always your debtor."

"I wonder." She looked at him. "Who controls you, Gracieux?"

He shrugged. "Who controls anyone?" The lieutenant's ghost looked knowing.

She smiled. "Who knows? It's clearer in some instances than others."

"Indeed."

"Did they really let go of you, the *undarii*?" He made no answer, keeping his face calm. She said, "It's said they kill their failures. Why didn't they kill you?"

"On account of my beautiful eyes, perhaps?" The ghost sneered. "Their ways are mysterious."

"Like yours." He bowed. "You know the answer." He was silent. "But you're not going to tell me."

He said, "Forgive me."

" 'It is forbidden'," she finished for him. "I always ask and that's always your answer. You're no small mystery yourself."

"That's my good fortune."

She laughed then and shook her head at him. "You trade on it, certainly." Her expression sobered. "Your kind is forbidden in this city."

"I'm sensible of your kindness to me."

Yvelliane said, "Tarnaroq has sent us a troublesome ambassador. Sigeris. Do you know him?"

"I know of him."

"If he was *undarios*, would you know it?" Gracielis was silent. "Him, or one of his retinue. An aide, perhaps?"

Still he made no answer, looking away from her, out over the city, over the river. They were too well matched, Yvelliane and Quenfrida. Clever Quenfrida, too clever to be caught out, for all Yvelliane's suspicion. There was a net here, and they would both weave him into it. He shivered and drew his cloak about him. He schooled his features to be expressionless.

Quietly, Yvelliane said, "Forgive me, but I need to know."

It was too dangerous. There were changes, hovering here over this city, which should be opaque to such things. Ghosts walked untimely. Changes were poised in the salt-fresh neutral waters of the river, which should not change. He had no way of knowing what imbalance Quenfrida might have found to exploit to Merafi's detriment.

He had agreed to help Thiercelin. He took Yvelliane's money on a regular basis. He said, "I . . . might." He was cold with it, with the heresy that might lead him to betray her. Quenfrida was confident enough in her power to come here, into this place whose ambience would not be manipulated by her kind, where her abilities (his abilities) were forbidden. The loving assassins, the perfumed ones, the priests of love and death. His name, spoken in scent about him, should have marked him one of them, had he had the strength. Quenfrida had it. Quenfrida *undaria*.

There was sadness in him that had to do with the chiming of silver bells, with bruised magnolia. He turned to Yvelliane and said, "If there is an *undarios*, they would know me."

"And if I asked you to look among the Tarnaroqui delegation?"

"I might locate him. And die for it." It was pointless to tell her what they both already knew, that his cautious and infrequent correspondence with her was in itself sufficient to purchase his death. All that stood between him and that end was that Quenfrida had never thought to ask him: *Do you still have dealings with Yvelliane of the Far Blays?*

If—when—she asked him, he would tell her every part of it and welcome the gift of death from her hands. Yvelliane did not know that and never would.

Who controls you?

Yvelliane was watching him. She said, "You could be given protection."

"Forgive me. I was inexact. I would want them to kill me. It can be very . . . sweet."

The lieutenant's ghost grinned, fingering its throat.

"The right death at the right moment."

"Yes."

She frowned, looking down at the roof-leads. "If I asked no names, would you tell me simply whether there is an *undarios* among the embassy?"

He knew already. Nevertheless, "Perhaps."

"It's a lot to ask." She hesitated. "I've never known: do you mind?"

He said, "You gave me a home in your city. Protected me from your prohibitions. You pay me well for information." Momentarily, he looked wicked. "You relieve my days with the balm of your presence."

The ghost looked supercilious. Yvelliane, however, merely shook her head at him. "There's a 'but,' isn't there? I heard it."

He met her gaze. "You've been my protector. I owe you a great deal. But I am, by birth, Tarnaroqui."

"Yes." Momentarily, she was silent. "I'm not asking you to do this for me yet. But later on, I may have to. In which case . . . ?"

"I'll tell you."

"Thank you." She pulled up her veil. He turned back to look at the river. The ghost shadowed him. She said, "Not a lot to see, at this time of year."

"No." He paused. Then, "The river is your lifeblood."

"Yes."

"If it . . . if it should turn against you, how would you fare?"

She looked at him sharply. "What do you mean?"

"I was wondering," he said, "if you're prepared for such a thing?"

She looked toward the river. "It would depend," she said, slowly. "For a short time, we would survive. But ultimately, I suppose, our kingdom would fall."

Iareth Yscoithi of Alfial could see in the dark. It was a small edge, even among her Lunedithin countrymen, who, whatever their strengths, lacked Yscoithi silence, Yscoithi patience. She had long ago assimilated and perfected the arts she required: waiting and quiet and the wisdom to recognize the apposite moment. She had learned, too, to subtract from her actions the wishes of her heart. She had gone that way once and, returning wounded, would not take that risk again. Besides, she was half-breed, and her father—who was not Yscoithi—had gifted her with tenacity.

It did not occur to her to be afraid as she crossed the hallway on silent feet. She took darkness for her part; she had a kinship with its properties.

The door to Kenan's suite opened soundlessly under her fingers. Before leaving her own room, she had heard the hall clock chime midnight. Kenan was at the palace with the ambassador and would be unlikely to return for another hour or more. The servants had all retired. She had time enough. She did not glance behind her before entering Kenan's rooms. She knew she was alone. She would have heard, had anyone approached.

The casement had been left open. Like all of his Orcandrin clan, Kenan did not care to feel shut in. Handmoon was near full. Cool light pooled across the floor. Iareth paused to allow her eyes to readjust. The first room was large. She crossed it without interest in its bureaus or any of its cabinets. She had known Kenan

too long to look for the obvious. Nor did she trouble
with the bedchamber. Kenan was clever enough to know
he was watched by his retinue and by the Merafiens
alike. He would be ready.

It pleased his arrogance to believe Iareth suffered simply by being here in Merafi. Merafi, where Valdarrien
d'Illandre—her beloved Valdin *kai-reth*—had died.
Kenan was mistaken. She had assimilated the need to
live with pain. And besides, it was a species of fortune
that Kenan let his spite blind him.

It would have delighted him to think she hated him.
Delighted, and fed his growing power.

She took care with her masks, lest he learn the truth.
She bore him neither hate nor malice nor ill-will. She
knew him all too well, had known him since his child-
hood.

There was a dressing closet set in the bedchamber,
behind a rose-paneled door. It was unlit. She let her eyes
adjust before beginning her examination. Servants came
and went in this room, as in any other. Anything too
obviously hidden would provoke suspicion.

Iareth's patience was of the predatory kind. She did
not trouble to study subtlety. She looked in front of her
eyes. Kenan's larger bags had been emptied and taken
to storage. But his saddlebags were still here, on the
highest shelf. She stood on the dressing stool and lifted
them down.

Their weight told her at once that she was right. It
was probable that Kenan had not bothered to unpack
them but had simply stored them away. Carefully, she
carried them into the bedchamber and put them on the
window seat. The knots fastening them were complex.
She took care to memorize the number and order of
loops. Removing the contents, she was similarly careful.
They must not look unnecessarily disarranged. If another
had asked this task of her, she might well have refused.
But she was not in the habit of refusing Urien Armenwy.
He was her commanding officer, for one thing. He was

the closest friend of Prince Keris, for another. Good reasons enough, by themselves. And then, both Queen Firomelle and Prince Keris were in poor health, making Kenan's actions all the more important.

Above all, Urien was her father, for all that their clan names differed. There were too few Yscoithi as it was: he had chosen never to make public the nature of their relationship, and it was known to very few people indeed. To be born half-blood, openly known to be of parents from different clans was even now a stigma in Lunedith. Such children were termed *elor-reth*, outclan, and found it hard to succeed. Iareth owed her position in the royal *kai-rethin* as much to Urien's protection as to her official clan status. And that protection was worth much. Urien was one of the very last of the clansmen whose blood ran pure enough to retain its ancient power. Few indeed in these days could claim as much. Once, before the days of Yestinn Allandur, the clansmen had been shapeshifters, each clan possessed of its own particular animal or bird form. The ability had been closely guarded, maintained by tight interbreeding within each clan. A child born of a cross-clan liaison lost the talent and was despised by all. But over the centuries, endorsed and sheltered by royal approval, more and more children had been born cross-clan. Their animal totems survived only as the symbols on their banners and brooches. Many clans had died out wholly: many of their children had abandoned the clan system altogether, becoming the ancestors of the Merafiens of Gran' Romagne. In Lunedith, clan names had survived and the habit of at least seeming to maintain intraclan marriage. But the old blood ran diluted almost everywhere. The subject was sensitive and few, now, were directly cross-clan. Once in perhaps three generations heredity would throw out a true shifter, and such were honored highly. Urien would never openly acknowledge Iareth, but he sheltered her, and that was sufficient to keep her status intact.

Her fingers were careful, laying out Kenan's secrets on the window ledge. No letters. Unfortunate, but not unexpected. A number of items of obvious significance to Kenan—his clan-brooch, his ring. A small pine casket, dyed blue and fastened with a bronze clip. A leather bottle. A sky-blue silk scarf. A deck of cards. A knife, small and wickedly sharp, sheathed in padded silk and hafted in old ivory. A copy of the one of the *Books of Marcellan*, the second, which dealt with the five domains of earth, fire, air, water, and darkness.

She frowned a little as she lifted the casket. It made no sound. Opening it, she discovered why. The contents—six small vials—were carefully wadded. Unstoppering one, her frown deepened. A smell of honeysuckle. Perfume. She had expected, dramatically, something else. The other five vials were differently scented, but also appeared to be perfumes. She replaced them and turned her attention to the cards.

They were not the standard Lunedithin animal deck, nor the five-suited deck used in Gran' Romagne for gambling. These were something other, a fortune-teller's deck, thirty-six cards in all. A card for each of the elemental domains, by the sun and both moons. A totem suit, from Allandurin eagle to Heliadrin serpent. A single run of court cards; clan-head, sword, diviner, mother, oblate. Her breath caught as she turned over the last, and despite all her hard-won control she was chilled.

The painted face of the oblate, gazing back up at her, was that of her dead lover, Valdarrien of the Far Blays.

Sky-eyed Quenfrida rolled over onto her back and stretched in one smooth motion. The thick toffee-gold hair spilled across her shoulders and breasts; she pushed it back with a hand. Lying beside her, his head pillowed on his arm, Gracielis watched with languid, darkened eyes. Too soon, yet, to feel the humiliation of what she could do to him. He was wrapped in repletion. Her perfume soaked him to the very bone. She reached across and ran her fingers idly along his side; smiled as he shivered under her touch. Her hand halted against his cheek. She looked at him. "So," she said, "you don't hate me today?"

His mind was a jumble of sensation and image; her mouth on his, her arms about him, hands provoking, bodies entwined. It was hard to capture any emotion save languor. He said, "I don't remember."

She laughed. "As I recall, you've always been better at love than hate." Her gentleness confused him. She had been waiting in his room when he returned from his assignation with Yvelliane. He had not stood a chance.

Release had left him weak. No other woman. Fragile under her touch, he said, "You know why. You know what happened."

She laid a finger across his mouth. "That is done with. The path remains."

His eyes widened fractionally. With his free hand he lifted hers away from him. The pulse in her wrist was swift. She might almost have been vulnerable. He said, "I failed, Quena. They closed the gate for me."

"The path remains," she repeated. "You might yet become *undarios*. There are sometimes those who linger a while by the wayside. You failed by omission, not commission."

"The seventh test . . ."

"You never attempted the seventh test. You fled."

Fled . . . Through the sacred garden, away from the gate of brass. Past the perfumed fountains, to the music of the bells. Petals of magnolia underfoot, falling like a benediction . . . Gracielis shivered. The lieutenant's ghost drifted into his line of sight like a lure. He said, "There's no going back."

"There is going forward." Quenfrida reached out to stroke his chest with careful fingers. Under the sheet, her leg rubbed against his. The first tendrils of reborn desire stirred within him, confused with the remembered bell-song and the scent of her. She moved closer, lips finding the sensitive place on the side of his throat. Her perfumed hair tangled across his face and shoulders. He groaned; felt rather than heard her laughter. His arms slid about her, caressing. She lifted herself on an elbow and looked down at him, smiling. She said, "There is yet time."

Her touch traced delicious pathways over his skin. He shivered again, eyes closing. Through the veil of her hair, he said, "I . . . don't know."

She kissed him. It was very disturbing. "Think about it."

Shortly thereafter, thinking became well-nigh impossible.

Early the next morning, Joyain looked up at the facade of the Far Blays townhouse and sighed. If only he had managed to curb his irritation. If only he had not let his prolonged service to Kenan get to him so. One of these days he was going to learn the art of thinking before speaking and stop getting himself into these ridiculous situations.

One of these days. Always assuming he got them. He gave his doublet a surreptitious tug, straightened his collar, tweaked at his hat, and raised a hand to the door knocker. Then he dropped it again and said, "Should we use the side entrance?"

His companion, a lieutenant like himself, sighed in turn. "Don't be daft. Are we tradesmen?"

"No, but . . ."

"Don't be so bourgeois." Elbowing Joyain to one side, Leladrien DuResne rapped smartly on the door and waited.

It was opened remarkably promptly by a very pretty maid. Leladrien smiled at her. "Lieutenants Lievrier and DuResne to see Monseigneur de Sannazar."

They were neither of them in uniform. It had not seemed politic. The girl looked at them. "Is monseigneur expecting you?"

Joyain opened his mouth to explain. Leladrien glared at him and said, "Of course," in his best charming tone.

She did not look especially charmed. However, she unbent enough to open the door. "Come in, then, messieurs. I'll inquire."

The hall was wide and beautifully appointed. Sinking into a chair, Leladrien looked about in satisfaction and said, "Well, at least you'll be killed by an aristocrat with taste, Jean."

"Shut up," said Joyain.

"Even if his method of arranging duels is a bit irregular. Properly speaking, I should be calling on his second."

"I told you, Lelien, he didn't name one."

"That's what I meant." Leladrien stretched his legs out in front of him, and looked at his boots. "I could get to like this lifestyle. Do you think there's a chance either of us will catch the eye of the famous widow?"

"No," said Joyain.

"Poor Jean. You were a fool to let yourself in for this."

"Oh, I know." Joyain said, with feeling. "And you don't have to remind me. I feel quite stupid enough already." Leladrien looked innocent. "I daresay it wouldn't have happened if I hadn't let Kenan Orcandros annoy me so much in the first place. He'd given me one hell of a morning. By the time Thiercelin of Sannazar showed up, I was ready to shoot my mother."

"You don't have to go through with it, you know," Leladrien said. "You've got a perfectly good excuse. Aristocrats are off-limits to us mere officers."

"A moment ago you were predicting he would kill me."

"Well, I like to look at both sides. And anyway," and Leladrien looked reassuring, "I never heard that Thiercelin of Sannazar was so much of a duelist."

"His friend Valdarrien d'Illandre was. And this Thiercelin's said to be a good shot."

"Valdarrien d'Illandre's dead. And shooting a target's

totally different from shooting a man." Leladrien paused, and frowned. "Usually."

"You're a great comfort."

"I try." Leladrien glanced at him. "Will you back out?"

"No."

"Well, it's your funeral . . . No, I didn't mean it that way! Shall I press for swords or pistols?"

"I . . ." Joyain began, but footsteps interrupted him.

The maid was back. "I'm afraid monseigneur is out, messieurs."

"Oh, well, in that case . . ."

"However, madame will see you both in the *petit salon*."

"But . . ." said Joyain. The girl ignored him.

She said, "Please follow me."

Sighing, Joyain followed. Leladrien, standing up, caught his eyes and said, "Which madame, do you think? I hope it's the young one."

"Ssh."

"They say she's . . ." Leladrien shut up, as the maid opened a door and gestured for them to enter.

"Lieutenants Lievrier and DuResne, madame," the girl said, and left.

The woman sitting in the large chair by the window was not the famous widow Miraude d'Iscoigne l'Aborderie. Clear brown eyes studied Joyain and Leladrien rather too sharply, as they made their bows. "Good morning, gentlemen." Yvelliane d'Illandre gestured for them to sit. Her tone bespoke polite interest. "How can I help you?"

Joyain sat. "Good day, madame. My business is with Monseigneur de Sannazar . . ."

"Yes, so I gather. You've just missed him. He's gone riding."

"Perhaps I should come back later . . ." Joyain began.

Leladrien interrupted him. "The fact is, madame, our business is rather delicate."

"Indeed?" Yvelliane arched a brow.

"I'm sure Lord Thiercelin would wish . . ."

"Well," said Yvelliane, briskly, "it can't be that delicate. I'm certain he hasn't dishonored either of your sisters, since he assures me that he has no mistress, and he's usually very truthful."

Joyain winced. "Please, madame . . ."

"And it's been a good six years since he was last so short of funds that he had difficulty meeting a gambling debt."

"Madame, I assure you . . ."

"So," Yvelliane said, "I can only conclude that he's decided to fight one or the other of you." Joyain looked down. "Please don't scruple to tell me. I have plenty of experience with matters of this type. My brother was renowned for it. Which of you is it?"

Very quietly, Joyain said, "Me, madame."

"I see." She rose and went to the mantel. "I've seen you before, haven't I? You're with the guard assigned to the Lunedithin embassy."

"Yes, madame."

She picked up a figurine, toyed with it. "I won't insult your honor by asking why you're fighting Thierry. However," and she paused, "I do question the wisdom of it. Your position attached to that embassy is sensitive. And dueling is impolitic."

Joyain said, "I'm aware of that, madame."

"Yes, I suppose you are, Lieutenant—Lievrier?" Joyain nodded. "However, as First Councillor . . ." Her sentence trailed off. She looked at him.

"I am entirely at your disposal, madame," Joyain said, wishing she would stop baiting him.

Her eyes were very keen. Quite unexpectedly, she smiled. "I don't want to cause any resentment," she said. "I do understand these affairs. But I'd be obliged if you didn't kill Thierry."

"I wasn't intending to, madame."

"No, I don't suppose you were." Again, a measuring look. "I won't interfere, but I suggest you arrange all this with his friend Maldurel. The Lord of South Marr."

It seemed to be some kind of dismissal. Rising, Joyain and Leladrien bowed. It was only as they were at the door that she spoke again. "Lieutenant Lievrier?"

"Madame?"

"One thing regarding my husband's visit to the Lunedithin embassy. I take it he was seeking Iareth Yscoithi of Alfial?" Joyain looked startled. Yvelliane nodded. "I thought so. Thank you. Good day, gentlemen."

5

THE SILK WAS TARNAROQUI. Under Gracielis' fingers there was a dust memory of warm air and clear skies. The loom rattle echoed through the weave with the sound of cicadas and the perfumes of summer. It was fine enough for a veil, or a shroud. The lieutenant's ghost hovered over it. Glancing up at it, Gracielis raised his brows and put the bolt back on the counter. The apprentice cloth merchant looked disappointed.

Amalie was studying two lengths of woolen stuff spread out on a table before her. Looking up, she said, "Which do you like, love, the brown or the blue?"

"Who can say?" Gracielis looked at the cloth, considering. "What hope can a mere color have beside your beauty?" The apprentice regarded him with an unfriendly air. The lieutenant's ghost pulled a face.

"Very pretty," Amalie said. "But even beauty needs to be dressed."

"Adorned." Gracielis smiled. "Sometimes."

She shook her head at him. "And you have no opinion on these colors?"

The apprentice fidgeted. Happily, Gracielis said, "Let's consider the nature of adornment. Is it a question of what is most becoming or what costs the most?" The apprentice began to look more hopeful. "Or is the premise false? Does a high price reduce the value of an object by virtue of the attempt to possess it?" He inhaled, intending to continue.

The apprentice said, "Perhaps madame would care to see some other fabrics? We have some fine brocades."

"No, it's wool I want." Amalie looked again at the two samples. The apprentice sighed.

Gracielis said, "Which do you prefer?"

"Brown is more serviceable . . ." She sounded doubtful. Gracielis wrinkled his nose at her.

"It's excellent value and very hard wearing," the apprentice put in.

"Adornment," Gracielis said, "shouldn't bore you, Ladyheart."

"But . . ." Amalie sighed, "it's to be a day dress. For work. Brown would be more sensible."

"And would depress you," Gracielis said. "Do you like the blue? You could have a brighter shade, or something with a pattern."

"In the shop?" Amalie laughed. To the apprentice, she said. "I'll have the blue. And a length of that cream silk for monsieur." The apprentice bowed and began to measure the cloth.

Gracielis said, "I don't need it." The ghost looked faintly sickened, as it often did when it came to matters of payment.

"No," Amalie said, "but should not beauty be adorned?" Gracielis bowed. " I like to give you presents. And you wanted that silk."

He took her hand and kissed it. "Where would I be without you? I'm always your debtor."

"Naturally," she said, laughing. She turned to pay the apprentice. "Have the parcels sent to my house on Bright Moon Street, please; and here's a little something for yourself."

"Thank you, madame."

The shop door swung shut behind them. Amalie slipped her arm through his. "You teased that poor boy. Was that nice?"

"He was insufficiently respectful to you."

"You nearly upset my bargaining."

"I'm desolated. I will make amends forthwith." Gracielis said. The lieutenant's ghost spat. "Command me."

"Later, perhaps."

"For you," he said, guiding her round a puddle, "anything. I'll kill dragons."

"Plural dragons?" She raised her eyebrows at him, eyes merry.

"Of course." His dyed lashes swept down. He looked at her sidelong. "So long as they're the stuffed theatrical kind."

"Very gallant!"

"Alas, I'm no hero." He sighed, elegant, melodramatic. The ghost made a gesture of contemptuous agreement. Gracielis made in return the slightest of bows. "On the other hand, I've never understood heroes. It is my belief that roses are a more appropriate gift than slices of dead dragon."

"Perhaps." Amalie feigned to consider. "Dead boar can be cooked and eaten, of course, but dead dragon would seem to have little purpose other than to stain my floors and force me to resand them."

"Dragons, therefore, are not a fitting gift." Gracielis smiled. "Perhaps I should slay snapdragons for you?"

She laughed. "I liked the roses better."

"Then it shall be roses." He looked wicked. "Sixteen dozen."

Amalie thumped him.

Three days had passed since they had walked by the river. Cold days, for the most part, with wet and misty nights to follow them. Gracielis had watched with eyes grown cautious, skin flinching from the ghost-touch of change. The air tasted to him of honeysuckle. He had not dared to speak of it to Quenfrida, lest he inform where he sought to be informed. He was afraid to do more than hint at what he sensed—rumors spreading everywhere of problems in the old docks, of the queen's failing health, of disturbances and discontent.

He was beginning to be alarmed. He was in danger of

becoming involved; he who should be indifferent to Mer-afi's fate. And Quenfrida suspected it.

You were ever better at love than hate . . . Hate had built the shapes in the mist and on the river. That and the heavy falling of water. By rights, he should have questioned Quenfrida when he had had the chance, re-sisted the silken enticement of her. He did not like what he was seeing and hearing.

The road underfoot was muddy. Amalie held up her skirts and teetered a little on her pattens. He made as clear a path for her as he might and conversed without full attention. There was something coming, something waiting in the mist and the infuriating rain. Even the lieutenant's ghost was grown wise to it, petulant with static, mist-laden. There were as yet several more shops and stalls to be visited. Amalie, despite her wealth, pre-ferred to do her own marketing. Gracielis obediently carried parcels, inspected fruit, and smiled at vendors. The ghost paced him, marching maliciously through those who lacked the blood to see it. Visible, here in Merafi, against nature, by day, and without two moons' light.

That went against Merafien nature, just like Valdar-rien of the Far Blays, who had no more right than the lieutenant to come back. The marketplace was damp, irritable with chill and mud and worry. Amalie's face looked pinched as she made her purchases, and the wares seemed dulled, spoiled by weather and waiting. She was as dependent upon the goodwill of the river as anyone else, and as likely to suffer should it turn.

As they made their way back to her house, he said, "Your ship isn't back yet." It was not a question.

She looked at him. "Yes. How did you know?"

"You're unhappy, save by odd moments. When you think no one is attending, you worry."

Her house was pleasantly warm. The street door opened straight into the shop. An apprentice was serving a customer at the high counter. Behind it, the journeyman cast up accounts at a lectern. They went through the connecting door at the rear and up into the kitchen. Amalie gestured for Gracielis to put her parcels on the table and sat on a stool to remove her pattens.

The housekeeper began to unpack the parcels. "No fish, madame?"

"It wasn't fresh. I thought we might use some of the salt meat instead." Amalie pulled a face. "I know it isn't popular with the boys, but . . ."

"Them!" The housekeeper could not have been more contemptuous. "They should be grateful you feed them so well." The lieutenant's ghost, who enjoyed her acerbity, shadowed her as she moved around the large room trying to look down her dress. "You're staying to eat?" she asked Gracielis. He looked at Amalie, who nodded. "Take those shoes off, then. Madame's chamber is no place for your mud." Amalie looked at her reprovingly. "Fresh cleaned, it is. And you can't sweep a polished floor with come-hither looks or pretty manners."

"I am," said Gracielis, "a mere parasite. Ladyheart, I beg you, persuade Madame Herlève to forgive me or I'll die of grief."

"And a nice mess you'll make doing it," Herlève said, flicking him out of her way with a hand. "Upstairs with you, Gracieux, and make madame smile. That's your job, isn't it?"

"I hear and obey." Taking Amalie's hand, he led her up the short flight of stairs to her large second-floor chamber. It was, if anything, even warmer than the kitchen. He evicted her tabby cat from the daybed and bowed. "Madame."

"Ridiculous creature! Whose house is this, anyway?"

"Madame Herlève's, surely?"

"You'd be forgiven for thinking so." The cat leaped back onto the couch and stood beside Amalie, looking disgruntled. The lieutenant's ghost, appearing suddenly through the floor behind them, made the animal jump. Gracielis frowned at the ghost. It looked unconcerned and dropped itself into the best armchair.

Sometimes, Gracielis wished he knew how it did that. It could not actually move any objects and generally walked through most of them. But from time to time it seemed quite able to treat them as solid. If he had the secret, he could tamper a little. He would enjoy watching the ghost fall through something unexpectedly.

Amalie said, "Bring me the chocolate set, will you?" He fetched it from the corner cabinet and then rang down for hot water. He sat on a footstool to watch her prepare.

Carefully, he said, "Your ship?"

"No news." She sighed. "I can stand the financial loss, but such events are bad for morale, especially in this political climate. And to cover immediate overheads I may have to sell one of my upriver contracts. Things may be tight for a while."

"Then you shouldn't buy me presents."

She shrugged. "It isn't that bad."

"Is something else worrying you, apart from the ship?"

The chocolate was made. She poured him a cup and passed it across. "There might be. You remember that my late husband's brother trades in the north? I buy some of my fur trim from him."

"I remember."

"Well, he's had worrying news from his Lunedithin agent. Apparently they're getting less willing to trade their fur and amber and a few other things under the terms of the present treaty. They say Prince Keris is getting old and forgetful. And then . . ." She looked at him, hesitated. "Well, I have reason to believe we're being undercut."

"You and your brother-in-law?"

"No. Not exactly. The Merafien Haberdashers' Guild."

"Ah." He blew on his chocolate. "That'll be my countrymen."

"Probably." Again, she paused. Then: "The heir to Lunedith is rumored to have Tarnaroqui sympathies. My nephew Jean is in his suite. He's keeping an eye on things for me."

"Shall I see if I can find anything out?" He often heard rumors through his fellow professionals, with their network of clients from all classes. "To date, all there is on the street regarding the new ambassador is that he's said to have rather odd tastes."

"I don't want to know. At least, not unless I need to resort to blackmail!" She smiled. Then she shook her head. "I've been meaning to ask, have you heard anything about the trouble there's been in the new dock?"

"A little. It's said it began with a fire in a riverside cabaret."

"Yes, I'd heard that, too. But . . ." She frowned. "My guild master has a ship down there. It came in just before the trouble started. Word is that the rioting is over, but no one has as yet been given access to any of their cargoes, or to the crews involved."

"That'll be due to the excise men."

"I daresay." She shrugged. "Didn't you tell me that one of the girls who works Silk Street has a lover in the Port Authority?"

"Chirielle, yes."

"Could you ask her about it? I'll pay, of course. I could use being owed a favor by the guild master."

"Of course." He bowed. "I haven't seen her lately, but I'll ask."

"Thank you, love." Amalie held out her hand. Rising, he took and kissed it. "That's nice. What would I do without you?"

He kissed the inside of her elbow. A little indistinctly he said, "Nothing so interesting as you do with me, I trust."

She shivered a little and stroked the side of his face.

The lieutenant's ghost watched in faint anticipation. He ignored it, bending down to kiss her throat. "I am to make you happy, am I not?" he said. "Madame Herlève ordered it. Shall I obey?"

"Lock the door first," said Amalie.

Thiercelin's game of solitaire was not coming out. He frowned at it, then shuffled the cards together into a heap. He sighed. That had been, by his count, the sixteenth game. None of the others had come out, either. Moodily, he began to lay out a seventeenth and poured himself yet another cup of bad wine from the carafe on the table. He stared at the cards and set blackly about trying to win.

He had been playing for perhaps ten minutes when a shadow fell across the cards. From behind him, an accented voice said, "You might, perhaps, move the double-coin."

Thiercelin turned. Gracielis stood at his shoulder, arms folded, head a little to one side. Annoyed, Thiercelin said, "Where have you been? I've been looking for you for days."

Gracielis was dressed for outdoors. Over his slashed doublet and breeches, he wore a heavy green-lined cloak, and on his head was a wide-brimmed hat. The odd-colored gloves of his calling were tucked through his belt. His shoes and stockings were grimy. He smiled. "I've been busy. My apologies." Sitting, he picked up Thiercelin's cup and drank from it. His lips were over the same spot where Thiercelin's had touched. "You've chosen poorly. My landlord has better wines than this. Of what were you thinking, when you dealt those cards?"

"None of your business," Thiercelin said. "If I'm going to be hungover, I might as well do it cheaply." Gracielis was taking off his hat. He raised his elegant brows, reproving. Thiercelin said, "Stop that." And then; "Busy doing what?"

The brows climbed higher. Gracielis said, "Shopping."

"Shopping?" Thiercelin could not quite suppress the slight rise in his tone. "All week?"

"Part of it."

"And the rest?"

Gracielis looked at him sidelong. "I had . . . commitments. Had I known you needed me urgently . . . Do you deal from the right or from the left?"

"The right," Thiercelin said. "Do stop fidgeting about that drowned card game! It isn't important."

"Games," said Gracielis, "can be of vital importance. Sometimes." And he looked down, his long lashes delicately set off against his white skin. He was quite ridiculously beautiful. "Is the deck your own?"

Thiercelin ignored him. He was not going to be vulnerable to that silken grace. He said, "I only want to talk to you, Graelis." He stopped as the diminutive escaped him and looked down.

Gracielis sighed melodramatically, placed one elegant hand over his heart. "Shall I be consoled?" And then, "Graelis?"

Thiercelin let the second comment pass. He said, "I'll buy you a drink. Failing that, you'll have to look to your current lady friend." He looked his companion over. "She seems to be able to afford you."

Gracielis turned his painted gaze upon himself, admiring, amused. "Perhaps."

There was an oval topaz brooch pinned on the doublet. Reaching over to touch it, Thiercelin said, "Certainly, I'd have said." Gracielis made no answer. He was looking at the solitaire, and frowning a little. "So," Thiercelin said, "is that a result of your shopping?"

"No. It was a gift from a lady."

"With whom you shop?"

Gracielis looked up. His expression was guarded. One hand dropped to cover part of the cards. He said, "There's more than one lady in Merafi. And not a few gentlemen."

Thiercelin gave up. Summoning a waiter, he ordered

a bottle of rather better wine and a plate of sweetmeats. "Not," he said, "as durable as topaz. My apologies."

"Not so." Gracielis mixed wine with an equal amount of water and drank. "It can't be pawned, so it's far more permanent."

Thiercelin looked thoughtful. "Perhaps I should buy you dinner?" Gracielis made a diffident gesture. Thiercelin laughed. "If the food here is edible?"

"It's excellent, of its kind, but you may think it plain."

"I'm sure I'll survive."

Across the table, Gracielis raised his cup in salute. "My thanks, then. But," and he smiled, "I wasn't hinting." He was charm to the bone. One might not resent it.

"I can afford it," Thiercelin said. He looked down.

Gracielis said, "Tell me about the cards."

"Why?"

There was a pause. Then Gracielis said, a little diffidently, "I can see . . . a something in them. But the deck and the spread are strange to me."

"It's a simple solitaire." Thiercelin picked up a card and studied it. "The general idea is . . ."

"I understand the principle. I wanted to know your thoughts."

Thiercelin looked up. "You're nothing if not persistent. If you must know, I was thinking about you."

The painted eyes widened the slightest fraction. With a finger, Gracielis traced the outline of one of the court cards. "The valet—a servant, a young man, a message. Aspected in stone, so the relationship will endure. And here, the sword, aspected in flame. Judgment and truth. And not a little danger."

"I don't believe in fortune-telling."

"Nor do I, when I do the reading." Gracielis said. "I have clearer vision for the past. The sword lies over another of its kind, aspected in wind, for the north. You've seen Iareth Yscoithi."

"That's a safe guess." Thiercelin, discomforted despite

himself, looked down and said, "And predictions of long acquaintance are doubtless good for your business."

"I have no idea," Gracielis said. "Perhaps I should try it." He paused, then added, "You are under no financial obligation to me, including your kind offer of dinner." Thiercelin was silent, playing with his lace. "It was your solitaire."

That much, at least, was incontestable. The rest . . . Thiercelin looked up, expecting to find compassion in the painted eyes and found instead that Gracielis was not looking at him at all. Rather, his gaze was fixed on some point to his right. Glancing over, Thiercelin could see nothing of interest. Quietly, he said, "I'm sorry."

Gracielis met his eyes and smiled. "It's nothing." His hand, passing over the cards, muddled them into a heap. "A game only. But you have seen Iareth Yscoithi."

It was a pretty hand and a graceful one. Watching it, Thiercelin said, a little absently, "Yes." And then, "Is it a trick?"

Gracielis looked inquiring.

"The card business. 'You'll have a fine heir and make wise investments.' All that."

"Have I said such events would occur?"

"No, but . . ." The persistence of it still troubled Thiercelin. "If it's not a trick, then . . . ?"

Gracielis had collected the cards into a neat stack. Picking them up, he weighed them in his hand. "You might call it a nervous habit."

"What?"

There were mysteries woven into the hazel eyes. It was nearly irresistible. Thiercelin shivered again. Gracielis said, "I'd read for myself to reassure you, but I always get my own cards wrong." He turned the top card over. "Thus. A favored second child, probably female, gifted in the numerical arts." He shrugged. "You wanted to talk to me about Iareth Yscoithi."

"I suppose so." Thiercelin felt dizzy, caught up in Gracielis' sudden changes of direction. Drawing in a long breath (and the air, too, was dizzying, heady with Gracielis' perfume), he said, "I saw her at the Lunedithin embassy. I told her about Valdin."

"Indeed."

"She . . . I don't know . . ." Again, Thiercelin hesitated. "She seemed so remote."

Gracielis said, "It's been six years."

"Yes, but . . . This must be important to him." Gracielis frowned. Thiercelin said, "Well, why else am I seeing him?"

"It's a matter of binding."

"Yes, I remember. But you said it wasn't me, so surely Iareth . . . ?"

"I don't think so." Gracielis rested his chin on his hands. "What I saw wasn't a person, or not exactly one, anyway."

Thiercelin sighed. "Iareth hardly seemed to care at all. It was just an oddity to her."

Gracielis rose and came around the table. He put an arm about Thiercelin's shoulders. He said, "I don't know Iareth Yscoithi. But it seems to me that it's her nature to disguise her feelings." He was very close. His perfume covered Thiercelin like a veil. There was a moment of stillness. Thiercelin could feel something beginning to uncoil within him. Not desire precisely, but some gentler thing, as though he had reached an acceptance without knowing it. There was a pulse at the base of Gracielis' throat, a blue vein beneath the translucent skin. It would be warm in that hollow, scented. Gracielis was leaning a little forward and the rose lovelock hung temptingly close. He was beautiful . . . In his mind, Thiercelin turned his face into those curls, breathed in their perfume, discovering if the fragile skin would really bruise at a touch. At a kiss. Gracielis' lips were parted. His breath grazed Thiercelin's cheek. His painted eyes were dark with concern. He had attention for no one in the room but Thiercelin. Thiercelin put a finger out to the

lovelock, stroked it, tentatively. Gracielis was quite still.
One might imagine anything from him. His skin would
taste of flowers . . . It was, after all, a matter of desire.
In the moment of realization, Thiercelin froze.

Yvelliane.

He had already betrayed her by seeking out Iareth
Yscoithi. To do this other thing . . . Swallowing, Thiercelin turned away. Some years ago, before her marriage,
Yvelliane had been seen regularly with Gracielis. He had
no rights over her past. And if, in her present, she preferred Firomelle's company to his, then it was still no
excuse for betraying her. She had never said she did not
care for him. Sometimes, before Firomelle had become
ill, in the early part of their marriage, he had begun to
believe that she might even love him. He should be
grateful that she made any space at all for him, given
all the calls upon her time. If, lately, she seemed no
longer to value him, it was only because she was so tired,
so anxious, so overworked. Perhaps this current temptation was in itself only a reflex of his love for her, a
seeking after comfort in arms that had once held her.
Better to think that than to believe he might simply want
Gracielis. And above all, he did not want to do anything
that could harm Yvelliane.

He said, "Graelis, please don't."

Gracielis drew away, leaving only a hand resting com-
panionably on Thiercelin's shoulder. Thiercelin ventured
a glance at him. Gracielis' face showed only kindness.
Thiercelin said, "Forgive me. It isn't you. I just can't
cope with this now."

Gracielis said, "But perhaps you'd like us to be
friends?" Thiercelin flushed, nodded. "So. Then it would
be wrong of me to take umbrage if sometimes you give
consideration to something more."

That was one way of putting it. Thiercelin smiled,
shaking his head, "I suppose so." The hand was still on
his shoulder, small and slight and narrow-boned. Thiercelin touched it. "But you will behave."

Gracielis removed his hand and used it to push back his hair. "I always behave."

"I'm sure," Thiercelin said. One of the inn staff was laying bread and plates and cutlery on the table before them. Watching her, he said, "You may be right."

Gracielis sat back down and looked inquiring.

"Iareth Yscoithi," Thiercelin said. "I'd thought, I don't know, that I knew her, I suppose. She was here for several months with Valdin. I spent a fair amount of time with them. She was . . ." He was reaching now for long-suppressed memories. Old wounds did not always heal clean. "She was reserved, yes, but not unapproachable. Whereas now . . . Perhaps I was wrong. Perhaps I never knew her. She's so cold."

Gracielis said, "She's Lunedithin. It isn't their way to be warm with those not of their blood."

That appalling, calm acceptance, with barely a hint of emotion at the mention of Valdarrien's name . . . Thiercelin said, "She's a stranger. I told her about Valdin. Yviane . . ." He hesitated. "I had to give my name at the embassy. When Yviane finds out, she . . ."

"Don't," Gracielis said. Thiercelin looked at him. "It doesn't help, hurting yourself."

"No, I suppose not." Thiercelin picked up a spoon and toyed with it. "I don't know what to do for the best."

"Wait, then."

"Yes. But Yviane . . ." Thiercelin shook his head. "I can't tell her about this Valdin business, not at the moment. She's so busy already, and the queen is ill. I can't explain my visit to Iareth without explaining things and giving her even more to worry about." Gracielis watched him in silence. He went on, "I have to deal with this myself. If I take it to her, she'll either think I'm incompetent or that I'm mad."

"I believe she values you more than that." Gracielis said.

"She has enough to deal with," Thiercelin repeated. If he could resolve this, it would be one small thing he could do to help Yvelliane, one small means of protecting her.

Gracielis was silent for a long time. Finally, he said, "As you wish." He paused again, and said, "As to Iareth Yscoithi, it may be difficult for her, being in Merafi." Thiercelin had not really thought about that. He nodded.

Gracielis continued. "It might explain her coldness. It's hard, being a foreigner here." There was an odd note in Gracielis' voice. Looking up, Thiercelin saw that his eyes were fixed again on the middle distance.

In all his thirty-three years, Thiercelin himself had never been more than eighty leagues from Merafi. He said, "Perhaps I should take you to see her. She might prefer to talk to you."

Gracielis shrugged, grace in the slender bones. "If you wish. But I doubt it. The Lunedithin have scant love for those of Tarnaroqui blood. Under their law we're heretics to a man."

"As are Merafiens, as I understand it."

Gracielis shook his head. "By their standards, you're sadly fallen away. You've permitted the blood of many clans to be mixed in your veins, instead of holding to the purity of each line. But that isn't heresy. Whereas the Tarnaroqui . . . Our blood isn't simply that of the clans, however mingled."

"But . . ." said Thiercelin, who knew his history, if rustily. "We're all descended from the clans. Who else . . . ?"

"Who else indeed?" It was growing dark. The landlord moved about the inn, lighting tallow candles. Shadows played across the planes of Gracielis' face, hiding his expression.

Thiercelin said, "I was told the old stories when I was a child. How Queen Firomelle's ancestor Yestinn Allandur broke the purity of the clans and forced them to intermarry. How, before he did that, pure clan blood supposedly gave people the ability to shape-change, each clan to a particular animal form. How . . ." and he swallowed, "in Yestinn's time there were other things, too, not born of the clans. Creatures of fire or air or stone or water, capable of taking on human shape but lacking our nature. But they weren't human. They couldn't interbreed . . ."

"Couldn't," said Gracielis, "or wouldn't?"

"The Tarnaroqui are known to be fey," Thiercelin said, "and to worship death and to make spies out of their priests. But I never heard that they—you— weren't human."

Gracielis smiled. "Fey," he repeated, slowly, "and strange. Ghostseers and prophets. Mystics and assassins." The landlord set a candle on the table between them. In its light Gracielis' face was austere, ascetic despite the paint. He looked at Thiercelin. "Impure blood—hated by those who still hold to the old clan ways. But," and the smile grew warm, "I'm not wholly inhuman."

He was beautiful in the candlelight and elegant and utterly to be possessed.

Thiercelin said, "You're shameless. And you know it." Gracielis bowed. "I may make you see Iareth anyway. I told her that Valdin spoke to us. She understood. But she won't tell me what he meant."

"Or can't," said Gracielis.

6

THE NIGHT SEEMED unnecessarily cold to Joyain, especially after an hour and a half spent crouched in concealment near the east door of the embassy. He felt foolish, and he was getting stiff. He should never have allowed himself get into this in the first place. If the Lunedithin wanted to spy on one another and break the curfew, that was their business. If he had any sense at all, he'd put a stop to it right now and go home. Not, he suspected, that Iareth Yscoithi would listen to him. And if his captain came to hear that he had left a foreigner to wander alone through Merafi at night, he could kiss any thoughts of comfort good-bye for the next three years at the very least. He would give it another ten minutes, and then he would tell Iareth that the whole thing was a monumental waste of time.

The door opened. Irritable, but mindful of his responsibilities, he drew back into the angle of the wall and held his breath. There was almost no light. Both moons were hidden behind heavy cloud, and the shutters of the embassy were closed. He could make out only a bare outline—a slight figure, cloaked and hatless. Closing the door, the figure set off at a steady pace toward the river. Joyain hesitated, waiting for some signal from Iareth. In this gloom, likely as not they would lose each other, let alone the man she wanted to follow. He started, as her hand touched his arm, but kept quiet. She squeezed his wrist then pointed toward the figure. Joyain took a step forward. She shook her head. Leaning forward, she whispered, "I will follow. Leave some fifty paces between us, then come after if you wish."

It was, finally, a chance to go home to bed. Unfortunately, his conscience troubled him about leaving a woman alone in the streets, especially with all the trouble there had been in the docks. "Are you sure it's Kenan?" he whispered back. She nodded once and faded back into the gloom.

Joyain counted to fifty and followed her.

He was long accustomed to Merafi after dark. He knew where he might go and where he had better not, how to evade the watch and how to detect evaders. And yet, trailing Iareth, he was aware of a strangeness. Mist had been rising from the river since sunset. It pooled across the roads like floodwater. In this murk even a native might have been excused a modicum of confusion. He counted side-turnings absently and tried to mind his footing (the mist was no help in that department). Ahead of him, Iareth was only the barest hint of a figure.

They were heading west and slightly south, down toward the old walled city. The mist grew thicker as they descended. It was far too late for the Kings' Bridge to be open. Kenan must be intending to cross by the Temple, which was always open for cash. It would be difficult for Iareth and himself to avoid attracting attention, since there would be a toll to pay, and too much delay would lose them their quarry. He wondered if Iareth had the necessary fee and began to rummage in his pockets.

They had come almost to the quayside when Kenan unexpectedly turned north along a narrow and evil-smelling passage. Not the old city at all, but the less respectable fringes of Silk Street. For Joyain, it was an area presenting few problems, but for Iareth Yscoithi . . . By default, only the least successful whores would still be plying their trade at this hour. She risked harassment, or worse. Quickening his pace, he climbed the last few steps and halted at the mouth of the passage. He looked right, then left. He could see no sign at all of Iareth. A few yards away, Kenan seemed to be negotiating with a woman. Joyain stepped back hastily and waited, hoping he hadn't been noticed. River bless, it was cold! And damp; the mist was seeping through his cloak. It deadened all sound. He could catch not one syllable of Kenan's interchange with the whore. Surely they hadn't followed him all this way just to witness a cheap liaison? Joyain wished he knew where Iareth had got to. Kenan had finished his conversation, and he and the woman had begun to walk toward a nearby house. Joyain hesitated, looking round, then followed them, hugging the wall. His breathing sounded thunderous in his ears. They were certain to notice him.

He nearly jumped straight out of his skin when a hand closed over his mouth. His own hand went to his sword hilt. He prepared to struggle. Then he recognized Iareth, obscure in the darkness of a shop porch. She held his gaze for long moments before removing her hand. He said, "What . . . ?"

"Ssh."

A door closed nearby, muffled in the fog. She hesitated, then whispered, "These dwellings. Is it possible to approach them from the rear?"

"I don't know," Joyain considered. "There might be a way in at the end of the terrace." The house into which Kenan had gone was in darkness. "I could look, if you like. But if he's just buying company . . ."

Despite the mist and the dark, he knew she smiled. "We speak of Kenan Orcandros. It's unlikely."

He decided to take her word for it. He said, "The rear will probably be shuttered, too."

She leaned against the porch. "If we do not look, we will never know."

He said, "Let's go and look, then." He was going to feel very stupid if, Iareth's view to the contrary, Kenan turned out simply to be tucked up for the night with some street-girl. Come to that, he'd feel more than just stupid if this little exploit ever came to the ears of his commanding officer. He decided to worry about that possibility in the morning and turned his attention to finding a route behind the houses.

In the end, it was Iareth who found it, a rickety half-gate set into the wall of the next-to-end house, leading into a tunnel whose level of uncleanliness caused Joyain to think nostalgically of the shantytown opposite the old docks. At least no one was sleeping in the noisome darkness. Even so, he didn't really want to think about what he might be putting his feet into.

They emerged into a line of partially fenced yards. Light showed from a couple of the houses. The sound of voices raised in anger came from the third—locals, from the accent. He looked at Iareth. She gestured to the rear of Kenan's house and began to pick her way fastidiously toward it. Shrugging, Joyain followed, doing his best to be quiet while climbing over barriers and avoiding the detritus of old barrels, sodden palliasses, and other assorted rubbish, all half-invisible in the mist.

There was no stair at the back of the house. All the shutters were closed, and no lights showed. "What now?" Joyain whispered.

"Ssh." She hesitated, then ran a hand over the wall. He watched. "The construction. Is it stone?"

He said, "No. Wattle, daub, and wood, mostly. This quarter was built rather hurriedly."

"There's no purchase." She sighed. "I had hoped . . . Of course, there is no guarantee that they are at the rear of the house."

Joyain could have told her that in the street and saved them both a lot of scrambling. However, one (probably) should not make such criticisms to a guest. Instead, he said, "Perhaps one of the shutters is loose."

She looked at him. "Is entering another's house without permission not a crime in Merafi?"

"Well, yes, it is. But I was trying to be helpful."

She smiled again. He was beginning to like her smile.

It had possibilities. She said, "Thank you." And then, "Lieutenant, could you lift me? I might gain a handhold upon a lintel."

He looked at her, thoughtfully. She was of medium height but slender with it, and he was rather on the tall side. "I can try."

"So." She pointed. "That ledge."

He nodded, making a stirrup with his hands. She steadied herself on his shoulder, then stepped up and reached over her head. She was lighter than he had expected. The end of her long, fair braid fell in his face. He said, "Can you reach?"

"Yes. Could you lift me a fraction higher?"

Joyain obliged. For a moment, her full weight was on his arms and shoulders, and he swayed. Then it was gone. A little trickle of plaster fell on him. He looked up. Iareth had managed to pull herself up onto a window ledge and was sitting on it, one foot hanging down, hands clutching the edge. She looked, despite the mist, as if she was thinking of laughing. He said, "Be careful!"

She *was* laughing, soundlessly. Taking one hand from the sill, she began to feel her way along the shutter. "Peace. The Yscoithi do not fall. Usually."

That was very comforting. He was stuck in someone else's filthy backyard, helping a foreign national with a little breaking and entering, and all she could do was laugh and talk about folklore. He withdrew into the shadows and waited.

The room was cramped and low-ceilinged, but its walls had been freshly painted, and the furnishings suggested an owner of a rather more elevated social rank than the average for the district. Kenan Orcandros sat in an overstuffed chair, a glass of red wine in one hand, and watched Quenfrida unbraid her hair. She took her time over it, separating each strand with care and smoothing it out over her white shoulders. He said, "Are you certain this house is secure?"

"Completely. Its inhabitants are mine, heart and soul." Quenfrida finished with the last braid and reached for a brush. "They see and remember only what I please."

"And you weren't followed?"

"No, my Kenan. I've been at this game for twice your lifetime and more. I am not easy to track or trace."

He frowned into his wine. "Even so . . . Wouldn't it have been safer to meet outside the city, on a hunt or a ride?"

"Thus breaking my reputation for indolence? Our aim is to go unremarked, after all."

"Yes, but . . ."

"Are you so sure you weren't followed yourself?" Lowering the brush, she looked over her shoulder at him. "You worry too much, my Kenan. Drink your wine and calm yourself."

No one had followed him. He was certain of that. He had found duties for the whole of his entourage to occupy them for most of the evening and had made a point of going to bed himself. And he was Orcandrin, sharp of ear and sensitive to changes in the air. He straightened his spine. "I know what I'm doing, Quena. We clansmen have ancient powers."

"Of course." Quenfrida turned her attention back to her mirror. He took a sip of his wine. He would have preferred the strong ale of his homeland, but she would not countenance that. It would be a change in the buying habits of this hidden household of hers, and that she would not permit.

She said, "I trust you took my advice."

"You know I've followed all your instructions at home and on the way here."

"So you have. But that was not what I meant."

He wished she would speak clearly. He disliked her habits of insinuation and indirection. A little gracelessly, he said, "About what, then?"

"The d'Iscoigne l'Aborderie chit. You must go to her

salon. She's a silly creature, but she has the most interesting contacts and she loves to be flattered. She could be very useful to you."

"I'll be going with Ambassador Ceretic."

"Good." There was a silence, broken only by the sound of Quenfrida working the comb through her hair.

Kenan said, "When is it going to start?"

"It has already started." Her voice was calm. "Did you not note how your touch affected the queen? You are poison to her. Soon we will spread that poison further. But there are preparations to be made first."

Soon. He had been waiting for this for six years, since he was fourteen, and she had come to his grandfather's court and introduced him to his birthright of ancient magics. His patience felt raw and stretched. He was tired of waiting. He said, "I hoped for something bigger."

"Even the greatest palace must be built one stone at a time." Quenfrida put down the comb and rose. "Think of how much we have already achieved. The power of the d'Illandre dynasty began to unravel from the moment you wounded Valdarrien d'Illandre six years ago at Saefoss." She came to stand behind his chair, resting her hands on his shoulders. "You lured him into that ambush, you fired the arrow that harmed him, you made sure his blood flowed there. Illandre blood on the same stones where Yestinn shed your ancestor's blood to create his binding. We are undoing it knot by knot."

It was so slow. Back then, he had dreamed of rapid glory, of himself at the head of a clan army riding across the great plains of Gran' Romagne to reclaim their ancient rights and liberties. But Quenfrida did not work with armies. Her trade lay in subterfuge and darkness, in poisons and tricks and manipulation. It was still not natural to him, even though he had seen how it could succeed. Her fingers dug into his shoulder muscles and began to knead. She said, "You disposed of that inconvenient captain that the Merafiens sent to escort you. You have clouded your grandfather's mind, day by day.

We need not wait much longer. We need only one more thing."

Her hands were warm and strong. She was *elor-reth*, outclan, and a Tarnaroqui witch to boot. She had taught him to crave her. He pulled away from her and rose, reaching for her over the chair.

She stepped away, shook her head. "Not yet. I have to tell you one more thing. You have one more task to fulfill."

"What?" He folded his arms, frowning.

"We've bound our working to Firomelle via the blood of her kinsman, but we need to bind it to her city, too. We need a piece of it, something that is part of its roots."

He did not understand. He glared at the floor and said nothing. She continued, "Merafi is an old city, my Kenan, if not as old as your Skarholm. Its people have reshaped it many times, but traces of its first form still remain. Find them."

He looked up. "How?"

She smiled. "Go to Miraude d'Iscoigne l'Aborderie's salon." She came round the chair and put her arms about him. "I'll send someone out to fetch us food. The cook at the nearest inn is surprisingly competent. And then, my Kenan . . ."

His hands knotted in her hair as he pulled her to him.

Iareth froze in position. Joyain opened his mouth to speak, and her brows drew together in warning. She was holding her breath.

He waited, listening. He could hear a dog barking a street or so away and water dripping off the neighboring roof. No voices. Iareth sat motionless for a few seconds longer, then pointed downward.

It took him a moment or two to grasp her meaning. Then he heard footsteps approaching the back door of the house. There was no cover in the yard. Even with the mist and the lack of moons' light, he was going to stand out like an obelisk. A bolt began to scrape open.

He dropped to hands and knees, and rolled into the lee of the next-door house. It had a flimsy lean-to kitchen jutting out perhaps two feet. He lay in its shadow and tried not to think about what he might be lying in. The door opened. Candlelight laced the mist, turning it soupy. He could hear a voice—from somewhere indoors, he thought—asking a question. A nearer one answered. Both spoke in a tongue he did not recognize. He held his breath and waited.

No one came out. After several minutes, a shadow cut off the candlelight. Then the door thumped shut and a bolt rattled. Joyain counted to ten, then breathed again. Venturing out on hands and knees, he looked up at Iareth, who hugged close to the windowsill. She held up her free hand, paused, then beckoned him back into the yard.

It had been too close. Frowning, he gestured for her to come down. She looked undecided. He made the gesture more urgent. She sighed, and began to turn herself round. It looked considerably more awkward than the original climbing had been. Joyain hesitated, then went to stand under the window and held his hands up to her. She looked down at him, face uncertain, then back at the narrow sill. She shrugged, and slipped off it, feet first.

He caught her. For the briefest instant, she stood in his arms, eyes meeting his in merriment, and he felt himself beginning to respond. Then she stepped free, and began to pick her way back toward the access tunnel. He brushed himself down belatedly and followed.

They were on the foggy quayside before either of them spoke. She said, "Thank you."

"My duty." Joyain shrugged. And then, "It was fun, sort of." She looked up at him, quizzically. "Why are we doing this?"

She said, "Your duty?"

"Yes, well . . . I suppose I meant: Why are you doing this?"

"Ah." Iareth sounded thoughtful. "I am Lunedithin." She did not seem to be intending to add anything to that.

Joyain waited long enough to be sure, then said, "Meaning I should mind my own business?"

"That would be a discourtesy." They had come to a junction. Iareth paused. "But it is not solely my secret."

He looked up the street to his left, toward the nobles' quarter and the embassy. Higher than the rest of Merafi, it was less misty. He could see lights shining from the mullioned windows of hillside houses. Somewhere, a clock struck three. He said, "Do you want to get straight back? I could use a drink."

"I see no urgency." She smiled. "Will anywhere be open at this hour?"

"Several places. Although," and he paused, "they may not be suitable for a lady. Some of them are rough. The nobility go there to gamble, and fights break out." Too late, he remembered her connection with the duelist Valdarrien, and stopped. "I'm sorry."

Her expression was neutral. She said, "Do you know an inn named The Pineapple?"

"In the old docks?" She was silent. He said "Slightly. It's an infantry place. Cavalry don't go there."

"Would it be open?"

"Probably." That inn was in a bad area, between the old customhouse and the shantytown. It was a fair distance from where they were now. He said, "I wouldn't recommend it. Especially for a . . ."

"A lady?" Iareth looked at him thoughtfully. "You have served how long in the Queen's Own Cavalry?"

"Eight years. Since I was sixteen."

"Consider, then. I was thirteen when I was first made *kai-reth* to Prince Keris. I have now some twenty-eight years. For all but three of the fifteen intervening, I have served as messenger and guard."

Joyain was still having trouble with Lunedithin terminology. He said rather slowly, "*Kai-reth* is guard, not kinsman?"

"It is both. Kin by blood and kin by vow."

"I see." She was four years his senior. She had served in an army over half as long again as he had. He said, "We could go to The Pineapple if you like, but . . ."

"Cavalry are not welcome?"

"No. And I'm not in the mood for brawling."

"Another time, then. Can you recommend some other tavern?"

He could think of one or two, although he still had reservations about taking a foreign envoy—a female foreign envoy—into any of them. He hesitated, then took his nerve in both hands. "I was thinking we might go to my lodgings. They're just over the river, and I have a couple of bottles put by." She looked at him. "I don't mean anything by it . . . that is, a drink, not . . . I mean . . ." Uncomfortable, he looked down. "It's a stupid idea, anyway." He was probably out of his mind. *Remember Valdarrien d'Illandre. The very dangerous (if deceased) Valdarrien d'Illandre.* "I'm sorry."

Iareth frowned a little. Her eyes assessed him. Then she said, "It is thus. Prince Keris and his chief adviser, Urien Armenwy, do not wholly trust Kenan. Prince Keris is in favor of remaining on friendly terms with your country. Kenan is not. He has formed close links with a Tarnaroqui who was for a time envoy to my homeland. She is now here in Merafi. Prince Keris and the Armenwy have asked me to keep watch upon Kenan and to notify them if he resumed his connection with her. Hence my wish to follow him."

It was a statement of trust. He said, "I wasn't making a pass. Well, not just a pass." Looking up, he saw that she was smiling. "Thank you," he said. She shrugged. He continued, "I'm not entirely disinterested myself. I have an aunt, a haberdashery merchant. She asked me to keep an eye out for Tarnaroqui interest in your party." Then: "Did you learn anything tonight?"

"A little." She took his arm. "Am I invited to share your wine?" He looked at her. She said, "Without any hidden meaning."

"Yes, if you like."

"I do not like overmuch to talk in the street. And it is a cold night."

He smiled then, and they began walking down toward the Temple toll bridge. Their talk was of desultory matters. It was not until they reached his lodgings over the shop of a minor sugar factor that she returned to the subject of Kenan.

"Do you speak Tarnaroqui?" Iareth asked. His room was tidy enough but sparsely furnished. There was only one chair. Iareth, rather to his surprise, elected to sit on his flat-topped tiring chest, and pulled up her legs tailor-fashion.

He lit the fire, then fetched mugs and a bottle from the cupboards. He said, "Not really, no. I can ask for bread, and ale. Oh, and I know the words for 'My subaltern's horse has cast a shoe.'" Iareth laughed. "Not desperately useful. Do you?"

She said, "A little."

"Was that the language they were speaking, the people in that house?"

"I think not, although one of them had the accent." Joyain handed her a cup. She took a sip before continuing. "You recognized the speakers?"

"No." Fog and distance had rendered them indistinct. "Maybe Kenan's whore has a protector."

"I think not." Iareth hesitated. "I had not before heard the voice of the one who opened the door. He may indeed be a servant, but not, I think, to a courtesan."

Joyain sat down and put the bottle on the floor beside him. He did not bother to ask if she was sure. Instead, he said, "Why not a courtesan?"

She smiled. "Two reasons. First, I know Kenan. He has strong views concerning intimate relations with *elorrethin*—with those born outside his clan. And second, I recognized the lady. She was for some time resident at the Lunedithin court. She became friendly with Kenan, although he was still a boy at the time."

"That woman who came to see him with the Tarnaroqui ambassador?" It made sense to Joyain. If Kenan had had some kind of *affaire* with her six years ago, he might well wish to renew it. It could be that. Or something more. Perhaps Amalie would understand better than he did. With the queen ill, it was only to be expected that Merafi's rivals would seek each other out.

"Quenfrida d'Ivrinez, aide to Ambassador Sigeris," Iareth said. They were both silent for several long moments. Then she said, "The Pineapple . . . Might we visit it on some other night?"

He did not understand. He said, "Of course. But . . ."

She seemed to realize what was puzzling him. She said, "Yviane Allandur told me of it."

"Yviane Allan . . . ? Oh, Yvelliane d'Illandre?" She nodded. "But . . ." Quite suddenly, understanding hit him. Coloring, he said, "I'm sorry, I didn't mean to pry. That was the inn where . . ."

"Where Valdin Allandur was killed, yes." Iareth's voice was flat; reflective even. "I'm not offended. Curiosity is understandable."

He stared at his feet. His boots were going to need considerable work in the morning. And as for the marks on his breeches . . . Very carefully, he said, "Is it a good idea to go there?"

"I know not. That is why I thought of it." Still in that thoughtful tone. Looking up, he saw that her expression was equally pensive. She said, "Although it would mayhap be better to go alone."

"I don't think so." She turned to look at him. "It really isn't a good place for a woman—even if she's also a trained soldier." He hesitated. "I'll take you, if you really want to go, but . . ."

She smiled faintly. "I think it most improbable that I would expose you to a fit of the vapors."

"No. That wasn't quite what I meant . . . Wouldn't you simply be upsetting yourself?"

"As I have said, I know not."

"Well, anyway, if you want to go . . ."

"I thank you, Lieutenant."

"Joyain. Or Jean, if you like."

"If you cease to call me 'mademoiselle.' "

"My duty . . ." Iareth gave him an amused look. He smiled. "On duty, that's the only way I'm allowed to address you. Otherwise . . ."

She nodded. "So. But it is Jean off duty? And you are now off duty?"

Well, he was drinking, even if his original reasons for accompanying her had been connected with his responsibilities to the embassy. He said, "It does rather look like it." Somewhere outside, a bell tolled the hour. Five. "Although I haven't yet completed it. I have to escort you home."

She was silent, looking at him speculatively with her cool green eyes. Then she twitched her braid forward over one shoulder and began to unplait it. "Might you not do that in the morning?"

He hesitated, then crossed the room and kissed her.

Halfway across Merafi, Thiercelin of Sannazar awoke with the sensation of being watched. He was alone. Yvelliane had presumably retired to her own room, if she had returned from the palace. Rubbing his eyes sleepily, he raised himself on an elbow. The chamber was in darkness. He could see nothing. Could hear nothing, except his own breathing and the steady patter of rain against the window. It was too early for his valet.

There could be no one else in the room. And yet, he felt watched . . . As his eyes adjusted to the gloom, shapes began to emerge around him, half-familiar, half-alien. The bed hangings were heavy with the possibilities of cloaked observers. The curtains cast a shadow across one chair, which might almost be the form of a man.

Thiercelin's sleep-fogged eyes filled in the remaining details. A patch of reflected moonlight made the planes of a face. A cluster of paleness (his own discarded shirt, perhaps) suggested the fall of lace over a slim hand. Brightness reflected off the polished chair arm, cold in the autumn night, nearly drawing the picture of light on a blade. Memory colored the rest. One booted foot on the floor, the other (across which the naked rapier lay) pulled up to rest on the opposite knee, arms resting along the sides of the chair, right hand with its lace toying with the sword hilt. Hatless—a darkness on the floor where the hat was dropped. Hair half-hiding the face, further shadowed by several days' growth of beard. The fingers of the left hand drumming silently on the armrest. Body slouched, indolent, bored. A faint glimmer of light, where an ear was pierced with gold . . . Thiercelin smiled in the dark and said, in a voice which mocked itself even as it spoke, "Will you never learn to knock, Valdin?"

In the night, in the darkness, the figure that was not there turned its head and looked at Thiercelin. "I do not," said Valdarrien d'Illandre of the Far Blays, "intend to submit myself to the tortured rituals of your conventionality, Thierry."

Thiercelin counted very slowly to ten. Then he sat up. "And just what," he demanded, "do you think you're doing?"

"At present?" Valdarrien lifted a hand and looked at it. "I appear to be talking to you."

"But . . ." said Thiercelin.

"I beg your pardon. Talking *at* you."

"You," said Thiercelin, "are unspeakable."

"Quite." Valdarrien seemed satisfied with his inspection of his hand. He lowered it again.

"River drown it, Valdin, just what . . ."

"It was rather my impression that we'd already discussed that. Honestly, Thierry, you might pay attention."

"What for?" said Thiercelin, stung. "You're not even really here!"

"Your eyesight," said Valdarrien, "appears to be failing."

"Valdin!"

"Thierry?" It was a tone of sweet reason. Exasperated, Thiercelin thumped his pillows. He did not need night sight to see Valdarrien's amused lift of a brow.

Slowly, carefully, he looked at the impossible mirage of his friend and said, "Valdin, you're dead."

"Hmm." Valdarrien inspected his other hand. "Oh, that. A touch inconvenient, I grant you."

"A touch inconvenient . . . !" Thiercelin realized he was spluttering, and shut up.

"But I'm working on that aspect." Valdarrien straightened in his chair. "Certain things are a little hazy . . . Did you tell me why you're sleeping in one of my guest rooms?"

"No, I didn't," Thiercelin said. And then, "As it happens, I'm not.. This is my room."

"So?" Valdarrien seemed to think about that. "I must remember to offer Yvelliane my congratulations. Or are you debauching my sister?"

"No, I am not," Thiercelin said. "Honestly, Valdin, you simply cannot be dead for six years and then wander in and start demanding explanations."

"Why not?"

There was no obvious answer to that. Thiercelin did not try for very long to think of one. Instead, he said, "I told her. Iareth Yscoithi, I mean."

"Iareth *kai-reth*." There was a smile in Valdarrien's voice, as though he spoke the name purely for the pleasure of saying it. "Yes. My thanks." He moved again, putting both feet to the floor, swinging the rapier to rest against the chair. "She understands, I think." He rose, gathering, impossibly, the shadow of a hat. "I'll bid you goodnight, then. See you later, Thierry."

"Yes," Thiercelin said, on a stupid reflex. And then: "Valdin, wait, I . . ."

But no one was there.

7

IARETH YSCOITHI OF ALFIAL to Urien Armenwy, called Swanhame, Councillor and Leader of the Kairethin: Greetings.

I send this by the swiftest means available, in the hope that it will reach you as soon as is possible. Yesterday, Kenan had a rendezvous with Quenfrida d'Ivrinez at a house in the oldest part of the city. With the assistance of Lieutenant Lievrier, I was able to follow him unremarked and to witness some part of their conversation. Watch over Prince Keris: they mean him ill, for all he does not wish to credit his heir with such behavior. They may also seek to harm the Allandur: I would most gratefully receive your advice as to how you would have me proceed.

Lieutenant Lievrier has been most helpful to me in pursuance of my observations. He did not, however, overhear the conversation between Quenfrida and Kenan, which was in Lunedithin, perhaps to avoid easy comprehension by such Merafien servants as may have been present in the house. As yet, I have told him only that it was with Quenfrida that Kenan met, and not the content of their conversation.

Father, I . . .

Iareth hesitated, pen in hand, and stared down at the paper. *Father, I . . .* Thiercelin duLaurier had come to the residence with word of ghosts. Of one ghost: Valdarrien d'Illandre, her beloved Valdin *kai-reth*. Quenfrida, too, had spoken of Valdarrien, there in her hidden house in

the city. Allandurin blood to work ill against the Allandurin city. *Father, I . . .* She struck out the last words and
recommenced.

*Quenfrida and Kenan seek to unmake the pact between
this world and that of ancient things. It appears that the
ambush at Saefoss, of which you know, was a part of that
working.* Again, she halted, staring sightlessly at the wall.
Urien had been there at the sacred waterfall when Kenan's partisans had attacked herself and Valdarrien. It had
been her hand that saved Valdarrien from death, but
Urien had been sorely wounded. Urien Swanhame,
shapeshifter, master of old ways, old powers. Did Quenfrida know that? Kenan certainly did. But six years ago,
aged only fourteen, could he have grasped its significance?
Iareth did not know. She did not know herself what meaning it might hold. Urien's swan-clan, the Armenwy, had
had no part in Yestinn Allandur's ritual all those centuries
before. Urien might have no influence over this new working. He would know. This last year or so, he had been
increasingly restless, speaking to her of changes imminent
in the taste of the air, the scent of the waters. That was
one of the reasons why Iareth had been chosen to journey
south with Kenan, to be her father's eyes.

She had not been reluctant. A city, after all, was only
stone and brick. It have never been her nature to evade
her duties. What was past remained past and might not
be changed. What was here and now must be faced. It
was simple. She did not fear Merafi, nor did she welcome
it. She was here, that was all. She was here and Valdarrien was not.

Except . . . She began to play, absently, with the end
of her braid. Urien had never approved her decision
to leave Valdarrien and return to Lunedith. Urien was
Armenwy: it was his nature to love deeply and but once.
The Yscoithi were not made so. They moved from lover
to lover without regret. If she had loved Valdarrien, if
she loved him to this day . . .

She closed her eyes. She was Lunedithin. To have

abandoned her clan, her people for that reckless, wild, passionate young man . . . Her duty had forbidden it, and she had done her duty. It was over and done and that was it. Valdarrien had asked her to stay, and she had answered him, "I cannot," and made herself believe it. It was only later, under Urien's reproving gaze, that she had understood. "Not *cannot*, Iareth *kai-reth*," said Urien, "but *will* not."

Well, it was done. Except . . . Thiercelin had spoken to her of ghosts, of Valdarrien walking this city as a shadow. Lunedithin to her core, Iareth did not think to disbelieve him. Ghosts were a part of the world she was lessoned to know, subjects of the domain of the Masters of Darkness. This, too, was news that Urien should know, if only in outline. *Tell Iareth kai-reth she was right.* Whatever it was that Kenan and Quenfrida had done, Valdarrien was as intimate a part of it as they.

And perhaps this offered her one more chance to see him, to speak with him. Iareth rested her forehead on her hands. If she had been wrong, done wrong six years ago, then perhaps . . .

No.

She sat up brusquely and opened her eyes. She would not go back, she would not regret. The situation at hand required her to focus, to be calm and firm and cold as she had always been. She had her duty. She would cleave to it. Such had always been her practice. And if she was alone, if she yearned for companionship, then there was always the habit of her clan to find comfort from strangers. She inhaled slowly, picking up her pen. Joyain was kind and straightforward and helpful. She liked him well enough. It would do.

That the ambush at Saefoss is key is indicated to me by another thing also. Thiercelin Llawrier, of whom you know, came to visit me . . .

By the time he had made enquiries in the thirteenth cabaret, a worried line was beginning to appear between

Gracielis' brows. The damp air made him shiver, and
tension crept along his nerves. The answer he kept receiving did nothing to soothe them.

The night's fog still had not cleared, even though it
was almost noon. It played tricks with his perceptions,
turning the familiar inhabitants of the quarter into shadowed mysteries. The lieutenant's ghost loved it. Its form
edged into color as it oozed through the half-drawn
world.

Gracielis could taste menace. The mist held a troubling stickiness, a sweet, cloying scent, reminiscent of
honeysuckle. His anxiety lent him a pretty air of deli-
cacy, but behind his smooth courtesies he was starting
to fracture.

There was something out of joint. He lacked the skill
to do more—or less—than be aware of it. He shuddered
a little as he turned along the north quay and the mist
grew heavier. Pulling his cloak closer helped not at all.
He could not avoid thinking of the film of moisture that
the motion trapped nearer to his body.

The lieutenant's ghost was drawn toward the river.
Glancing sideways, Gracielis caught upon its face a sort
of optimism. By looking through it, he could glimpse—
just—less concrete forms hovering close to the river's
surface. This was getting worse. He would have to ask
Quenfrida and risk the cost. All around him, Merafiens
went about their business, blind to the changes that
paced them.

He was beginning to feel queasy. He crossed the street
and went into the Royal Repose coffeehouse, less out
of any hope of finding his quarry than to put walls between him and the river.

The coffeehouse was only just starting to fill. The hostess was still polishing tables, and only one of the three
waiters was on duty. A small knot of guildsmen clustered
in an alcove. Two more men leaned on the counter. A
lone woman sat close to the fire. Gracielis raised his hat

to her and bowed politely. She acknowledged him with a curt nod.

He said, "May I join you?"

"I don't see why not." Her tone was graceless. He looked at her sharply. "Well, you're too early to scare off business."

"Thank you." He drew up a stool and dropped his hat and two-colored gloves onto a table. The lieutenant's ghost took up position leaning on the mantel, turning rose in the firelight. He said, "You're early yourself, Sylvine."

"I came in to get warm." She was dressed skimpily. Her face looked pinched. Even so, she glared. "I don't need handouts from you, Gracieux."

"Of course not." It was harder for girls like her, he knew, who were not especially pretty, illiterate, ill-educated. She depended in large part upon the patronage of troopers, apprentices, and clerks. At this season there would be fewer of them willing to brave the cold and the curfew for a fast and mercenary embrace. He said, "Would it be charity to buy you breakfast? I don't like eating alone."

"Save your manners for the gentry." Sylvine coughed. "I'll let you pay for me, but I don't want your airs."

"As you wish." He summoned the waiter and ordered for both of them. The lieutenant's ghost watched with envious eyes as he handed over two silver coins. Catching its expression, he shrugged.

"The rain isn't hurting your custom, anyway," Sylvine said a little spitefully.

He looked apologetic. "Regulars."

"What else?" She coughed again and rubbed her arms. "I wish it'd stop, though. The side streets are turning into swamps."

And worse. He kept his face neutral. "It's inconvenient."

"There's an understatement!" The food arrived. She

broke open a roll and reached for the preserves. "You didn't say what you wanted in here."

He looked at her sidelong, eyes limpid. "Breakfast." The lieutenant's ghost pulled a disgusted face.

"You can get breakfast at your lodgings." He said nothing, letting candor write itself across his face. She said, "Besides, I know you. You never come in here unless you're looking for someone."

His lashes swept down, playing surprise. "I didn't realize you made such a study of me." Looking up, leaning toward her, he added, "I'm flattered."

She snorted. "Only by yourself. I don't waste that much time on you." He drew back a little, hand going to his heart. She said, "You owe me, remember?"

"I remember." He sat back and looked down at his crossed ankles. "How may I serve you?"

She hesitated, playing with the butter knife. "I don't want charity."

"I wasn't offering it . . ." He looked at her thoughtfully. Over her shoulder, the lieutenant's ghost made a suggestive gesture. He ignored it. "But you may have another piece of information which I need."

She smiled. "I hear things. You know that."

"Yes. And what's better, you remember them." He pulled out his purse and took out a coin. "You're right, of course. I did come in here to look for someone." Her expression did not alter. He added a second coin. "Chirielle."

Her shoulders sagged. Disappointment showed on her face. She shook her head. "I haven't seen her. No one has, for days."

It was what he had heard everywhere that morning. Even so, he did not put the coins away. He sipped his chocolate in silence for several minutes. Sylvine finished her roll and reached for another. The lieutenant's ghost folded its arms and sat down on the hearth. Gracielis said, "The trouble in the new dock. Have you heard anything of that?"

She regarded him speculatively. He returned the look with innocent eyes. "I might have," she said.

"I thought so." She stared at the coins. He said, "I have a . . . friend with customs troubles. She's concerned."

"And you want to soothe her. How charming."

He bowed, trailing perfume. "I do my humble best." The lieutenant's ghost gagged.

She hesitated. Then she said, "I don't know anything about customs." She frowned. "I did hear about the rioting, though."

"Oh?"

She looked at the coins again. He added a third. She said, "I had a client, a couple of nights ago. A trooper. His regiment had been active down there. He said . . ." She stopped, glanced over her shoulder at the knot of guildsmen. Then she leaned forward, lowering her voice. "It wasn't just the usual kind of trouble. That's why they're keeping it so quiet. My trick said . . ." Again, she paused. "He said it centered on the new dock itself. Someone—some people—started firing the jetties. And then . . . oil got poured on the river and lit. He said they were trying to hurt the ships."

Then why not simply set fire to them? But Gracielis did not ask that. Burning oil, burning through the mist on the river. Air, water, fire comingled . . . He shivered, and Sylvine looked at him curiously. Clearing his throat, he said, "Is that all?"

"Most of it. There's been looting, of course, and fighting. My trick did say that some of the rioters were acting funny."

"Drunk?"

"He didn't think so. Some of them seemed to be seeing things . . . You've heard that there's a sickness in the shantytown?"

There was always a sickness in the shantytown. However, Gracielis said, "Your client thought it might be connected? A fever with delirium, perhaps?"

"He said his captain thought so."

"I see." He pushed the coins toward her, then, hesitating, added a fourth. She took them and slipped them into a pouch at her waist. He said, "Do you think Chirielle became caught up somehow in the riot?"

Sylvine shrugged. "Who knows? Her landlady hasn't seen her, but all her stuff's still there, so if she's flitted, she's done it with nothing."

There was little he could add to that. Looking beyond her, at the lieutenant's ghost, he said, "This trooper. Is he a regular?"

"No. Just a pickup."

"A pity. I'd be interested to hear more of his experiences."

"No one gets everything they want. Not even you."

"True, alas. He didn't name any of the ships involved?"

"No."

It was better than nothing, although it would not answer all of Amalie's questions. He reached for his hat. "Did he say when the area would be reopened?"

"Two to three days, I think."

"So." Rising, he pulled on his gloves. The lieutenant's ghost stood also, looking resigned. "Thank you. You've been very helpful." He raised her hand to his lips. "If you should happen across Chirielle . . ."

She took her hand away. "I'll tell her you're looking. But that'll be another one you owe me, Gracieux."

"I wouldn't have it any other way," said Gracielis.

Thiercelin was enjoying a late breakfast in bed, and carefully not thinking about his dreams, when there was a tap at his door. Through a mouthful of croissant, he said, "Come in," and put down a rather tedious epistle from his boot maker.

It was Yvelliane. Coming to sit on the edge of the bed, she pulled off his nightcap and dropped a kiss on the crown of his head. "Good morning, Thierry."

He looked at her in some surprise. "It must be earlier than I thought."

"It's quarter past eleven."

As far as he could see, she was not dressed to go out. A little worriedly, he said, "There's nothing wrong, is there?"

"Not so far as I know." She helped herself to the rest of his croissant. "I'm sure you get better service out of the cook than I do. How do you manage it?"

"My winning smile?" He rescued his morning tea from his wife's attentions and then, after a moment's thought, put the whole tray onto the side table. "Haven't you had your own breakfast? If I'd known you were still in, I'd have gotten up and eaten with you."

"At seven?" He shuddered. She smiled. "I'd be cruel to expect it. Besides, I like to think of you sleeping peacefully."

"Glad to oblige. Any time." He returned the smile. "Tickets for the spectacle are available from my valet, but for you I might just be able to arrange free admission."

"That would be nice." She tapped him lightly on the nose with a finger. Catching her hand, he kissed her palm. She said, "When for?"

"It's a nightly event." Holding on to the hand, he leaned over to kiss her cheek. "I must say, you're a nicer sight at this hour than my valet."

"I should hope so." Her smile faded and she rested her head on his shoulder. He put his arms around her.

"You're working too hard."

"You know why I must."

"Yes, but . . ." He sighed. "Well, I have you here with me now, anyway."

She looked up. "What do you mean?" Her expression was suddenly defensive. He put his hands on her shoulders and looked down at her, noting the shadows under her eyes, the fine lines between her brows. If she would only confide in him . . .

He said, "I'm here." And then, as her eyes filled, "What is it?"

"Nothing." She bit her lip.

He hugged her. He said, "You can talk to me, Yviane."

"I don't want to talk, I don't even want to think anymore." She buried her face against him and, after a moment, slid her arms round his waist.

Leaning his cheek against her soft brown hair, he said, "It's all right. I promise."

"I wish you could make that real," she said rather indistinctly.

He tightened his hold on her. "I can do my best."

"I know. But yesterday . . ."

"What happened? Is Firomelle worse?"

"She's always worse." She straightened. "But she tries . . . She's seeing the city guild masters today. That's why I'm home. I haven't been too popular in that quarter since I increased the glass tax."

"Well, I'm sure she'll manage without you."

"So am I. That isn't what . . ." She shook her head. "I'm just tired and silly."

"Umm. All that early rising." He smiled at her and dropped a kiss on her brow. "You could always go back to bed."

"At this hour? Thierry, I . . ."

He kissed her shoulder, just at the point where the lace of her collar met her skin. "Why not?"

"Well, I . . ." She stopped and shivered as his lips traveled the length of her collarbone. "Thierry, that isn't fair!"

"It isn't meant to be." He halted, raising his head to kiss her mouth. "But since you've got nothing better to do and you want to stop thinking . . . I don't like this dress."

"What?" She sounded a little breathless. "I'm not saying that isn't nice, but . . . What's wrong with my dress?"

"Neckline's too high." Reaching round behind her, he began to undo her bodice with careful fingers.

"Oh, honestly!" Despite herself, she was laughing. "Thierry, I wanted to talk to you . . ."

"Am I stopping you?" Pausing in his unlacing, he kissed her neck. "Are you in any great hurry, since Firomelle doesn't need you today?"

"It's just not . . ."

"Not what?" The bodice was undone. He began to push down the tops of her sleeves. "Ah. Now, that's an improvement."

"Thierry!"

"Yviane?" He had turned his attention to the small buttons on her top petticoat.

"I just wish you'd . . ." She halted, face irresolute. "Oh, you're hopeless."

"Hope*ful*," he amended, rather muffled. She gasped as he bit her gently. For an instant, she hesitated, then slid a hand along his rib cage and began to tickle. He jumped. "Stop that!"

"Make me," said Yvelliane.

She was safe. Just for this brief instant, she should be safe. Yvelliane lay with her face buried in Thiercelin's neck, his arms tight about her, his face in her hair, the reassuring scent of him all about her. The line of his collarbone made a familiar pressure against her skin. She was warm, she was held, she ought to feel safe.

Somehow, she could not make the feeling stick with her. Even in the midst of their lovemaking, the fear and the worry had not deserted her. They hovered on the fringes of her mind, taunting, tormenting. Valdarrien was dead. Firomelle was dying. And Thiercelin . . . She did not want to think of it, yet the thought would not leave her. He had called on Iareth Yscoithi without telling her; he had involved himself in a duel. There was something between him and Gracielis, something he would neither explain nor forgo. Everyone she loved was leaving her alone. She dug her fingers into his shoulder, and he made a sleepy noise of surprise.

She swallowed. He said, "What is it?"

She did not want to ask. She did not want to know. She wanted—oh, how she wanted—to be safe. He shifted against her, half-turning so that her head rested on the pillow. He frowned. He said, "Talk to me, Yviane."

She did not want to talk. She wanted comfort and silence, if her thoughts would only let her be. Thiercelin said, "I know I don't know much about politics, but I can listen. And I won't tell anyone."

"I know." Rolling over on to her back, Yvelliane stared up at the canopy of the bed. She said, "It wouldn't help."

"It might."

It would not. Once she opened this topic with him, once she spoke of Iareth and Valdarrien and Gracielis . . . She said, "Leave it, Thierry."

"If that's what you want." He sounded hurt.

"It's just better that way."

There was a silence. She could hear his breathing, regular and steady. For six years, he had been there, quiet and undemanding. She had never questioned that. She had never asked him why, she had just assumed . . . Perhaps Firomelle and Laurens were right; perhaps she had neglected him.

There had always been so many other things that seemed important—trade agreements and budgets, negotiations and diplomatic correspondence. Valdarrien had never wanted to know about any of that, yawning when she mentioned it. She had always assumed that Thiercelin felt the same. And now . . . She inhaled and made herself turn to look at him. "Have I been hard on you lately?"

"Not really." But he would not meet her eyes. "I know you're busy. It doesn't matter."

"It should. Forgive me?" She reached out, touched his face.

"Always." He kissed her palm. "You know that."

"I wonder." She bit her lip. She was embarking on dangerous waters. "Sometimes I can't see why you stay with me."

"You know why. I've loved you since the first time we met. You ignored me completely."

"I didn't mean to. And I still do it, don't I?"

"Don't, love. It's all right."

"I just can't help it." She sighed. "Even today. I didn't come to you to make love. Only to ask questions. And I keep wondering how far I can go before you stop loving me. I drove Valdin to his death."

Something changed in his face. Despite the warmth of the bed, she went cold. He said, "That wasn't your fault. Valdin never could keep hold of his blasted temper. It was his responsibility. It was nothing to do with you."

"Valdin's fault? He'd stopped all that—stopped dueling. Until . . ."

"Let it go, Yviane." Thiercelin spoke sharply, turning his face away from her.

There was something here she did not understand, did not want to understand. There was something he was hiding from her.

He had seen Iareth Yscoithi. He had been in contact with Gracielis. She could not face it, not now. She did not want to be hurt any more. She pulled away from him and began to grope on the floor for a petticoat.

Thiercelin said. "Yviane . . . there's something I should . . . That is, I . . ." He sounded anxious, almost afraid. This was it. This was what she did not want to know . . .

She sat up, pushing the covers away. "Iareth Yscoithi," she said bitterly. "You've seen her. I know all about it."

"You do?" His voice was alarmed. "Listen, I . . ."

She cut him short. "Valdin loved her. He'd have done

anything for her. And she abandoned him." Fear caught in her throat. She pushed it down, counted her breaths.

"She had a duty to her family. Valdin understood."

"Did he?" She stood. "Not to my recollection. The only thing he understood was that he was hurting."

"Iareth was hurt, too."

"I doubt it." Anger. That was easier by far than fear. She reached out to it, let it warm and sustain her.

He said, "Be fair, Yviane."

"Why? She wasn't fair. Valdin adored her, and she broke him."

"Valdin dramatized everything. He had no sense of proportion. He was getting over it."

"Really?" Yvelliane finished putting on the petticoat. She reached for her skirt and began to fasten it. "That's easy to say."

"It's true."

"I'm happy you can think so. It must be a great comfort to you."

Thiercelin sat up. "And just what is *that* meant to mean?"

"What do you think?" She turned. They glared at each other for long moments. "You haven't exactly been slow to run after her now that she's back in Merafi. And I doubt she's discouraging you."

"Yviane!"

She ignored the outrage in his voice. "Valdin wasn't enough for her, clearly. And you're making it easy for her."

"I made," he said, "one courtesy call on her. I haven't seen her since, nor do I expect to."

"Oh, really?"

"Yes."

"I don't believe you."

"Your choice." His voice shook.

Yvelliane drew on her bodice with jerky movements. Her fingers fumbled over the stiff buttons. "And what about Lieutenant Lievrier?"

"Who?" Momentarily, he seemed baffled. Then he blushed. "Oh, that. It's unimportant. And it's none of your business."

"None of my business? When my husband goes fighting duels with an officer assigned to the Lunedithin embassy?" He was silent. "Did you really think you could keep it from me? He called on you here, you know."

With an effort, he said, "It's nothing, Yviane. A silly disagreement."

"Call it off, then."

He looked away.

She said, "Well?" She made herself hold his gaze. She must not back down. She could not be hurt, not again, not now. She had her anger to hold her, to protect her . . .

He said, "I . . . It's a matter of honor. However little I may want to fight him, I can't back down without losing . . ."

It was Valdarrien's answer. Somewhere, beneath her fury, Yvelliane felt pain creeping up on her. She fought to keep her voice cold. "Losing what? Your life, like Valdin?"

"Please don't."

"Why not?"

"Well, I . . ."

She ignored him. "Iareth came here six years ago, and it cost Valdin his life. Now she's back, and you're risking yours."

"It isn't like that."

She looked at him. "Prove it. Call off the duel."

He closed his eyes. "I can't."

"Can't, or won't?"

"Can't. Yviane, I . . ."

She cut him off. "You're right. I don't understand you *or* Valdin. As if any of the things you fight over actually matter!"

He looked up. "I'm not in the habit of dueling. As you know."

"Then why now?" He was silent. "Because of Iareth Yscoithi?"

"No."

"Then why? You have no other reason, have you?" Thiercelin still said nothing. She sighed. "Don't you care, Thierry? She killed Valdin as surely as if she fired the gun."

"That is *not* true."

"It is."

"River rot it! Is that all you wanted this morning, to play off a jealous scene?" He glared at her.

"I'm not jealous." She lifted her chin.

"You certainly could've fooled me." She made no reply. "That's it, isn't it? Iareth did what you never could. However much you bullied him, Valdin wouldn't behave. He just went right on quarreling and fighting. But she tamed him."

"I hardly think . . ."

He interrupted her. "You always have to be in control. Of me, of Firomelle, of Valdin . . . He could never do a drowned thing right for you. You censured everything he did—his friends, his pastimes, his manners. If he was wild, is it any wonder?"

"You tell me! You were fast enough to encourage him in all his games. Almost from the moment he set foot in Merafi, you were there, introducing him to all the rakehells and gamblers, and letting him keep you, half the time. Sometimes I wonder if it really was *me* you were in love with!" She stopped. She had not meant to say that. Had never meant to say it. If it were true . . . Her throat was tight; her eyes threatened tears.

"Indeed?" Thiercelin rose and made her a small bow with offensive precision. "I'm surprised you waste time thinking about it. I'm sure Firomelle has better uses for you."

"Now who's jealous?"

"I have no idea."

"Oh, really?" Her voice was contemptuous. "You begrudge every minute I spend away from you."

"Well, that would be most of your life, wouldn't it? Why don't you tell me something, Yviane? Tell me: why did you bother to marry me, if all you want is a man for an hour or two every couple of months?" he said. "Or is it that I'm cheaper than Gracielis?"

She looked round at him and, despite herself, her eyes were wet. He reached out to her. She ignored him. She said, "Well, you should know *his* current going rate." And swept from his room, slamming the door behind her. She heard Thiercelin curse, then a crash as he flung something at the wall. Halfway down the corridor outside, she stopped, pressed a hand to her mouth. Her heart pounded in her ears. Her eyes stung. *Why did you bother to marry me?* She had dared not answer that, not when he was so angry, so willing to hurt her. *Because I was so alone. Because I felt safe with* you. She half-turned, looking back at his door. She might go back, try to explain. She could still smell him on her skin, dearly familiar. She wanted to go back.

He was still angry. She might only make things worse. He had seen Iareth; he was seeing Gracielis . . . She had pushed and argued with Valdarrien all his life, and it had made no difference at all. He had never heeded her. She did not know how to deal with those she loved, only with numbers and intrigues and dry papers. Swallowing hard, she rubbed her hand over her eyes and made herself go down the stairs to her office and its piles of work.

Alone in his room, Thiercelin buried his face in his trembling hands. "Drown you, Valdin," he said, very softly. "Oh, drown you."

Miraude smoothed out the folds of her gooseberry silk afternoon gown, and contemplated herself in her longest mirror. The dress was new, but she had horrified her *modiste* by requiring it to be made in a countrified style.

The round neckline was cut high, and the plain sleeves fitted tightly to just below her elbow, without ribbon or frill. On another woman, it might have been dowdy. On Miraude . . . She looked charmingly serious, a modest jewel in the casket of her suite. Her acquaintances would wonder at her for a day or two: she could afford that. In a week, at least a third of them would be wearing garments in the same mode.

It paid, she had learned, always to appear completely confident. Inside, however, she felt uncertain. Kenan Orcandros was a different kind of challenge. She had always been able to rely on her charm and her beauty to steer her to her goals. Kenan was unlikely to be so easy. She frowned at herself. Today, she must be quiet and modest, careful and scholarly, and hope that the simple fact of her nationality would not prove an insurmountable barrier. She wished Thiercelin were coming to her salon. But he had stalked from the house at lunchtime, face set and shoulders rigid. Yvelliane was locked away in her study and refusing to answer her door. Miraude's frown deepened. Something was wrong in her home, and she had no idea why.

She had no time to find out right now. However much she disliked it, it would have to wait. Giving her gown a final pat, she went through into the drawing room attached to her boudoir. Chairs had been arranged in a series of small, intimate circles about tables or before the hearth. A long white sideboard bore a selection of cold refreshments; on a square table close to the door were set decanters of wine and goblets. Maids would be ready in the kitchens to bring in tea and chocolate. The air was scented with fresh flowers and with pinewood. Books of prints, of poetry, of philosophy were on hand for debate or diversion. Atop another table was a ready supply of paper, quills, and ink.

It was not necessary to be well-born or wealthy or even well-mannered to be admitted to Miraude's salon. She had realized early on that one might meet one's social peers anywhere. Interesting conversation was much rarer. From the first day she had set up the salon, that had been her goal. Her regulars included indigent writers, wealthy dilettantes, priests and scientists, philosophers and painters, aristocrats and musicians and travelers, actors, mathematicians, scholars, and anyone who intrigued or amused the hostess. Yvelliane was an occasional visitor; Thiercelin had always refused to attend. "I don't mind listening, Mimi, but someone might expect me to say something clever."

"Mal comes," Miraude had pointed out.

"Yes, but Mal never minds looking like an idiot," Thiercelin had said, and retreated to the stables.

Today's program included a recital of several new poems, a piece performed by a shy young harpsichordist, and a discussion of a treatise upon the nature and meaning of the Five Domains written by a skeptical university doctor. She had chosen them with care, seeking to engage the attention of her most particular guest, Kenan.

He was among the last to arrive, accompanied by the Lunedithin ambassador, Ceretic. She met them at the door and dropped a neat curtsy. "Your Highness. Thank you for coming."

"We do not use titles in Lunedith." He looked over her head as he spoke.

"That must create an admirable informality of conversation."

"We find," said Kenan, "that individuals know their place without constant reminders."

Miraude lowered her eyes and introduced him to the deputy priest of the temple of the flame.

She made it a principle to talk little at her gatherings. She found she learned more that way. She passed among the guests, listening a little here, smoothing over an irritation there, smiling and gracious and demure. By the time she made her way back to Kenan, he had been joined by a scholar from the university, a priest, a satirical writer and a merchant-chemist who made it a point never to believe in anything he had not seen or measured or tested for himself. She paused beside them, leaning gracefully against the back of the writer's chair, opposite Kenan. She knew she made a charming picture, the eggshell walls setting off the fragile color of her gown and the creamy gold of her skin, the late afternoon light striking deep blue notes in her hair, one long ringlet falling forward to kiss her cheek.

The chemist said, "In the light of our new scientific knowledge, you have to accept that the old beliefs are metaphors. Our ancestors couldn't grasp the world the way we do, they lacked our techniques. But all these tales of living rocks and shapeshifters . . . They're just ways of expressing our feelings and fears about the natural world. They don't literally exist. It's not possible."

"The *Books of Marcellan* say otherwise," the priest said.

"Marcellan was a primitive. The work being done at our university and at those in the Allied Cities have clearly demonstrated that . . ."

"In Lunedith," Kenan said, cutting across him, "we are not so contemptuous of our past."

The chemist blinked. The scholar said, hesitantly, "Of course, all these things are open to interpretation . . ."

"Fact is fact," Kenan said.

"But that's precisely my point. Science gives us facts. The *Books of Marcellan* merely give us stories," the chemist said.

"Stories believed by many people over many years," said the priest.

"Facts," said Kenan, folding his arms.

The chemist stared at him. "But, young man, no one has ever seen such things."

"Perhaps," the writer said, quietly, "we need better eyes."

"I've seen them," said Kenan.

There was a silence. The scholar picked up his tea,

cup rattling against the saucer. The priest said, "Well, of course, there have always been accounts . . ."

"Delusions," said the chemist.

Miraude said, "Isn't that often the first response to new discoveries?" She smiled at the chemist. "I remember you telling us how your brother reacted to your early findings. As you always say, proof before pronouncement."

"The Lunedithin maintain closer links to our common past than we do," the priest said. "And, of course, the Tarnaroqui . . ."

The chemist interrupted. "None of this is testable, gentlemen."

"Perhaps," Kenan said, "your city is simply too young. You clear away your past in every generation. How can you know anything of your origins like that?"

"Without progress," the chemist began.

"Truth," said Kenan, "is not to be found in perpetual changes. You have neither depth nor faith nor any real past here." He leaned forward in his chair. "Merafi was founded by an unbeliever. It was made to be blind. You have nothing here older than two or three centuries. My family have lived in the keep at Skarholm for a thousand years."

"The Old Water Temple . . ." said the priest.

"Was rebuilt by the queen's great-grandfather after the west city fire," said the writer.

"There are tunnels." The scholar put down his cup. "Under the butter market and along the line of the old city wall."

Kenan turned toward him a little too sharply. That was interesting. The scholar continued, "And under the Old Temple there are ancient foundations. It's possible they may belong to Yestinn Allandur's original fortress, if the early maps can be trusted."

"I didn't know that," the writer said.

"I've been engaged on a program of investigation,"

the scholar said. "A cellar was damaged in that temple last year, and the priests very kindly invited me to excavate."

Kenan's face was neutral, yet the line of his shoulders bespoke intent attention. Watching him sidelong, Miraude said, "I should very much like to see that. History fascinates me."

"It's dark and dirty . . ." the scholar began.

She came to stand beside him. "And you would be there to teach me."

"Well . . ."

"It would," said Kenan, "be of interest to see if any part of Merafi has true antiquity."

Miraude placed her hand over that of the scholar. "With Prince Kenan and you to watch over me, I'll feel perfectly safe. And," And she smiled again at Kenan, "We might come closer to finding the proofs that our chemical friend requires."

The scholar lifted her hand and kissed it. "If you wish it, then."

"I do. It will be our adventure."

Across the table, Kenan raised his cup, hiding his mouth. She was pretty certain he smiled. Well, that was his privilege. But there was something he wanted here, and Miraude had every intention of ensuring she was with him when he found it.

The lieutenant's ghost preened, watching Gracielis with colorless eyes, aping his every movement. Pushing his wet hair back, Gracielis smiled and then shook his head, spraying water across the floor, through the ghost. He said, "You waste yourself, haunting me. You should haunt children. You're the ideal excuse for wicked behavior." It stared back at him, contemptuous.

He shrugged and stepped out of the bath. His skin was flushed with heat. He stretched and reached for a towel, enjoying precious time alone. Well, almost alone. The ghost sneered at him. He bowed to it. Then, wrapping a robe about himself, he sat down to the glass and began to comb the tangles out of his hair. Unpainted, his face had a curiously unreal quality, as though he withheld his opinions even from himself.

He had not found Chirielle or much information to add to that he had bought from Sylvine, but Amalie had been pleased with what he had been able to tell her and his expenses had been more than met. There was a new ring in the ebony box on his dresser. And, more importantly, his words had eased some of Amalie's worries. It pleased him to please her and to spare her anxiety.

It was evening. For once, it was dry. Both moons shone unimpeded by cloud, and he was blessedly free from any sense of impending change. Perhaps, after all, it had been simply imagination. Perhaps there was nothing strange below the surface of the river. *Don't ask too hard why Thiercelin should see ghosts unseasonably, in opaque Merafi. Call it fluke, only; or attribute it to unacknowledged old blood.*

Perhaps it was all over.

He did not trouble to turn when the knock came at his door. One of his landlord's staff, no doubt, come for the bath. He called, "Come in," and returned to the important task of applying his perfume, spelling out his name. "You're prompt. Thank you."

"I wasn't aware I was expected. Or did you see it in a card game?" The voice belonged to Thiercelin. The words were a little slurred and the tone sardonic. "Am I disturbing you, Graelis?"

Gracielis turned and smiled. "Of course not. You're welcome. Sit and I'll call for refreshment."

Thiercelin sat down astride a chair and folded his arms along the back. "Wine, I hope. It's too late for chocolate."

"As you wish." His face showed only welcome, but behind the calm courtesy Gracielis was calculating. Thiercelin's clothing was rather disheveled and he was flushed. He was also frowning. Gracielis drew his robe a little tighter and padded barefoot into the hall to attract the attention of a waiter. The lieutenant's ghost followed him. It grimaced in anticipation. Gracielis arched his brows at it. He had nine years' knowledge of the drunkards of this city. He did not think Thiercelin had it in him to become violent. Nevertheless, he was cautious. The marks left by Quenfrida were fading, but he felt no need to acquire new ones.

Returning to his room, he sat down on a stool and said, "So. How may I serve you?"

Thiercelin shrugged. "I don't know. I was in the neighborhood. I thought I'd visit."

"I'm honored." There was a silence.

A waiter came in, bearing wine and water. He placed it on the sideboard and bowed. "I'll send the boy up for the bath, Gracieux."

"Thank you."

Thiercelin picked up the bottle and examined the label. "Not cheap. I'm too drunk to care, you know." He paused. "And I may have to write an IOU for it. Somehow I lost most of my ready money at The Wheel."

Gambling was a pastime that Gracielis took care to avoid. However, he shrugged and said, "These things happen. Let it be my treat." The ghost made a disbelieving gesture. He ignored it. "Your health, monseigneur."

"Thierry," said Thiercelin. He poured wine for himself and drank.

Gracielis had poured water for himself, not wine. He watched Thiercelin, disquieted. After a moment, he said, "I'm about to dine. Will you join me?"

Thiercelin gave him a sharp look. "I'm not that drunk."

"I didn't think that. But I'm hungry." It was not quite true, but Gracielis played candor, and after a second Thiercelin relaxed.

"Why not?"

"I'll arrange it, then."

*   *   *

It took perhaps fifteen minutes for the bath to be removed and food provided. The lieutenant's ghost hovered over it in impotent longing, and cast resentful looks at Gracielis. He paid it no heed, concentrating upon calming Thiercelin. The latter showed no special interest in the food, but he ate well enough.

Even so, Gracielis took great care not to touch him.

"Who pays for all this?" Thiercelin asked him, waving a hand at the room. The meal was over, and the Lord of Sannazar had settled into the single armchair. "Or is that an impolite question?"

Gracielis sat on the rug before the fire, letting its heat dry his hair. "The question is reasonable. The answer is: I do."

"And who pays you?" Gracielis looked at Thiercelin reproachfully. "Am I being indiscreet?"

The ghost bared its teeth in silent laughter. Gracielis said, "A little."

"Forgive me, then. I just . . . wondered."

"I have several regular clients. I wouldn't be treating them well if I revealed their names."

"No, I suppose not." Thiercelin sighed. "And it doesn't bother you, living like this?"

"You believe it should?"

"I don't know. It would bother me, I think." Thiercelin looked down. Gracielis watched him. "I disturbed you tonight, didn't I?" Behind Thiercelin, the ghost nodded, jubilant.

Gracielis said, "You did not. As you see, I was unoccupied."

"That isn't quite the same thing. I don't know why I came here."

"You were passing."

"Did I say that?" Thiercelin said. "I was lying. What time is it?"

"I don't know. Around ten, perhaps. I haven't heard the curfew."

"I'd thought it later." Thiercelin shook his head. "You lose your sense of time in places like The Wheel. It was midafternoon, I think, when I went there." He smiled. "With Mal—Maldurel of South Marr. That's why I lost, of course. Valdin . . . Valdin always said Mal was bad luck. That's one of the reasons I stopped gaming. Almost stopped gaming. Do you disapprove?"

"No."

"And if you did, you wouldn't tell me." Thiercelin drew in a long breath. "Do you lie to me, Graelis?" Gracielis looked down. "I'd like to know."

Gracielis thought. Carefully, he said, "Not in general." And then, looking up, "Vanity is not one of your traits, I think."

Thiercelin smiled. "Meaning that no flattery is necessary? Or is that flattery? That's too complex for me right now." Thiercelin grew serious. "If I asked you something, would you answer me honestly?"

It would depend . . . But Gracielis could not say that. He said, "Naturally." The lieutenant's ghost pulled a face at him.

Thiercelin looked speculative. "About Yvelliane. You told me there had been nothing between you. Is that true?" Gracielis hesitated. Thiercelin added, "I think I need to know. We . . . quarreled."

"That's a poor reason."

"Perhaps. But I need to know all the same." Thiercelin's face was open. The ghost gloated at his shoulder, and Gracielis knew a flicker of anger.

If this was friendship and not one of his carved and contrived connections, then he should be honest. He watched the fire for long moments. Thiercelin said, "Graelis, please."

Gracielis said, "You didn't quarrel on my account?"

"No. Not really. It was about Iareth, I think. Or Valdin." Thiercelin's voice was bleak. "Or simply because Yviane can no longer be troubled to maintain the pretense of affection."

"It isn't pretense."

"How would you know?" Gracielis was silent. "It's true, then. You *are* her lover."

"No." Gracielis looked up. "I'm her informer."

Thiercelin looked puzzled. "Informer? About what? I thought discretion . . ."

"I don't inform on my clients. But I hear things. And I transmit them, when it seems desirable."

"What sort of things? No, I don't want to know. Did you tell her about me, about Valdin?"

"No."

"Will you?"

"No. You don't wish it."

"Is there more?"

"To me?" Gracielis smiled. "Of course." He stretched, letting the firelight gild his skin. The ghost made an obscene gesture. "What would you know?" Not everything. Not even a friend might know that. Quenfrida was not given to sharing her secrets. Nor did his own needs, his fragile pride, permit any revelation of his dependence on her. He said, "I speak and read five languages—six, if you include old Lunedithin. I dance beautifully. I have excellent taste. And," and his eyes danced, "I can play the spinet. A little."

Thiercelin said, "I dread to think!" And then: "How little?"

"Very little."

"I'll remember that." They smiled at each other. "And Yviane?"

"I don't know. Does she play the spinet?"

"That wasn't what I meant."

"I feared not." Gracielis drew in a long breath. "I'm not her lover now."

"Not 'now'?"

"Not . . . Not since the death of Lord Valdarrien. Before that, yes, for some two and a half years."

"I see." Thiercelin sighed.

"It does not help you, knowing."

"No, not really." Thiercelin looked at the fire. "And even if she was . . . if you and she still . . . It wouldn't be my business, would it?"

Carefully, Gracielis said, "Have you been faithful to her?"

"Yes. Does it surprise you?"

"No. You love her."

"Oh, that." Thiercelin waved a hand through the lieutenant's ghost. It snarled at him. "It's what I do. I love Yviane. I always did, even before . . . It doesn't change anything."

It was Gracielis' opinion that it changed a goodly number of things. He said, "Does she know that?"

"It wouldn't make any difference."

Gracielis said, "She isn't given to thinking of herself as lovable. Just as useful. She doesn't make such things easy."

"She makes it impossible." Thiercelin rubbed his eyes. "I can't make her hear me, I can't reach her, and I've tried for so long. And now . . . this business of Valdin and Iareth Yscoithi. I can't burden her with all that." He covered his face. "I'm a mess, Graelis. There's more." Gracielis was silent, waiting. To the floor, Thiercelin said, "There's you." He looked up. "Can I stay, tonight? I don't want to go home."

"You should, nevertheless."

"I can't, not yet."

"If you wish, then."

"I don't mean . . . That is, I want the company, but I don't . . ."

Gracielis smiled. "There is," he said, "no obligation."

"Thank you," Thiercelin said. And then, "You're making a habit of this, aren't you? Being kind to me." Gracielis looked away, discomforted. Thiercelin said, "That night, when Valdin was killed . . ."

"It was nothing."

"It was a great deal. And the other things more recently, to do with him." He paused. "I saw him again . . . He spoke, this time. He seemed so real . . . It's no problem of yours."

Gracielis looked at the lieutenant's ghost. His share of the burden left by careless Valdarrien. However much he might wish to avoid it, he was bound into this, even without Quenfrida's schemes and temptations. He did not pretend to understand. Because he had been silent a little too long, and Thiercelin was watching him, he smiled, and said, "One likes to keep in practice. Such opportunities aren't common, here in Merafi." The ghost grinned.

"Or anywhere, I'd have thought."

"Merafi especially." Gracielis spoke without thinking. Thiercelin looked inquiring. "You know the old tales? Regarding places where . . . things not wholly human might more easily manifest?"

"There's something about it in the legend of Yestinn Allandur. His rival, Gaverne Orcandros, had a . . ." Thiercelin seemed to be searching for a word. "He was supposed to have found a woman who had no clan blood, or some such. Is that what you mean? The creatures born out of flame or stone?"

"Something of the kind. The stronghold of the Orcandrin was at one of those vulnerable places. That's how he was able to find his . . . his lover."

"I never heard any tales of that kind regarding Merafi."

"No indeed. Merafi is an opposed place." Gracielis hesitated and then added, "Legendarily. It is supposed to have a property—a kind of opacity—to such creatures."

"Ghosts," put in Thiercelin.

Gracielis looked at the lieutenant's ghost, and nodded. "Ghosts, for instance. It's said that some quality of this city—the mingling of salt and fresh water, perhaps—produces that opacity. That's why Yestinn is supposed to have chosen the site to build his capital. His old stronghold wasn't opaque. And he'd attracted negative attention from . . . inhuman things."

"Do you believe it?" Thiercelin's tone was hard to read. He sounded almost anxious.

Gracielis hesitated. After a moment, he said, "Well, I am Tarnaroqui . . ."

The disclaimer had the desired effect. Thiercelin relaxed and smiled.

All over Merafi, curfew rang. In the Lunedithin residence, high on the northwest side, Iareth Yscoithi of Alfial made her preparations for bed. On the floor below, Tafarin Morwenedd opened a second bottle and raised a glass to absent friends. Joyain declined to join him, and wondered how long it would be before he would be relieved of this duty. Kenan had gone out before lunch and once again not returned. This would be the second night he had been absent.

Kenan was no child, no prisoner, and no fool. It was his business, if he elected to spend a night in foreign arms (whatever Iareth might say about his proclivities). And it was not—could not be—Joyain's fault, if he lacked the same unconcern demonstrated by the Lunedithin charges. It was not part of his orders to know their exact whereabouts at all times.

It had, above all, nothing to do with any lingering sense of guilt Joyain might have regarding his own behavior. Valdarrien of the Far Blays was dead. If his friend Thiercelin was to fight Joyain tomorrow, it still had nothing to do with Joyain's congress with Iareth Yscoithi. Everyone involved was an independent adult.

He had no intention of indulging in guilt. He had nothing to feel guilty about. Kenan was guaranteed to turn up safe and sound, probably at the most inconvenient moment possible and full of unreasonable demands for attention. Everything was perfectly in order.

He hoped that Leladrien had managed to make

proper arrangements regarding guns. He hoped that Thiercelin's second would remember enough about military law to bribe the park keepers to look the other way tomorrow morning. Otherwise . . .

His spurs clicked as he turned and started back down the room. It was fine. He was not worrying. He had nothing to worry about.

He could not help it, all the same.

Beside the fire, Tafarin poured more wine and smiled. Upstairs, Iareth put out her candle and opened the casement.

A few streets away, Yvelliane of the Far Blays sat in the dark, pretending to herself that she was not waiting for Thiercelin to return. Maldurel of South Marr, in his lodgings, put the finishing touches to his toilette, thinking of nothing in particular. Miraude sat up in bed, head bent over a volume on the early history of Gran' Romagne.

The night was clear. Two moons, out of phase, lit the city. In the new dock, the last of the fires were nearly extinguished, the last rioters almost subdued. The river flowed on, thick with mud and fallen leaves. The air smelled of coal and autumn. No ghost rode the starlit aisle to the Rose Palace. Down in the shantytown, the sinkholes ran saltless for the first time in a week. In Amalie's salon, the master of the Haberdashers' Guild sipped sweet wine. Word from the coast guard spoke of ships finally expected home now that the weather had improved.

In Quenfrida's house in the old city, Kenan Orcandros smiled.

Thiercelin could not sleep. It was, he was aware, nobody's fault but his own, yet for all that he could not escape a vague sense of resentment. He lay in Gracielis' bed and wriggled, staring into the gloom. The room was lit only by the dying fire. Before it, Gracielis stretched out. He had his back to Thiercelin and his blanket pulled up to his chin. Probably, he was asleep. Thiercelin turned over again and suppressed a sigh. Think of nothing. Think of something neutral . . . Not of tomorrow's duel, not of Yvelliane. Remember Valdin, that time in the Old Palace, fighting in a gallery. How he cursed the polish on the floors! Of course, it was different with swords; such duels took longer. A pistol shot . . . *Don't think about it.* His opponent—what was his name?— Lievrier was a cavalryman. Had to be a fair shot, then. Maybe better used to muskets . . . Thiercelin should not have drunk so much today, risked a hangover. River bless that Gracielis had made him eat. One thing Yvelliane would not have to reproach herself with. . . . Don't think about it.

It was much too warm. Thiercelin wondered if Gracielis would mind if he opened a shutter. The fire was going out, of course, but . . . He wriggled some more and tried to get comfortable. He could smell Gracielis' scent on the pillows and sheets. He lay in the very place where Gracielis himself must usually lie, hair tangling with the memory of auburn curls. *Don't think about that, either.* Had Yvelliane ever felt this same confusion? Not since Valdin died, Gracielis had said, but Thiercelin could picture it anyway, Yviane here in this room, in Gracielis' arms. He shivered with a jealousy that was part pleasure.

Gracielis had not lived here six years ago, prompted the rational side of his mind. Remember, he roomed down by the old docks, in that inn where Valdin . . .

It could only hurt so much, a gun wound. Only last so long. How short a time, between the shot and Valdin's death . . . *Don't think about it.* This bed was too soft. Typical of Gracielis. How old was he? How old had he been, when Yvelliane . . . *Don't think about that, however tempting.*

However erotic. Thiercelin buried his face in the pillow and managed not to groan. Gracielis' perfume folded about him like a shroud.

There was movement in the room. Then Gracielis said, "Monseigneur?"

"Thierry," said Thiercelin, into the pillow. His pulse was racing . . . this was the worst kind of foolishness. He was, rot it, married. He loved Yvelliane. Gracielis could be no more to him than a passing temptation. He could master it. He had to. "What is it?"

"Is something wrong?"

Thiercelin was not going to turn round. He was, above all, not going to look at Gracielis lying half-naked in the firelight. *Think of Yvelliane.*

That hurt. He could only see the anger on her face, the bitterness as she accused him. She would never understand, and he was failing her. He could not think of a way out of the tangle. He had never meant to hurt her, only to solve this problem of Valdarrien. He was unfit to do anything by himself.

He could not take it to her, not now. He could only go on and hope for the best. Perhaps it would all turn out well and she would forgive him. Perhaps two moons would become one. He said, "I can't sleep. I didn't mean to disturb you."

"I wasn't asleep. Do you want to talk?"

"Not particularly." It would serve no purpose, not now. Perhaps tomorrow Lieutenant Lievrier would kill him and he'd be out of the whole mess. He tightened a hand into the sheet.

"Very well." Thiercelin heard Gracielis lie back down. There was a silence.

It was still too hot. That was something safe to focus on. Thiercelin pushed at his covers. "Graelis?"

"Yes?"

"Do you have something against fresh air?"

There was a pause. Then Gracielis said, "Your Merafien winters . . ."

"It isn't winter yet."

"No, I suppose not." There was almost a hint of resignation in Gracielis' voice. "I'll open the window."

"Not if you don't want to." Thiercelin halted and sighed. First he had to quarrel with Yvelliane, and now this . . .

Gracielis said, "It's no trouble."

Thiercelin turned over to look at him. Gracielis was propped on one elbow, silhouetted by the fire. His auburn hair hung loose over his shoulders. His blanket had slipped down. The slim frame was better built than Thiercelin had expected. Yvelliane could have told him, no doubt, but he was not going to think about that. Gracielis stood, wrapping a sheet around him, and went to the window. His skin was very fair, far paler than Thiercelin's. Thiercelin caught himself wondering how it would feel, touching that skin; whether it would taste as exotic as its perfume. He set his teeth and averted his eyes. This was no time, no place . . .

Gracielis opened the shutter and looked out. He seemed almost surprised. He said, "It still isn't raining."

"Why should it be?"

"No reason, I suppose. I just . . ." Gracielis shook his head. "You're right, of course."

"Oh, thank you." Thiercelin stopped, then added, "I'm sorry."

Gracielis sat down in the armchair. "You're troubled."

"No." Thiercelin pulled himself part upright. "All right. Yes. But it's not important." Only a duel and a quarrel and now this new confusion. "How old are you, Graelis?"

Gracielis looked at him sidelong. "How old do you want me to be?" Thiercelin looked away. Gracielis said, "I'm twenty-six."

A year older than Valdarrien had been when he died. Thiercelin buried his face in his hands. He said, "I've a duel, tomorrow, with some cavalry officer. It's stupid, but I can't stop thinking about what happened to Valdin. Or about Yviane or about you."

"In which order?" Gracielis asked.

Thiercelin looked up. "What?" Gracielis smiled, teasing, beautiful. Thiercelin said, "Explain."

"Well . . ." Gracielis said. Then he stopped, and began to laugh. Thiercelin stared at him. "I'm sorry. It's just . . . In my experience, people staying in my rooms don't usually think of me in association with duels. Or with their wives."

"Considering the circumstances of our first meeting," Thiercelin began. Then he caught Gracielis' eye. "It isn't funny."

"No. Not at all." Gracielis looked down. "Merely unflattering."

"I hardly think . . ." Thiercelin said, then he gave up. "You did that on purpose."

"Worry was stopping you from sleeping."

"I'm still not asleep," Thiercelin said. Gracielis was silent. "Any remedies for that?"

"Several. But you've forbidden me to mention most of them."

It was going to be a mistake. He was going to feel dreadful come morning. It was the only way left to him of forgetting, if only for an hour or two. Thiercelin leaned back against Gracielis' pillows, amid Gracielis' scent, and said, "Come here."

Gracielis hesitated a moment. Then he rose, and came to the bedside. "Are you sure?"

To his eternal shame, Thiercelin blushed. He said, "I think so." Gracielis did not smile. Rather, he reached down and brushed back Thiercelin's hair.

He said, "Revenge is a poor motive." He did not quite look at Thiercelin.

"Who mentioned revenge?" There was no answer. "Are you saying no to me?"

Gracielis said, "I think so. It's better that way."

Some of the tension was beginning to ease. Thiercelin inhaled. He said, "Is that sound business practice?"

"Oh, yes."

"Yes?"

"Indeed." Gracielis put his head to one side. "Consider. In the first place, you're more likely to come back for more, if the thought of me doesn't make you feel guilty. And in the second, the strength of desire is seldom harmed by a little frustration."

"What?" said Thiercelin. Gracielis looked demure. "If you think I . . ."

"I think you're upset," Gracielis said. "You don't really want me, monseigneur. Not at this moment."

The worst of it was that he was right. Thiercelin said, "I do wish you'd stop knowing quite so much about me."

"Forgive me."

"I just don't like feeling idiotic."

"Then don't." Gracielis smiled. "There's no need." He went back to the fire. After a moment, Thiercelin turned to watch him.

"Thank you."

"You're welcome." Gracielis settled back on the rug. Twisting, he gave Thiercelin a coy look over one shoulder. "Any time."

"I'm sure," said Thiercelin.

It is night. Merafi lies asleep, quiet under two moons. In her narrow house in the old city, Quenfrida sets down a bowl of meltwater upon a polished floor and raises to her wrist an obsidian blade. Kenan watches with eager eyes.

As the first drops of her blood fall into the water, all the candles go out.

8

GRACIELIS STOOD BAREFOOT, naked to the waist, hair unbound around him, listening to the melody of sweet silver bells. They were strung in their thousands through the tree branches, each one named, each one a memory. Under his feet, bruised magnolia petals clogged the air with their dying. His senses were heady with it, sound and scent; his body was drunk with fasting. The mist filling his eyes granted him a sight clearer than clear daily air. The world sang beneath him, within him, in the myriad voices of the bells.

He turned slowly, feet barely touching the ground, after the fashion of dreams. He knew the path that wound, snake-wise, beneath the carpet of magnolia; knew how the sun could strike, the night fall aslant through the branches. A knife now filled his hennaed hands, wicked with edge and poison. He knew the path, and the brass gate to which it led, and the place beyond.

Seven tests—and beyond them the great mysteries to which he had been given no key. Seven, to measure strength, and heart, and soul, to turn him from acolyte to *undarios*-priest, the first of Quenfrida's training and stone proud to prove her. His blood had run thin and cold at the thought of them. Seven. The first had come easy to him; and the fifth; the second less so, and the third, which he had thought to find simple, went disastrously awry. Nervous tension unbalanced him for the fourth, which already he had dreaded. The sixth was a blur in memory and limb. The seventh lay ahead, last and greatest—the test of death and life.

He had not followed the path, had not passed the brass gate. Terror had gathered him like a discarded cloak, bundled him over the wall. Later Quenfrida had found him and scorned him and bound him with the silken strands of his need. Then she had flung him forth, to live as best he might. He had never essayed the seventh test.

And yet . . . Now, his feet bore him over the petal-sweet ground, along the path, his hands slick on the bone-handled knife.

Human bone, they said. He had taken care never to ask the truth of it. The blade was hot to burning. Blood to seal his fate, to set upon the wind the song of his bell. Blood not his own, or else wholly his and all of it, to take or forge his life, to feed the perfumed soil of the garden. He had been seventeen. He had feared to die, feared to kill, feared failure. His hand shook as he set it on the latch of the brass gate. His foot hesitated on the threshold. From this step, there was no returning.

He crossed.

The world fell apart about him. He was drenched under a torrent of ice-chill water. A mighty waterfall thundered beside him, behind him. His vision blocked, blurred under the flow. He stood on slick hard stone, treacherous with rough edges, canted water-wards by centuries of pounding. Between him and the water there was a haloing silhouette. A man's head and torso, naked and muscular, swan wings beating where his arms should be. *That's not real, I'm seeing it wrong, he's a man, a man, but the swan is within him.* . . . A sharp pain cut his shoulder, like fire, like acid, the kick of an arrow through flesh. Gracielis fell, rolled, felt his hair slap damply across his face. It was black, that hair, and straight as pain. *Not me, not my past, my memory.* Through the haze of water, he caught sight of shapes closing in, men on foot armed with bows or spears and swords. A swan-cry cut the air, and for a moment it seemed as if the waterfall paused, turned to strike out at the ambushers. Gracielis—no, this must be Valdarrien— struggled to his feet, reaching for the sword at his hip. A man rushed him and he twisted sideways, jarring his shoulder. A feint and he cut low, taking his opponent on the thigh. The man staggered but did not fall, rushing him. Another twist took Valdarrien off-balance: he slipped, fell, sending red pain through his injured shoulder. His opponent bared broken teeth and closed. No time to rise . . . the blade came down for him, swift and sure and he closed his eyes . . .

Liquid splashed his face and neck, a thick sour splattering. He gasped, opening his eyes. His opponent was down, an arrow opening his throat. Valdarrien pulled himself to kneeling and met the cold level gaze of Iareth Yscoithi. She nodded, once, and turned, already taking aim at another man. Beyond her the spare form of Urien Armenwy closed with two spear-fighters. Valdarrien pulled himself to his feet. How many were there? A quick count: one downed by Urien, one dead, another lying stunned in a pool of water . . . A flash of orange caught his attention and he whirled, feet sliding on the rocks. Beyond the waterfall, half-veiled by spray, a small figure crouched, hands upraised. Red hair . . . The boy Kenan . . . There was no way to reach him. Valdarrien's pistols were in his saddlebags. They'd be of little use anyway in all this moisture. Perhaps Iareth, with her bow . . .

Another man closed on him and he turned. Another, and another behind him . . . surely there were too many for the three of them to withstand . . . Gasping, grasping for balance, Valdarrien parried and cut, cut and parried. His shoulder burned, he felt himself sway, dizzy, exhausted. Something was wrong, there was a scent in the back of his throat like honeysuckle. The redhead laughed.

His foot slipped again and he fell heavily. He was too

stunned to evade the descending blade. He could feel it
already, the bite of steel, the sticky, sharp parting of
flesh, the grind of bone. . . . *This is wrong, it didn't
happen this way, he lived, Valdarrien lived* . . . There
were swan feathers all about him, acrid with blood and
that cloying honeysuckle haze. Kenan's face swum above
him, triumphant . . .

"Graelis."

. . . He was inhaling the water and the blood and
the sweet ghost-memory of her perfume, swan-tangled,
cruel Quenfrida . . .

"Graelis!"

. . . mingled now with the falling of the blood from
the wound in his borrowed body, Allandurin blood to
feed a force that should, even now, be left bound and
sleeping . . .

Hands were upon him, jolting his aching shoulder,
shaking him aware. Awake. Mist of water clearing from
his eyes, washing away the debris of another man's
memory. Gracielis looked up into worried brown eyes.
Thiercelin of Sannazar. His body protested with remembered fear and borrowed pain. His shoulder felt oddly
clammy. Thiercelin said, again, "Graelis?" And then,
"Are you all right? You were dreaming."

He was going to be sick sometime in the next few
minutes. He pushed Thiercelin's hands away and groped
for his robe. Thiercelin said, "Can I get you anything?
Water?"

Gracielis shook his head, regretted it. The room was
cold; mist seeped in through the open window. Rolling
upright, he bolted for the stairs and the yard beyond. It
was dawn, sun close to rising, air still very chill. He clung
to a tethering post, gulping, fighting for mastery of his
body. Ghost-sight lay weighty upon him, cloudy with images. Around and through the lieutenant's ghost, shapes
contorted, closing grotesque barbed hands around the
city . . . something happening, something wrong . . . His
stomach heaved. He doubled up, retching. He was cold

with fear, with rejection; his skin was slick, clammy. The lieutenant's ghost hovered on the fringes of his vision, where it might make him dizziest. Amidst nausea, he cursed it softly in his own tongue, and then, because the price was already paid, spoke the word that would free him of it for a few hours. He almost welcomed the wave of sickness that drove awareness of the misty shapes from his mind.

Gentle hands were laid upon him, soothing, supporting. He leaned into them, let them turn and lead him away to where he could sit. A voice said, "Wait," and the hands were gone, briefly. They were back before the mist could have him, putting a cup into his hands. "Drink."

There was no perfume to spell out a name. Gracielis opened his eyes and looked through the mist at Thiercelin. Gracielis said, "It's happened. She's working. I can feel her. Something's happening, something's wrong . . . Thierry, I . . ."

"Slowly," Thiercelin said. His words were halting. "I can't follow you when you speak so fast."

The mist was full of claws . . . Their sting was inside him, like a poison. Gracielis tried to control himself. He wanted Quenfrida more than he could bear to admit. The air tasted sweet, wrapped around him in honeysuckle fronds. It was not her scent, but the feel of her was mixed with it, horribly. Thiercelin's hand closed over his and he fought an urge to pull away, as the cold and the strangeness bit into him. There was something terribly wrong . . . Thiercelin held onto him and said, "What is it? What's wrong?"

It was too much for him to see at once. There were swan wings in the mist and another, more menacing shape behind them. Throwing an arm across his eyes, Gracielis whispered, "No." And then, "I can't. I don't know how. Oh, let go . . ." Thiercelin took the cup from him and pulled him to his feet. Disoriented, he struggled.

Thiercelin shook him lightly. "Stop it." Over his

shoulder, Gracielis could see the mist closing in. Thiercelin said, "Calm down," and his voice held no fear. Gracielis tried to look at him, to avoid the mist-shapes and found his sight blurring. "All right," Thiercelin said firmly. "I'm taking you inside. Come on." Those same strong hands drew him into the inn's cramped back-kitchen. Gracielis leaned into them, shaking, and felt Thiercelin's warmth through his thin robe. He almost panicked when Thiercelin let go, heart pounding. Then he realized that the other was simply closing the door. He rested on the wall, shutting his eyes, breathing deeply. His mouth tasted foul. He was so cold.

"Drink, now," Thiercelin said, putting another cup into his hand. This time Gracielis obeyed, rinsing his mouth, then spitting into the slop bucket. The water tasted bitter. For a moment he shivered, wanting to put it from him. Then he inhaled and made himself swallow.

Thiercelin said, "Better?"

"A little," Gracielis said, and realized that they were speaking Tarnaroqui. Switching to Merafien, he said, "Forgive me."

"What for?"

"Disturbing you." Thiercelin made a noise of derision. Gracielis said, "I am very sorry."

"Don't be ridiculous." Thiercelin took the cup away. "You're frozen. Come back upstairs." His hands were kind rather than firm now. Gracielis welcomed the support. He was so tired, so confused . . . His room, his precious, safe room, was colder than it should be. He halted on the threshold, and his eyes widened in alarm.

The mist, coiling, winding, clinging, somehow here in his sanctuary . . . He must have tried to back away, for he collided with Thiercelin and caught at him, shaking. The window was open . . .

Thiercelin stared at him in consternation. Gracielis' voice nearly refused to obey him. Desperate, he said, "The window. Please close the window."

Thiercelin looked concerned, then said, "All right.

Don't worry." Watching him, Gracielis was aware with every nerve of the danger. Yet nothing touched Thiercelin as he walked, oblivious, across the room and shut the window. No resistance to him, no barrier . . . "Better?" he asked. Gracielis nodded.

"In you come," Thiercelin said briskly, and shut the door behind them. Gracielis made a vague movement toward a chair and Thiercelin caught him. "No, you don't. Bed."

"But . . ." Gracielis said.

Thiercelin stared him down. Gracielis let himself be guided to the bed. The sheets were still warm. Thiercelin pulled them around him ferociously, then sat down on the edge. "So," he said. "What happened?"

Gracielis' head pounded. He said, "I ate something, I suppose." Even to his ears, this sounded feeble.

"Hah," said Thiercelin. And then, "I know enough about you by now. You saw something?"

"I . . ." Gracielis began and stopped. It was too cold, too close. He could not describe it, not yet. He said, "A dream. I was dreaming . . ." He rubbed at his shoulder, almost absently, and found it damp. He shuddered. Too many memories. Too many memories not his own. "An old nightmare." Partly true, anyway, if no more than partly. He rubbed his shoulder again, then looked at his hand, lest it prove bloodstained.

It was not. He looked at Thiercelin. "I'm sorry. I woke you."

Thiercelin looked thoughtful. "Just a dream? To do this to you?" Gracielis was silent. "Do you want to tell me about it?"

"I don't know."

"It's just—you talked in your sleep. You said," and Thiercelin frowned, "at first, it was just 'no,' and something about bells, but then . . . You called out a name."

Gracielis turned colder. The air full of death, and the river turning . . . He was as caught here as any Merafien, and his memory was no longer inviolate. He looked at

Thiercelin, whose needs had brought him to this moment, and saw only kindness. It was too late now to turn back. "Quenfrida," he said. "She is . . . She's someone I knew at home."

But Thiercelin shook his head. "No, it was a man's name. Urien Swanhame."

Swanhame. A man built slight and gray with swan wings behind him. Gracielis said, "I know no one of that name," and shivered anew.

Thiercelin said, "I know him. Urien Armenwy. He was a friend of Valdin's, someone he knew in Lunedith." His voice was entirely flat. Looking at him, Gracielis saw that he was afraid. Thiercelin continued, "I met him once or twice."

Gracielis held a hand out to him. "I don't read minds."

"Not even the minds of the dead? Valdin and Urien . . . were close." Thiercelin took the hand and held it. "Iareth, too, I think."

Iareth Yscoithi. The archer of his dream, who had saved Valdarrien's life beside a waterfall, in the presence of swan-eyed Urien. In the presence of a red-haired boy with mocking eyes . . . Allandurin blood, falling onto water and stone . . . Gracielis shuddered. He knew his dreams of old: the garden and the path and the unopened gate. He knew how it should end. Not like this, in this nightmare of water and blood. *Now I know. Now I know what binds him, and it still makes no sense . . .* Out loud, he said, "Will you see her again?"

"Iareth? I don't know." Thiercelin's hand was cold. He was clad only in a thin shirt. "Why?"

Gracielis drew in a deep breath. "It was an old nightmare, and yet it was not. At its end there were changes. She was in it. You must ask her . . ." He hesitated, recalling the mist, the unclean feel of it. He could not bear to speak of that, not yet. Quenfrida's touch in it, somehow; and something more. He said, "Ask her about Lord Valdarrien and a waterfall and this Urien."

"You think he's the source of the binding on Valdin?"

I don't know . . . "It's possible."

Thiercelin relaxed. "I'll try to see her. Though it would help if you came, too."

"No!" Gracielis spoke more vehemently than he had intended. Thiercelin stared at him. "If you please, I'd rather not."

"Well . . ." Thiercelin looked down at him and his expression softened. "I'm sorry, I shouldn't have asked. After all I've already done to you."

"Tonight wasn't your doing." It was nearly true. Gracielis found from somewhere a smile. "It was . . . old experiences of my own." Thiercelin looked unconvinced. Gracielis sat up carefully and took his other hand. "It's the truth, I swear." Thiercelin was shivering a little. Despite the fire, the room was cool. "I've usurped your bed. Let me return to the hearth."

"No," Thiercelin said. "It was your bed to start with."

"That's different."

"I beg to disagree."

They stared at one another for a few moments. Then Thiercelin said, "This is daft. As if it mattered. I'll take the floor."

"You will not. You are my guest." Back on familiar territory, Gracielis added, "This bed is wide enough for two."

"You're ill. I'll disturb you."

"I'm much recovered. And you're cold. It'd be hard for you to sleep on the floor." Gracielis made room. "And . . . I think I might appreciate company. A ward against dreams." Perhaps Thiercelin's very normalcy could shield him a little. Thiercelin still hesitated. Gracielis looked demure. "I'll behave, I promise."

Thiercelin's lips twitched. "How?" Gracielis made no answer. "I may not sleep well, anyway. This duel . . ."

"Forgive me. I'd forgotten."

"You had reason."

"Yes, but . . ." Gracielis stopped and shrugged. "I fear I have no remedy for that trouble."

"No more than I have for yours." Gracielis looked down. Thiercelin hesitated a moment longer. Then, "To the river's bed with it!" he said, and climbed in. Despite the gap between them, Gracielis could feel how cold he was. There was silence. Gracielis turned over and saw that Thiercelin's face was wet.

It was late. He was tired. Not his problem, this business of Valdarrien. (*Don't think of the lieutenant's ghost.*) Not his past. His part was restricted to a brief, half-instinctive act of kindness. There was no room amidst his own fears, his own bitter memories, for this added confusion. Very gently, he said, "It will be well, monseigneur. Thierry." And wrapped his arms about Thiercelin and held him, as the fire turned the room warm and the gray dawn began to filter through the shutters.

9

"**B**ANDAGES," SAID LELADRIEN. "Smelling salts. Change for the toll bridge. Spare cloak. Pistols . . . Have I forgotten anything, Jean?"

Joyain looked at him in irritation. "How should I know? You're the second."

"So?" Leladrien pulled a face. "Your merchant origins are showing. Calm down."

"I am calm."

"Oh, really?" Leladrien put down the gun he was cleaning and leaned on the table, folding his arms. "Tell that to my floor. You'll wear it out if you keep pacing up and down like that."

"I'm not pacing." Joyain said, reaching the window and turning. "I'm exercising."

"Of course." Leladrien's tone dripped sympathy. Joyain glared. "Training for your Big Event."

"Do stop it, Lelien."

"And fail in my duty?" Leladrien looked offended. "As your second, it's my job—my vocation—to ensure that you stay calm, stable and prepared."

"By annoying hell out of me?"

"Better annoyed than afraid." Leladrien's expression shifted two degrees toward the smug. "And I'm succeeding so far, aren't I?"

Joyain came to a stop halfway down the room. "That isn't the point."

"It isn't?"

"No." Joyain caught himself beginning to pace again. "And, moreover, I don't appreciate your suggestion that I'm scared."

"Did I suggest that?"

"Yes."

Leladrien looked at the cleaned pistol thoughtfully. "You're sure? I have a pretty clear memory of calling you annoyed. And you _are_ annoyed."

"Yes, but . . ." Sighing, Joyain looked at his friend. "You're supposed to help me."

"I know." Leladrien smiled. "And it seemed to me that the best way would be to take your mind off it. Of course, if you'd rather worry . . ."

"Not really." Joyain made a deliberate decision and sat down. "What time is it?"

"Nearly eight."

"Two hours . . . How will we get into the Winter Gardens?"

"Whatsisname has access. Lord of South Marr. He's got a contact in the watch. It's all arranged."

"Good." Joyain looked at his boots. "That's all right, then."

Leladrien hesitated. "Jean . . . if something does go wrong . . . is there a letter you want delivered?"

"No." Joyain had considered writing to his family and rejected the notion. Better to leave it impersonal. That way, fewer questions would be asked. And as for Iareth Yscoithi . . . "Thanks, Lelien."

"My pleasure." Outside, a clock struck the quarter hour. Joyain sighed again. Leladrien said, "Look, let's go and get some breakfast."

"I'm not hungry."

"No, I suppose not." Leladrien smiled. "But I am. Come on."

Joyain shrugged and complied.

*　　*　　*

"All set?" Thiercelin hoped he sounded more cheerful than he felt. It was horribly cold, and the mist still had not lifted, even though it was now half past nine. Not that anyone could tell that, from the state of Maldurel's sitting room. The air was still smoky from the fire, and the candles had yet to be changed.

Maldurel regarded him with a jaundiced air. "Who knows?" he said. "At this hour."

"You should, for one. Looks as if you've been up all night." Thiercelin leaned on the mantel. "Or are you just getting old, Mal?"

"Hmmph," said Maldurel. And then, "What kind of a time d'you call this, anyway?"

"Breakfast time," said Thiercelin, "usually."

"What? You're getting staid, Thierry! Breakfast before noon! I make it a point never to rise before eleven-thirty."

"So I see."

Maldurel ignored him. "It's bad for the constitution. Bad for the complexion. You might," and he yawned, "have fixed this little *affaire* for a reasonable hour."

"You chose the time," Thiercelin said, stung.

Again, Maldurel ignored him. "Like Valdin."

"I have the clearest recollection," said Thiercelin, "that Valdin had a reprehensible predilection for fighting at dawn."

"Nothing wrong with that. Good sense, in fact. Get it over with before going to bed. Gets it out of the system. No lying awake worrying. No inconvenience to the seconds."

"But you haven't *been* to bed yet," Thiercelin said, outraged, "so . . . ."

"That's not the point." Maldurel climbed to his feet. "I didn't expect you to appreciate it. Just like Valdin. Bloody maniacs, the pair of you."

Thiercelin bowed. "Enchanted. Shall we go?"

"May as well, I suppose." Maldurel's valet brought in

his cloak. "Will this take long, d'you think? I have an appointment at two and I shall have to get ready."

Thiercelin said, "I doubt even I can manage to prolong one duel for four hours."

"Good."

The valet ushered them out the door. Silence fell as they began to make their way along the street. At the first corner, Thiercelin said, "Do you have the key to the gardens?"

"Of course." Maldurel patted his pocket. "Picked it up last night."

"Right."

Again, there was silence. About halfway there, Maldurel said, "What's it about, then?"

Thiercelin's mind was elsewhere. He said, "What?"

"I said," said Maldurel, "what's it about? This duel."

"Oh, that. A matter of diplomatic protocol."

"What?" Maldurel seemed to find the information indigestible. "What d'you want to go fighting about that for? Hardly seems very significant."

"It seemed quite important at the time."

"Oh. You were drunk, then." Maldurel considered. "Funny thing, that. Reminds me of something I meant to tell you."

"What?" said Thiercelin, who was beginning to feel rather lost.

"I'm coming to that."

"What are you talking about, Mal?"

"What?" They stopped, and stared at one another. Rather defensively, Thiercelin said, "I wasn't drunk."

"What?" said Maldurel. And then, "Oh, then. I was."

"You were what?"

"Drunk."

"You weren't there."

"Yes I was. Stands to reason I was. Man can't see a thing if he isn't there, can he? That's only sense."

"I think," said Thiercelin, "that we'd better start this

conversation again. Where were you drunk and when; and why are you telling me about it?"

Maldurel wore the expression of a man at the extreme of patience. "A sennight since. At the Rose Palace. It was a funny thing. Thought it might interest you. Gave me quite a turn, or at least I expect it would have done if I'd been sober."

Thiercelin put his head in his hands and wailed. "Will you *please* make sense?"

Maldurel looked at him. "Nothing to tear your lace about. As I said, I was drunk. It was queer, though. I was on my way home, minding my own business, and not thinking about much. And there he was. Large as life. Same bloody sneer on his face, and lurking about in corners trying to give a man a start. Typical, if you ask me."

"Mal, who are you talking about?"

Maldurel sounded like a man explaining himself to an idiot. "Valdin, who else? The emperor of Tarnaroq?"

"You saw Valdin?"

"Yes. I just said so, didn't I?"

"Valdin himself? Near the Rose Palace? In the aisle?"

"Yes. But I was drunk. Nothing to get so excited about, Thierry. People are always seeing things when they're drunk. My cousin saw a dancing cow once in the fish market. At least he thought he did."

Thiercelin cut him off. "Did he say anything?"

"The cow? How should I . . . ?"

"No, Valdin, idiot!"

"I see," said Maldurel, "no cause for abuse." And then, more kindly, "But I suppose you're wound up about this duel. He did, actually."

"What?"

"What?"

"*What* did he say?"

Maldurel looked faintly affronted. Carefully, he quoted, " 'Still hungover, Mal?' "

Thiercelin was still laughing when they reached the Winter Gardens.

His opponent awaited him outside the gate, together with his second. Suddenly sober, Thiercelin exchanged bows. Then he looked at Maldurel.

Maldurel gazed back at him. "What, Thierry?"

"The key?"

"Oh, yes. Of course." Maldurel began to rummage through his pockets. The two army officers were silent. Uncomfortable, Thiercelin shuffled, then pretended to be cold. The opposing second caught his eye and smiled wryly.

He said, "Cold enough, for autumn."

"Yes," Thiercelin said. "I hate to think what the winter will be like."

"Worse, I should think," said Maldurel. And then, "Aha!" He grinned broadly and brandished a large brass key. "Got it! Well, gentlemen, shall we go in?"

It was still misty. The garden, sloping down to the river, was empty, lawns half hidden in fog. It had a half-kempt air. The dead leaves had not been raked away and moss had begun to colonize the gravel paths. Vapor coiled about the tree boughs. Thiercelin shivered a little. The seconds were examining the guns; his opponent had wandered away somewhat and stood staring into the distance. Against his will, Thiercelin remembered Valdarrien, anger-lost and vital, sword light in his hands under these same trees. The grass was damp today. That was going to be a nuisance. How young they had been, the first time Valdin fought here. Ten years ago, maybe twelve. The air was moist, unkindly warm. Thiercelin inhaled and tasted honeysuckle. Valdin had been half-drunk, almost laughing as he fought, barefoot on the spring grass. Thiercelin could not, for the life of him, picture the face of the other man involved. The affair had been friendly, to first blood only, and there had been a large and amicable breakfast afterward, by the riverside. The other man had fallen at one point; that was it. Thiercelin could see Valdarrien's half-smile as he helped the other up. It had to have been about cards, then. Valdarrien had always been blasé about money. That duel had been fought closer to the river, down at the bottom of the wood. Thiercelin remembered the feel of bark at his back as he leaned on a tree to watch the sport. The other second, a young provincial, had watched with him, wide-eyed with delight and shock. Even then, he had had the name for it, nineteen-year-old, reckless Valdin, the troublemaker, the duelist, laughing on that spring morning on the river's edge. Thiercelin looked away through the fog-bound trees, as if he might somehow see through them into that happier past.

There was nothing there, save mist and garden. He sighed and turned away.

His companions were ready for him. Maldurel coughed and looked serious. Thiercelin raised his brows and waited. Maldurel frowned. "Drown it, Thierry! Some of us are trying to do this properly."

"Sorry," said Thiercelin, meekly.

"Bad as Valdin. Worse. Leastways, he usually paid attention when people waited for him." Thiercelin looked down. "Right, then," Maldurel's tone turned formal. "Monseigneur of Sannazar, Lieutenant Lievrier, you are here to answer to one another in a matter of honor. If either of you wishes to reconsider or retract, please do so now." There was a pause. Thiercelin looked at Joyain, who stood blank-faced. It had been a part of their tacit agreement, long ago, that dueling was Valdarrien's province and that Thiercelin held it foolish. Yet here he was on the edge of the same abyss. He risked his life. He risked his relationship with Yvelliane. Perhaps he had already damaged the latter beyond repair. Opposite him, Joyain looked down briefly, then raised his head and shook it. Thiercelin paused, then did likewise.

Maldurel looked slightly disappointed. "Oh. Well, then . . ."

The other second said, "The weapons."

"Of course." Maldurel held them out for inspection by the principals. "If you gentlemen would care to make your selection? Or should you shake hands first?" Maldurel looked at the other second, who shrugged.

"Shake hands, choose pistols, walk ten paces, turn and fire. Is that so much to remember, Mal?" The voice came from amidst the mist-bound trees. Three of the four men turned toward it, expressions between outrage and confusion. Thiercelin did not dare look. Instead, he glanced at his opponent. Joyain had gone white.

Maldurel said, "That's nice, coming from you!" And then, as he began to realize what he was seeing, "River bless!"

Thiercelin turned. Against a nearby tree, a slender figure leaned, watching them. Mist swirled about him; he seemed to be smiling. Thiercelin gulped thick air and said, "You can't do this, Valdin."

"Clearly, I can." Valdarrien's tone was light and a little sarcastic. "Haven't we discussed that before?" Thiercelin was silent. "But don't let me interrupt you. You were about to shake hands with this gentleman. What are you fighting about, anyway?"

"None of your drowned business." Thiercelin realized that he was in effect bickering with a ghost and sighed. He looked across at Joyain. "I'm sorry. This is a fiasco."

Joyain jumped. His gaze did not leave Valdarrien. He said, "What?"

"I," said Maldurel, who appeared to be feeling ignored, "have just been insulted by a dead person, and you only call it a fiasco. Thierry, I hardly think . . ."

Joyain tore his eyes away and looked at Thiercelin. He said, "Monseigneur, you may be unaware that this duel is in breach of military regulations. Under the circumstances, perhaps we . . ."

Thiercelin said, "It was my fault. I behaved poorly. I offer you my unreserved apologies." He bowed. "And I regret this disturbance." Behind him, he heard Valdarrien snort. Ignoring him, he added, "My cousin is too young to be aware that certain jokes lack taste. I'll ensure it doesn't happen again." Daring Valdarrien to make anything of this, he held a hand out to Joyain. The latter hesitated, took it in an uncertain grip.

Joyain looked back into the trees. Rather shakily, he said, "A joke?"

"Yes," Thiercelin said, firmly. Then, lowering his voice, "I may need to call again upon Iareth Yscoithi. Will that inconvenience you?"

If anything, Joyain grew even paler. But he merely said, "Of course not," and saluted. Thiercelin watched as he and his second made their way from the gardens.

Maldurel said, "Never heard you had a cousin in town."

"He doesn't," Valdarrien's light voice said. "He was being tactful. Covering for me as ever." He bowed. "My thanks to you, Thierry."

"I don't want them," Thiercelin said. This could not be happening. He needed a drink. He needed help. Maldurel, gawping, was worse than useless. "This can't happen, Valdin."

"I don't see why not."

"Because . . ." Thiercelin hesitated. "I don't know why. But it can't. People just don't . . ."

"And when," said the erstwhile Lord of the Far Blays, "did I ever do what 'people' do?"

"I don't know, but . . ."

"Someone's coming," Maldurel said. "I heard the gate bang." And then, "Come to it, Valdin, I'll thank you to be a little more polite. I've stood by your good name these last years, I'll have you know."

Valdarrien shrugged. "I owe you, then. How will you collect, Mal?" Something in the tone bespoke malice. Thiercelin laid a restraining hand on Maldurel's arm. Valdarrien continued, "I don't think Yviane will let me into the family coffers just now."

"It's nothing," Maldurel said.

Thiercelin added, "Call it habit, Valdin. We all do it, even Mimi." He paused, inhaled. "We'll say good-bye, now. We've matters to attend to elsewhere."

"Oh, do you?" Valdarrien sketched a bow. "Later, then."

He had said that before, two nights since. Thiercelin's skin was cold. He pulled gently on Maldurel's arm and said very quietly, "Start walking. I'll join you." Maldurel looked at him curiously but didn't protest. Thiercelin waited until he was a few yards away, then turned back to Valdarrien. He said, "You owe me, too, Valdin."

"Possibly."

Thiercelin sighed. "I want you to tell me something. Tell me about Urien Armenwy and a waterfall."

"Whatever for?" Valdarrien sounded surprised. Thiercelin was silent. "I knew Urien in Lunedith. We were ambushed together. What more do you need to know?"

How these matters are involved in your presence here. But Thiercelin could not ask that. He said, "The subject came up recently."

"With Yviane?" Valdarrien seemed to smile. "No, she wouldn't discuss her diplomatic work with you." Thiercelin bit his lip. "It was Iareth, then. My Iareth *kai-reth*." Again, his tone bore menace. "You'd do well to stay clear of her, Thierry."

"You told me to contact her."

"I did?" There was brief puzzlement in Valdarrien's voice. "I don't remember . . . There's been a lot happening. Urien, and the waterfall . . . Kenan Orcandros set a trap for us. Alongside the big waterfall . . . Iareth said it was a special place, dangerous. We won, but Urien was badly hurt and I was shot in the shoulder. Iareth saved my life . . ." He looked up. "Forgive me, Thierry. I forget myself. *You*, of course, are to be trusted with her."

"You're too kind." Thiercelin could not quite keep bitterness from his tone. "Is there anything else?"

"Perhaps." The fog was beginning to lift. Valdarrien's

voice sounded thinner. Looking across at him, Thiercelin could see that his shape had lost some definition. Valdarrien said, "It's hard to be sure. There's something. Something I need . . . I can't remember." His eyes met Thiercelin's and he was, for a moment, the old, beloved Valdarrien. "Help me, Thierry."

How many times had Thiercelin heard that? It was too familiar. It stung, the old grief like acid. He swallowed tears and said roughly, "I don't know." This should not be happening. He wanted Yvelliane. "It's different now. Things have changed." He could see almost down to the river as the mist cleared. Valdarrien's shape was all but gone. "I'm sorry, Valdin."

"Yes." The voice was a thread. "Later, then." A few raindrops began to fall. Valdarrien seemed to turn away, toward the water. Then he stopped. Thiercelin was not quite sure he could still see him. Valdarrien's voice said, very indistinctly, "Iareth's father. Urien's her father." Then he was gone.

Thiercelin stared after him, shaking.

In an inn a few streets away, Joyain sat with his head in his hands and tried to control his shaking. He felt sick. The memory of Iareth Yscoithi—in his room, in his bed, in, river protect him, his arms—swam before him. He could not think. It made no sense. He could not have seen Valdarrien of the Far Blays.

He was alone: leaving the Winter Gardens, he had shed Leladrien, pleading duty. He could not face company. He remained unsure if he could face his duty, either. Not now. Not after . . . It was hardly the kind of thing one might tell a woman, even Iareth; *I have seen your lover, who is dead . . .*

Thiercelin of Sannazar had taken the whole thing in his stride. Perhaps it really had been only a jest. A dishonorable one, to avoid the duel . . . The theory sat poorly with what Joyain knew of Thiercelin's reputation. All right, not a deliberate ruse, but the thoughtless act

of a third party, of the claimed "cousin" . . . Leladrien
had believed that tale, certainly, laughing at the idiocies
of the aristocracy. Capable of anything, the lords from
the hill.

Joyain could choose to believe it, too. Chalk it up to
the vagaries of life, ignore it, forget it. Forget, above all,
two nights' since, in his room above the shop of the
sugar merchant. Forget Iareth Yscoithi.

He could say nothing in any case. He would only look
a fool.

Business as usual, during altercations.

It took several hours before Gracielis could bring himself to open the casement. The mist outside had turned
into solid rain. To his eyes, it was heavy with pain. He
was fevered, a little, and edgy. He had no desire to leave
his room, to expose aching head and seared nerves to
whatever lurked outside. His solitude was no protection,
although he had sought it deliberately. At his own request, Thiercelin would not return before tomorrow, at
the earliest.

He wanted Quenfrida, desperately.

He needed to see the river and the city also to discover the extent of the change he felt. In the end, he
wrapped himself in his darkest and warmest clothing and
forced himself to go out. The lieutenant's ghost shadowed him, for once neither mocking nor contemptuous.
Gracielis shivered and marveled at the insensitivity of
the people crowding the streets. The air was full of immanent danger and yet they remained blind.

The ghost knew. He could see the knowledge in every
uncertain line of it. That was no reassurance. He knew
he could simply leave Merafi. Yet images of lovers past
and present danced through his memory. Lovers to
whom he owed, perhaps, the chance to flee. Amalie.
Yvelliane. All the others, through nine years. The air
tasted foreign, weighted with a power that should not
run here. A power whose course would serve all too

well the requirements of his Tarnaroqui masters, if not deflected. It was not for Gracielis de Varnaq to gainsay them. He should rejoice at it.

He could neither rejoice nor leave. He had lived too long in Merafi simply to abandon its people to their danger. He had no more desire for death at twenty-six than he had had at seventeen.

He did not want to run away again. He was caught into this, bound almost as surely by the place as by Quenfrida. His charm was perhaps beginning to desert him, his grace to break down and leave him open. He was ceasing to be himself.

If, indeed, he had ever been anyone at all.

He climbed the one hundred and thirty-two steps of the River Temple and went out onto the wet leads. The city lay all around him, mantled in rain. The river was hazy, the south channel all but invisible. The main course, which he had crossed to reach this tower, ran dark and swift. To the west the river ran high. To the east it faded into indistinctness. Clouds hung over the docks and the shantytown. The river felt wrong. It felt ominous, here in the middle of the city it sustained. Death by water, slow, sleepy, almost painless save at the last, when the body labors and panics for breath. The inhabitants of Merafi were drowning in their own complacency, and they would never know.

The voices on the streets had held no hint of concern or trouble. People were accustomed to unrest in the docks, distress in the shantytown. No one cared. He was alone in his perception of despair.

Perhaps he had run a little mad, in the hollow place behind his masks. Perhaps there was nothing in it beyond fear and the natural mists of autumn. He leaned on the parapet. The ghost hovered beside him. Everything was coming apart. Across the rain-swamped river, shapes broke and swirled.

This was beyond him. Too many possibilities, too many threads of need and power and loyalty. Pain throbbed behind his temples. He rubbed them with his left, black-clad hand. Water turning bitter in the city and water falling in a dead man's eyes.

He took his gaze from the river and looked instead at the lieutenant's ghost, half-hidden in the rain, a fragment of a man he had barely known. Today there was no contempt in its colorless eyes. "So," he said to it, "what would you do? Have done?"

It shrugged. He sighed, "It's your city." There was no response. He turned again and let a hand cover his eyes. It had been nine years and more since he had allowed himself the luxury of weeping. He would not weep now.

Tell Iareth kai-reth *she was right* . . . Words with little meaning, little sense save to that same Iareth, who would not decode them.

He might perhaps go to Yvelliane and warn her and watch her fail to understand him. He might go to Thiercelin, who was powerless. Iareth, then, as alien here as Gracielis, and in whose eyes lay madness, to trap him into another man's past. Gracielis flinched from it, cold, afraid. For all her small treacheries, there remained only Quenfrida. Only and always Quenfrida.

He left the tower, trailed back through the streets to his lodgings at the Jade Rose. His room was empty. He paced it, uncertain. He possessed no sure way of summoning Quenfrida. She only came when it pleased her, and left as lightly. A message would likely meet with silence. He might wait an hour or a week or a year, before she saw fit to seek him out.

No means to bring her, unless . . . He was bound, in his blood and hers, to forbear from certain things. Bonds the severing of which would not go unremarked by her.

It was wholly forbidden. There was no other way.

His painted eyes turned to the lieutenant's ghost.

In the embassy on the hill, Iareth Yscoithi sat on the wide sill of a first-floor window and let her level gaze fall on the rain. She had sat thus for close to an hour, unmoving. It was not time yet for word from Urien. Her letters could not yet all have reached him. Her body was still, but her thoughts turned, and for the first time she knew regret that half her blood was Yscoithi. Not even for Valdarrien would she compromise it before, yet now with bitter hands she might have spilled it, if the loss could have released the rare power locked in the Armenwy half of her blood.

Kenan had returned and there was joy in him like a light set in alabaster. She could find no reason for it, but he had been with Quenfrida. Alarm ran in the clanblood of Iareth's veins. She was not Merafien. Her calm was only skin-deep. Animal-wise, her sense of impending danger ran edged with instinct. Urien would know. Urien would see beyond the alabaster chill and the new wound at Kenan's throat to the truth, however strange.

She had warned him, her sire, her commander, of her failings, and he had chosen to discount them.

It was not for Iareth to gainsay him.

Only, perhaps, to fail.

Gracielis did not have all he needed. No incense to sweeten the air and darken his limpid eyes. No bowl of virgin silver. No wicked bone-hafted knife to slice skin and memory. Candles he did have, for the fifteen pillars of the heavens, and a half-handful of fingernail-sized bells and a grief as deep as any trance. He had repainted his eyes with gold and emerald green, replaced wool and cotton with silk. He wore no rings on his fingers. His feet were bare on the smooth wood floor. His hair was left to fall, for once uncurled, to his waist. The lovelock, retinted forest green, kissed his cheek. His pulse points were warm and perfumed with his name. In the full rite, he should have fasted two days in advance and held silence for one. His present state would have to suffice. He was as pure as his flawed nature might permit.

He had performed this ritual only once before. It was the fourth test of the seven and much to be feared, lest ghost-sight see too deeply into oneself. Full sibling to the act of exorcism, which might be performed by a lesser priest. An act not of interdiction, but of absolution.

Absolution of the condemned. He sat down cross-legged and looked into the colorless eyes of the lieutenant's ghost. It watched him with wary amusement. Across his knees he held his one and only knife, a pretty thing intended more for adornment than use. Its blade had been honed sharp by his baffled landlord. Gracielis ran a finger along the edge and watched as his blood welled from the cut, breathing slowly to master fear.

He disliked the sight of blood. His fingertip throbbed faintly. He averted his eyes as the blood trickled toward his palm. Instead he looked at the ghost. He said, "We must be close to friendship, you and I. We have been scarcely separated at any time." Blood from his finger dripped onto the floor. The room was quiet. No sounds drifted in from the taproom below. The ghost began to drift closer to him.

Gracielis looked back at the knife blade. "It is strange, really, since I don't recall ever learning your name. Although you were free enough with mine, living." He spoke a little too swiftly. He sought mastery. He drew another finger along the edge of the blade. "We weren't friends then, I think." The ghost was less than two feet away, watching. The knife edge was discolored. He lifted it and looked at the point. It glittered. He shivered, throat dry. "Of course, hate is very powerful." This time, his tone was nearly level. "Strong enough to bind a living man." The knifepoint was against the small blue vein in his left wrist. He looked from it to the ghost. "Living, or dead."

The blade bit into flesh, deep, deeper, deep enough. Into the vein, evading the artery and the tendons. There came a white flash of pain, freezing his hand and knotting his stomach. He bit down on his lip, forced control. Then he spoke one word in another tongue.

There was a moment of stillness. It lasted just long enough for him to register that the colorless eyes of the lieutenant's ghost were actually blue. Gracielis looked into those blue eyes, drew in one long breath, and reached.

He was forty-two years old. A soldier all his life, an officer on merit, not through birth. Tough and too proud of it, contemptuous of gentleness, of need, living to be seen to be strong; drinking hard, brawling, brutalizing where he might have been tender. And inside a bitter hollow, soured by desires that might find expression only in violence and disdain. Filtered through that bitterness, Gracielis could see himself, also, younger, foreign and vulnerable in his first days in Merafi. *I remember*, murmured that part of him which remained discretely Gracielis, *I remember the cheap inn, the soldiers who mocked and bullied and sometimes paid* . . . But he had surely never been so beautiful? A heart-searing loveliness of grace and silken charm the lieutenant hated and resented and feared and wanted with an aching intensity. Looking back at himself, Gracielis said, "I never knew." Felt the agreement, the confirmation of desire denied. Desire soured by fear and control into a furious contempt that burned the tormentor almost as much as the victim. In borrowed memory, Gracielis watched his own eyes grow wide with alarm and shuddered with the fierce pleasure of it. So fragile. How sweet a bruise would be, worn along that high cheekbone. The lieutenant's hand was raised to strike and Gracielis fought for control. To show kindness instead of foreign disdain. In memory, he redrew understanding and desire upon his features, in place of fear. This was almost beyond him. He lacked the strength, swamped in ancient dislike and water falling in swan eyes . . . His hand clenched about the knife blade and he rocked back with the pain, forcing clarity. Holding out the bloody hand to the lieutenant's ghost, he said, "Forgive me. Forgive me my blindness, that I did not realize that I should come to you."

He felt shoulders that were not his shrug and start to turn away. Heard his own voice, all silvered over, say, "The fault is mine. Won't you let me atone?" Felt his foreign body turn again and step forward into arms that were warm and open and then suddenly absent with the wrench of bonds tearing.

He was flung back abruptly in on himself, temples pounding, cold, alone. The lieutenant's ghost was gone. Blood from his wrist and hand dripped upon the floor. His eyes were muzzy and unfocused. Rain drummed against the closed shutters like a reminder. He forced himself to stand. The candles must be extinguished, and he should find a bandage for his hand. He had to wait for Quenfrida. He had to hide from her the full extent of his weakness. He expected at any moment to lose consciousness, fought it with what strength remained to him. The thin silk clung to him, clammy, uncomfortable. One by one, he managed to put out the candles, to tear a strip from a shirt to bind his bleeding hand.

A chair stood nearby. He fell into it, locking his good hand about the arm to hold himself upright. He had to wait for Quenfrida. The room felt very empty. In all the last six years, he had never been wholly alone.

He realized with dull surprise that he was crying.

The river ran slowly. Across its surface, mist formed and congealed. Its patience surpassed that of mortal things. It encompassed its own disturbances and admitted no conscious knowledge of human action. In the shantytown the air tasted foul. Debris lapped at the fringes of the settlement and the inhabitants shivered as night fell. In the embassy on the hill, Kenan looked up from his book and did not smile. Pain cramped through his hand. He rubbed it and touched alarm.

Dancing, Quenfrida pulled away from her partner and gasped. Across her palm was a deep gash fully three inches long.

*   *   *

Gracielis had forgotten that he was afraid of the dark. He had forgotten how it felt to be utterly alone. It was too cold in his room, and he shivered. Quenfrida would not come. He had transgressed and she would not come. She knew him too well.

The light was fading. Behind heavy clouds, the sun set. The moons rose unnoticed. He sat with his back to the shuttered window. He could think of nothing. His mind was empty of everything save the fear and the knowledge that he must wait.

She came into his room at deepest night. She perfumed the darkness. She encompassed all that lay within it. She was too beautiful. He gazed on her in need and yearning, while her sky-blue eyes held him in contempt. He reached out to her with his bloodied hand.

She ignored it. Softly, she said, "I should kill you where you sit."

He said her name because it was necessary. She looked at the blood on the floor and said, "What have you done?"

"I needed you." He was desperate. "*Chai ela*, Quenfrida. Quena, the air is full of death."

"I do not," said Quenfrida, "require you to teach me that. I am not blind."

"It frightens me." Death in the air and the taste of a power he almost knew. Honeysuckle and a strange face in his cards. He said, "You frighten me."

"Do I?" She held his gaze until he was forced to look away. "Do you think that matters? You forget yourself. You broke your vow."

"I had no choice."

"You had every choice. You elected to do that to which you have no right."

He was crying again, humiliated before her. He said, "The city will die, Quena. The people."

"Merafiens. They are no concern of ours."

"They live."

"Death is the right of everyone."

"But not this death. Their river . . ."

"Why not?" Quenfrida laughed, showing her teeth. "They have chained it long enough. Now it takes its turn."

It should not be possible. It was against the nature of the place. He said, "Stop it, Quena. Please."

She smiled. "Stop what?" He made no reply. "Do you reproach me for my anger with you? Is that it?" He shook his head. "What, then?"

"Last night . . . I felt your hand, working."

"So?"

He inhaled and forced himself to look at her. "You and someone I don't know. Another of your making. I, too, am not blind."

She regarded him curiously. There was a short silence. Then she said, "So I see. But how are you sure it's only two?"

"I know you." He could barely bring himself to say it. He could not quite keep the fear from his voice. "I know your history. The hierarchs distrust you. And I have seen . . . I have seen your second acolyte." She was smiling now, but there was menace in it. Too late to back down. He said, "I read your past."

Her eyes narrowed. Softly, viciously, she said, "You could not."

"I did."

They looked at one another in silence. Then he said carefully. "Forgive me. It was cards . . ."

Her smile broadened. "Cards?" He nodded. "Cards only? And what did you see?"

"The other one. I saw you had taken another."

"Is that all?" She studied him for a moment. "Yes. You will not lie to me at present. So I have a new acolyte. What of it?"

He looked down and said, "Stop this working. I beg you."

"Why?" She came closer, so that her perfume made him dizzy. "Tell me, my Gracielis. Our kind are banned from this city. If we are found here we risk death, or worse. Not death of our own device or selection, but the dishonorable death of strangers. Why, then, should we trouble ourselves over them?" He was silent. "This city is not our concern." Her voice was no longer angry. Rather, it was patient and weary.

He caught her hand and drew it to his face. "There are those who have been good to me . . ."

She smiled. It was not a kind smile. "You are free to warn them. I grant you that much. If they will believe you."

He looked down, no longer able to sustain the sight of her. He said, "Why not?"

She began to stroke his hair with her free hand. "We need them to be weak, my Gracielis."

Almost inaudibly, he said, "I don't."

Her heard her sigh. Her lips brushed his brow. "Always so gallant. But the truth is that we must consider the wider political need." She took her hand from his and sat on the chair arm. "Have you thought about what I said to you?"

He was lost, he was reeling. He said, "I don't understand."

"The seventh test."

Magnolia and the chiming of silver bells. Water falling and a man with swan wings beating in his eyes. The cold smile on the lips of a redheaded stranger . . . He said, "I don't know. I don't think I can."

She put an arm around him, gentling the pain. He wanted so much to turn his face into her shoulder, to hold on to her and never let go. She said, softly, sweetly, "I offer you a bargain, my Gracielis. Undertake and overcome the seventh test and join me. And then perhaps I may lighten my hand on this city, if you still wish it."

His hair mingled with hers. Through the mixed curtain, he said, "But how . . . ? We have no temple here."

"None is needed. I've learned other ways." He could hear her smile. "All you have to do is kill someone for me in the right place and fashion. You have the access. It will not be as hard as you think. One death only."

"Who?"

"Yvelliane d'Illandre of the Far Blays."

He shook his head, tried to pull free of her.

She said, "You have the access."

He found his voice. "No. No longer. I don't see her or any of her family."

Despite his resistance, her hands were on his shoulders. Such small hands, such strength. She said, "Two things, my Gracielis. First, Thiercelin of Sannazar spent last night in your room. And second, you've corresponded with Yvelliane since your eighth month in Merafi. You have no secrets that I don't know. You are mine to your soul."

He said, "No," although whether to the deed or the knowledge was unclear.

She leaned against him. "But I wish it."

Again, he said, "No." And then, "Quena, please."

"Merafi or Yvelliane. What would you?"

She was beautiful and deadly and false. He would fail and she would not withdraw her hand from Merafi. He said, "I cannot." He pulled himself to standing. "She has been my protector."

"And what am I?"

He met her sky-eyes. He said, "I beg you, Quenfrida *undaria*. Ask anything else of me. But I cannot do this."

She said, "You never could. You were never adequate. I should have let you pay the price of your failure." She rose in turn and went to the door. Opening it, she said, "I'm your death, Gracielis. One day. But you'll never know when or how."

He had known it forever. She was leaving him in anger; she was abandoning him. He was too weak to catch her, to hold her, to follow. He reached out for her even as the door began to close. He could hear his own voice, begging, tear-swollen, outside of his control, saying what he had thought he would never say.

"Quena. Quenfrida. I love you."

She was gone and the mist would have him and he was always alone, for she had taken away his center.

The knife of his ritual was still very sharp. The touch of it along his narrow wrists was sweet as a benediction.

So much blood.

So much peace.

10

JOYAIN HAD NEVER FELT any great affinity for
paperwork, but after the alarming events of the
aborted duel (about which he was determinedly not
thinking), he was unexpectedly comforted by the pile of
unit business that had collected for his attention. He had
found himself a carafe of watered red wine and settled
down in his closet to work his way through the heap.
The residence staff bustled about in the hall outside,
exchanging gossip with each other and the guards. Joyain
found worrying about the correct form of address for a
clerical third cousin of the queen (and how was he supposed to know that?) was a splendid displacement
activity.

He wondered vaguely how long this duty was going
to last. Leladrien had opined that the trouble in the new
dock was more or less over. It seemed possible that Joyain might be relieved in the next week or so. He had a
friend who had bought out of the regiment a year ago
and married into a small estate to the south. He'd had
an invitation to visit for some time. He might well take
it up. Get away from the city, catch up on news. Don't
think about what he might be leaving behind. In particular, anything that had occurred this morning.

He was three quarters of the way down the paperwork
(and all the way down the carafe) when someone
knocked on the half-open door. He called, "Come in,"
without looking up, and went on trying to balance the

figures for his unit's expenditure. Absently, he said, "Ensign, what's fifteen multiplied by seven?"

"One hundred and five," came the answer. "Is the number important?"

It was not the ensign. Joyain controlled a start, hearing Iareth's voice, and looked up. "Only in a financial sense. Can I help you?"

She had taken a seat. She smiled. "Possibly, yes."

"Right . . ." Joyain found it impossible not to return the smile. "I'll be with you in a moment . . . one hundred and five?"

"Indeed."

Joyain added up the column of figures, checked it, caught himself beginning to recommence the whole calculation from scratch and forced himself to initial the item instead. He put down his quill, wiping it carefully, recapped the ink, made sure that his two sets of papers were in neat, separate piles, sharpened the spare quill, straightened his collar, fastened a button on his cassock, and realized that he had run out of excuses to avoid eye contact. He sighed and looked up. "Now, how may I help you?"

Her cool green eyes were thoughtful, watching him. She said, "You had other duties this morning?"

"Something like that." Joyain found himself looking down again. It was nothing to do with him, her past relations with Valdarrien of the Far Blays. It would stay that way, if he could manage it.

"Kenan has contrived to injure himself," Iareth said.

"Seriously? Has a doctor been sent for?"

"It was minor: he has treated it himself."

"He . . . I trust it wasn't deliberate . . . An insult to an important visitor would be . . . Or involving him in a . . . an incident, or a . . . duel . . ." Joyain realized he was making no sense and fell silent. He began to fidget with the quill. "Very embarrassing for us, too."

Quietly she said, "People are exiled for insulting diplomats and princes. I have reason to know it."

Joyain shut his eyes. Once again, he'd walked right into the obvious. It had been a diplomatically embarrassing duel (with a Tarnaroqui aide) that had led to Valdarrien being sent to Lunedith, where he had met Iareth Yscoithi. He said, "I'm sorry. I didn't mean . . ."

"I have said it before. I am mistress of my past."

"No, I . . ."

"There is no cause for you to feel embarrassed. I make no assumption of commitment."

"That isn't . . ." Joyain looked up, and sighed. "It isn't that. I've just had a rather . . . unusual day. I have no right to inflict it on you."

"It matters not." She smiled. "I have had a somewhat unusual day, also."

"Prince Kenan?"

"Indeed. The matter of his injury . . ." She shrugged. "It can only have been an accident. It is nothing over which you should worry."

Joyain looked at her sharply. She was frowning. "But you should?"

"Perhaps." She paused then shook her head. "How long does it take your couriers to travel from here to Skarholm?"

"It depends on the weather. A fast courier is supposed to take eight to ten days."

"So." Iareth appeared to calculate. The outcome seemed to displease her. Joyain, already uncomfortable, began to think he was being downright unfair.

He cleared his throat. "Would you like a drink?"

"Thank you, no."

"I can ring for chocolate."

"No. It is unnecessary . . . Something troubles you, I think?"

"Of course not," he said. And then, "Yes." She looked quizzical. "Something odd happened this morning."

She rose and came to stand behind him. He looked up at her. She said, "You wish to tell me?"

He hardly knew. She was almost a stranger, even now. And besides, ghosts were not commonplace in Merafi.

Thiercelin of Sannazar had seemed almost to be expecting it.

Joyain sighed, and said, "I had an . . . an affair of honor this morning. It was interrupted."

"A legal problem?"

"No . . ." He sighed again. She rested a hand on his shoulder. "A . . . friend of my opponent turned up. It was rather unnerving."

"Indeed?"

"Yes . . ." Joyain swallowed. She stroked the nape of his neck. A little nervously he said, "Valdarrien d'Illandre is dead. That's common knowledge."

"That is so." Iareth's hand stilled.

"Yes. Only this morning, the person who interrupted was him."

She leaned forward so that she could see him clearly. Her face was thoughtful. "Valdin Allandur?"

"Yes. Thiercelin duLaurier spoke to him."

"Thierry?" To his surprise she smiled. "He said something to me to that effect, when he visited." Joyain stared at her. "Forgive me. You are Merafien, of course. These matters are distressing to you."

"And they aren't to you?"

"Yes, but it's different." She sat on his desk, and put her hand on his cheek. "Will you honor me with your trust, Jean?" He hesitated, then nodded. She said, "It is not wholly unexpected. And it involves Kenan. I must have further speech with Thierry."

Joyain caught at her hand. "You're not worried? I'd have thought . . ."

She interrupted him. "I am more than worried. But there is no use to that. I am not unpracticed at waiting."

Joyain was confused. He started to say something, but nothing of meaning would come. He shook his head, then, and rested his forehead against her.

*   *   *

Something is wrong . . .

Gracielis hurt. His head echoed with pounding blackness. Fragmented memories tumbled, mingled, distorted. Magnolia and the thunder of falling water. Mist-shapes reached, pursued, surrounded him, dream-beleaguered. Swan wings beat across a rain-drenched sky, fell silent under the torrent of bell-song. Long hair, silken, unbound, dusty-fair golden, spread across the pillow like a shattered rainbow; lemon-scented to speak the syllables of a name. Hunted through the long aisles of a garden, the dark reach of the mountains, looped back upon himself in fear and blood and death. Blood that pooled on the rock, and on the straw, on the polished boards, to trickle over his hands. So very sharp . . . *they say the haft is cut from human bone* . . . So cold, so very cold, and the bitterness seared him. It was too hard for him; he could not face learning to live without Quenfrida. He faced a darkness so profound as to overturn all confusion, unknown, unknowing, afraid . . .

There was too much to control, to recall. Impossible to bind it all into a cohesive whole. Instead, strands within him unraveled into separate broken threads, slipping too easily between his impotent, helpless fingers.

The river is turning . . .

His eyes opened onto an expanse of painted ceiling. Flowers, smoky with age, entwined along the beams and bordered the static dancing figures. He frowned and blinked at the ceiling. He wanted to raise a hand to rub those same eyes. He met reluctance, pain stinging his arms. The inside of his mouth tasted sour. His lips were dry. He began to turn and was arrested by dizziness. He shut his eyes again and groaned.

Someone spoke his name. He opened an eye to see a fuzzy silhouette bending over him. A woman's voice. He made himself open the second eye. She smiled at him.

It was Amalie, and the ceiling belonged to her personal chamber.

She said, "How are you feeling?"

There was something that threatened her, which she should be told. He could not quite remember. He said. "I've felt better."

"Poor love." Her hand caressed his hair. "Do you want anything?"

He could make no sense of it. He said, "I don't know. May I sit up?"

"If you like." She moved pillows, made to lift him. He tried to help himself and pain lanced down his wrists and arms. He gasped. It took a moment or two before he was ready to look about him.

He was in her old-fashioned high-post bed. Light filtered through the windows and a fire burned in the hearth. Amalie sat beside the bed in an upholstered chair. She was dressed simply, and there was an embroidery frame on her lap. She said, "Better?"

He hurt all over. He found a smile and said, "A little." And then, "What happened?"

She looked worried. "Don't you remember?" His face must have answered that, for she continued, "You tried to kill yourself. I don't know why."

It almost explained his lassitude. He looked away from her and noticed another lack. He began to shiver. "When?"

"The night before last . . . I went to your lodgings to leave you a message and found you. It seemed best to bring you here. The landlord helped me. He won't tell anyone where you are." She hesitated. "I hope you don't mind."

Almost on reflex, he said, "Your concern honors me." But in truth, he hardly heard her. Through the window, he could see the rain falling; watching it, he let himself slide backward into the memory. Sickness in the city and in himself. No cure. No solution, only the sly bargains of Quenfrida.

I am your death . . . She had promised that and taken
from him the comfort and horror of her presence. She
had left him, and he had said . . . had said . . . had taken
up the knife from the floor and hacked through both
wrists with it. Across Amalie, he said, "You should have
let me go."

She put down her embroidery. Tears stood in her eyes.
"Oh, love, why?"

He knew he should comfort her, but he could not. He
said, "The river is turning. There's death in it." She
reached out a hand to him, then stopped halfway, uncertain. He said, "She wants my collusion." For nine years
he had not wept at all, and now it seemed he could not
stop weeping. Amalie watched in mingled concern and
fear. He could not bear that. Looking down, he said, "I
should have died."

She put her arms about him. Her touch was familiar.
It was not the touch he longed for. She said, "Hush,
dear one. It's over."

It was not over. He swallowed hard and said so. Her
arms tightened around him. He said, "If your ship comes
in, you must burn the cargo."

She withdrew a little. "What do you mean? I need
those goods."

"No. You don't understand." He shivered. "There's
sickness."

"In the new dock? There always is."

"Everywhere." Turning so that he might see her face,
he said, "Ladyheart, do you trust me?"

Her fingers twisted in the blanket. But she nodded.
He said, "Listen, then. There will be plague. Flooding.
You must leave Merafi now and not return, not for
years. There's a . . . a power here, which should not be.
It's awake, and inimical. If you remain, it'll harm you."

She looked away, at her lap. Very carefully she said,
"You're overwrought. It's understandable . . . There was
just a minor disturbance and a small flood in the
shantytown . . . There's nothing wrong, you'll see."

She did not understand. She knew nothing of his old life in Tarnaroq. She interpreted his alarm, quite naturally, as sick fancy. And he had no means to prove to her that matters were otherwise. He was not Quenfrida, to play games with perception. He had none of the little skills, the showy ones of light, of fire. He could see ghosts and the past, sometimes. Useless to read for her. She had told him so much of her life already. It would be a charlatan act, lacking truth.

He was too light-headed to plan clearly. He thought of Thiercelin, who might give more credence to his fears, and then remembered that Thiercelin might even now be dead. A duel . . . He inhaled and said, "Have there been any important deaths recently?"

"I don't think so." Amalie looked at him, puzzled. "Why?" And then, "Love, surely that wasn't it? A suicide pact?" She sounded frightened. She had moved as far away from him as she might. Rather too lightly she continued, "I know I'm not your only patron, but . . ."

He interrupted her. "It was nothing of that kind." She looked unconvinced. "I promise you. I asked about deaths because a . . . friend of mine was due to fight a duel."

She relaxed a little. "I see. No, I've heard nothing of that."

Thiercelin was safe, then. As safe as anyone might be now in Merafi. Gracielis said gently, "Thank you." And then, for she was still afraid, "Ladyheart."

She looked at him. "You're not going to tell me why, are you?"

"No. I cannot. I made a . . . vow once, and I may not break it."

"I see."

He was too weak to reach out to her. He said, "I wish you would believe me about the river." He could read for someone else, Herlève, perhaps. "There's a reason, connected with my vow. I studied certain matters once. I learned to see certain things, conditions, and bindings, and sometimes the past. You've praised my insight a time or two. It's something of that nature."

"I don't know." Amalie spoke almost too quietly to be heard. "There are stories, about Tarnaroqui witches, but . . ." She had been gazing at the floor. Now she turned. "You?"

"Not precisely." He was so tired. "I might show you, perhaps, if I were stronger."

"I don't know if I want that."

"No."

"It's just that . . ." She stopped. Her face grew determined. "I don't really know you at all, do I? I thought I did, but . . ."

"You do."

"No. You did this—" she gestured at his bandaged forearms, "and I can't think of the least reason for it. And now you tell me you have, I don't know, magic powers . . ."

Unexpectedly, it hurt. He looked at her, distressed. "I'm still myself."

But she would not look at him.

Thiercelin shut the door with unnecessary force and swore. He had had two very frustrating days, and was in no mood for being obstructed. Especially by such persons—innkeepers, for example—who should know better.

He was also rather tired. Somehow, in the wake of his abortive duel, he had been unable to face going home. Pictures in his mind, of dead Valdarrien following him in. Not that Yvelliane would be there to see, of course. She probably had not noticed his absence yet. She would hardly have time for such trivia as her brother's ghost. Thiercelin had ended up accompanying Maldurel to a party and making a night of it. The following day, hungover and rather embarrassed, he had hired himself rooms in one of the large inns in the hill district. A lackey had been dispatched to summon his valet and to arrange for his luggage to be brought to him. Thiercelin doubted the event would cause any surprise at home. The story of his quarrel with his wife was guaranteed to have reached the servants' hall at double speed. He could not quite face communicating his temporary address to Yvelliane, however. He told himself that he needed time to think and carefully put the issue to one side. He would solve this business of Valdarrien by himself. Perhaps that would prove to her that he was a capable, responsible adult. Perhaps she might finally believe that he loved her and not her late brother.

In the late afternoon he had paid his promised visit to Gracielis and found the latter absent. Thiercelin had left a note and gone back to his temporary lodgings.

Conscience had provoked him to return the following morning. But when he tried to go up to Gracielis' room, the landlord of the Jade Rose intercepted him. Monsieur de Varnaq, he said, was away.

"When will he be back?" Thiercelin asked.

"I have no idea, monseigneur."

"Do you know where he went?"

"I couldn't say, monseigneur." And the landlord bowed and excused himself.

Thiercelin, on the whole, disliked being stalled. He liked it even less when, after the landlord, left the taproom, one of the serving maids had tapped him on the arm, and said, "Regarding Gracieux . . ."

"Yes?" Thiercelin hesitated then remembered. Some coins exchanged hands.

"I didn't see him leave, monseigneur, but he's been gone two nights and that's a fact."

"Two nights?" Surprise caused Thiercelin to raise his voice. The girl shushed him, giving an anxious glance at the door to the kitchen. He spoke more softly. "You don't know where he is?"

She shook her head. "No, monseigneur. He comes and goes a lot." She paused. "There's someone, though. One of the professional kind . . . She might know." The kitchen door opened. The girl started and said loudly, "I'm sure I don't know." A swift glance over her shoulder. Then in a lower voice: "Sylvine."

Then the landlord came over and rather frostily asked Thiercelin to leave.

Hence the necessity of slamming the door.

He was halfway back to his lodgings at the Phoenix when he began to have the feeling he was being followed. The streets were as busy as ever; a brief halt and a look around from a shop doorway gave him no real clues. Even so, he was increasingly uncomfortable as he set off again.

He almost leaped out of his skin when, on the corner of Coopers' Street, a hand was laid on his arm. He looked round in alarm, to find himself staring at a young woman in a rather unsuitable dress. The hand on his arm was gloved in brown. The other, resting on her hip, was in green. She smiled (revealing uneven teeth) and said brightly, "Good day to you, monseigneur."

"Quite," said Thiercelin. And then, "And to you, demoiselle." A professional named Sylvine . . . It was possible. "Demoiselle Sylvine?"

"At your service, monseigneur." She curtsied.

Thiercelin hesitated. This was a busy junction, and the girl was not of the type with whom a lord should be seen consorting. Not before dark, anyway. He raised his brows at his own hypocrisy and looked around him for somewhere to take her. He said, "Perhaps I can buy you a glass of wine? I believe you may be able to help me." And then, "If you could recommend a local cabaret?"

She could, of course. Possessing herself more firmly of his arm, she led him down two alleys and into a small tavern. The wine she ordered was not cheap, and when it arrived, it looked to have been watered. Watching the clientele, Thiercelin came rapidly to the conclusion that the owner did not expect his customers to be overly bothered by such considerations. At least there was a steady traffic of couples up and down the rickety stairs.

He could not help thinking that Valdarrien would have loved it.

The girl Sylvine drank two glasses of wine rather quickly and smiled at him. "So. You think I can help you?"

"I'm looking for the Tarnaroqui who rooms at the Jade Rose. Gracielis de Varnaq. Do you know him?"

She nodded. "Gracieux. Everyone knows *him*."

"Yes, well, he seems to be missing."

"It's possible." Sylvine studied her gloves. Her expression was calculating.

Thiercelin said, "A girl working at his inn thought you might know something."

"Possibly." She sighed, dramatically. "It depends, rather. He's my friend. I'd need to be sure your interest in him was . . . friendly, too. If you see what I mean."

He rather thought he did. He put a coin down in front of her. She looked at it without interest. He added a second. Her eyes narrowed a little. He hesitated, then added a third. "Two's the going rate for an hour's conversation. Or so I gather from Gracielis."

She laughed. "He charged you that? You were had."

"Was I?" Thiercelin looked rather pointedly at the coins.

"He's a class item, Gracieux. But just for talking!" She shot him a shrewd look. "Or was there more?"

"Not your business, I think."

"Oh, I don't know. I tipped him off about your interest in the first place. I might be due a cut."

"Well," said Thiercelin, "you seem to be collecting it, don't you?"

"So I do." Again, that shrewd look. "But this is information, not conversation."

"And I thought you said this was too much just for conversation." He smiled at her sweetly. "Shall I ask your going rate?"

She pushed her hair back behind her shoulders and inhaled. Her bodice was a little too tight. The glance she

gave him was arch. Then she coughed. Thiercelin looked
sympathetic. Her expression turned irritated. "I've nothing you'd want. You don't look the kind to come
slumming."

Gently Thiercelin said, "The information?"

He could almost hear her calculate as she looked him
up and down. She paused then said, "Twenty livres."

"Robbery. I've bribed the watch for less."

"Eighteen, then. The watch don't know where he is."

"I'll bet they could find out, though. Five."

"I thought you were his friend. Fifteen."

"Seven."

"Twelve. Don't you want to know where he is?"

"Ten." Thiercelin stared at her, hard.

She looked uncertain. Then she sighed, and said,
"Ten, then."

"Good. So, where is he?"

"Where are my ten livres?"

Thiercelin counted them out slowly in front of her.
He wondered rather how he was going to replace them.
His income from his Sannazar estate had never been
quite enough, and he had already spent more than thrice
its total this year. He would have to speak with his man
of business. He was not going to apply to the Far Blays
revenues for funds until this mess was sorted out. Sylvine
held out her hand for the money. He shook his head
and said, "Tell me, first."

"Half up front."

He pushed five coins over. They disappeared into a
pocket. She said, "Do you know a haberdashery company called Viron? On Bright Moon Street?" He shook
his head. "Owner's a widow. One of Gracieux' regulars."

"He's with her?"

She ignored him. "Word is he was carried out of the
Jade Rose two nights since and taken off by her. Don't
know if he's at her place; my source said he looked half

dead. But I expect a lord like you can go and ask Madame Amalie Viron what she's done with him."

"I daresay I can." Thiercelin handed her the rest of her fee. Then he rose and put on his hat. "Thank you. It's been an experience." He bowed to her. "Good day, demoiselle."

"Aristos," said Sylvine.

It did not take him long to locate the shop on Bright Moon Street. He asked for the owner. A courteous apprentice offered him a chair in the shop and went upstairs to inquire. A few moments later he was conducted up two flights of extremely clean stairs and shown into a small salon. It was furnished a little more elaborately than he personally liked, but it was warm and comfortable. The woman standing by the fire was not young, nor was she pretty, but her figure was trim and her smile attractive. She dropped a curtsy and said, "Monseigneur de Sannazar? This is an honor."

Thiercelin bowed. A little awkwardly he said, "You're Madame Viron?"

"Yes." She gestured to a chair. "I'll have some wine brought up." Thiercelin sat. "Now, how may I help you?"

He waited until she, too, was seated, then said, "I'm looking for someone. A friend . . . Gracielis de Varnaq."

"What makes you think I know him?"

"A . . . colleague of his mentioned it. Forgive me if I'm being indiscreet."

She was silent. Thiercelin hesitated, looking at his hands. Then he said, "Do you know him?"

She said, "May I ask you a question?"

"Certainly."

"What interest do you have in him?"

"He's my friend." She looked surprised. He twisted a button on his doublet. "We met in rather unusual circumstances, but it's true."

"I see." She rose, and went to the window. She said, "When you last saw him, how did he seem?"

Thiercelin let go of the button. "Not well."

Her voice was almost too quiet to hear. "Suicidal?"

"No, I wouldn't say so. He'd a fever, but . . ." Thiercelin stopped. "River bless."

She turned to look at him. "You should know, I think, that two nights ago he tried to kill himself. I don't know why."

"Neither do I," Thiercelin said. And then, "Did he . . . ?"

"He lives. The doctor says there's no immediate danger."

Thiercelin found he was holding his breath. He released it and said, "Do you know where he is?"

She paused, studying him. Then she seemed to reach some kind of a conclusion, for she nodded, and said, "He's here."

"May I see him?"

"I don't know. Wait here, please, monseigneur." She went out and he heard her climb the stairs. The clock ticked on the mantel. Thiercelin played with his gloves. Several minutes passed before she returned. She said, "He'd like to see you." She did not sound entirely happy at the prospect.

Thiercelin rose. "You're very kind. Thank you."

The room to which she led him was furnished in the same style. She did not enter with him. He advanced a few paces and hesitated. Gracielis looked to be asleep. The door closed. Thiercelin sat on the edge of a chair, and Gracielis opened his eyes.

They looked vast, bruised in the narrow face. Thiercelin said, "Well, that was a sensible thing to do."

Gracielis smiled palely. "It's a good thing, monseigneur, that I'm not dependent upon you for sympathy."

"Thierry," said Thiercelin, out of habit. And then, "So, will you tell me why?"

Gracielis looked away. "Forgive me. I can't."

There was a silence. Then Thiercelin said, "Does it have anything to do with me? With me and Valdin?"

Gracielis sighed. Then he said, "Not in the sense you mean." He hesitated. "Thierry, I . . ."

"Yes?"

"There is a thing I can't ask of Madame Viron . . ."

"What?"

"There is a weaver on Little Mill Street, trading under the sign of the blue orb. Could you take a message to him?"

"I don't see why not."

"Thank you. Could you tell him, please, that Gracieux will do what was asked. He'll understand." Thiercelin raised his brows. Gracielis caught his eye and looked momentarily wicked. Then he said, "You're good to me."

"I owe you."

"No more, I think." Gracielis paused. "We should talk . . . Not today."

"No." Thiercelin rose. "I'll come again. You'll be here?"

"It seems probable."

Outside, it was raining.

"Be careful of your heads." Lantern in hand, the scholar lead the way through a low doorway, "And mind your feet: the stairs are worn and quite narrow." The undercrofts of the Old Temple were cool and dark and dank, redolent of old wet stone and stale air. The higher layers had been filled with chests and closets, wine racks and barrels, braziers and lamp stands and rows upon rows of shelving. Down here, the detritus was sparser. Fractured wooden bones hinted at long-forgotten trunks or cabinets. Lampions clumped together in rusting heaps. Shelves sagged or hung by one end. Miraude wrinkled her nose: her mouth was sour with damp and dust. Her boots were already grimy from the upper floors. Here, the moss and slime attested the closeness of the water table. Well, she had been warned, and had dressed *en cavalier* as a precaution. The scholar waited at the stair foot, lamp held up. She picked her way downward in its pool of yellow light. Behind her, Kenan's steps were firm and confident. In all the times she had been inside this temple, she had never known that its roots reached so far. Its public face was smooth and elegant, dressed stone and curving graceful pillars. The walls of this undercroft were built of irregular stones, clumped together and held in place with a thick mortar. Some showed signs of old decoration: a trace of painted lettering here, a smoothed edge there. As Kenan joined them at the base of the stair, the scholar said, "This is thought to be the oldest part of the current temple, but its original function was probably something else. Our earliest records suggest that in the reigns of Yestinn and his first three successors, the temple was rather to the north of here. This building seems to have been erected as a store or perhaps a communal warehouse, probably at the time when the first fortress was extended on the eastern side. The remains that underlie this area represent a part of that fortress which was demolished to admit the expansion."

Miraude said, "Why did they do that?"

"It was toward the end of the Long War. The holdings of the kings were increased, and that meant an increase in the size of the royal household."

"And," Kenan said, coldly, "doubtless an increase in the number of hostages and prisoners." He looked around him. "I fail to see anything remarkable in this room."

"Oh, the interesting remains are farther in." The scholar beamed at them, and offered Miraude his free arm. "Shall we?"

He guided them diagonally across the undercroft, ducking under the low vaulting and steering Miraude around those places where the floor was slippery. From around halfway, a crack appeared in the flagstones, splintering into veins as they neared the wall. Several of them continued upward into the fabric of the latter. To the right of the widest, a section of floor was cordoned off and covered with an oilcloth. "Damage from the landslip," the scholar said. "And here . . ." Releasing Miraude's arm, he lowered the lamp. "You see at the base? That's where we found the first traces."

The crack ended in a gap approximately two feet high and eighteen inches wide, giving onto a dim space. In the light of the lantern, Miraude made out a piece of smooth wall beyond, extending down into the darkness. "The current wall has been built across the base of that former one," the scholar said. "One of the junior priests was able to wriggle through and found a considerable space beyond, heading underneath this undercroft. So we took up a section of the flagstones, over here." He gestured to the oilcloth.

Kenan said, "I fail to see any indications of age."

"Indeed. But you haven't seen our main discovery." The scholar said. "If you would take the lantern for me . . . Thank you. Now, over here, we have the real find." Handing the lantern to Kenan, he lifted part of the cordon and pulled the oilcloth aside, revealing a hole some four feet square with a ladder leading down from it. "Now—Prince Kenan if you could bring the lantern a little closer—you'll note that there are marks on the stones that we lifted." He gestured. "Here and here. They're very worn, but this seems to be the wings of the Allandurin eagle, while over here we have what looks like the paw of a bear or similar creature. I speculate that at one point the priests retained some responsibility for what lies beneath here. Long forgotten, of course and I haven't yet had time to examine their records fully . . . However, shall we go in? I think you'll find this fascinating." He took the lantern back from Kenan. "Be careful of your heads. This first area is low and the floor is rather uneven." Stepping down into the hole, he offered his free hand to Miraude. Aware of Kenan, sour and judgmental, she smiled and stepped down neatly without aid. A cold draft came from underneath the flags. She tugged her sleeves down, making sure they were properly tucked under the long cuffs of her gloves.

Under the floor, a low space extended away into darkness. The floor had one been smooth-tiled, but centuries of stress and subsidence had reduced it to rags and lumps. Here and there stretches of tiles remained, patterned in faded blues and browns. The walls were dressed stone, thick and solid—the remains of foundations. A series of columns, all now broken off, marched the length of the area. As the scholar had warned, the ceiling was low. Miraude could just about stand upright, but both men had to bend. The scholar guided them onward, pausing from time to time to point out a maker's mark or the site of a find of pottery or bone. Stubs of walls interrupted their progress, marking out the limits of long-neglected chambers. In the gloom, it was hard to make out the dimensions of the space. It had to be many times larger than the undercroft. Miraude guessed that it must extend out well beyond the boundaries of the Old Temple, but in which direction she was unsure. They seemed to turn several times, but the low light and the old stone gave away no clues. Left to herself, she was not certain she would be able to trace her way back to the entrance, but the scholar went on with a steady pace.

He halted in front of the stump of a particularly wide pillar and held up the lantern. "This is my prize find," he said. "If you come round the back . . ." On the reverse of the pillar, a flight of steps led downward. The cold draft strengthened. There was a taste of stagnation, or ancient damp, biting through the dust and dirt. Miraude shivered. Beside her, Kenan swayed and put out a hand to support himself. The scholar said, "Prince Kenan? Are you unwell?"

For several moments, there was no reply. Then Kenan

straightened and inclined his head. "Dust in my eyes."
He pointed to the stairs. "Let us descend."

There was something lying on his stomach. Gracielis
opened an eye and peered down, cautiously. Biscuity-
yellow eyes stared back incuriously. Then they blinked,
as their owner yawned and began to wash a back foot.
Gracielis considered. The pain was gone from his head,
and with it much of the mind-numbing dizziness. He
opened the other eye and tried moving. It hurt a little,
but nothing insupportable. The cat, disturbed, glared at
him. "I beg your pardon," he said, politely.

Someone snorted. Turning, he saw Herlève making up
the fire. She said, "That dratted animal. She's not to be
let in here—I keep telling Madame. Let me take her
out."

"It would be a discourtesy,"

"I'm sure. Well, you're clearly feeling better." She
studied him. "The doctor says you're to eat and can get
up if you want to." She sniffed. "Madame says you can
join her in the salon."

"That's kind."

"I daresay," she said. "But don't you go upsetting
her again."

"No," Gracielis said meekly. "I'm very sorry for the
trouble."

"So you should be." Herlève came over and thumped
his pillows with unnecessary force. "Right, up you come.
No, don't lean on that. You'll start the bleeding again,
and think of the work that'll make." Gracielis held his
tongue and let her lift him. She put a tray in front of
him. "Now, you'll eat all of this."

"Yes, Madame Herlève."

She glared. "Can you manage?"

"I believe so."

"I'll thank you not to spill it on Madame's bed linen."

"When is it? What time?"

"A little before noon. You slept through, after Monseigneur de Sannazar left." She paused and looked at him, "And there's another thing. Poor Madame!"

"He isn't my lover." She looked disbelieving. "I swear it."

"So what is he? Your cousin?"

"No, he . . ." Gracielis hesitated. "We met a long time ago, through a duel. He's my protector, after a fashion."

First I've heard of it, said Herlève's expression. But she made no comment. When he had eaten, she took the tray away and said, "Your clothes have been sent. You can dress and go through." She paused then added, "Monsieur Jean is here. So behave yourself." Without awaiting a reply, she whisked out of the room. He heard her talking to someone outside.

His robe had been laid out on a chair, freshly washed and ironed. Putting it on proved a little complicated and infuriatingly slow. He was still slightly light-headed. At the fringes of consciousness he heard rain drumming on the window. That made him uncomfortable. He took his mind from it. Time enough, later . . . He made his way to the mirror and set about untangling his hair.

That hurt. His abused wrists protested. He needed to use one to brush, the other to support himself against the mantel.

He nearly lost his balance when the door opened and Amalie came in. She gazed at him aghast, then rushed over. He leaned on her as she steered him to a chair. She said, "What were you doing?"

"My hair." He gestured at the mirror. "You have company."

She laughed and took the brush from him. "Let me." And then, "Herlève says you're feeling better."

"Indeed. Thanks to your care." She patted his cheek and began brushing. The cat jumped into his lap and began to purr.

Amalie said, "Is that you or her?"

"Both." He smiled at the cat.

"Hedonist."

"Who wouldn't be, possessing your undivided attention?"

"Hedonist *and* shameful flatterer." Amalie bent and kissed him. "You've cheered up. I'm glad."

He twisted round to see her better. "I've distressed you. Forgive me."

She paused, winding one of his curls around her finger. "Did you mean all that, about the river?"

He looked down. She resumed brushing. After a moment she said, in a slightly altered tone, "It's over its banks in parts of the low city and the shantytown. Jean told me."

Flooding. The window was at his back. Gracielis did not try to look at it. He could still hear the rain. He sank his fingers into the cat's fur and said, "Do you have a set of playing cards?"

"Yes." She was surprised. "Why?"

"There is something I'd like to show you, with Monsieur Jean's permission."

"Card tricks?"

"Not precisely."

"Well, if you wish." She finished combing and fetched a hand mirror. "Will that do?"

His reflection showed him a sharp edge to his beauty, as though something of his true nature was beginning to break through. He smiled at Amalie. "Thank you, Ladyheart."

She kissed him again. "Come and see Jean. I've made chocolate, and the room is warm." She helped him to stand, then slipped her arm through his. He kissed her hair.

In the salon, Joyain sat in a wing chair by the fire, staring at his immaculate boots. He looked up as they entered and nodded. "Gracieux."

"Monsieur le lieutenant." Amalie made sure Gracielis was comfortable on the daybed, then went to see to the chocolate. Gracielis continued, "You are well, I hope?"

"Yes. And yourself?"

"I'm much recovered, monsieur." Gracielis risked a smile. "Thanks to Madame."

Joyain made a noncommittal answer and turned to receive his chocolate from Amalie. Gracielis watched him. They had met several times over the years and preserved a relationship of guarded neutrality. Like most military men, Joyain neither approved nor condemned prostitution and possessed the virtue of refraining from interfering in Amalie's affairs. On the other hand, Gracielis suspected that, like many of the better mannered of the officer class, he felt a quiet dislike of overtly charming and gilded masculine beauty. Gracielis knew relatively little about him. He would make a good subject.

Amalie brought Gracielis chocolate and sat down herself. Into the small silence he said, "There was the mention of cards . . . ?"

"Of course." Amalie rose and opened a box on the dresser. Joyain looked surprised. She handed them to Gracielis. "Here."

"Would monsieur le lieutenant shuffle them?"

Joyain looked even more surprised, but did not demur. Gracielis added, "Could you discard the numbered cards, apart from the aces?"

"Well, if you like." Joyain sorted through them. "Now what?"

There was a small table next to the daybed. Gracielis pulled it toward him with a foot and put his cup on the floor. He said, "Could you bring them to me, please, monsieur?—No, Ladyheart, please do not touch them—and might I borrow some small possession from you? A kerchief, perhaps?"

Looking puzzled and faintly put out, Joyain brought over the cards. He had no kerchief, but a little rummaging produced a spare button. Gracielis thanked him and began to lay out the cards, Mothmoonwise, in the pattern called the star, which anchored past and present.

He turned the cards singly, carefully, beginning a commentary. Joyain's had been a simple life, uncomplicated by entanglements or grief. Nothing in the early youth to remark upon. His principal was stone, for dedication and inner stoicism. His gifts were aspected by Handmoon; unapplauded and treated practically by their owner. His family held him in affection and had no difficulty in letting him go. The past was good.

Amalie had come to sit beside Gracielis, her thigh against his. He could hear her breathing, gentle and steady. Joyain stood to one side, arms folded, face cynical. Gracielis paused in the reading to smile at him and turned up the next five cards.

The present. Harder, for it was mutable. To left and right, shading into past and future. Stone and steel—for duty—crossed by water-quartered Mothmoon and by a slender figure with level eyes and careful, balancing hands . . .

Gracielis had seen her before, in Thiercelin's reading. Her nature running counter to her role, her strengths born out of contradiction. He looked into Joyain's eyes and said softly, "You know Iareth Yscoithi."

The eyes narrowed. "That's an easy guess. My aunt has probably mentioned that I'm stationed with the Lunedithin embassy."

Amalie had, but she had not gone into details. In the spread, Iareth's card lay shadowed, between fire and water. Gracielis shivered. She lay over the place of the heart. He looked swiftly at Amalie, then back at Joyain, and said, "She is your lover, and will burn you."

Joyain took a step back. Gracielis added, "Forgive me," and turned up the next card. Water-hallow, threatening. Death in the air and in the river. Death here, too, in the cards, although perhaps not for Joyain. Stone surrounded by troubles unknown and only half-realized. It bordered on the future and Gracielis could see but poorly. He passed it in silence and turned up another card.

His hand pulled back. He said, "No." He had been here before, but sky-eyed Quenfrida had been the subject. His second self, his rival, close enough to Joyain to touch him and bound intimately in the reading to the death in water. Gracielis said, "There is a man, a new acquaintance. One who sees."

"I don't know what you're talking about."

He has power over water. Unbidden, the dream-memory rose. Water falling and swan wings and mockery in hostile eyes. Gracielis said quietly, "He has red hair and blue eyes and you dislike him. It's mutual. He holds your lover under his hand. Do you know him?" Beside him Amalie gasped, but he did not look at her. To Joyain he said, "You've been granted to him, unwilling, and your role is ambivalent. Who?"

Joyain said, "I don't think . . ." And then, "What is this?"

Gracielis held his eyes a moment longer, and turned up two more cards. The first made him smile, obvious as it should have been to him. He said, "Thiercelin of Sannazar," but its role was near past and there was no danger in it. The other, sword-handed, was expected also, given the pivotal role of Iareth Yscoithi. "And Valdarrien d'Illandre."

Joyain sat down rather suddenly. He said, "How did you know? Who told you?"

"No one." Gracielis made his voice gentle. "I have simply seen it."

"You can't." Joyain looked past him at Amalie. "This is a joke, yes?"

She said, "No, I swear." And then, "Gracielis, does this mean they're true, the things you told me yesterday?"

Turning to her, Gracielis took her hand and kissed the palm. "Yes, Ladyheart." She looked down. He turned back to Joyain. "You should try not to care for Iareth Yscoithi."

"I don't think that's any business of yours."

"Indeed, and I ask your pardon." Gracielis hesitated. "Will you tell me who this might be?" His hand lay again on the card of the red-haired acolyte. "It touches on more than you."

"Is Iareth in danger?" Joyain seemed to ask almost against his will.

"I regret I don't know. This isn't her reading."

"I see." Joyain sighed. "It's Prince Kenan, I suppose. Kenan Orcandros, the Lunedithin heir. You're right: I don't like him."

"Thank you." Gracielis hesitated, then turned back to the cards. He knew too little of Quenfrida's activities during her time in Lunedith. He turned up the last five cards and sighed. The future, and only confusion. Water crossed with stone . . . He made no sense of it. He shrugged and turned away, suddenly tired.

Joyain said, "No sudden wealth or good fortune?"

"No." Gracielis mingled the cards. "I don't do the future. I don't have that sight."

"Indeed?" Joyain was trying to sound sardonic. It did not quite work.

Amalie drew in a long breath. Then she said, "Why?"

Gracielis looked down. "You wouldn't believe me."

"No." He felt her put an arm about him. She said, "Lie down."

He obeyed, closing his eyes. He was a little afraid of what he had done. Of the patterns that repeated themselves everywhere. Amalie said, "Could you do that for me?"

"No."

"Why not?"

He opened his eyes. She watched him, worried. He said, "I know you too well, Ladyheart. I wouldn't be able to see clearly." It was not quite true, but he could not bear to be more honest. He was too scared he would hurt her. "It would hold little interest for you. I'd see nothing you wouldn't expect me to know. And I can't do the future."

"How unfortunate," said Joyain, nastily. Gracielis was silent.

Amalie said, "I think we all need a drink. I'll have Herlève bring wine."

"That has appeal," Joyain said.

"I'll fetch glasses." Amalie went out. The two men sat in silence, apart from the clock on the mantel. Gracielis stared at the ceiling. He had a name now for his rival and a means of learning more. He might act, save that he lacked strength and training and knowledge. It would be no fair fight, himself against Quenfrida and Kenan. Especially if Kenan was *undarios*. Assuming, of course, that a person with clan background could become *undarios* in its fullest sense.

There was no one else who would help Merafi. He was Tarnaroqui. It was not his problem. It was beyond him. He sighed and closed his eyes. He had made his choice when he sent his message to Yvelliane via her estranged husband. He would have to live with it.

Amalie interrupted his thoughts. She spoke a little too cheerfully, and he knew he had again distressed her. She was saying, "Do go in, monseigneur," and then, "Do you know my nephew, Lieutenant Joyain Lievrier? Jean, this is Lord Thiercelin duLaurier of Sannazar and the Far Blays." Gracielis opened his eyes. Thiercelin stood in the center of the room. Joyain, too, was standing. Amalie said, "We were about to have a drink—a little early, I grant you, but—would you care to join us?"

"Thank you," Thiercelin said, bowing to Joyain. "I already have the honor of knowing the lieutenant."

"Really?" Amalie steered him to a chair.

Joyain said, "We met through official channels. The embassy." His voice held a curious edge. He avoided looking at Thiercelin.

"Oh, of course. Madame of the Far Blays is First Councillor," Amalie said.

The conversation turned on desultory matters for the next half hour or so, mostly between Thiercelin and

Amalie. Gracielis found it easier to listen than to partici-
pate, and few remarks were directed at him. Joyain, too,
was largely silent. At the end of the half hour he rose,
kissed Amalie's cheek, bowed to Thiercelin, and excused
himself. Amalie showed him out, then, returning, said,
"I believe you have matters to discuss. I'll be in the shop
if you need me."

Gracielis said, "I can't steal your room . . ." But she
only smiled and shook her head at him as she left.

There was a small silence. Thiercelin broke it. "You
look better."

"Thank you."

"I delivered your message."

"You're kind." Gracielis hesitated, trying not to fidget.
He did not look at Thiercelin. "It was Lieutenant Lievrier with whom you dueled, wasn't it?"

"Yes." Thiercelin sighed. "Except that it didn't happen. There was an interruption . . . Valdin . . ."

"Yes, I know." Gracielis spoke with thinking. He
sighed, and looked at Thiercelin.

Thiercelin rose and came to sit on the end of the daybed. "I doubt the lieutenant told you."

"No." Gracielis had no intention of elaborating. He
said, "Have you seen Iareth Yscoithi again?"

"Are you going to tell me what's going on?" Thiercelin made himself more comfortable. "I have all day.
I'm wholly at your disposal."

Gracielis let his lashes hide his eyes. "You're appro-
priating my line, I think."

"Hmm," Thiercelin said. "Tell me, Graelis. Or are
you meaning not to?"

"No, I'm prevaricating." Gracielis smiled. "It's hard.
It touches upon matters which are in some wise . . ."

"Forbidden?"

"Yes." Gracielis hesitated then switched to Tarnaroqui. "You know what is meant by *undarios*?"

" 'Perfumed-death,' " Thiercelin translated absently,
back into Merafien. "No, I don't think so."

"It's a matter of belief. A species of religious order."

"The famous assassin-priests?"

"Yes, and more. It's a discipline. To be *undarios* . . . It's to possess a certain type of understanding or vision."

"Seeing ghosts?"

"Amongst other things. One doesn't have to be *undarios* to have that or other, lesser powers." He caught Thiercelin's eye. "Card-reading. Poisoning. The manifold arts of pleasure."

Thiercelin folded his arms. "Now, why does that sound familiar?" Gracielis looked reproachful. "All right, Graelis, I'll control my credulity. You're telling me you have this discipline."

"I have some of the training." Gracielis felt some of the old bleakness settle upon him. "I lack certain strengths . . . I have sight, but no power." He forced himself away from it. "I was taught always that the forces open to my kind may not be awakened in Merafi. Well . . ." He hesitated, looking toward the window. "I was misled."

Thiercelin's eyes narrowed. He said, "Explain."

"Something is awake here, which doesn't belong and which intends you harm." Thiercelin's brows lifted. Gracielis said, "You've already seen a forerunner of it."

"Valdin? He's alarming, I grant you; but he's hardly a citywide threat."

"He no longer belongs here. But he's come. And where he's come, others may follow. Will follow. Forgive me."

"I wasn't assuming this was your fault." Thiercelin said. "Is this why you . . . ?"

Gracielis looked at his maltreated hands. It would be easy to lie. He said, "No." He was cold. He was too close to betrayal. "To be *undarios*, to enter upon that path . . . There are bonds formed. There's someone in the city I've known almost all my life. Three nights ago, when I dreamed, and after, I felt a working, colored by her touch. After you had gone, I . . . summoned her. I can't tell you how, but the means weren't permitted to me. I hoped to persuade her to undo what she'd done. I succeeded only in angering her." He shivered. "She refused."

Thiercelin said, "And that's why . . . ?"

"More or less." It might not be said, even to Thiercelin. It could not be explained. He could not bear to be laid so open. "She rejected me." He would not break. He would not grant to her that power, not from memory alone. He had no other choice.

In any case, he had been replaced. Kenan stood now where he had in Quenfrida's regard. Unless he chose to buy that back in blood and treachery. He said, "You must be careful. She isn't finished. There'll be sickness and flooding and death."

"This friend of yours is *undarios*?"

"*Undaria*. Yes, and she has at least one colleague."

Thiercelin looked at his hands. Then he said, "As an informer, shouldn't you be telling this to Yvelliane? Or didn't she believe you?" Gracielis was silent. "I'm sorry, Graelis, but this all sounds so . . ."

"Un-Merafien? As it happens, I've already taken steps to do that." He sighed and added, more to himself than Thiercelin, "It will have to suffice, if she grants the time . . ."

"What?" Thiercelin said. And then, receiving no reply, "There is no place, Varnaq. I looked it up on the official maps of your country."

Gracielis looked at him in surprise. "Does it matter?"

"Yes . . . I keep thinking I know you. But you see things, you deal with powers . . . you report to Yvelliane—and no doubt to this countrywoman of yours—Who are you, Graelis? I think I need to know."

It no longer mattered. His life was counted out in the measure of Quenfrida's convenience. Gracielis reached out a careful hand to Thiercelin. "I can't tell you my birth name. I was never told it. But in the temple whose property I am, I'm Gracielis *arin-shae* Quenfrida." His

lips quirked. "Varnaq is one of the minor places of punishment, in Tarnaroqui belief. Reserved for those who
cheat at cards and commit crimes against taste." Thiercelin frowned. "I am, as you have known me, Gracielis
de Varnaq, gigolo and spy." Thiercelin's hand tightened
on his. Gracielis inhaled and changed the subject.
"When you see Iareth Yscoithi, would you ask her about
another in addition to Urien Armenwy? Kenan
Orcandros?"

"The envoy?"

"Yes." Gracielis hesitated. "I need to know about
him."

"You could come with me and ask Iareth yourself."

A memory of water falling and of level green eyes . . .
It was not his past, and he would not succumb to it. He
said, "No." And then, more gently, "At present, as you
can see . . ." He indicated his abused wrists.

"Later, maybe. Your Madame Viron tells me the injury is minor."

If Quenfrida allowed him a later. Gracielis smiled a
little. "Perhaps."

Thiercelin looked down at their hands, and his face
was strange. But he said only, "I'll hold you to that."

Power. Kenan could sense it, feathering across his
skin, lighting sparks of recognition. Down there, down
in the depths something waited for him, old and strong
and valuable. This was what Quenfrida had meant when
she sent him here. This was the root of Merafi, waiting
for his touch, his blight upon it. He doubted that the scholar
who had led him here had the least idea of the significance of the place. The man had walked down the shallow steps and along the passage beyond chatting about
sally ports and lower guard chambers. A fool, but a useful one so far. Kenan could already see several ways in
which that usefulness could and would be extended. The
girl—Miraude—was less useful but potentially interesting. Handled correctly, she might be employed to dis-

cover something of the plans of Yvelliane d'Illandre. Following at the rear of their small procession, Kenan watched Miraude almost with approval. Slight and silly and no threat to him. He could, he decided, afford to expend a little more time on her. Besides, he found her body appealing. Ahead of him, she tripped on the uneven floor, and he put a hand under her elbow. She looked back at him in surprise and he smiled thinly. "Be careful."

"Thank you." She freed herself gently, returning his smile.

The passage was cut into the rock, sloping down toward the river, following the line of a low rock spur. There were similar tunnels under the keep at Skarholm, carved out into the crag long before the days of Yestinn Allandur, the breaker of covenants. At the base of those tunnels lay the heart of Skarholm itself, the Chamber of Clans, once the assembly place of the clan-heads in the time before Yestinn invented kings. Perhaps Yestinn had built this echo of it here as a sop to the weaker clan leaders of his time. The scholar's pool of lantern light reached no more than a handful of feet ahead. Had he the choice, Kenan would have extinguished it. He was Orcandros. His eyes were apt in darkness. His ears were sharper still. They were higher than the river, but he could hear it, distantly, dropping and gurgling along its course, back-noted by the steady slow brush-brush of the tidal estuary. Two waters, one salt, one sweet, and rock, all close, all entwined. This place hallowed Merafi and sealed its opacity to ancient powers. In this place he could enact a working to match what he had begun with Valdarrien's blood six years before.

He would not need Allandurin blood this time: that was already present. He could taste it in the sour air. He just needed to give matters a gentle push.

The passage came to an end on a long, smooth ledge. The scholar ushered them onto it and held his lantern up high. The light shivered, rippled out into the gloom.

They stood on the side of a long oval cave, carved not by hand but by water, its sides whorled and smooth. Here and there, light struck sparks from crystals of quartz. The floor was muddy: small pools of water glistened in the lowest spots. Diagonally from where they stood, a cleft led on into further darkness. "Obviously," the scholar said, "the cave itself is natural. I speculate that after Yestinn it was used as a cold store of some kind or perhaps a guard point above a water gate, although of course the river has moved its course somewhat since the early period, and the branch that would have come closest to here is heavily silted now. But if you look at the ceiling, you can see that the cave must have been used by Yestinn himself or one of his early heirs." He raised the lantern as high as he might.

Miraude gasped. Kenan hid a smile behind his hand. Across the roof animals were painted in wide bands of faded color. Allandurin eagle, Orcandrin otter, Artovanin bear. Each of the clan signs marched there in appointed order, following each other round in a flattened circle, all save the eagle, who flew in the center.

At home in Skarholm, the animals were carved into the rock, showing proper respect. At home, no creature came ahead of any other. That was as it should be. Kenan intended to ensure that those days would return, for Lunedith, at least.

"You note," the scholar said, "the clan badges. The same creatures appear on the tapestries in the Grand Audience Chamber of Rose Palace and on the wood panels in the Great Hall of the Old Palace. It recalls our joint past, of course." He made Kenan a small bow. "I understand there are similar decorations in Skarholm."

"Indeed."

"Perhaps you might describe them to me some day."

"Of course."

Miraude peered across the cave. "It's very cold. What did Yestinn do in here?"

"It may have been a council chamber of some kind, or a place of meditation. That crack you see over there leads into the cellars of the Old Palace, although the passage itself is blocked off. I've been able to make a temporary exit close to the Mercer's Bridge: a shop owner has kindly allowed me access to his cellar. We'll be leaving that way. This room retained some use after the first fort was abandoned. I'm hoping to spend the winter working through the household documents from some of those reigns, if I can gain access to them."

"I'll speak to my sister-in-law." Miraude shivered and stepped closer to Kenan.

He offered her his arm. "It is indeed cold. When we leave, you must allow me to buy you some spiced wine." She smiled up at him, taking his arm. He smiled back. This would do. This would do very well. He turned to the scholar. "Shall we continue?"

It was dusk when Thiercelin returned to his new lodgings. His valet was not in evidence, and the candles were still unlit. Perhaps he should have left instructions with his new landlord. He had not thought about that, earlier, wrapped in his concerns. He deposited hat and cloak onto a chair, and began to hunt for tapers. If Gracielis was right, if he was not mad . . . There was something, after all, that he might do for Yvelliane, if he could expose this Quenfrida and her accomplices. Perhaps then she would understand that he was not Valdarrien, that he loved her, that he could support her. Finding a taper, he nearly dropped it again when a voice spoke to him from the shadows.

"Hello, Thierry."

It was as if his thoughts had summoned her. He was mistaken. Turning, the lighted taper in one hand, he found himself looking at Yvelliane.

He took a step toward her. "Yviane."

"I'm glad you're so pleased to see me."

"I didn't mean it the way it sounded. I . . . You startled me. I was just thinking about you." He lit the nearest lamp. "I'm glad you're here. How did you find me?"

"Your valet." Yvelliane took a seat nearby and looked at him.

"I was going to send a note . . ." He carried the taper round to the remaining lamps, then sat himself. "Can I get you something? Some wine?" She looked even more tired than the last time he had seen her. He wanted to go to her, to hold her. She sat with her spine straight and her hands folded in her lap, cool and forbidding.

She said, "Nothing, thank you."

"Are you sure?" She nodded. He went on, "Listen, Yviane, I . . ."

She cut across him. "You weren't here when I arrived. You'd gone to visit Gracielis." Her voice was chill.

"That's nothing. He's ill and I just . . ."

"You clearly care for him a great deal. Perhaps I should have applied to him to ask you to cancel your duel."

She was still angry. He would never get through to her. Thiercelin ran a hand through his hair and sighed. He said. "Please don't. I don't want to argue."

"Nor do I." But her face belied it. "You chose not to come home. I understand."

"I just wanted . . ."

Again, she cut through him, "I do, however, want something from you."

"You do?" He gazed at her in new hope. "Anything. You know I . . ."

"It's nothing personal. Royal business."

"Oh." Firomelle. Always and always Firomelle. Thiercelin looked down. His boots were dusty. She had once again retreated behind her armor of duty, and he could not touch her. Nothing changed. Nothing between them ever really changed. He said, softly, "What?"

"There's to be a ball at the Rose Palace next week. I

need you to escort me. Tell Gracielis that I want him there, too: I'll provide him with a partner. That's all."

Thiercelin said, "About Gracielis . . . There's something you should know, something he told me . . ."

"I don't want to know." She began to put on her gloves, tugging each finger smooth with precise, short motions.

He was tired of barbed remarks and riddles. He wanted simple human contact and kindness. He looked at her with a kind of desperation, and said, "Oh, Yviane, must you?" He rose, made to reach out to her.

"I don't have much time, Thierry. Firomelle . . ."

"Needs you. I have that one engraved on my heart."

"It happens to be true." She rose and began to put on her hat. "Don't see me out. I'll expect you at the ball. If you can bear to oblige me."

That was unfair. Thiercelin forgot that it might be advisable to placate her, and said so. She favored him with a brief, contemptuous glance. Defensively, he added, "You know you only have to ask. I'm not Valdin."

"I thought we'd already discussed that."

"I didn't mean . . . Oh, to the river's bed with it!" He sighed. "Yviane, we need to talk."

"I don't think so. And, anyway, I haven't the time."

Obliquely, he remembered Gracielis' face, speaking of the woman who had rejected him. Such bleakness . . . He could only hope he did not betray himself so clearly. He looked at his feet and said, "Would you talk to me, if you did?"

"Would you listen to anyone but yourself?" Yvelliane went to the door.

"Yes," Thiercelin said desperately.

She smiled at him, and frost crystallized in his veins. "How tolerant," she said, and walked out of the room.

Outside in the street it was cold. A hint of mist crept in from the direction of the river. Climbing into her carriage, Yvelliane leaned back against the seat. Her maid said, "Madame?"

"I'm all right. I'm tired."

The girl fell silent. Yvelliane closed her eyes as the carriage began its swaying way up the street. She had handled it all wrong again, she had mishandled Thiercelin just as she had always mishandled Valdarrien before him. No wonder he had left her, no wonder he had turned to Gracielis, faced with a wife who did nothing but snap and demand. She did not know what else to do.

He said he loved her.

If he loved her, why had he not come home?

She could not make him. She could do nothing save continue on her set course. She tried to take comfort in that, found it dry and hard and stale. *But,* said the weasel voice in the back of her head, *he wanted to talk to you* . . .

There was no time. She had to be back for the evening council.

He wanted you to listen . . .

If he came home, he'd find plenty of opportunities.

But you're hardly ever there . . . The voice choked her. *If he's gone, whose fault is it, Yviane?*

Who killed Valdarrien?

Will I never learn?

11

IN THE DARK OF THE LOST HALL beyond the
undercroft, Kenan sat with his eyes closed and
counted down the seconds to sunset. Awareness of light
and dark, sun and moons ran through his clan-blood.
Quenfrida's teaching had shown him how to awaken it,
dilute as it was. He would never have the otter shape of
his ancestors, but somewhat of their other skills lived on
in him. He sat cross-legged on the floor, upper body
naked, hair drawn back into a tight braid, hands resting
loosely upon his knees, his breathing regular and slow.
The priests had no idea he was here: he had slipped in
from the scholar's private entrance in the shop owner's
cellar. The shop owner would never again remember
that entrance. Quenfrida's instructions had included the
art of clouding minds. And the scholar . . . He would
never know anything again. As the last light slid below
the horizon, Kenan stirred and opened his eyes. It was
time.

His tools were laid out before him. A handful of earth
from the temple grounds, a glass bottle filled with water
from the river, a tallow candle, a stick of red pastel, a
bundle of hairs—his own, his grandfather's, and strands
from various of his *kai-rethin*—and his thin bone-
handled knife. He had not Quenfrida's art of lighting
candles with a look: for that he must use flint. In its
flickering light, he drew a rough circle on the floor
around himself with the pastel and placed the candle

carefully beside him. Then he sprinkled the earth in
front of him, shaping it into a small mound. The city,
stronghold of Firomelle and her line, heart of Gran' Romagne, which held his homeland in thrall. He held his
hand over it, describing it in Lunedithin, first of tongues.
Merafi, in small, for him to work his will upon. With the
tip of the knife, he scratched a shallow trench around it,
digging into the dirt of the cave floor. He untied the hair
bundle and wrapped the strands about the base of the
mound. Then he uncorked the bottle. All around him,
the eyes of the painted creatures watched him. He saluted them and dripped seven drops slowly onto the
mound. "River water, mother of the city, vein of its lifeblood, hear me." Another seven drops. "River water,
born of the mountains, born of the sea, sweet and salt,
to shelter the city and keep it secure." Seven more
drops, "River water, taken by me and summoned by me,
be mingled in blood and break your bindings." He set
the bottle aside and picked up his knife. The edge shone
slick and cold in the candlelight. He held his left wrist
out over the mound and put the knife to it. "Blood of
my body, clan-blood, old blood, enact my will on this
river and city." He looked up at the paintings and nodded, once. "Clans of my fathers be my witness." And
drew the knife along his vein.

Blood dripped down. Kenan held still, his breathing
steady, counting his heartbeats from one to ten. And
then . . .

The mound shivered, quivered. Water began to seep
from its sides. Kenan lowered the knife and with his
bleeding hand extinguished the candle in the heart of
the soil. There was a moment of stillness.

A bear growled, low and angry. Wings beat, lifted,
stirred into life. Hoofbeats tapped over the ground. The
call of an owl answered the bark of a fox, the cry of a
wolf. The hall floor shivered as thin red lines spread out
across it, overlaying the natural patterns of earth and
water. In the darkness, Kenan smiled. They had heard

him, the totems of his past, and they concurred. Clan-
blood had spoken. It was time for Merafi to fall.

This was not a good idea. No, being brutally honest,
it was a stupid idea and a fitting end to a humiliating
and unsatisfactory day. Joyain scowled as he wended his
way down toward the old docks. That had its advantages.
At least it caused people to get out of his way.

He was not in uniform, but that was no guarantee.
Someone in The Pineapple might still recognize him.

The very last thing he needed was a fight.

She will burn you . . . Joyain put no faith in fortune-
telling. Gracieux was a meddler and a charlatan, nothing
more. What Joyain chose to do was no one's business
but his own. And if he chose to accompany Iareth Yscoithi on some bizarre pilgrimage into the disreputable part
of the old dock, well, then . . . He was off duty. He
could do as he pleased.

It was morbid. What he really wanted to know was
why she couldn't simply pay a visit to the Far Blays
family mausoleum like anyone else?

It was not a question one might ask, not without seeming even more graceless than he felt already. He risked
a quick glance at her. Her face was impassive.

The streets grew narrower as they neared the south
channel of the river. They were rougher too, and none
too clean. In the dim evening light it was sometimes
hard to pick a course across the dirty cobbles. The
houses lining them had a hunched quality, united against
intruders. A sour smell blew off the river.

He turned right just before the quay and followed the
dim alley under the edge of the old wall. The torches
of the sentries made occasional flashes of light as they
patrolled, throwing weird shadows over the roofs. Joyain
felt uncomfortable.

The Pineapple was set against the angle of the wall,
with a wide yard between it and its neighbors, and a
high rounded arch. Once, it would have accommodated

travelers arriving by the nearby East Gate. Now most of
the livery buildings were derelict, along with the top two
floors of the inn itself. The taproom was vast, crowded,
and smoky.

The ale was famously awful.

If Joyain had been Valdarrien of the Far Blays, he
would have picked a better place to die in. He hesitated
outside and said, "Are you sure about this?"

Iareth had been gazing upward, watching the slow-
pacing torches. She said, almost absently, "No," and
then unexpectedly smiled at him.

"We don't have to go in. . . . It was out here that
he . . . That the duel took place."

"So." She held out a hand to him. "But I would enter,
even so."

Joyain shrugged, taking her hand. He had to duck
under the low lintel and nearly came to grief on the
uneven step down. He had managed to forget about that,
of course. The place was busy, loud, and wholly without merit.

He found them a corner table, looked suspiciously at
the bench, dusted it down, then sat with his back to the
wall. The clientele was mainly infantry, half still in uniform. There were very few women and none of them
respectable.

All in all, it was a very unsuitable place to be.

A servant made his way toward them. Iareth raised a
questioning brow. "The ale's bad," Joyain said, "but the
wine's worse."

"Ale, then."

He ordered for both of them and tried not to look at
it too hard when it came. Iareth tasted hers and her
eyes met his. Her expression altered not one jot, but her
opinion was plain in every line of her. Joyain smiled. He
said, "You were warned."

"Even so." Her clear eyes laughed. He was aware of
a sudden disastrous warmth for her.

She will burn you . . . He looked away and sipped his

ale. It tasted worse than he remembered. He shuddered and pushed it away. Beside him, Iareth dipped a finger into hers and stirred it. When he risked looking at her again, she was oblivious. He found himself moving a little farther from her, a little farther from that calm self-control.

Another woman might have wept. Iareth was not like the other women he knew. She was herself only; and seeing that, he was aware also of the memory of Valdarrien of the Far Blays. The chance remained that she was even now the same woman for whom his erratic lordship had lived and died.

Well, Joyain wasn't intending to die for her or anyone else. And he had no sympathy to spare for dead Valdarrien. Whatever else the interrupted duel with Thiercelin had been, it had most assuredly been a sad breach of manners.

It fitted admirably the reputation of the late Lord of the Far Blays.

Beside him, Iareth rose. He looked up at her. She said, "Let's leave."

"Of course." He gathered his belongings and joined her. She wore a curious air of severity. Some of the infantrymen looked as she passed and, to a man, turned away as though discomfited.

Outside it had grown foggy. The light from the tavern gave the night a curious quality, like walking through smoke. It was cold. He drew his cloak about him. The thick air bore a faint sweet smell, like overripe fruit. Or honeysuckle.

They passed a handful of people in the alleys, but once they turned toward Change Street, they were alone. Iareth said, "No, I have no understanding." She spoke more to herself than him. "I had hoped . . . It is a lesson, I suppose. One cannot always learn as much as one wishes."

Joyain could think of no sensible reply to that. She hesitated, then added, "Forgive me. I had hoped to reach understanding of the choice made by Valdin Allandur. But there is nothing for me in that place."

Or for anyone. "You might ask Monseigneur de Sannazar," Joyain said. "He was present."

"So. He has told me a little."

He did not want to discuss this. He stared into the fog and said, "Are you cold?"

"No."

Conversation died. They followed the length of Change Street, turned left, and made for the Glass Bridge, named not for its materials, but for the guild that had paid for it.

He walked into her without meaning to. In the fog he had failed to register that she had stopped. He said, "Whoops," and staggered a little.

"Hush." She held up a hand. He could barely make out the gesture.

He could hear nothing out of the ordinary. The creaking of a shop sign. The trickle of water off the eaves. A woman's voice, singing somewhere. "I don't . . ."

She put her right hand on his arm. Her left rested on her knife. Joyain looked over his shoulder down the street. Nothing, only fog.

Iareth shoved him. He stumbled and went down, breaking his fall by reflex. Iareth dived to her right, rolled. Something whistled through the space where they had stood and thudded into a wall. Joyain swung to his feet and drew his sword.

He could see almost nothing. She rose to a crouch, a knife in either hand. Silence. He exhaled. "What in the . . . ?"

A dim shape grabbed for Iareth. She half-turned and cut upward. He took a step toward her. She followed up with a feint to her right. Her attacker moved to parry and stumbled, as her left hand came in under his rib cage.

Came in, and went right through . . . Joyain shivered.

It had to be the light. He had to be wrong. It was not possible. Iareth stepped back, moved into middle guard, and waited.

The figure straightened and reached for her. And divided itself in two.

Joyain swallowed. Half of it looked at him, and it had not even turned round. He had to be dreaming. Or drunk. Or mad. Such things did not happen in Merafi.

A sword that had not been there only moments before cut at him in *quarte*. He parried and prepared to follow through. It cut back at him from the other side. He wasn't fast enough for this. He parried, then used his cloak-wrapped left arm to block the next blow, protecting his chest. It was going to hurt, even if it didn't get through. The fog hid Iareth from him.

The impact left him breathless. He staggered. His arm was numb, but the pain was dull. No blood, no tear. The sword edge was blunt. Gasping, he twisted away from a flank cut and used the impetus to drive home a thrust into his opponent's thigh.

It met no resistance. His blade cut air. Nothing there . . . He fell back, in low guard, and put the wall behind him. His spurs dragged on the cobbles, striking sparks.

His opponent recoiled.

Joyain nearly lost the advantage, gawping. The thing could not be hit. It could not, presumably, be disarmed. But that brief flash had alarmed it. He reflex-parried, thinking. Creatures out of fog and damp and chill. He hardly had time to waste lighting fires, even if they did fear it.

The alternative, however, did rather look like being bludgeoned to death. He tried to remember the layout of the street. No taverns—private houses, mostly, and tenements—a small temple. A bakehouse . . . He was half-turned around by the mist. He risked a glance at the building against which he was backed. Bare wall and the edge of a door with a lion-head knocker. Where *was* he? He parried twice and began to move out to his left. Still no sign of Iareth. Wall. More wall. Blows raining on him. His right wrist ached. His left arm was still numb. Still more wall. Another two parries. His breath sobbed in his chest. If only he could see better.

Abruptly there was nothing at his back. He stumbled and cried out as a blow connected with his sword arm. The shock ran up into his shoulder. Already cramped, his grip slipped, and his saber dropped to the cobbles.

Oh, river bless . . . He lacked breath even to curse. He had to choose, now, between retrieving the sword and investigating the gap. Always supposing, of course, that the creature did not simple relocate itself behind him. He glanced rapidly over his shoulder. Faint, yellow-shadowed mist.

Yellow-shadowed. He remembered the aura around the torches of the sentries and gasped in relief. Somewhere in that yard, there was a light. Or a fire. He had only to get to it.

He was unprotected. He fell back, dodging. If only there was no gate . . . He reached back. Nothing. Nothing. Something mingled with the honeysuckle scent of the air.

He was at the side of a bakehouse. The public bakehouse, whose ovens were always lit. He looked briefly at his insubstantial opponent, then turned and ran. The yard was straw-strewn, the footing treacherous. Slipping and stumbling, he ducked round the pump and misjudged the distance. He nearly collided with the woodpile for the ovens. He had just enough time to grab up a length of wood, to use as a makeshift shield against the blows that pursued him.

He could feel the heat of the ovens, away to his right. They would be banked for the night. He was going to be unpopular. He had no choice. Wishing his gloves were thicker, he found the latch to an oven door and cranked it open.

Firelight spilled out, turning the mist golden. Joyain,

his hands stinging, crouched as close as he might, and tried to make out his surroundings. The sudden transition from cold to hot made him shiver. He controlled his breathing and took a pace forward. Nothing. Another. Two more. On the sixth, something struck at him. He recoiled. Not banished, then, only waiting. But the fire kept it at bay.

He might stay here till dawn, and abandon Iareth. Or he might act. Somewhere there had to be something he could use as a torch. His lodgings were no more than three streets away. There he had candles and a good hearth. If he could make it that far . . . He groped around him until he found a bundle of medium staves. The fire would scarcely be hot enough . . . His army issue flask held pure spirit. He fumbled it from a pocket and doused one end of a stave. Thrust into the oven, it spluttered and caught fire.

He held the torch aloft as he made his cautious way toward the street. He could hear nothing, apart from the creaking sign, the leaking gutter. Nothing came near him. He said, quietly, "Iareth?" and tried to hold alarm from his voice. How long had it been? The fog was still thick. He almost lost the torch when he tripped over his discarded saber. The metal was chill as he snatched it up. He called again, "Iareth?"

This time he thought he heard a reply. He advanced, called a third time. From his left her voice said, "Jean?"

"Over here—no, I'll come to you."

She stood on the porch of one of the private houses, panting. He said, "Are you all right?"

"I have bruises . . ." She was pale in the uncertain light. "Nothing worse."

"What *were* those things?"

She smiled. "I have not the slightest idea."

"Well, whatever they are, they don't like fire." He hesitated. "This torch won't last long. We wouldn't make the bridge. My rooms are nearer . . . I have candles, and I could borrow a lantern to get us up to the embassy."

"Certainly." Iareth stepped out into the street cautiously. "Let us go."

By mutual consent they ran. The streets were empty. Two candles burned in the sugar merchant's shop. The torch was almost gone. Joyain passed it to Iareth and took a candle to light them upstairs.

His hands shook so much that it took him three attempts to light the fire. Iareth, meanwhile, lit all the candles she could find. That would be expensive in the long run, but he could not bring himself to care. He found the small bottle of spirits Amalie had given him on his name-day, and poured two rather large portions.

"Fire inside and outside," Iareth said, gasping at the taste.

Joyain began, painstakingly, to unlace his left sleeve. "It seemed appropriate."

"Indeed." Iareth dropped her cloak on the chest. The gray fabric was torn but she seemed unharmed. "Are you hurt?"

"I'm not sure." He winced, tugging the sleeve free. She put down her cup and came to help him. He said, "Thank you. I used it to block . . . I don't think it's broken."

"Can you move your fingers?" He could. She frowned. "Urien has more skill than I. Or Kenan, for that matter. But in their absence, I must suffice."

"Rather you than Kenan!"

She smiled. "You may change your mind on that." She unlaced his cuff and rolled up his shirtsleeve. Then she felt along his arm carefully. It hurt less than he expected. "I think you are bruised only, but I will bind it for you."

"Thanks." He sat, while she found bindings; then let her strap his forearm. Her touch was sure and impersonal. After a while he said, "Were you expecting what happened?"

She looked up. "No."

"But . . ." He sighed. "It isn't possible, you know. What happened." No more possible than the details a deck of cards had revealed of his life. "There has to be a rational explanation. That terrible ale . . ."

"You drank almost none of it."

"Some humor in the air, then." He was not convincing even himself. He stopped and looked at her. "I don't like all this."

"No. I dislike it also."

He said, "Tell me about Valdarrien d'Illandre." She raised her brows. "Well, he's dead, but I saw him. And now we've been attacked by something that wasn't there . . . Perhaps there's a connection. Even if it's simply that I'm going mad."

"Then I am mad also, after tonight." She hesitated. "Why would you hear of him?"

"I don't know. I'm trying to understand what I'm mixed up in."

"So." She shifted position so that she sat more comfortably, and hugged her knees. "It is hard to define someone in words. Yviane Allandur called him wild. Urien said that he was merely thoughtless. He had a . . . a quality to him, of assurance. He did not think overlong about his actions." She watched the middle distance, calm, considered. "He had a most ungovernable temper; and yet he also understood pain and honor and loyalty. His death was a great foolishness."

Joyain could think of nothing to say. It seemed to him that he was the fool for asking the question. She still loved Valdarrien and Joyain Lievrier was in grave danger of making an idiot of himself.

For lack of anything better to say, he said, "I'm sorry." And then, as she looked up, "It was brave of you, going to The Pineapple."

"On the contrary, it was cowardice. I should not need to question my past."

He didn't understand. He said, "It can't have been easy."

"It was an indulgence."

He said, "Gracieux warned me off you, today."

"Who?"

"My aunt's lover. He's Tarnaroqui, and he tells fortunes. He said you'd hurt me."

She frowned. "And you think him wrong? You may be misled. You know I can offer you comfort only?"

"Yes." He looked down, unable to sustain her regard. "But warnings tend to have a bad effect on me."

She laughed. "That is a poor reason."

"The worst."

"When Kenan's embassy ends, I shall leave Merafi. I have no intention of returning. It is against the laws of my people to form any but a casual liaison outside one's clan."

"I know." He looked at her again. Her face was serious. "I'm prepared for all that."

"Are you?" She hesitated. "Valdin *kai-reth* . . . It is true, I was less clear with him than duty required. It is also true that I permitted my . . . my preferences to cloud that duty. But it remains a fact that I must share guilt for his death. I did him an ill service when I became his mistress. It is a mistake I cannot afford to commit again. And then, Urien . . ."

"What?"

She shook her head. "It matters not. I'm concerned simply that you do not expect anything of me that I cannot give." Still, Joyain was silent. She looked at him, and said, "May I stay, this night?"

"Of course," he said, and held out his hands. But although her touch was gentle and her body compliant, it was not his name she whispered in the warm candlelight.

"Yviane?" Something tugged at Yvelliane, sending a sharp pain up through her neck and shoulders, "Yviane?" Another tug. She shrugged, trying to ease the pain, and realized she had been asleep. Miraude stood beside the desk, dressed in her nightgown and a heavy brocade overrobe. "Yviane, it's four in the morning. You should go to bed."

She had fallen asleep over her papers again. The ache in her neck, the twist in her shoulders bore witness to that. Her eyes felt dry and sore. She sat up cautiously and rubbed them. Miraude handed her a cup of water. She sipped at it, then stretched.

She said, "Four A.M."

"Yes."

"And you just got in?"

Miraude nodded. She perched herself on the edge of the desk. "I saw the lamp was lit, and I need to talk to you. But you're tired. It can wait."

Yvelliane drained her water. "No, now is fine. What is it?"

"Kenan Orcandros. I told you he came to my salon and he was interested in the archaeological remains at the Old Temple?"

"Yes."

"We visited them, the day before yesterday. I wanted to tell you earlier, but you've hardly been here."

"Firomelle . . ."

"I understand." Miraude picked up a pen and toyed with it. "He didn't seem that interested once we were there. I mean, it was as if he wanted to make it clear how recent everything here is. But there was one thing that was odd. There's a cavern, maybe an old council room, I think. Just before we went in, something strange happened with Kenan."

"Oh?" Yvelliane took the pen away.

"It was as if he felt something, was reacting to something that we couldn't see. It was weird."

"There's a cave like that under Skarholm, too. Valdin saw it. It's used for clan rituals." Yvelliane frowned. "I wonder . . . I wish I knew more about the *undarii* and their skills."

"I could see if there are any books . . ." Miraude sounded doubtful.

Yvelliane shook her head. "There's someone I need to write to. Thank you, Mimi."

"I'm due to go to the theater with him later this week. I'll let you know he if hints at anything."

"Um." Yvelliane stared at her papers. Perhaps Kenan had simply been reminded of something, taken by surprise by such a clear link between Merafi and his homeland. It was possible, but she doubted it. She would write to Gracielis and inquire . . .

Gracielis. Her hand went to the back of her neck, rubbing it slowly. Miraude said, "What's wrong?"

"I'm stiff."

"Yes." Miraude slipped off the desk and came to stand behind her. Her small hands closed over Yvelliane's. "But that's not it, is it? It's Thierry."

"Don't, Mimi." Yvelliane did not want to talk about him. She did not even want to think about it. There was not the time, not now. She had Firomelle and Quenfrida and the tales of unrest in the low city to worry over. Thiercelin would have to wait. She could not take more pain.

Miraude said, "What happened?" Yvelliane made no reply. Miraude continued, "He told me there's nothing between him and that Tarnaroqui. I believe him."

"I don't," Yvelliane said, and pulled away.

"I could go and talk to him."

"I'd rather you didn't."

"Yviane, I . . ."

Yvelliane stood up, forcing Miraude to step back. "Not now, Mimi. I'm going to bed."

Miraude shook her head. "You have to sort this out sometime."

"Not now," Yvelliane repeated, and left the room.

Iareth Yscoithi of Alfial to Urien Armenwy, called Swanhame, Councillor and Leader of the Kai-rethin: Greetings.

It has started. Kenan has done something. Creatures rise from the river. They seek harm to all who live here. This night, Lieutenant Lievrier and I were

*attacked and he took a slight wound. They cannot
be damaged with weapons, but Jean discovered that
they retreat from fire. Things go very ill here in
Merafi, and I do not know how to stop them, or to
whom I should turn. I do not think Yviane Allandur will receive me: she still bears me ill will.*

*Father, I need your counsel and your aid. Come
here. I beg you, come.*

The river continued to rise. By the end of three days
the landslip to the south of the estuary was all but submerged, and the south artisans' quarter was unpleasantly
damp. In the low town, well water began to smell rank.
People drank it anyway, but some of them boiled it first
and complained it tasted sweet. The mood in the shantytown, trapped between the south and main channels, was
hostile. Tempers frayed as the inhabitants of the nearby
old docks glared out over the remains of the wall and
the embankment built by Firomelle's ancestors.

On the third night, someone set fire to the plank
bridge linking the shanty isle to the main city. It burned
poorly in the damp, but the insult was sufficient. By
dawn, there were twenty dead.

Every morning saw more bodies in the streets of
the old city. Garbled reports spoke of masked gangs pa-
trolling after dark. No one seemed to credit anything
supernatural. Joyain wrote a careful report of his own
experience, then tore it up. He did not want to think
about it. He had taken care not to discuss it with anyone,
not even Iareth. She was quiet and calm as ever, but she
had not sought him out since that night. In fairness, he
had made no move to spend time with her, either. *She
will burn you.* He did not know what to think or feel.
Perhaps he would be better off away from her, away
from all the Lunedithin.

There was sickness in the new dock, in the shanties,
in the low overspill. Joyain heard of it from Leladrien
on the afternoon of the fifth day. There were barricades

in the old docks, erected by the tenants against the threat of the shanty-dwellers. The watch and guards seconded from other regiments had orders to tear those down, but this had no effect. The barriers were simply rebuilt, sometimes by the troopers themselves. By the fifth day, no one tried to cross them. Leladrien's company had been ordered onto the isle—such of it as was still above water—to investigate. As cavalry, they had been more concerned initially with the inappropriate nature of the job than the actuality. "Until we got there," said Leladrien, white-faced in the mess. "Ever been in the shanties, Jean?"

"Not lately."

"Hmm. Well, most of it's gone. The entire east end is awash. It must've been abandoned a couple of days ago. The rest . . ." He gulped the remainder of his drink and said, "Is there any more of that?"

"I expect so." Joyain fetched a refill and watched as Leladrien drank it straight off.

"Not sure that helps. All the same. . . . The rest of shantytown is empty, too." Leladrien licked his lips and looked uncomfortable. "Those river-damned barricades! Some people got out, I guess, before the bridge was swamped; or maybe into the old dock in the first day or too. Though where they are now . . . Have you heard of any increase in vagrants?"

"No."

"Well, you wouldn't, up there with the aristos." Leladrien sounded bitter. Joyain looked at him in surprise. "You and Her Majesty both!"

"Lelien!"

"All right, all right. I won't shout." Leladrien sighed and helped himself to Joyain's drink. "I'm sorry, Jean. It's just this morning . . ."

"You're trying to tell me the shantytowners are dead?"

"Everyone we found, anyway. Women and children, mostly. They'd tried to bury some of them, but in the end I suppose it was too much work. Pray for a north wind, Jean. We had to burn the lot." He looked up and smiled unkindly. "It won't do for the queen's guests to be disturbed by the smell of burning flesh, will it?"

His animosity was making Joyain uncomfortable. "You don't have to tell me if you don't want to."

"I have to tell someone." Joyain looked down. Leladrien continued, "I don't know. . . . How many bodies did the watch pick up this morning?"

"Eighteen, I think. All but four have been identified."

"Right. Some of the corpses in shantytown had gone that way. Bludgeoned. But the rest . . . There's been some kind of plague down there. Half of those I saw were rotten with it." Leladrien rubbed a hand across his mouth. "Probably as contagious as all hell, but the captain's too scared of a panic to make anything official. And I don't imagine it would do any good by now anyway. Some shantytowners got out. Even if they did leave their families behind." Again he smiled, but this time it seemed to be an attempt at self-conviction. "It's a good thing I'm not sentimental, that's all. You wouldn't have stood it, you cry when you have to shoot a horse." Joyain said nothing. "So, what's your news? Taken your foreigners to any good parties lately? I hear you're screwing one of them." Joyain tried to stare him down. "Well, what am I supposed to say to you? I spent this morning counting bodies. It's hardly comparable."

"I'm sorry," Joyain said.

"Not your fault, I suppose, although I'll run you through if I ever hear you bitching about your luck again." Joyain started to reply. Leladrien cut him off. "I know, you think you should be doing something. Except I don't think you'd like it if you did."

"Is that the point?"

"The point?" Leladrien shook his head. Then, horribly, he began to laugh. "Drown it, Jean! There isn't any point. There never has been. That's the whole of it."

People were beginning to look at them. Leladrien's

voice was too loud. Joyain said, "Hush." And then, "You need to stop thinking about it."

"Certainly. Any suggestions?" Leladrien said, "I've taken two baths, and I can still smell it. That really concentrates the mind."

"What do want me to do about it?"

"What can you do?" Leladrien was cynical. "As little as ever, I expect." Joyain winced. "Maybe you could ask your dear friend Thiercelin of Sannazar and the Far Blays to exert some pressure upon his beloved wife, and get us some kind of official guidelines. We're still operating on standard procedure, because the captain's a scion of a noble family and has no bloody idea what to do unless he's been told how. Or perhaps your equally dear friend the heir to Lunedith could raise it with the queen the next time they take chocolate together?"

"Not him," said Joyain. "It would ruin his chance to gloat." And then, "You know I didn't ask to get stuck up there."

"Yes," Leladrien said, savagely. "Doesn't help."

"I'm sorry."

"I know, I know." Leladrien put his chin on his hands. "Get me another drink, will you?"

Joyain complied, suppressing misgivings. Returning, he said, "I've asked several times for a transfer. The Lunedithin don't need me. But protocol dictates . . ." He sighed. "And I suppose I hadn't realized it had gotten this bad. There's so often trouble and sickness down there."

"Yes." Leladrien sipped his drink. He had begun to look less angry than tired. "I thought so, too. Until this morning." He made a visible effort to pull his mind off the subject. "How's the north channel?"

"Still low. The drainage is better up there and the cliff helps. Though I did hear that the Lesser Horse Bridge has been damaged."

"Terrific." Leladrien's family lived on the north side.

"I haven't got up there recently, but I . . ." He shook his head. "Forget it."

"I'm going to ask for that transfer again."

"Yes." Leladrien looked at his hands. "You'll probably get it, too. There's going to be more trouble—people are going to panic when this shanty business gets out."

"It's that bad?"

"Honestly?" Joyain could not return the look Leladrien gave him. Leladrien continued, "I don't know. I've sent a warning to my family . . . But I don't know. I hope not. I hope I'm overreacting because I'm tired and pissed off. But it might be . . . You should tell that aunt of yours to leave."

"She's had a warning." Joyain hesitated, afraid of disturbing already troubled waters. "Gracieux told her. He knows something. He warned her nearly a week ago. I'm not sure she believed him. He was ill, and . . ."

"Ill?" Leladrien did not give Joyain time to answer. "He lives off Silk Street, doesn't he? The plague can't have got up there already. The surgeon said . . ."

"Shut up," said Joyain. Leladrien looked astonished, but obeyed. "He'd had some kind of accident. Or maybe the watch captain beat him up; I don't know." Leladrien relaxed. "I've heard nothing about sickness anywhere in the north or west quarters. Nor in the middle city, for that matter. Only in shantytown, the new dock, and parts of the south overspill."

"Good." Leladrien stood. "Pray it stays that way. You won't like burning bodies in the Old Market."

"No. Where are you going?"

"Back down. I was given three hours' furlough four hours ago. See you, Jean."

"Yes." Joyain rose and held out a hand. It was ignored. "Go safely."

"If possible." Leladrien waved and turned. In the doorway he stopped and looked back. "Jean?"

"Yes?"

"Don't ask for that transfer."

"Why not?"

"Just don't, that's all." And he was gone, leaving Joyain to brood.

He stood at the foot of the bed . . . Iareth smiled in
the midnight dark and sat up, her hair falling unbound
around her. The embassy lay in silence. She inhaled and
said, "Give you good even, Valdin *kai-reth*."

His eyes were keen upon her. She had forgotten nothing, no line of him, no shade of look or gesture or tone.
He moved fractionally, and she saw the tension beneath
his scrutiny. She patted the bed. "Will you sit?"

His weightless form made no dent. He was all longing
and desperation. Though he did not need to breathe, he
wore the air of a man who holds his breath at a wonder.

We are kai-rethin *and one and always; that changes
not.* Thus she had sworn to him six years before, and,
on that vow, left him. Within the space of six more
months he had died. She had grown accustomed to the
loss. But not, and never, to the longing.

Her Yscoithi kin had approved of her action, her sire
had not. Urien Armenwy had himself transgressed that
law in begetting her. His nature was Armenwy, pure and
simple. Like all his clan he chose one mate only, and
that for life. Iareth might perhaps have made her choice.
But she had been raised Yscoithi, trained Yscoithi; and
that clan was dwindling. Caught between Valdarrien's
love and her duty, she had chosen duty.

She looked at him, and said again, "Valdin *kai-reth*."
Kai-reth by vow only, and not by the necessary blood.
It had been all they had. It was not enough.

He said quietly, "Iareth. Iareth Yscoithi *kai-reth*."

"Peace. I am here." Her words were calm, but she
was not calm. Another woman might have wept. Iareth
only counted her heartbeats and said, "I am forgotten,
then. You have been here several weeks and have not
sought me."

"I couldn't find you."

"You have found me now."

"Yes." There was triumph in the word. Gazing at her, he said, "You were wrong."

"How so?"

"When you left me, you said we wouldn't meet again. But here we are."

"I wasn't wrong. This is no true meeting." Her voice was cold as she spoke. He shivered at it a little and drew back. She stifled the impulse to comfort him. "There was a choice made. And I am still bound by it."

"Binding isn't wanting," Valdarrien said, and there was need in his voice.

"One doesn't have to gratify every want."

Unexpectedly he smiled, dark, sardonic. "We always did differ on that point." His gaze turned speculative. "But you don't deny the wanting."

"We are *kai-rethin*, you and I. There should be no deception between us."

"And no treachery." He began to reach out to her. Then he stopped.

"Forgive me," Iareth said, softly.

"You did what you had to. I never blamed you for it." He looked bleak. "I couldn't, somehow. Not even . . ." He halted and shook his head. "I can't remember."

He had died in Thiercelin's arms, speaking her name, and of that she would never be shriven. She said, "It was necessary."

"I know. You were always fair with me." He looked down. "Has that changed?"

One could not bargain with the dead. One could not change the immutable. Honor allowed no alteration in the vows that held her to him, sanctified by his death. She did not think of Joyain. Her mouth dry, she said, "No."

" '*Kai-rethin* and one and always,' " he quoted, almost absently. "You remember?"

"Yes."

"But it was abstract." He looked up. His face was stricken. "Always one, and always apart . . . I love you, Iareth *kai-reth*."

"Peace," Iareth whispered. "I haven't changed."

"I know. That's part of the horror of it."

"You cannot do this. You must let go. You haven't the right . . ." She gestured at him. "You cannot come back like this." He looked at her, and she saw that he did not understand. "The dead have no rights, Valdin *kai-reth*."

"So Thierry tells me. Do you think I asked for this?"

"I don't know."

"*You* promised me always. Urien made me promise to live." He sounded petulant. He broke off and shook his head. "Any way I say it, it sounds childish."

"I've never rescinded my promise."

"No. But I wanted . . ." Again, he shook his head. "I'm finding a way out of this . . . Do you know what's the worst of it?" She was silent. He looked at her, and his eyes were despairing. "I can't even touch you. I have to change that or change you. Don't you see?"

There were no routes back from death. She said, "I don't understand," and he closed his eyes, shoulders sagging. She said, "I have not ceased to love you."

He opened his eyes again and glared. "Do you think that helps?" he said, and disappeared.

12

"**I** HOPE YOU REALIZE that this is unorthodox?" The cavalry commander tapped Joyain's written request for transfer with a finger.

"Yes, sir." Standing as upright as he might, Joyain stared straight in front of him. He had expected this matter to be processed by his captain. It had never crossed his mind that it would come to the attention of the colonel. He was uncomfortably aware that his boots were not as clean as they might have been, and that there was a darn on the right hem of his cassock. This was going to look just beautiful on his record.

"Leading the guard of a respected foreign visitor is hardly an unimportant post, Lieutenant."

"I know, sir." The back of Joyain's neck was starting to itch. It probably meant that his hair needed trimming. "But with all due respect, I wasn't the officer originally intended for that position."

"So?" The colonel had disconcertingly sleepy eyes. One expected him not to notice most of what went on around him. One certainly did not expect him to care a bent copper for the opinions of a junior lieutenant of minor family and without significant connections at court. The colonel said, "You've been able to handle the job, haven't you? I've had reasonable reports of you." Joyain knew better than to acknowledge the compliment. "Perhaps you'd care to tell me the cause of your discontent?"

"Well, sir," Joyain hesitated, and cursed his lack of resolve. "I believe I can be of more use elsewhere."

"Aren't I the best judge of that?" The tone was soft, but without the necessity of standing to attention Joyain would have been staring at the floor in embarrassment. "Well, Lievrier?"

"Yes, sir. But . . ." Joyain gathered his courage in both hands and looked the colonel in the eyes. "I've seen the reports on the shantytown, sir. I want to be of more immediate assistance."

"Oh, do you?"

"Sir, there are other equally capable officers. And I have personal reasons for wishing to be elsewhere." If he was going to earn a black mark for questioning his orders, he might as well make it a nice big one. "The fact is that I believe I'm becoming too attached to one of the Lunedithin party."

The colonel studied him. "That's honest, at least." Joyain stayed silent. "When were you transferred to this regiment, Lieutenant? Three years ago?"

"Four, sir."

"Family in Merafi?"

"An aunt by marriage only, sir."

"Hmm." The colonel steepled his fingers. "What makes you think we need your talents in the old docks?"

The fact that I've fought a part of what we're facing, and I know that it isn't human. He could not say that, either, not without being dismissed as a lunatic. Joyain said, "I just think I'd be better away from the Lunedithin, sir."

"The cavalry aren't here to rescue you from your mistakes."

"Yes, sir. I know."

Again, the colonel studied him. Finally, he said, "How do you think you'd be at quelling panic or supervising mass burials?"

"I can do it, sir."

The colonel sighed. "Lieutenant, I'll be honest with you.

We aren't short of men, and you're doing a good job where you are. However," and he looked at the letter again, "there are indications that we may need reinforcements at some point, particularly to handle night patrols. In which case," and he looked up, "I'm prepared to grant your request, effective from the day after tomorrow."

Joyain could breathe again. Saluting, he said, "Thank you, sir."

"Don't be too hasty about that." The colonel watched him. "Some of your duties might be unpleasant."

"So I've heard, sir."

"Have you? Well that's as may be." The colonel rose, and nodded. "All right, Lievrier. Dismissed."

Joyain saluted again and turned to go. At the door, the colonel called him back. "One thing. Where did you meet Yvelliane d'Illandre?"

"At the palace, sir." Among other places. But not even Leladrien was gossip enough to have spread that little item around.

"I see." The colonel frowned. "Forgot to hold the door open for her, did you?"

"Not that I recall, sir."

"You'd do well to remember that she has a long memory, Lievrier, and a good deal of influence. Try not to get across her again. It looks bad on your record."

"Yes, sir." Joyain suppressed a sigh and tried his level best to look baffled. "I'll bear that in mind, sir."

"You do that. As it happens, I've chosen not to pay attention to her comments. But if she complains again, I'll have to act."

"I understand, sir."

"Yes, I suppose you do." The colonel smiled. "Run along then and tell your friend duResne that he's to have a companion in his misery." Joyain tried very hard not to look surprised. The colonel laughed. "And tell him that next time he's to bring his gripes to me in person. It saves time."

"Yes, sir," said Joyain.

*   *   *

Standing on a doorstep, Gracielis tried not to fidget with the bandages on his wrists. The day was damp and chill. The air tasted sour and corroded. He did not want to be here. He had had no choice. Thiercelin had descended like a tidal bore upon Amalie's house almost before breakfast was over and swept him off to visit the Lunedithin embassy. "You're upright and reasonably coherent," declared his lordship. "So let's get this over with."

They were admitted by a servant and shown into a small salon. Thiercelin sat down on a high-backed chair, and removed hat and gloves. Gracielis remained standing, back to the window. He was armored in the trappings of his younger profession, feeble weapon against the danger that was Iareth Yscoithi. Iareth, who should be wholly strange to him, yet who haunted his nights, mirrored through a memory that was not his. He tugged at his lovelock and tried not to dwell upon the possibilities attendant upon this meeting. That way lay madness. He was face-to-face with his own inadequacies.

The servant returned and ushered them upstairs. Gracielis was silent, listening to the twin pulses of fear and alien need. In the landing mirror his reflection was foreign to him, beneath an expectation, an ancient desire. Deep within the shredding fabric of himself, he summoned the memory of Quenfrida's power over him as a protection against Valdarrien. Through his gloves he dug his nails into one bandaged wrist, letting pain tie him to himself.

Iareth Yscoithi stood in the room's center. Gracielis bowed without looking at her, holding tight to courtesy. Beside him, Thiercelin said, "Good day," and his voice was diffident.

"And to you also. You received my message?" Her voice held all the strangeness of the north. The sound caught at Gracielis. How long had Valdarrien mourned the loss of this woman before his violent end? Thiercelin was kissing her hand. Irrational jealousy shivered through Gracielis.

"A message?" Thiercelin said. "No. I've been away from home; it hasn't reached me. But if there's something I can do for you?"

"It is possible," Iareth said.

"This is Gracielis de Varnaq. I told you about him."

"So."

Unable to deny the moment any longer, Gracielis looked up. Level green eyes met his. Double vision, as memories met and mingled, of a younger Iareth, in *kairethin* gray. She looked tired and mysteriously older. He had forgotten how tall she was.

He had forgotten nothing, no part of her, the touch of her, the scent, her speaking silence and her dispassionate watchful gaze. Gracielis reached out to her without volition and the words were already forming, to follow: *Iareth* kai-reth, *oh, my love, oh, my heart . . .*

In her native tongue, Iareth said, "Valdin Allandur spoke but little Lunedithin."

He said in the same language, "I don't speak so very much of it myself."

"So. But it serves our present need."

"Thank you." It was too late to recall his manners and kiss her hand. Besides, he feared to touch her. He said, "How did you know?"

"I shall always know him. It's in the nature of the bond." She looked at him. Her matter-of-factness was comforting. "It seems to me, however, that you must find your own control, for Thierry has no knowledge of this tongue."

He had no control; that was not his gift. He began to say so, looking down in shame at his two-colored gloves. Abruptly he remembered Valdarrien's ghost in the royal aisle, and heard again that distant command. *Tell Iareth* kai-reth *. . .* He smiled and looked up. "You were right," he said to her in Merafien; and then, inside himself, "peace, be still."

Iareth gestured. "Will you sit? I believe Thierry has business to discuss."

"It's Valdin. In part," Thiercelin said, sitting. He looked down at his crossed ankles. "I've seen him—and talked to him—again."

"I, also." Iareth said. At Thiercelin's gesture of surprise, she added, "It was to be expected."

"I suppose so." Thiercelin frowned. "Graelis should explain, really. It's his theory."

Gracielis had sat down with his back to the window. He looked away, then said, "I'm content to be in your hands."

Thiercelin glared at him. "He thinks someone is trying to harm Merafi, and that Valdin is somehow involved. It sounds daft put like that, but . . ."

Iareth said, "There are many odd tales regarding the Tarnaroqui and their abilities. And others, of old powers." She looked at Gracielis without curiosity. "There are those of my people who hold such things unholy."

"Unholy," said Gracielis, "is preferable to absurd. It's less insulting."

Iareth said, "Tell me."

Gracielis looked at Thiercelin, who outlined the situation as they knew it. He avoided no part of it, not even the name of Kenan Orcandros. Iareth listened without comment. At the end of the account she was silent a moment; then she turned to Gracielis. "You saw a binding in water?" He nodded. "And you dreamed of Urien Armenwy, called Swanhame?"

"Yes." Gracielis hesitated. "And of you and someone whom I believe to be Kenan Orcandros."

She looked at her hands. After a moment, she said, "I wondered what it meant, that Valdin Allandur should tell me I was right. But now I think I understand." She rose and walked to the window. "There is a place in Lunedith, a waterfall named Saefoss. It is unhealthy. We seldom go there. But six years ago, I traveled there with Valdin and his party, and with Urien. By the side of the fall we were ambushed and several of us injured, including Valdin." She turned. "Do you know of this place?"

Gracielis smoothed his lace. Then he said, "I can hazard a guess." The tale was familiar to all of his training. Yestinn Allandur had enforced control on the old powers at one of their places of greatest potency, and then moved his own center to opaque Merafi. He had slain one of his own by treachery, by the side of the living fall. Gracielis said, "It is the place of Yestinn's compact. Where he shed the blood of his enemy, Gaverne Orcandros." He considered. "Was Kenan one of the ambushers?"

"Yes," Iareth said.

"And he was injured there?"

"Yes." She hesitated. "He had a hand in the wounding of Valdin *kai-reth*."

Gracielis shivered. An ancient pact, built on Orcandrin blood shed unwillingly at the hands of an Allandur. And now, Allandurin blood shed in the same place, equally unwillingly, by Orcandrin hands. Kenan's Orcandrin hands now linked in a working with the trained mind and strong gifts of Quenfrida.

Everyone was descended from the old clans except a handful of the Tarnaroqui. A handful whose ancestors had also struck bargains long ago, with old powers. But those bargains had not been for control. At the bidding of those distant priests, parts of the old power had put on human seeming and lain with humans to breed the likes of Quenfrida. The likes of Gracielis, too. The *undarii*, who could see the past and bind the dead and make use of the gifts offered by the awakening of old things. Those ancient powers lacked discrete awareness or individual consciousness, but they were strong and dangerous and they could, at a cost, be manipulated. By those who had the right blood.

Not wholly inhuman.

Kenan and Quenfrida had woken the past. Bound in blood and water and betrayal . . . It was a possibility

only half-credited even among the *undarii*. But Gracielis found no trouble in seeing where the temptation
lay. It would call loudly to Quenfrida, who had lost much
of her human power by choosing his flawed self as
acolyte.

She had another now, Lunedithin and Orcandrin, and
his touch lay alongside hers in the working that threatened Merafi.

They had woken the old power of water, and the river
was turning. Gracielis looked at Thiercelin and said,
softly, "No," and then, to the floor, "It's over, then."

"Oh, Graelis," Thiercelin said. Iareth was silent. Rising, Gracielis made himself go to a window and look
out. They were high here, on the hillside. On a normal
day he should have seen all Merafi laid out before him.
It was not a normal day. The tripartite course of the
river was shrouded in mist. Haze hid the west quarter.
Blue smoke drifted from the south, although the angle
of the house did not permit him to see that part of the
city well. Only the tower of the temple raked upward to
affirm the cityscape, and its shape was blurred.

Gracielis rubbed at his shoulder and sighed. He could
do nothing. For him there were no more choices. For
these others . . . Without turning, he said, "You must
leave."

"Oh, must we?" said Thiercelin.

Gracielis said, "Your river is turning." And then,
"Monseigneur, do you trust me?"

There was a pause. Then Thiercelin said, "I suppose
so. I asked you to help with my ghosts. And I haven't
strangled you yet."

"I'm grateful." Gracielis paused, looking at the temple.
A few short days ago he had stood on its roof with Yvelliane and asked idly about the river. "If you trust me, then
you must believe me. The troubles you already experience
will worsen." He turned, looked at Thiercelin. "It's simple.
The world you have known is ending."

Thiercelin's brows drew together. "Just like that?"

"Yes."

"Then we'd better do something about it." Thiercelin's voice held all the confidence of aristocracy. He stared at Gracielis, and his expression would brook no contradiction.

Gracielis looked at Iareth for support. Her face was neutral. Gracielis said, "But . . ." Then: "You don't understand. Monseigneur—Thierry—what you suggest can't be done."

"Why not?"

"Well . . ." Gracielis fumbled for words. He looked down at his bandaged wrists. "It isn't possible. You lack the knowledge and the resources. It's been too long since the old ways were credited here."

"Then I'll get help elsewhere," Thiercelin said.

"Where from?" Gracielis sat down on the window seat, and realized that he was shaking. "You'd have to find someone both willing and competent to undo what's been done. A high adept of the *undarii*. There's no one within three months' ride of here. Will you go all the way into the heart of Tarnaroq and try to convince them?"

"If I must."

"They won't believe you." Gracielis gestured hopelessly. "It would go against their interests, even granted that Quenfrida has probably acted without their knowledge. And if they did agree to help you, you lack the necessary time. Three months there, and three months back, without calculating how long it might take to convince them. Merafi won't hold so long. The tidal bore at next moon-double will destroy you. It's too late. I'm sorry."

Thiercelin inhaled. "Valdin tried to warn me. I owe it to him to do something."

"Lord Valdarrien's ghost is nothing but a side effect of the power that awakens," Gracielis said. "His blood was shed to arouse it. You've already done a great deal, but . . ."

Thiercelin cut him off. "I doubt it. I haven't even told Yviane most of what I know."

"There's nothing she can do."

"How can you be so sure?" Thiercelin leaned forward and glared. "Do you know everything about us all of a sudden?" Gracielis looked down. "She taught you well, your Quenfrida. Don't cross her. Don't question her. Take her every action as irrevocable and infallible." Behind his curtaining hair, Gracielis closed his eyes. "That's a counsel of impotence, Graelis. I won't follow it. I won't believe it until I've tried everything I can think of first. You may be right, but I swear by all your superstitions that I'll die before I just give in. And if I don't do any good, at least I'll have tried. Which is more than I'll be able to say for you."

"Forgive me," Gracielis said, into his hands.

"Help me," Thiercelin said right back.

Gracielis was still, listening to the pulse beat in his marred wrists. He said, "I can't."

"Because it's forbidden? Or are you simply scared?"

Iareth said, "Do not."

Thiercelin ignored her. "Well, Graelis?"

Gracielis said, "I'm not capable. I'm not *undarios*." He met Thiercelin's eyes. "I lack the knowledge needed." He paused, then added, "We aren't adequate to this task."

Thiercelin looked down. Iareth said, "That may be true only in part. Might not assistance be sought?"

"The distance . . ." Gracielis began.

She shook her head. "I have already written to Urien Armenwy. He is wise in many things." She hesitated. "He is not of your *undarii*. But he has the old clan gifts." She looked at Gracielis. "He has the knowledge you speak of. And he will come; I am sure of it."

"When?" Thiercelin said.

"Soon."

Thiercelin nodded. Then he turned back to Gracielis. "You feed information to Yviane. Am I so different?"

"No."

"Then help me."

There was a long silence. Gracielis looked away, toward the window and the mist. He wanted no part of this. He was inadequate. He had lost her already, sky-eyed Quenfrida. His death was written. He had no need to court another.

If he refused, it would be graceless. If he accepted . . . Quenfrida could only kill him once. He was not safe, whatever he did. There was no sanctuary deep enough to guard him from waterborne death and Valdarrien.

He glanced at Iareth. She sat motionless, watching the floor. The long line of her, curved through head and spine, bespoke serenity. Merafi was no more her city than it was his.

He would not let himself think about that. He would permit himself nothing regarding her, for she was no part of him.

Dead Valdarrien had come back. To warn or to take or to try again to possess Iareth Yscoithi. If Gracielis refused, he would place no obstacles in the path Valdarrien sought importunately through his own dreams and flaws. Yet, if he helped Thiercelin . . . There were no guarantees. He doubted there was anyone within a thousand miles with the power to force Quenfrida to give up what she had gained.

He twisted his lovelock round a finger, and said, "I'll do what you want. I'll help you. But it won't work. I lack the strengths you need."

"We'll see," said Thiercelin.

Dusk was falling as Thiercelin and Gracielis made their way back to the Phoenix Inn, where Thiercelin had taken rooms for them both. It was raining again, and cold. Thiercelin at first tried to keep up a conversation, but he received only monosyllabic replies. Gracielis had withdrawn, swathed in a cloak. He walked quickly. To his surprise, Thiercelin had to lengthen his stride to keep up. When they reached the inn, Gracielis excused himself and vanished into his own rooms. His presence prickled at the edges of Thiercelin's awareness, like the first hint of a storm. Thiercelin changed for dinner and snapped at his unfortunate valet. He had hoped, despite himself, for some word, some sign that Yvelliane missed him. There was nothing. Well, he would prove himself to her anyway. He would face this nightmare that Gracielis saw and fight it and show her that he was not Valdarrien. He would help her even if she did not seek it of him. Perhaps he would never be able to make her love him, but at least she might see him as he was and not as simply her brother's shadow.

He had to send a message in to remind Gracielis to come and eat. On his arrival, Gracielis looked absently at the meal laid out in Thiercelin's private parlor and said, "I don't think I . . ."

"Sit down," Thiercelin said. Gracielis obeyed. "When did you last eat?"

"Yesterday. But . . ."

"But nothing. I don't want you fading out on me." Gracielis pulled a small face, then inclined his head in graceful resignation. He raised a hand to push his hair back. The bandage on his arm looked bulky. Thiercelin studied him, then said, "Won't work. I don't have time to feel sympathetic."

"Or cause, I think."

"Quite." Thiercelin began to serve himself. "Moreover, I've as much reason to feel sorry for myself as you, and I'm not indulging in self-starvation."

"No." Gracielis picked up a piece of bread and looked at it. "I'll eat. To please you." He spoke softly. His outrageous eyes held Thiercelin's. It was a deadly beauty. Thiercelin looked away and added unnecessary beans to his plate.

They ate in silence, Gracielis sparingly. Thiercelin caught himself watching the movements of the bandaged hands and had to force his attention away. He was mar-

ried to Yvelliane, however little she might want him.
This was a foolishness only, a product of loneliness and
confusion and the artifice of painted eyes.

He had asked and been refused. Better to remember
the wisdom in that refusal and think of something else.
How Valdarrien would laugh. Would have laughed, cal-
lous as ever before another's difficulty.

He could hear the rain pounding down outside. Gracielis' fair skin was golden in the candlelight. He would
taste of honey. *Think of Yvelliane, think only of
Yvelliane* . . . In four days he would see her again. Thiercelin poured himself wine and drank it off in one
draught. This was folly. Gracielis reached for the wine,
and his perfume enveloped Thiercelin like a veil. His
eyes met Thiercelin's. He arrested the motion.

Despite the wine, Thiercelin's mouth was dry. He
said, "Well?"

Gracielis said, gently, "Thank you. You were right to
make me eat."

"And drink?" Thiercelin gestured at the wine. "I
thought you didn't."

"I don't. Usually." Deliberately, Gracielis poured himself a half glass, and raised it. "Shall I toast your
health?"

"If you want to."

"So. Your fortune, monseigneur." Gracielis drank.
Then he put the glass down and said, "You know what
I am. My profession."

"Meaning what?"

"This." Gracielis lowered his beautiful eyes, and
looked sidelong. "It's a part of it. Those who would be
undarios are trained in seduction."

Gigolo and spy. And something more. Practiced, tried
and tested; designed to please. Thiercelin said, "Is that
supposed to help? I don't know what to do."

"It's supposed," said Gracielis, "to explain."

Thiercelin said, "I love Yviane. I don't need complica-
tions. My marriage is shaky enough already." Gracielis

watched him, and his eyes were kind. Thiercelin sighed. "You're not helping."

"No." Gracielis rose. "I'll go." His half-finished drink stood on the table between them. "I regret the inconvenience."

"Do you?" There was no reply. Thiercelin hesitated, then said, "Am I being unfair?"

"Not really."

"This afternoon—I pressured you. I know it can't be easy . . . to try to do what's needed to help Merafi."

Gracielis laughed. It was so unexpected Thiercelin stared at him. Gracielis paused, then said, "Forgive me. It was the understatement. 'Not easy,' in place of 'impossible.' "

"I wish you wouldn't keep saying that."

"Forgive me," Gracielis repeated. He went to the door. "Good night, monseigneur."

"Thierry. Good night, Graelis."

The door shut. Thiercelin stared at it for long moments, trying to order his thoughts. He might call it spite or resentment, that he was tempted in the wake of Yvelliane's coldness. Honesty forbade him. He had not forgotten a touch, an embrace. Bred to seduction . . . The opening hung there, tantalizing as Gracielis himself, offering an excuse. Thiercelin picked up Gracielis' discarded glass and drained it. He was old enough by now to take responsibility for himself.

To choose for himself.

He did not knock on the connecting door. Gracielis met his eyes and said nothing. His fair skin was soft and flushed at a touch, although the taste of him was jasmine and not honey. His hands were gentle. Shivering under them, Thiercelin said, "Don't ask," and felt laughter run through the slight frame.

"Never, I swear it," said Gracielis.

13

L ELADRIEN HAD WARNED HIM. Joyain tried
not to remember that, as he gazed around him. He
had wanted this duty. He had spent the last two days
in restless anticipation of it. It could not be as bad as
it looked.

It was raining. Ash and debris collected in the gutters,
greasy, malodorous. The unpaved roads were treacherous underfoot: a man could easily come to grief. Looking
down toward the remains of the local almshouse, he re-
pressed a shudder. Leladrien had been right. This kind
of thing was beyond him.

There was almost never any trouble in this part of
Merafi. Built outside the south part of the old wall, it
sprawled out onto the flood plain. It was neither prosperous nor prestigious: a quarter for lesser artisans, for respectable shop laborers, for shabby-genteel widows, and
retired, impoverished clerks.

It was a smoldering mess.

Joyain had not expected this. He looked back over his
shoulder at the southwest gate and caught the eye of the
ensign. He said, "When did this start?"

"I don't know, sir," the ensign said. Joyain looked at
him in disgust. "I was off duty last night."

"And you don't read reports?"

"I haven't had time, yet, sir. We've been busy."

"Clearly. What happened to last night's duty officer?"
The ensign looked uncomfortable. Joyain said, "Well?"

"The sergeant said he didn't report in, sir. The sickness . . ." The ensign reddened under Joyain's gaze. "The watch are overstretched."

"So I keep hearing." Joyain looked back at the fires and sighed. At least there had been no wind last night. The flames had started somewhere on the west edge and spread slowly, hindered by the damp. Even so, about half the district was a blackened ruin, and an infantry patrol was picking its way through it disconsolately.

The fire had started during the night. The watch had not reported it until noon. That they were overworked was undeniable, but all the same . . . Joyain sighed again and rubbed his palm against his thigh. "Well, done is done. I'm not blaming you, Ensign. But I recommend that you start collecting some eyewitness accounts. The captain will want an explanation."

"Yes, sir."

"Get on with it, then." Joyain began to walk back toward the guardhouse. "I'll be down here all day—you can send witnesses to me as and when. And I'll want casualty figures." And after that, the gravedigging would have to start. He'd think about that later.

"Yes, sir," the ensign said.

The office at the guard post was not of the largest. Nor the tidiest, for that matter. Whatever division of the watch held it did not seem to consider the place a high priority. Joyain suspected that personnel had been quietly creamed off from here to help with the more serious problems in the shantytown and low city. And if the duty officer had taken sick . . . That, too, should have been reported immediately, but it was beginning to look as though the overnight staff had been two troopers and an elderly sergeant.

Against procedure, of course. But in the current state of affairs, understandable. Hard luck for the watch that their laxity had happened to coincide with a night on which someone had let their cooking fire get out of control.

It took him several minutes of concerted searching, but eventually he located the sergeant's report. The fire had been noticed a little before dawn, and a man was dispatched to investigate. There was no record in the report of his having returned. Joyain made a mental note to follow that up. No comment was hazarded as to the origin of the blaze. However, the sergeant had remarked on the surprisingly sluggish attempts of the local inhabitants in trying to combat it and the general reluctance to approach the area. The center of the fire was believed to have been in a small dip toward the edge of the district, which might explain why the guard post had been so slow to notice it.

The fire had begun to die after a heavy shower around dawn.

Joyain finished reading through the notes (the spelling was appalling) and leaned back in his chair. Local disinclination to help was nothing new, of course, but in this area it was a little surprising. Surprising, too, that someone would have been careless when fuel was so expensive. Drunk, perhaps, or asleep. It could not have been arson, not here. No profit for any of the gangs, and precious little incentive. No sickness down here, either, as yet; or so it seemed. No other immediately obvious reason for fire-starting . . .

Mist gathered in dips, especially beside the river. Mist thick and arcane with formless enemies, who battered and crushed. Who retreated before fire . . . The thought was insidious. Joyain resisted the urge to push it away, and frowned. All right, suppose he was correct. The attack suffered by himself and Iareth had been real enough; and the toll of bodies found in the low city suggested that the experience was not unique. Admittedly he had seen no official reports of anything like the event he had witnessed, but he had himself deliberately elected to play ignorant, as least officially. He probably wasn't unique in that, either.

So far nearly all the victims had been drunkards or

vagrants. People with no walls to put between themselves and the night.

The army high command cared very little for such people. While waiting in the colonel's antechamber two days before, Joyain had overheard two of the aides-de-camp expressing relief at the fortuitous "cleaning out" of shantytown.

There had been no reports of anything odd or dangerous from north of the river. No bodies in the west quarter or on the aristocrats' hill. The worst incidents had been from areas close to the southernmost of the three river channels, such as the shantytown and the new dock and this district.

No, it was ridiculous. There was always discontent in the low city. There was always sickness in the shanties and the docks. There were always street gangs.

What if he had not been the only person to discover that the mist creatures would retreat from fire? What if there was someone scared enough to fire an entire district in order to drive away night terrors?

He was out of touch, that was the problem. Stuck in the Lunedithin embassy, he had lost track of mess gossip. Once his half-troop arrived down here, he'd take a trip up to the barracks and see what he could pick up. Maybe Leladrien would have heard something. There was almost certainly a perfectly rational explanation for what had happened to him.

There was a knock at the office door. Looking up, Joyain called, "Come in."

The ensign entered. He saluted, and said, "You asked for witnesses, sir."

"Yes."

"I've found someone. He lives here, and he seems pretty respectable."

"Good. Show him in." Joyain gave a surreptitious tug to his cassock and put his gloves back on. He could do nothing about the disorder in the room, but at least he could look tidy and efficient.

The man who was ushered in was elderly and looked tired. His clothes were impeccable if outmoded, and showed signs of much diligent mending. Bowing stiffly to Joyain, he said, "Good day, Lieutenant."

"Good day, Monsieur . . . ah . . ."

"Banvier."

"Monsieur Banvier. Please be seated. It's good of you to give up your time." Joyain waited for the old man to sit down before continuing. "I'm trying to find out how last night's fire got started. I understand you saw it?"

"Not the beginning. I didn't see that. But when it started to spread . . ."

"Of course. Can you tell me what time that was, approximately?" There didn't appear to be a blank piece of paper anywhere in the desk. Joyain turned over an old duty roster and looked for a pen. "It woke you up, I expect?"

"No, I wasn't asleep." Monsieur Banvier leaned forward. "I don't sleep at night now. I was at my prayers."

"I see." Joyain found a pen, albeit very battered, and dipped it in the ink. As he expected, it was scratchy and blunt. "So this would be about when . . . ?"

"I couldn't hear the bell. The wind wasn't blowing and I don't own a clock. But Handmoon was starting to set. That's when it's most dangerous."

Joyain looked up. "What do you mean?"

Banvier nodded at him. "You're not with the watch, are you?"

"I'm a staff officer in Her Majesty's household cavalry."

"I thought so. I was a stores clerk in the arsenal. I couldn't tell the watch this, you understand."

"Of course," said Joyain, who didn't. "Please go on." This assignment was getting weirder by the minute. And he'd found the Lunedithin a strain. "Handmoon-set, you say?"

"That's right." Banvier looked at him. "My brother went for a priest, nigh on fifty years ago. He's dead now, but he told me a thing or two, and I've remembered. That's how I knew when to be careful." He met Joyain's eyes. "The old kind are coming back, like in the stories. Neither dead nor alive, neither man nor beast, killing and maiming because they know no better. They killed my neighbor. He'd gone outside, you see, near the river."

"Near the river?" said Joyain, who was getting confused.

"My brother told me about it. How there used to be creatures made of mist and air. But the old kings bound them and drove them out and so we've been safe. But not anymore. I saw it, you see. About a week ago, written on Mothmoon." Banvier sighed. "Death in the water. First in the shantytown and the docks, as ever, and the low city. Then here, and next . . ." He shrugged. "Who knows? Someone should tell the queen."

"Umm," said Joyain. He had stopped writing. None of this made any sense. It was worse than the things Gracieux had thought up to frighten Amalie. He said, "And the fire?"

"They run from it, those creatures. I saw them through the cracks in my shutters. I watched and I prayed and I kept my own fire lit." Banvier said. "Beautiful, in a way, but not like us. I've never seen anything like them, and I've seen some strange things. Dead things, even, and traces." Joyain suppressed a shiver. "I'm telling you the truth. You do believe me?"

Creatures of mist, inhuman, which retreat from fire. Gracielis' tales, of river-borne danger . . . Joyain said, "Well, it's unusual . . ."

"But true."

"Your brother told you about these creatures?" Joyain knew he was buying time, trying to put his thoughts into some species of order. "And he was a priest?" If this was priestly knowledge, why had there been such a silence from them? They were usually all too happy to find excuses to call attention to themselves.

"Yes, and no," Banvier said. "They don't believe, there on their island. These are old things, I told you."

"Yes, of course."

"My brother saw things too, more than me. That's why he went there, but they had no use for that. He used to read, looking for explanations. He said that some of the old books talked about it." Banvier hesitated. "You could look there, if you don't believe me. Or find a Tarnaroqui. They're fey. They'll know all about this. They'll be laughing."

Joyain was beginning to feel irritated. First Gracieux, now this. The ensign had called the man respectable, but the ensign had reason to be less than delighted by Joyain's presence here. Either something was so wrong that the city itself was losing its senses or he was getting the runaround.

He said briskly, "Well, that's very interesting." Kenan Orcandros had some kind of relationship with a Tarnaroqui aide, Iareth had said . . . It was scandalmongering. A few high tides, a lot of unseasonal rain, and tongues began to wag. He wouldn't be at all surprised if Gracieux turned out to be an agent provocateur . . . Out loud, he said, "Do you have Tarnaroqui blood yourself, Monsieur Banvier? Or Tarnaroqui contacts?"

"Oh, no." Banvier looked shocked. "I'm Merafien born and bred these five generations. You're doubtful; I can see it. So I'll tell you something. I wasn't going to let anyone know this. No point. But when I saw you, I thought you might credit me. I could see it, you see, behind you. You've been touched by them, those mist-things. Their feel is on you. So I thought I could tell you. It'll happen again. First this, then the sickness."

"I see." Joyain rubbed his eyes.

Banvier rose. "The watch know about the creatures too, but they won't admit it. If you stay overnight down here, you'll see. But you must stay inside and keep your fire lit."

"I'll bear it in mind. Thank you."

"You're welcome." Banvier bowed, and turned to go. In the doorway he halted and looked back. "Oh, the fire. I'd forgotten. I've an idea where it started, although I didn't see, as I said." Joyain, resigned, raised his brows. "There's a girl—was, I should say—who lived on the west edge of the district. She made her living sewing. She often sewed half the night, and burned a fire. But she always left her shutters open. The fire will have started at her place, I'll warrant."

"Thank you," said Joyain automatically, as the door thumped shut. He put his hand over his eyes and sighed. Then he looked up and yelled for the ensign.

"It's so slow," Kenan said. He pushed his chair back from the table and stood. "I'd thought that by now . . . I'd hopes of something more immediate and dramatic." A smile twisted the corners of his mouth. "I've waited so long."

"In your terms, perhaps." Quenfrida was disapproving. She put down her embroidery frame and looked at him. "You're losing your sense of perspective, my Kenan."

"Am I?" Kenan frowned. "You credit me with overmuch interest in your goals. You forget that I have my own expectations. I've waited all my life for the moment when I might free my homeland from the hands of the Merafiens."

"And I have waited four times your lifetime." She spoke calmly, but her face was mocking. "Patience. You're not dealing with human things now. The old powers are not swift to waken. They've slept a long time."

"Rain and mist and paltry deaths." Kenan walked to the window and stared out into the rainy darkness. No lights showed in the houses around the courtyard. A depressing smell of rotting vegetation mingled with a sickly tang of caramel from a nearby confectioners' shop. He drummed his fingers and sighed. "Is that all?"

"It will escalate." Quenfrida rose and opened a small cabinet with a key from a chain at her throat. She took out a decanter and two glasses. The firelight played pretty games with the color of her skin. "The time is right for us now, by moons and by water. It won't be much longer."

Kenan watched the rain. "Yet meanwhile, I still see nothing."

"That, too, will come." She hesitated. "Ghost-sight isn't everything. It isn't essential."

"Your first disciple has it."

"And it is of no use to him." She came to the window and laid a hand on his shoulder. "Forget him, and drink with me." The air was abruptly heady with her perfume. "Waiting is its own art."

"I can so nearly touch it." Kenan pushed her away from him. "I feel what is out there, but it remains outside my reach. I've made my compact, yet my hands remain unfilled." He hesitated. "Perhaps the bloodletting at Saefoss was insufficient. Perhaps injury and what I did in the the old clan hall weren't enough. Perhaps I should take a life in the ritual."

"That rite unlocks power only in those with the right blood. You're clan-bred. It won't serve you. You have other powers, clan skills he can't ever attain."

"And now? What do we do?" Kenan looked at his hands. "You speak of death in Merafi. Yet when I walk its streets I see nothing, sense nothing."

"You are its master. It dare not come near you." She took his arm. Placing one of her small hands under his, she formed it into a hollow. As he looked down at her, she smiled. She said, "As to now, you practice; and you observe." Heat danced along the edges of his palm, signaled in wispy smoke. Quenfrida lowered her eyelids, and the candles grew dim. The room was very still: he could hear only her breathing, regular as any clock. She said, softly, "Work through me. Conjure it."

He placed his other hand under hers, and fought to

bring his breathing similarly into line. Her heat blistered him, but the force of her would not permit him to remove his hands. Closing his eyes, he sought his way to it, along the patterned channels of his blood, clamorous with confusion. Shapes twisted away from him, limping. He clutched at them with hungry fingers, trying to turn them outside their nature. Clan-blood, structured in the material world; none so pure, perhaps, but unbearably human. His hands convulsed with the effort. Quenfrida stood beside him, unmoving as dead air. He could barely feel her, beneath the heat, the pain. He made one last, immense effort, and felt sweat soak him, His head pounded. The shutters banged and slammed in a sudden gust of wind. The room quivered in unexpected cold. He could touch nothing new. His head fell back; he gasped. Quenfrida forced his hands away, and the room seared with a light so intense he could see it through his closed lids. He stumbled back, panting, dropped to his knees. The floor was damp, sticky: opening his eyes, he found himself slumped into a pile of decomposing leaves. Quenfrida watched him. He could not quite bring himself to look into her eyes. Into the brightness of her, sky-shaded. Light danced around her, weaving caresses into her creamy complacency. She shook the toffee-gold hair back from her brow, and color shivered from it to illumine the walls. Flames danced in her upturned hands. Within Kenan, some animal remnant awoke, urging flight, cringing before the drenching odor of honeysuckle and ash. He licked dry lips. He said, "Quenfrida. Quenfrida *undaria*." His voice betrayed him, edged with the fear bound into his otter-clan-blood.

She looked down, and the flames were extinguished. She placed a palm against a pane of window glass, and the wind died. She drew in two sharp breaths, and the room returned to its normal temperature. She looked at Kenan, and for the briefest half-instant, swan wings shadowed her sky-blue eyes. He shivered, still on his knees, and brought his seared hands in toward him. They were whole, unharmed. He cradled them against him and watched her gather her skirts to her. She looked in some distaste at the floor.

He said, "It was already raining. Your wind brought the water in."

"Most likely." Her voice was perfectly controlled. She smiled at him, and her eyes were clear. "Come: we'll find a drier room."

The hand she held out to him was small and shapely, no probable vessel for the powers she juggled. Climbing to his feet, he took it and found it sweet and cool. He said, "What did you do?"

"Party tricks. Bring the wine." She had gathered up the glasses; obediently he collected the decanter, and let her lead him upstairs.

He said, "I can do none of that. Not one part. It remains beyond me."

"That is due to your clan-blood." Quenfrida took them into a large chamber. Placing the glasses on a chest top, she pulled open the tapestried hangings of the high-post bed and sat down upon it, dropping off her shoes. "It's to be expected. But not everyone of the *undarii* has the ability to work with those ways, anyway. I am aspected in sky, and wind: those tricks are strongest in that quadrant."

"But *he* can do it."

"As it happens, no." Quenfrida smiled beautifully. "Pour me a drink and come here, my Kenan. It doesn't matter what Gracielis can do."

Kenan said, "To you, perhaps. It's different for me."

Laughter danced in her clever face. She leaned back on her elbows and looked at him sidelong. "Jealous, my heart?"

"I think not." He handed her the wine. "Not, at least, in the way you insinuate."

"I can expect, then, no rivalry over my person?" Quenfrida laughed, then sat up. "He could not do what you've done: bind the old powers to his will."

"Naturally. He lacks Orcandrin blood. You keep reminding me that such is the major requisite for that deed."

She placed a thoughtful hand on his chest and looked up at him from under her lashes. "Any of the Orcandrin can bleed. But few have the necessary forcefulness to compel binding. What I was alluding to was his lack of strength." Her voice turned gentle. "You can't do conjuring tricks. But you are *undarios*. He failed. You can forget him."

He put his hand over hers and looked at her pensively. "You're most insistent on that point, Quena."

"Well, it happens to be true."

"Mayhap. But I recall that you never discard anything. Don't play games with me."

"I'll consider it." Her voice was indolent. She tugged at a button on his doublet speculatively. "If you behave likewise regarding me."

"Think you I would do otherwise?"

"Perhaps." Quenfrida pulled away from him, and began to unpin her hair. He watched. After a moment, she said, "You're wrong, by the way."

"Concerning what?"

"The extent to which our working has progressed. You ignore the extent of symptoms already present here."

"I would have the power to see it."

"There are more forms of vision than those of the eyes." She finished with her hair, and began to undo her bodice. "Help me, please." He complied, a little stiffly. "So prim!" He avoided her gaze. "You are very nervous, these last few days."

"It is to be anticipated, a little impatience. The queen has men stationed in my house to watch me. My entourage are restless."

"Indeed." Quenfrida stood and stepped out of her dress. She started to unfasten the rosettes holding up her stockings. "Your impatience is in itself a sort of vision. You don't see it, but you feel it."

"You believe so?" Kenan considered, not wholly displeased with the notion.

"Yes." She turned to face him, loosening her petticoats with slow deliberation. "You're good on feeling, my Kenan."

"So," said Kenan and swept himself into her scented embrace.

There is a whirring of wings, a steady beat driving the air down away before them, across the sky, across moons, painted in reflected light and memory. The sky is clear at his back. There is mist before him. He cleaves it, straight, stark, bright with alien beauty. This is his world, more than any other. He knows it at gut level, along the vein, through the nerve; it strengthens within his hollow bones. None closer, none more directly born into it. The waterborne changes are flagged bright for him, tasting danger through bird senses. Full circle, back again to the very starting point of his delicate, long race-memory. They have troubled his rest. They have tampered with the rhythm of his serene days, and he will find them and see for himself the nature of their broken revolution.

His is no ordinary fear of changes. The wind may blow as it will, for all of him, but he cannot help but feel its teachings. His shadow is long, occluding the disk of Handmoon, long as his balancing, killing hands.

He is Urien Armenwy, called Swanhame, drawn down from the north.

There is a chill wind blowing.

14

YVELLIANE SHOOK OUT HER SKIRTS and regarded her reflection. The russet gown was neat
enough, if not showy, and at least she looked competent.
She had forgotten to bring any of her good jewelry.
Well, there was no one she particularly needed to im-
press tonight. She would do. Of course she would do.
There was a faint line between her brows, and her eyes
were dark-circled. There no longer seemed to be sufficient hours in any day. So much that needed to be
done . . . She put the thought from her, that personal
problems might have contributed to her fatigue. She had
overseen too many years of Valdarrien's wildness to be
ruffled by the minor vagaries of Thiercelin. Jealousy was
a petty thing, and spite was worse. Thiercelin was hardly
property, at his age. They both had the right to make
their own courses. She had other concerns. She had to
keep thinking that. She might afford no weaknesses.

Greater concerns. Think of Firomelle, grown so frail.
Think of murders committed by night in the low city,
and sickness, and discontent. Think of all that, and turn
away from the intrusion of private matters. A marriage
was not worth more than the safety of a state.

There had been stones thrown at her carriage today.
That was enough to worry over. It was only tiredness
that pulled her thoughts back to Thiercelin. She sighed
and lifted her chin. It grew late. It was time for her to

present herself in the Grand Audience Chamber, with calm demeanor, dancing in the face of civil adversity.

The Chamber was filling when she sailed in. Firomelle had not yet appeared, nor could Yvelliane see any trace of Thiercelin amidst the throng. She schooled herself against irritation. His distaste for these affairs was renowned; and both Gracielis and Miraude (who was to partner him) were capable of taking many hours over polishing themselves for public display. Yvelliane paused in the door, smiling, then joined a fellow councillor.

The Tarnaroqui ambassador bowed to her. She curtsied in return and avoided his eyes. Quenfrida hung on his arm, and her smile glittered with malice.

There was no time to spare for this ridiculous obsession with Thiercelin. Yvelliane turned her back very firmly to the door and began a conversation with a colleague regarding the measures being taken in the city by the watch.

It was past eleven by the time the footman announced the rest of the Far Blays party. Firomelle had appeared and sat with Prince Laurens by the fire. She looked pale and strained and she coughed too often. Laurens was plainly perturbed. Yvelliane had not as yet had a chance to speak with either of them. Now she glanced once more at the queen, put her glass down on a table, and drew in a long breath. Her companion said, "Your sister-in-law gets lovelier every time I see her."

Yvelliane permitted herself to look round. Miraude glittered in the doorway, dramatic in crimson and black, Thiercelin and Gracielis flanking her. Yvelliane said, "You should tell her. I'd say she's wearing half the annual military budget in rubies."

"At least."

Miraude waved. Yvelliane nodded in reply and waited as her sister-in-law towed her escorts through the crowd. Thiercelin looked bored and sensible in the same burgundy doublet he had worn to the last five royal soirées.

He clashed with Miraude, rather. He would not meet Yvelliane's eyes. Gracielis, surprisingly, wore black. He looked directly at her and smiled outrageously.

"Such a crush," said Miraude, arriving at Yvelliane's elbow. "I shall lose my breath completely." She sounded rather pleased by the prospect. "Goodness, Yviane. You're looking very . . . practical."

"I'm going hunting right after the party." Yvelliane wrinkled her nose. "You look splendid."

"Thank you."

"As usual. And you're late."

"As usual." Miraude looked deliciously guilty. "I couldn't find my earrings. Blame Thierry, he rushed me."

"Hmm. Always fatal." Yvelliane looked at her husband. He returned the gaze and kissed her hand. To her companion she said, "You know my family, of course, Lord Yvaux?"

"Indeed." Yvaux had made his bow. Now he kissed Miraude's hand and nodded at Thiercelin, who had gone back to looking bored. "A pleasure, as always."

"And Monsieur de Varnaq?" Yvelliane completed the introductions, faintly distracted. Something in Gracielis' demeanor was bizarrely familiar. Some echo, in stark black, half recollected. She did not recall having formerly seen him dress his hair away from his face.

Miraude said, "Did I thank you, Yviane?"

"I don't think so. What for?"

"My escort." Miraude looked from one to the other. "Even if Thierry doesn't go with my dress."

"You're welcome," Yvelliane said. And then, "Such vanity, Mimi!" Miraude blushed. Across the room, the Lunedithin party was announced. Yvelliane looked up to see Kenan, scowling and pale, accompanied by Tafarin Morwenedd and Iareth Yscoithi in green and cream. Beside her, Yvaux said something, but she barely heard it as memory fell into place. Iareth in green, and Valdarrien sulky at her side in black, hair drawn back, ear pierced by a single diamond. Six years ago and more. It could be coincidence only. Light caught on the stud in Gracielis' left ear and fractured. The bow at his nape was velvet.

It made no sense. Gracielis did not even look at Iareth. Yvelliane was imagining things. She smiled at Yvaux and said, "I beg your pardon?"

"I was merely commenting on the heat," he said.

"Appalling, isn't it?" Yvelliane fanned herself, still only half-listening. Thiercelin would not look at her. Kenan was moving toward them. The Tarnaroqui party had dispersed about the room. Miraude touched her sleeve, murmured "I need to talk to you later." Yvelliane nodded. Gracielis looked at her, and smiled. There were hollows beneath his eyes and he was perhaps a shade too pale. Yvelliane said, "I didn't know you liked black."

"I don't." Gracielis looked down at his gloves, one dark, one light. His scent covered him like a cloud. "It was an impulse only." He looked at Miraude. "And a most fortunate one."

"Evidently," Yvelliane said. "Thierry was less lucky." Miraude raised a brow. Gracielis favored Yvelliane with a speculative look, then his long lashes swept down.

Thiercelin said, "Someone has to be the loser. Come and clash with me on the dance floor, Mimi, since Graelis seems to have forgotten to ask you." He still did not look at Yvelliane, holding out a hand to Miraude, and leading her out. Gracielis kept his eyes downcast.

Graelis . . . It was of no import, whatever there might be between Gracielis and her husband. Only Firomelle mattered. Yvelliane looked up to see Kenan only feet away, and suppressed a sigh.

Gracielis said, "Monseigneur de Sannazar has stolen my partner." And then, "I shall have to steal his." The hazel eyes were wicked. To Yvaux, he added, "If monseigneur has no objection?"

"Go ahead." Yvaux was amused by his dramatics.

Gracielis bowed flamboyantly then offered a scented

hand to Yvelliane. "Dance with me, madame, or my heart will break."

"That," said Yvelliane, "I should like to see." Gracielis clutched at his chest. Kenan had almost reached them. Shaking her head, she said, "Oh, very well. If it'll stop you playacting."

He led her onto the floor. She said, "I'm not dressed for this."

"Perhaps not. But it makes no difference. You'd be beautiful in sackcloth."

"Oh, naturally!" The figure separated them, and she took a promenade on the arm of a senior nobleman. Returning to Gracielis, she looked into his pretty eyes and said, "I've something to ask you. You haven't forgotten your promise, I hope?"

"Your every word is engraved upon my heart." Gracielis paused to complete a turn, then continued, "Shall I recite them back to you?"

"It hardly seems worth it. Tell me, is there any special significance attached to clan halls in your beliefs?"

"There could be. It would depend on the circumstances."

"I see." They changed places. "I'll present you to the Tarnaroqui party after this dance."

"As you wish." The dance again parted them. Returning, Gracielis said, "The redheaded gentleman in gray is the Lunedithin prince, isn't he?"

"Kenan Orcandros, yes. What of him?"

"Nothing I may tell you on the dance floor." The words were serious, but the accompanying glance most certainly was not. "Perhaps I might reveal myself to you in the long gallery? Or some other private place?"

"I'm sure you might." The figure called for her to place her right hand in his. "But I've other concerns at present."

Gracielis looked at her sidelong. "Will I survive your indifference?"

She turned in a swirl of satin skirts. "Probably." His

eyes played tragedy. She said, "Do you know any of the Tarnaroqui delegation already?"

"It depends." Gracielis took two paces back, executed a series of complex steps, and offered her his light-clad hand.

"On what?"

"The circumstances in which we find ourselves."

"I see." The dance again separated them. Yvelliane danced a measure with a fellow councillor, then returned to Gracielis for the promenade.

He said, "You should dance more often. It suits you."

"I've better uses for my time."

"Forgive me," Gracielis said. "You were smiling until I reminded you of your duties." She looked away, counting steps. He said, "Lord Thiercelin misses you."

"That's nice. Are you a go-between, or are you just being tactful?" She could see Thiercelin dancing in the next set. He appeared utterly oblivious to her, laughing at something Miraude had said. He had no need of a harassed and scratchy wife. No more than she had need of him. He had brought Gracielis to live with him at the Phoenix. She courted censure, dancing with her husband's lover. She snapped her gaze away from Thiercelin.

Gracielis said, "He misses you and you are missing him. Be kind: it becomes you."

She could not be distracted by this, not here. She said, "Not now. Don't meddle."

"As you wish." But Gracielis was disapproving. As the dance ended he bowed over her fingers. "You needn't introduce me to your Tarnaroqui. I can tell you all you want to know without that."

"I daresay, but I rather wanted to see how they react to you."

To her surprise, he laughed. "You'll cut yourself. Let me do this my own way. Prince Kenan is looking at you."

"How nice for him." Yvelliane did not trouble to re-

turn Kenan's gaze, searching the crowd for the Tarnaroqui group. "I have considerable diplomatic experience
of my own, you know."

"I know." Unexpectedly Gracielis kissed her hand.
Then, holding on to it, he said, "The one you want is
Quenfrida. I'll tell you anything you want to know about
her, if you'll present me to the Lunedithin heir."

Yvelliane looked at him, surprised. He returned the
gaze levelly. She asked, "Does she know you? Quenfrida, I mean."

"Oh, yes." Something, some emotion, gilded his
voice. "Intimately."

"And Thierry?" It was not the question she had intended to ask.

He said, "Come into the gallery," and slipped her
hand through his arm. Even in high shoes, he was fractionally shorter than she was. She let him lead her, aware
that this was not the result she had intended. Across the
room, Thiercelin had passed Miraude to another courtier
and was heading for the gaming room. Yvelliane wondered if he had yet outrun his quarter's allowance. The
room was far too warm.

The gallery was cooler. Gracielis, who had the trick
of appearing familiar with his surroundings wherever he
found himself, drew her into a convenient curtained embrasure, and handed her on to the window seat. He said,
"You can do nothing to Quenfrida. It's too late for
that."

"What do you mean?" Yvelliane fixed him with a firm
eye and tried not to glare. He twisted his rose-colored
lovelock about a finger. She said, "She knows you intimately?"

Gracielis took her hand in his and looked down at it.
"My whole life. But you must trust me all the same, for
I've made a promise and I'll keep it."

She took her hand away. "You'll forgive me if I'm
skeptical?" He spread his hands before him, graceful,

diffident. "I don't have the time right now to play games."

"So." Sitting down beside her, he hesitated, rubbing his shoulder. "I'll honor our agreement. But it does no good. You recall what you said, when I asked you what would happen if the river ever turned against Merafi?"

"Yes."

He turned to face her. "It's happening."

Such things did not happen, save in stories. Such things did not happen in Merafi. She said, "Tell me."

He told her in level, measured words, and she listened without interruption. She knew enough of him to recognize his sincerity. He was more than half *undarios*. If she had not believed in the rumored powers of the *undarii*, she would not have been troubled by the presence of Quenfrida. Flood, rain, murder, plague; all out of season. She said, briskly, "Then we'll have to turn the river back to us, won't we?"

Gracielis shook his head. Then he pulled a face, and said, "Merafiens!"

"What did you expect me to say?"

He shrugged. "I don't know."

"Well, I'm not going to give up." Yvelliane rose. "And I intend to start by doing something about your Quenfrida."

"She isn't my Quenfrida."

"If you say so," Yvelliane said. "Did she send you to tell me?"

"No."

"Then let's go and start the relevant proceedings." Gracielis looked uncomfortable. She said, "Come on."

He was looking at his feet. "About Kenan Orcandros . . ."

"He doesn't like non-Lunedithin. However beautiful they might be." Gracielis looked suitably desolated. "And I doubt he likes men either."

"I'd very much like to meet him anyway."

Yvelliane said, "I'll make a bargain with you. I'll introduce you to him, if you'll let me watch Quenfrida's reaction to meeting you in my company."

He frowned. "She already knows there's a connection between us."

"I don't doubt it. Humor me anyway." Still he hesitated. "I don't imagine she can do you any real harm in so public a place." He looked down, hiding his expression behind his lashes. "Come on."

He took her hand with good grace and let her draw him back into the Chamber. Quenfrida sat amidst an attentive circle near one of the long windows. Reflected candlelight burnished her hair and struck lights from her jewels. She glanced up as they approached, and her face showed nothing beyond the most perfect politeness. She said, "Good evening, Lady Yvelliane."

"Good evening," Yvelliane said. Quenfrida made room beside her on the chaise longue. Her perfume was stifling. Yvelliane prevented herself, with a slight effort, from pulling her skirts against her, and said, "I've brought one of your countrymen to meet you."

"Really?" Quenfrida did not trouble to look at Gracielis. "How thoughtful."

"I do my best. We must look after our guests, after all." Yvelliane gestured to Gracielis. "May I present Monsieur de Varnaq?"

Gracielis was pale beneath his paint, and his practiced smile was a little forced. He bowed elaborately, trailing lace and perfume.

Quenfrida looked at his two-colored gloves, and her smile widened. "I'm always delighted to meet a friend of the councillor."

Gracielis said, "I also. Especially one who is both so fair and a compatriot."

"I might say the same."

"You're too kind."

"But no. I'm never too kind. Only kind enough."

Quenfrida's smile this time was cruel. Yvelliane felt rather than saw Gracielis flinch before it.

His voice was steady. He said, "Then perhaps you'll be kind enough to dance with me?" He held out to her his left hand, the light one. Quenfrida glanced once at Yvelliane, and her eyes were amused. Then she took the hand and followed Gracielis into the dance.

He danced beautifully. But beside Quenfrida, he was unexpectedly angular. Yvelliane watched them for a few moments, then rose, intending to seek out Firomelle.

Instead she found herself looking round for Thiercelin. He was nowhere in sight. Gracielis had not answered her question on that subject. She had to stop herself from thinking about it. The survival of a marriage could never be more important than the safety of a state. She would need a full and detailed report from Gracielis; and she would have to have Quenfrida's expulsion papers drawn up. Plenty of time, later, to find Thiercelin. Miraude swept up to her in a flurry of silk and said, laughing, "I'm all out of breath. I must be getting old."

"Oh, indubitably." Yvelliane could not help smiling. "I can see the gray hairs."

"Charming." Miraude smiled back, fanning herself. "You stole my partner, Yviane. I shall sulk!"

"I'm sorry, Mimi. I needed to talk to him. Didn't Thierry look after you?"

"Not him. One dance, then he fled into the gaming room." Miraude pulled a face. "I'm quite abandoned." Her face grew serious. "I have something for you. It may be nothing, but . . . The university scholar who showed Prince Kenan and me round the Old Temple remains has vanished."

"There have been a number of odd deaths in the city recently."

"Yes. But he seems to have been one of the first to go missing." Miraude looked across at Kenan. "I saw Prince Kenan a day or two ago, and he pretended he'd

found the archaeological site dull. But I'm not sure. He's
done something, I'm sure of it. If I could get closer to
him, I might be able to find out more . . ."

"If he's behind that man disappearing, maybe you
should back off for now." Yvelliane took Miraude's
hand. "Be careful, Mimi. I can't spare you."

"I'm always careful." Miraude squeezed her fingers
and looked at the dance floor.

Yvelliane followed her gaze. She could still see Gracielis amidst the dancers. There was a curious hesitance
to his movements, as if he sought too hard for some
form of control. Yvelliane looked away again and found
Firomelle's eyes on her. The queen raised an inquiring
brow. Yvelliane gave her a small nod and turned back
to the dancers in time to see Gracielis come to a complete halt, displacing the measure. Quenfrida said something, and Gracielis replied, before pulling away from
her with a violence that ripped all grace from him.

The disruption rippled out over the dancers. Quenfrida smiled and shrugged, returning to her seat. Miraude said, "And there's another mystery."

"I'll tell you later." Catching Firomelle's eyes, she
held up three fingers and saw the queen nod in reply.
"I have to go."

"I'll try to talk to Thierry. He should come home."

It could do no good. But Miraude was gone before
Yvelliane could say anything. She possessed herself of a
bottle of wine from a buffet and let herself out through
a side door. She found Gracielis standing in a window
embrasure in the corridor. His forehead was pressed to
the glass. His arms were wrapped about himself. He did
not look around.

She said, "Well?"

He was silent so long that she began to think he would
not answer. Eventually he drew in a long breath and
said, "Does it matter?" His accent was pronounced.

"You tell me." She kept her voice light. "There's a
private room just over here."

He looked around. He said, "Very well," and accompanied her into the chamber.

She poured wine for both of them and sat. He stood staring into the empty fireplace. She said, "Will you tell me?"

"I don't know," he said. And then, "I wish it would stop raining."

"What?" Yvelliane said.

"Nothing. I rather wish you hadn't done what you just did."

"You know the reasons."

"Yes." He sighed. "Forgive me. I made a scene."

"I've seen worse."

He hesitated, then tugged off one of his gloves and began to rub at a wrist. It was bandaged. She looked inquiring, and he shook his head. Then he said, "Quenfrida . . . The worst thing is that she makes humiliation almost into a pleasure. She'll kill me for this."

"We can give you protection."

"Not against Quenfrida." He smiled a little. "You should look to yourselves, in that department."

"We will."

He studied her in silence. Then he said, "In the long term, you know, it doesn't matter which of you wins. You can't undo what she has done."

"I'm concerned with the short term. And I don't like absolutes." She hesitated. "What did she say to you?"

"Nothing of significance . . ." He sighed and picked up his wine. "She told me what it's like to bed with her newest disciple."

"Does that matter?"

"Yes." He sat, and looked at his hands.

Yvelliane said, "Do you want to go? I can excuse you to Miraude."

He shook his head. "No, that would be a discourtesy. She—Quena—is finished with me, I think." He lifted his wine and studied it. Rather abruptly, he drank it off. "And I have yet to be presented to Kenan Orcandros."

Yvelliane watched him, noting the effort that was restoring composure. He was stronger than his airs suggested. She said, "I'll arrange it. But there's another I'd have you meet first."

He wound the lovelock about a finger and smiled at her, his old, polished smile. "Why not?" he said.

No one was watching Iareth Yscoithi. No one noticed when she made her way from the hot room onto the terrace outside. It was raining. The terrace was empty. She stood on the stone, with her head tipped back, and let the rain soak into her hair and gown. The stars were hidden from her. To the west she could just make out a fragment of Mothmoon, disk near-covered by cloud. Handmoon was a faint, unshaped nimbus. She raised her hands to the sky, restless with heat and tension, and from the shadows at the terrace-edge a voice said, "Iareth *kai-reth*."

She had half-expected him. She turned, green eyes adapting to the dim light, and said, "Valdin Allandur."

He stood with his back to the torchlight. His tall figure was cloaked in darkness. His eyes were very clear. He said, "Rain becomes you."

"I thank you."

He stepped forward, dressed in black, hair tied back, diamonds bright in his ears. He said softly, "Dance with me?"

They could not touch. But she did not say that. She looked up into his eyes and smiled. Music spilled from the building behind her. His face held a need that spoke louder than any word. She hesitated, then said, "Certainly."

He bowed, and his insubstantial hand reached out. She held hers over it, not quite touching. There was an instant of stillness, then the measure took hold. Two steps, and turn; two more, and bow. They might not make the lifts, the quick, joint-dependent swings. She circled him on silent feet and heard that he made even less noise

than she. He leaned over her and cast no shadow. She
moved under his arm and shivered as the end of her
braid went through him. He seemed not to notice. Light
patterned them from the windows. He was almost gone,
stepping into it. Then he emerged in stronger color from
the other side. They danced on, unspeaking, untouching,
and she was serene in the damp night.

The music stopped. She had her back to him, arrested
part way into a measure. She looked back, suddenly
afraid, and his gray eyes smiled at her. He said quietly,
"I shall always be waiting for you." She found she could
not speak. He smiled at her and said, "We'll be together
again. I swear it."

The door banged behind them. He leaned toward her,
as if he would leave her with a kiss. She said, "Valdin
kai-reth . . ." and saw him warm to her.

He said, "Soon," and he was gone.

Perhaps it was only the wind that brushed her cheek.

Yvelliane had left him alone for a few minutes. Gracielis was grateful, mindful of his need to reacquire his
self-control. He sat in silence, teaching his breathing to
become slow once again and sipping at the wine she had
left him. His hands were not quite still. He was not quite
safe. If he ever had been.

Quenfrida had known, of course; she had always
known. She had doubtless rejoiced at the charade. He
sought to put from him the memory of mocking, sky-
blue eyes.

It hardly mattered. It was already too late. Even his
death would lack meaning.

It was not that which frightened him, though he had
hinted such to Yvelliane. What truly alarmed him was
that he had no memory of how he had come to be in
the corridor where Yvelliane had found him. An image
of Quenfrida, smiling at him coldly, choosing the next
weapon with which to assail him. And then . . . glass
cold against his brow, body shaking, half-governed; and

in his mouth an aftertaste of anger, lacking any words to trace it.

A few minutes only. But enough for a man to lose himself. There was no mirror in the room, but the curtains were open, and he could see his reflection in the window. He stared at it for long moments, then shook his head. Stern black, severe, reminiscent not of his own taste, but of that of lost Valdarrien. He smiled and said, "Well played," to himself, or perhaps to another. "But not quite well enough." The earring was paste. He reached back and untied the velvet bow, shook his hair forward. He rubbed one marred wrist. It seemed, after all, that it was not death that he feared.

So. He poured himself a third glass of wine and considered it. For now at least he must live, mad or sane. He owed that to Thiercelin. He was stronger now than he had been at scared and homeless seventeen. It was what he was bred to, this game of watchfulness and silken deceit. He was unlikely to win it; but he could try to do what he had promised.

When Yvelliane returned to fetch him, he favored her with a smile of devastating sweetness and offered her his arm. She looked skeptical but accepted the arm. She said, "Better now?"

"I'm much restored by your kindness."

She laughed. "Not by my wine?"

"What vintage can compare with your presence?"

"Several, to my certain knowledge. It's a subject you might discuss with Thierry."

"I might not. It would hurt him."

She looked down. There was short silence. At she said, "We should go." She led him to a door at the end of a corridor. She knocked, awaited a response then opened it. Taking her hand from Gracielis' arm, she said, "Go in. I'll wait for you."

It was not a large chamber; nor was it richly furnished. Dark curtains were drawn across the windows. Light came from two candelabra standing on a long sideboard.

The face of the woman who sat at one end in a high-backed chair was hidden in shadow.

There had been no cause in his nine years in Merafi for Gracielis to be presented to its queen. Making his living from her gentry and nobility, he moved far beneath her ambit. Nevertheless, he did not at once make obeisance, born of another race, subject to another dynasty. For long moments they regarded one another. Then a draught set the candles a-flicker and he caught sight of her face.

One might not feel pity for a queen, however tired, however ill. But one might perhaps feel a brief instant of recognition of a burden shouldered and held unflinching. The oak-paneled room was alive with it. He could feel the echo of her past pain beneath his fingers, even through his gloves. As the candles burned down, he knelt, as he would to the emperor of Tarnaroq.

Firomelle looked at him. "Gracielis de Varnaq?"

She had not given him permission to stand. To the floor, he said, "Yes, madame."

"You may rise." He stood and waited before her. She said, "Yvelliane d'Illandre tells me you will do us a service."

"Yes, madame." In the dim light, one might make out the kinship between Yvelliane and Firomelle.

She said, "Yvelliane would have you write and sign a sworn statement regarding the woman Quenfrida d'Ivrinez."

He said again, "Yes, madame."

"You are willing?"

It was pointless. The expulsion of Quenfrida could not save Merafi, not now. It was too late. It could not turn the river back, or halt the rain. He could say none of that to Firomelle, face-to-face with the extent of her pain. She had as little time as her city. He looked at the floor and said, "I am willing, madame."

"Thank you," Firomelle said. "I've taken the liberty of having the papers prepared. You'll find them in that bureau." She pointed. "It isn't locked. There's pen and ink, so that you may amend it, if you wish."

He opened the bureau and took out the papers. Whoever had readied them had a beautiful hand, as neat and clear as his. He hesitated, then removed a glove and let his naked palm touch the paper, smelling fresh ink and sand, hearing the regular scratching of the pen. Local paper, made fine and heavy. He felt the secretary's anxiety, hurrying to meet Yvelliane's deadlines, and only half-conscious of what he—no, she—copied. She might have shared the secret of his dual nature, had not duty come between transcription and comprehension. He was glad of that.

He put the glove back on and concentrated on the words. Behind him, Firomelle called a servant to fetch the witnesses. They were both strangers to Gracielis. Making his bows to them, he kept his eyes downcast. An informer and a whore had scant honor in his own house, let alone that of another. They watched as he added a line or two to the statement, confirming that Quenfrida was *undaria* and naming Kenan as her accomplice. Below that, he signed all his names in full, lest at some future time his identity be questioned. Firomelle signed next, then the witnesses. Looking up, Gracielis found Yvelliane watching him. She must have come in during the signing. She smiled at him.

Firomelle thanked and dismissed the cosignatories. Then, to Gracielis, she said, "Thank you."

He bowed. She held out a hand. The rings she wore seemed too large, too heavy for it; her long sleeves were almost as much a disguise as his. Her bones were beautiful. He could see the sickness that gnawed them. He knew he should tell her of the danger to Merafi. He could not. She bore too much already. He had warned Yvelliane, and that would have to suffice. He said, "Good night, madame."

She smiled. "Good night, Monsieur de Varnaq. Fortune attend you."

"And you also, madame," said Gracielis. He wished he had the power to make it come true.

Kenan sat on the edge of the dance floor and considered. It was only duty that had brought him here tonight. Tafarin might find such parties amusing, but he did not. He would have left an hour since had it not been for the chance that had alerted him to the presence of his rival. Quenfrida had given him no warning, and he had been less ready than he might have been. A measure of his inability, of the defect in him—in his clan-blood—which left him blind where he should see.

Quenfrida's shuttered face had given him the clue his newer senses had failed to provide. At last he had identified the other, the rival, the supplanted acolyte, Gracielis. Kenan watched the side door through which Gracielis had gone with Yvelliane d'Illandre an hour since. Gracielis was said to be a whore. No surprise, then, in finding Yvelliane consorting with him. He could make use of his acquaintance with her to meet Gracielis and see for himself what manner of weakling he had replaced.

Tafarin arrived beside him, breathing wine fumes. Kenan looked at him in distaste. Tafarin slapped his shoulder. "You miss all the fun, Kenan *kai-reth*."

"So?"

"The loss is yours, of course; yet I would persuade you otherwise. You might learn something, even."

He stood between Kenan and his view of that side door. Smiling with an effort, Kenan said "Peace, Tafarin *kai-reth*. You know well my pleasures lie in different directions. Enjoy this night on my behalf, as well as your own."

"As you please." Tafarin made him a salute and swirled off into the throng. Kenan sighed and looked back at the door.

It was open. Typically, those he sought had returned while his attention was elsewhere. He forbore to curse.

Instead he rose and attempted to scan the room. Almost impossible, of course, in the crowd.

He was unable to repress a start when a familiar voice spoke at his elbow. "Ah, Kenan. We haven't yet said good evening, I think?"

Yvelliane. She could not know, of course, that he had been looking for her, but he could not help mild irritation. Turning to her, he did not trouble to disguise this, neglecting to salute or bow. "Good evening, Yviane Allandur. Since the greeting is necessary."

She looked at him without liking. She said, "I have someone here who wants to meet you." Her tone suggested that she found the desire inexplicable. Kenan followed her gesturing hand, and came up short.

Auburn curls and fair skin. A scent blended at pulse points, to speak to those who might hear in it the syllables of a name. Kenan stood motionless. He did not look at Yvelliane, who surely had no knowledge of what she had just done. He was not himself conventional within *undarii* bonds. He did not choose to proclaim his identity to the knowing world in tones of perfume. His Lunedithin blood protected him from suspicion. This painted toy of a man could not know him for who—or what—he was.

He smiled. Yvelliane said, "Kenan Orcandros, may I present Gracielis de Varnaq, a Tarnaroqui . . . entrepreneur."

The eyes of Gracielis de Varnaq laughed deliciously, glancing sidelong at Yvelliane. Kenan nodded and said with conscious politeness, "An honor, sir."

"For me, also, monseigneur." Gracielis had more of an accent than Quenfrida. He smiled, showing white, even teeth.

Yvelliane said, "I need to speak to the prince consort, so I'll leave you, messieurs. Good night." Kenan acknowledged her departure with no more than a glance. Gracielis bowed elaborately over her hand.

Kenan said, "You are not a member of the Tarnaro-qui delegation, I believe?"

"No. I reside in Merafi."

"So? You have abandoned your homeland? I am not myself overwhelmed by the opulence of Gran' Romagne."

The corners of the carmined lips twitched. Gracielis said, "Choice isn't given to every man. You're fortunate, monseigneur."

"Doubtless."

"For myself . . ." Another overstated gesture, trailing scent. "I'm sure you're sufficiently acquainted with my history." His hand was abruptly over Kenan's. His eyes were immense with delight. His fingers crooked in the sparse lace at Kenan's wrist. "*Chai ela*, Kenan *istin-shae* Quenfrida."

There was something shadowing him . . . Through that touch, skin to skin, Kenan felt the unformed ability chained in the other's alien blood, bound, asleep in all but small ways. Something crossed it, some fleeting taste, almost familiar, which did not quite belong. Keeping face and voice neutral, Kenan said, "That knowledge is mine, I concede. And I know also what you are not. I am proof against your abilities, Gracielis *arin-shae* Quenfrida."

"Naturally." Taking his hand away, Gracielis looked down, cloaking his too-readable eyes. "I would expect no less."

Kenan in turn looked down at the small tear in his cuff. Then he laughed. Gracielis was still, silent. "You will not drink with me, I assume?" Kenan asked.

"Why should I not?" The beautiful eyes swept up. "We are, after all, almost brothers."

15

WHEN THE INFANTRYMAN finally forced open the door, Joyain was unable to stop himself taking a step back. Then, swallowing, he said, "What *is* that?" A heavy, sweet smell wafted out toward them, sticky with decay. Like rotting flowers . . . rotting honeysuckle. The air inside the temporary guardhouse was hazy, even though the nearby river was relatively clear.

The soldier said, "I don't think there's anyone here, sir." He choked, coughed, and began to back off. "Perhaps they didn't get down here?"

"Then where are they now?" Joyain asked, finding shelter for his own uncertainty in sarcasm. "Not a single member of that patrol has been seen in eighteen hours."

"Maybe their relief . . ."

"The relief patrol was diverted to help deal with the fire in the Artisans' quarter." Joyain sighed and pushed back his hair. He was sweating, and his palms felt sticky. "Well, let's get on with it, since we're here."

It was nothing like a proper guard station. After the desolation of the shantytown and the illegal, desperate severing of the half-rotten bridge that had connected it to the main city, this nearby old warehouse had been hastily turned over to military use. The official reasoning, passed down from high command, was to put down any further trouble in the area around the new dock. In the barracks and in the officers' mess whispers hinted at a different cause.

Leladrien had said that there were no more people left alive in the sodden ashes of the shantytown. Rumor suggested that someone in headquarters meant to make sure of that.

From the stone steps of the warehouse, greasy with soot, Joyain could see nothing to hearten him. The remains of the shantytown steamed and smoked on the opposite bank, already partially underwater. The piles of the bridge were gone, either covered or swept away. The water was evil with mud and refuse. The remnants of the floating dock tugged and splintered at their moorings. Beyond it, the wide artificial basin created for the use of shallow-draft boats was an empty swirl of scum and foul vegetation. The debatable land between that and the raised road to the southeast gate was also vacant, not even a stray dog nuzzling amongst its mud and wrack. The river ran high. To Joyain's left, the confluence of the middle and northern channels was a pounding rush of filthy water, swollen by too many days of rain. Scant wonder no ship had tried to moor. The landslip below the north cliff was gone, underneath those tumbling waters. High above it, some lights still shone. Distant images of torches hung in pleasure gardens and avenues used by the nobility. Still dancing and playing, as the city sank into decay around them.

The burned-out shell of The Pineapple was only a few hundred yards away. Joyain did not look at it. Two days and a night in a Merafi deluged in rain and mist and panic had left him remote in feeling from the Lunedithin embassy and Iareth Yscoithi.

It had been a cold gray going. He was desperate for sleep. His hair and clothes smelled of sweat and ash. By rights—as if he, or any other common-born officer, had rights!—he should have gone off duty eight hours ago. But the fire had broken out anew in the Artisans' quarter, despite the river-cursed rain; and Joyain's exhausted, resentful unit of mixed watch and infantry had had to man their post until it was extinguished again.

After that, the rank and file had been allowed to go
to their beds. The laughing fates had not, however, forgotten Joyain Lievrier. Tired as he was, his recompense
had been a short interchange with his captain, and the
charge of coming down here and checking up on the
progress of this scratch garrison. "I haven't time to go
myself," the captain had said, "and besides, I suspect
you'll get better results. DuResne has charge there, and
he was in no very cooperative mood when I sent him."

"Leladrien wouldn't mutiny, sir," Joyain had said,
stiffly. "I'm sure he has a good reason for his silence."

"Doubtless." But the captain's tone had given lie to
the word. "And a reason too, I'm sure, for why it is that
no one in or around that area has seen him, or any of
his men, for twelve hours." Joyain, lacking permission
to speak, had maintained a resentful silence. "Well, he's
a friend of yours. Get down there and sort him out for
me. There's a unit seconded from the Garde-Rouge outside. Take them with you."

More infantry, and from a provincial levy . . . Ideal
material to take orders from a worn-out cavalry staff
lieutenant with a headache and a sensation of being ex-
ploited. Joyain had sighed, saluted, and said, "Yes, sir."

It had been the only reply he could think of that
wouldn't land him in the military prison. Now he poked
at the dirt on the warehouse steps with a booted foot
and tried his hardest not to be aware of the honeysuckle
smell clinging everywhere.

"Lieutenant, sir!" The call came from inside the warehouse, and apparently upstairs. One of his party of
searchers had found something.

Joyain put his hat back on and called back, "Yes?"

"I've got something, sir, if you'll come up."

"On my way." Rubbing his soiled toe cap on the back
of his calf, Joyain tugged at his cassock and straightened
his shoulders. The reek inside the building was far worse
than he'd imagined. He wanted to throw open all the
windows and gulp what passed for fresh air. The stone

floor was wet. All the fires were dead. The makeshift grates looked as if they'd been put out with buckets of water. The temperature was at least ten degrees too high to be compatible with the lack of fire and the weather outside. Against his will he recalled bitter man-forms in a night-mist and shivered.

The soldier who had summoned him was waiting on a second-floor landing. Peering into rooms on his way up, Joyain had seen no life beyond his own unit; no sign of anything other than chilly abandonment. The soldier saluted him and said, "In there, sir."

He indicated a narrow door made out of cheap deal, standing ajar. There was something wrong with his face . . . Joyain looked at him curiously, awaiting further explanation. He received none. After a moment, he shrugged, and said, "Right. You carry on, then." It would help if he had the least notion of the names of any of this unit . . .

The soldier made no effort to accompany him. Joyain pushed the door open and understood why.

Originally, he supposed, it had been a clerk's office. A crook-backed slip of a room crushed under the eaves and lit by a single unglazed window. The army had imported a cot and dragged the desk away from the window. The scuff marks were still barely visible on the floor through the overlay of mud and bloody vomit and water. There were no words adequate to describe the smell. Something that Joyain did not intend to investigate too closely lay half behind the desk. It might once have been a man. If he had looked—but he wasn't going to look—he might have been able to theorize about the cause of death. (Obviously, it was dead. No one could live in that many pieces. He was not even going to begin to imagine what might have come to chew and tear limbs after that fashion. Half the gut must be missing, apart from what had fallen across the floor.) Joyain found he was rubbing his hands up and down his thighs convulsively. Drawing in a long breath, he forced himself to stop and clamped one hand around the hilt of his saber instead. That was nearly reassuring.

Then he looked up. Something in the pit of his stomach protested dimly, while through his mind rattled a dry military tally of the room and its contents. Bed, one; chair, one; body, one . . . no, two, another shape hidden beyond the desk in the unlit corner of the room, a disjointed bundle of a man dropped from too high, and left to lie in a congealing puddle of his own fluids. *Unrecognizable, of course,* said that same dry voice in Joyain's mind, even the uniform too marred and mangled to lend any identity; skin blackened and discolored, flesh torn and seared, some wounds still weeping light thick fluid into the mess on the floor . . . Scanning upward past the wrecked chest, past the pitiful ends of rib protruding from the broken skin, past the crushed forearm flung out as if it would protect the head, look up, look up, and look away quickly . . . On one side, the skin had been ripped clean away from the throat and jaw, exposing teeth which were still strong and good; and, on the upper right-hand side, the face was also torn off, no cheek, no brow, no eye. Joyain was shaking, he could barely breathe, he was trying so hard to look away anywhere but down; his loins were cold and unmanned, he was—river rot it—shaking! He was . . .

The ruined jaw moved, and Joyain started back, banging his thigh against a corner of the desk. Under the blood and the knotted, matted hair, a single eye opened and looked straight at him. He could see the effort in the bared muscles, the convulsive swallowing in the gullet. Sweat ran down his own neck, and he breathed fast through his mouth.

A voice he did not want to recognize said, "Hello, Jean."

"No," Joyain said. He could no longer stand. Sinking back, he leaned on the desk, gasping.

"Sorry . . . about the mess." Leladrien's lips were partly gone. The muscular rictus where they should have been was a vicious parody of a smile. "Things you . . . should know." Joyain knew he should do something, say something, summon help, anything. He could not move at all. He wanted to cry. He had forgotten how. Leladrien said, "We were . . . mostly dead, before they came. The . . . things. Look in the cellar. It's a sickness. But the things . . . are real. Not phantasms." His voice was ghastly, a sobbing thread caught up perpetually on the angles and floods of its own pain. Black fluid dribbled from the edges of his mouth and between his teeth. "Burn this place. Promise me."

"I . . ." Joyain said, and swallowed bile. "Lelien."

"Promise, Jean." Joyain was afraid to speak. He nodded, chill, wan. Leladrien said, "Good." And then, "Other matters . . . Don't touch anything. Not without gloves. You still there, Jean?"

"Yes," Joyain whispered, eyes tight shut, hand hard on his sword.

"Jean, listen. You must . . . You must shoot your deserters . . . Hear me?"

"Yes."

"If they go into the city . . . they'll spread it."

It made grim sense. Although it was surely too late . . . How many of the watch and the city garrison lived in the Artisans' quarter, or the low city, or over the shops in the business district outside the wall? Joyain swallowed again and said, "Yes, Lelien."

"Good man. Good thing they sent you. Thought so, last night, before the things came . . . Jean will be down for us, sooner or later." Leladrien's single eye was no longer seeing Joyain. He coughed, or tried to, and nausea knotted in Joyain's stomach.

Joyain said, "What are the things?"

Leladrien ignored him. "I watched the lights . . . on the hill. You can see so much, when the sickness has you . . . They were dancing last night in the palace . . . Couldn't even see the fires in the streets from up there . . . Laughing, I suppose. Loud enough to drown

the cries . . . It won't rise so high, the river, to drown
them too . . . D'you see it, Jean?"

His mind was wandering . . . No surprise. Through set
teeth, Joyain said, "No," denying the memory of late
torchlight on the cliff top. Leladrien made a sound that
might, perhaps, have been meant for a laugh.

"They'll learn, our aristos." Leladrien paused. Then,
"Last thing, Jean."

"Yes," Joyain said, "anything." There was a pounding
in his ears. Dully, he realized it was his heart. Oh,
river bless.

"Jean," said Leladrien, "shoot me."

Stone buildings were hard to burn, harder still in pouring rain. In the end, Joyain had to commandeer a wagon-
load of oil from a tavern, and even then the fire was
difficult to set. Knowing that he might not fairly ask one
of his men to face what lay in the cellar, Joyain took
upon himself the task of soaking and torching the bodies. It was worse, almost, than the eaves room, between
the smell and the shadows and the overpowering heat.
Too many men made inhuman by plague and death. He
reemerged pale and trembling, and his tone with his unit
was savage with misery.

He could not bear to think of Leladrien or of what
he had done in that narrow attic room. Nail down the
knowledge, seal it, and concentrate only on the now,
the necessary.

He had thought there could be nothing worse than the
odor in the house. Mingled with wood ash and charring,
spoiled flesh, it proved him wrong. He was not the only
one to stagger back from the warehouse, choking, although unlike some of his men he managed to control
his nausea.

It was only the acrid smoke which caused his eyes to
water and sting.

He was dimly aware that this conflagration constituted
a second court-martial offense to his credit. He shied

away from that thought, too, from the memory of a much wanted, illegal coup de grâce. It could not go unreported. He had no choice, caught up by duty and necessity. By awareness of how loudly a pistol shot could echo in a largely empty building.

The unit sergeant was at his elbow. Joyain pulled his distracted attention away from the fire and looked at him.

"What next, sir?"

The flames had attracted few onlookers. Joyain suspected that sickness and violence had driven most of the local residents away. He supposed he would have to check the surrounding building for further evidence of the destruction suffered by Leladrien's garrison. More silent houses. More blackened, mangled, and decomposing people—people, not bodies. He felt himself pale, fought vertigo. He must not show any part of his distress in front of his unit. He said, "Clear the crowd and get any statements you can about what's been happening down here. Have some of the men go through local houses and check for further casualties. I'll need the details for HQ."

"Very good, sir." The sergeant moved off and began to pass on the order. Joyain sat down on a nearby mounting block and struggled to collect his thoughts.

Things from the river—mist-born, night-bound death. Iareth Yscoithi had been calm in the face of that strangeness; and Gracielis de Varnaq (who knew too much) had warned Amalie to leave Merafi, as if he had known what might be coming. Neither of them were native, neither of them had much reason to care about the city's fate. Joyain shook his head and tried to settle his information together.

A warning of old things, stirred impossibly from the past to haunt and delude the present. Find a Tarnaroqui, old Banvier had said. Or ask a priest . . . He should go to a temple and pay for prayers for Leladrien, slain by water, consumed by fire . . . Enough, perhaps, to burn

away the taint that had destroyed him, if it was true that
these . . . whatever . . . feared fire.

It was ridiculous. He was ordering his intentions along
a course of superstition and legend. Plagues happened,
in docklands. Street gangs used night and fog to cloak
their actions. A dying man might easily come, through
delirium, to believe his death was caused by more than
just sickness.

No illness known to Joyain came equipped with teeth
sharp and strong enough to disembowel and half-flay
a man.

There had to be some reasonable explanation. There
must be. He must disbelieve the testimony of his own
eyes and look for a rational solution. There could not
be danger on the scale hinted at by Leladrien and old
Banvier. The queen and her council had issued no special orders. The nobility were content to continue their
pleasures. There was, then, no cause for alarm.

Shoot your deserters. How many men and women had
been in and out of this area in the last twelve hours?
How infectious was this plague, anyway? *Touch nothing
without gloves.* He must report back, yet he might already be a walking contagion despite having handled
nothing directly, if the air itself was contaminated and
the water as well. He sighed, temples pounding. It was
beyond him. He was not made for this kind of thing.

The sergeant returned. Joyain said, "Yes?"

"We've finished searching, sir."

"Good. And?"

"Sixteen dead, sir, and two or three close to death, all
in houses within thirty feet of the river. No one admits
to having seen anything unusual in connection with Lieutenant DuResne's unit."

"Anyone seen anything odd on their own behalf?"

"Not that they're telling us, sir." The sergeant hesitated, "At least . . ."

"Yes?"

"One woman—who used to work at the inn that was

burned two or three nights back—swears blind she's
seen an aristo hanging about the remains."

"So? Who is it?"

"According to her—not that she looks too reliable to
me, sir—it's the Lord of the Far Blays."

Thiercelin duLaurier. Joyain suppressed a sigh. "The
councillor's husband? Well, that might not be such a bad
thing. Bring it home to them what's happening down
here."

The sergeant looked uncomfortable. He said, "Not
that lord, sir—the last one. Valdarrien d'Illandre. And
what's more," and his voice swooped up as the annoy-
ance of a sensible man forced to report nonsense broke
through, "she says she can only see him when it's
raining!"

It was cold. That was the only possible reason Joyain
could have for shivering. He looked at the outraged sergeant and said, "Did you check her breath?"

"Yes sir. You could have lit a torch from it."

"Well, there you are, then." Joyain made himself
smile. "Anything else of that type?"

"Not really . . . A child talked about seeing a dead
grandparent, but the father tells me it's the fever."

"Nothing regarding street attacks?"

"Nothing new, sir." Joyain glanced at the man.
"You'll have heard some of the stories the watch have
been spreading? Lot of rubbish designed to cover up
their own shortcomings, I'd say."

"No. I've been on detached duty." Joyain forced himself to keep his tone light. "You'd better tell me."

"Very good, sir. Some of their patrols are claiming
that the deaths in the low city aren't to do with the
gangs, after all. Say they've seen creatures that creep
about in the fog and attack people. That are conve-
niently impossible to catch or kill, I might add. Trying
to get themselves off the hook, if you ask me."

"Sounds likely," Joyain said, distracted. Barracks talk,
filtered by skepticism and expedience before it reached

the officers, the high command, and, presumably, the royal council. "Thank you, Sergeant. Carry on." Joyain rose. "I'm going up to HQ to report. Make sure that fire is watched and doesn't spread."

"Right, sir." The sergeant saluted, and turned to go. Joyain watched him, frowning, then headed into the city.

He needed a drink. Stopping at a favorite tavern in the middle of the old town, he had two as a species of valediction. Then he called for pen, ink, and paper, and set himself to write a suitable account of the fate of Leladrien's unit, and of his own actions in respect of this. It was easier than he had expected. He included everything, including his conversation with Banvier, the fight he and Iareth had had with the mist creatures, Leladrien's testimony, and the stories picked up by his sergeant. He ended with a stark admission of his offenses against military law, and an offer to resign his commission and present himself before an appropriate disciplinary board. A half-livre to the potboy ensured that it would be delivered safely. After that, he had another drink. Then he took a fresh piece of paper, addressed it to Amalie, and wrote on it, quite simply "Leave Merafi" and his name. The potboy would take that, too. Joyain added a further half-livre to the fee and finished by buying himself another drink.

He had a superstition about doing anything in even numbers. That suggested to him a fifth drink. After downing it, he rose and went out into the street.

It had been years since he last visited a temple, save on official occasions. Something, some sense of what was appropriate, directed him toward the small chapel set two streets away from where Leladrien lodged. Had lodged. There was only one priest in attendance, and the floor had not been swept. Joyain bowed to the flame and dipped a nervous hand into the well, before finding himself a seat. He was out of the habit of prayer. It seemed needful, yet at the same time it was hard to assimilate. Perhaps his dilemma showed in his face, for the priest came to stand beside him, placing a hand on his shoulder.

Joyain looked up. The priest was surprisingly young; a reason, perhaps, for his service in this minor shrine. Joyain said, "Did Lieutenant DuResne ever come here?"

"From the tenement above the chandlers'?" Joyain nodded. The priest said, "No."

"Well, he never will, now. He's gone to the flame." The priest was silent. His expression did not change. Joyain said, "How many have turned up dead, near here, these past few days?"

"Enough."

"Naturally dead or murdered?" Again, that silence. Joyain twisted his hands together. His knuckles were dirty with soot and ink. He looked at them, square and familiar. He said, "No one asks questions. No one bothers so long as it touches nothing important." The priest was motionless. Joyain was cold despite the ale he'd drunk. "Does that mean that it doesn't matter? That death doesn't matter?"

The priest said, "I don't know."

Joyain turned to look at him. "Who does, then?" There were too few candles burning in the chapel, and the narrow, high windows gave little extra light. Shadows ran away into the corners, mocking. The air was full of waiting. Joyain had never felt so alone. He said, "The evidence is everywhere; but no one does anything." The priest watched him. "No one talks about it, or acts. No one ever will. Do you understand me?" The priest was still silent. Joyain stood, and stepped away from him, shaking. His voice was no longer under his control. "Do you?" The priest made a gesture of pacification. "It's all over, d'you hear? The streets are full of death. The living are dying, and the dead are coming back."

The priest looked down. Then he sighed, and said, "What of it? What cannot be changed must simply be accepted."

Joyain said, "There has to be another way."

"Why?"

"Because . . . I don't know . . . We can't just let ourselves die, surely? We have to fight back."

The priest gestured at Joyain's uniform. "That is the choice of your life. It is for you to decide whether it makes any difference." His tone was gentle but his eyes were bleak. Behind him, shadows stirred.

Joyain said again, "How many dead?" And then, "Don't you care?"

"Yes. But my care won't change anything."

"Then why bother to begin with?" Joyain inhaled. "Why waste the time?"

"Why not?"

"But . . ." Joyain said, and shook his head. "I don't know. You're counseling despair. Will we all simply wait for death?"

"We all die."

"Yes, but . . . Not like this, surely?" There was no answer. Joyain rubbed his eyes. "Why won't you help me?"

"Do you need help?"

"Yes," said Joyain wildly. And then, "My best friend is dead."

"I'm sorry for your grief."

"Is that all?"

"Yes."

"Then why," said Joyain, gesturing round him at the chapel, "all this?" He received no reply. "Why anything? The city is falling apart around us, and the council does nothing."

"That is on them, not you or me."

Joyain stared at the priest. "You're just waiting? Waiting for death to find you?"

"Yes," said the priest. "Like you."

It was almost nothing, which drew Iareth out from the embassy with the first hints of dusk. An edge-of-vision thing, an ill ease in the blood, calling to her of open spaces. She rode out through the northern boundary, uphill, with her back to the river, toward the great road that led north. The sky was low and gray; intermittent rain darkened her hair. There was no wind. A steady stream of traffic threaded its way along the road; carts, in the main, many of them heavy-laden, all heading away from Merafi. There was a smell of burning.

A mile or two beyond the city she took a turn away from the road toward the low hills between the city and the sea. Perhaps a half mile farther on she reined in and dismounted. Tethering the horse to a scrub oak, she lifted down her saddlebags and walked to the brow of the next rise. She looked back toward Merafi.

It was heavy with mist. Toward the river's main channel, the haze was hedged with orange: moisture infected with fire. No light to it, no beauty, but a sullen quality of waiting. The rain looked to be heavier there than here in the hills.

She had ridden here years ago with Valdarrien. A Valdarrien who could touch her, as he had not, last night, on the terrace. From Valdarrien her thoughts turned to Joyain, and she sighed. He was out there somewhere under the mist, and she had done nothing for him.

In the hollow, her horse whickered. She turned and caught sight of a pale shape against the sky. Her Yscoithi eyes, sharpened on darkness, saw farther than many. She narrowed them now, looking north. Her restlessness shifted toward a keener anticipation.

Swan wings clove the rain, strong as iron, and near as certain, borne in through the heavy air from the north and the land of her birth. Iareth stood tall on her ridge and waited, scarlet and gray cloak drawn about her. The swan moved in. When it was some few hundred yards away, she raised her left and primary hand and saluted. Hand on sword hilt—I serve you. Hand over heart—I reverence you. Hand held out, palm up before her—I am yours.

The swan banked and began to turn, coming in to land. The huge wings tilted, braking, bracing against the impact with the ground. Come at last to stillness, they did not fold. The line of them bisected the twilight, blinding white. An arching, then, through the hollow bones, a reaching, as the head reared back and the wings tried for the horizons. Feathers stirred and shredded. The body narrowed, lengthened, growing upward. The outstretched wings grew into arms, flung out sideways. The proud eyes of the swan held Iareth's as the neck shortened into human proportions and the head grew out into that of a man. He stood naked before her, a slight-built form with graying hair, and eyes as level as her own.

She opened the saddlebags and held out to him the tunic and trews they contained. He took them and dressed. Then he smiled and said, in Lunedithin, "Report."

Iareth gestured at the city behind her. "It is as I have written to you; disturbance of their river, worked in spite and ritual witchery. Kenan's doing and that of the Tarnaroqui Quenfrida d'Ivrinez."

"I remember her."

"There is as yet little sense of it among those who dwell here. The Allandur has a wasting sickness. Her council looks too keenly to the future."

Urien said, "I would not, as yet, have Kenan know I am here. I shall need money for lodgings and further clothing."

They began to walk down toward her tethered horse. Urien, barefoot, seemed unconcerned by the damp or the harsh, short grass. He said, "And Tafarin?"

Iareth smiled. "Tafarin *kai-reth* has been occupied in researching taverns." Urien, in turn, looked amused. She said, "What of Prince Keris?"

"He begins to heal, in body, at least. But your news of Kenan has disturbed him greatly."

"I regret it."

"Indeed. But better that he knows and is able to protect himself from those whom Kenan has stationed to harm him. They have been removed."

"I am glad of it." Iareth untied her horse and offered it to Urien. He shook his head. Leading it, they walked toward the road. Handmoon was rising behind the clouds. Iareth said, "We must make good time. Parts of the city are no longer safe by night." She hesitated. Then she said, "I have seen Valdin Allandur twice now. And I am not alone in that." Urien looked, inquiring. "He has spoken to Thierry, who was formerly his friend, and to another, a Tarnaroqui in Thierry's employ. And Jean—Joyain Lievrier, of whom I wrote to you—has seen him also. He brings warning of the disturbance of old things." She glanced at Urien, "I do not find myself altered in respect to Valdin Allandur."

Urien said, "You have long known my mind on that matter."

"So." She sighed. "But I am not, by nature, wholly Armenwy. It is laid upon me to roam, where Armenwy are lifelong faithful." Urien said nothing. A little defiantly, she said, "One may not live between two clans. Choice is necessary."

"Mayhap." Urien was neutral. Then he said, "A Tarnaroqui?"

"Yes. I know him but slightly, but he has *undarios* sight, and he has undertaken to aid Thierry. It might be well for you to meet with him. He has knowledge of this Quenfrida." Urien nodded. She hesitated, reached out a hand to him. It was the first contact between them since his arrival. "It is good that you are here."

"Let us hope so," said Urien.

16

"I THOUGHT," SAID THIERCELIN in a tone of mild accusation, "that you didn't usually drink."

Gracielis, at the window, said, "I don't." He was dressed negligently, with his hair left to fall straight down his back. He turned to look at Thiercelin and added, "You're right."

"There's a comfort." Thiercelin was in no very good mood himself. He was mildly hungover and rather depressed; Gracielis' abnormal behavior was beginning to tell on him. "So it's my wife's doing?" Gracielis looked away. "I don't blame you. Yviane would drive anyone to drink." And then, "Oh, do stop doing that!"

Gracielis jumped. "Doing what?"

"Drumming your fingers on the sill. You've been doing it for the last half hour, and it's driving me to violence."

"Forgive me." Gracielis lifted his hand and looked at it in slight surprise. His sleeve fell back, showing the bandage underneath. "I didn't realize."

"Evidently." Thiercelin's barb missed its mark. Gracielis merely folded his arms and went back to gazing out of the window. Thiercelin said, "I don't get it, Graelis, you've been staring out there almost all day. What are you doing?"

"Thinking."

"Helped by the view?" Thiercelin knew he was being

petty. Uncomfortable, he added, "I can understand you feeling unwell, after last night, but . . ."

"I'm not hungover."

"Oh, really?" Rubbing a hand across his eyes and pretending to ignore his own headache, Thiercelin said, "You don't look very healthy."

Gracielis rose and turned. Crossing the room, he sank cross-legged at Thiercelin's feet. He took Thiercelin's right hand and kissed the fingers. Then he said, "Forgive me, monseigneur—dear monseigneur—I'm selfish."

Thiercelin glared. "Stop that." Gracielis looked baffled. "I'm not ill, and I don't need sympathy."

"Naturally."

"And don't humor me either."

"Shall I be briskly supportive?"

Thiercelin swore. Then he said, "Do you have to do that? No, don't tell me. I don't think I can stand to know. Do you have any idea how much money I lost last night? I'm supposed to be economizing, but . . ."

Gracielis leaned against him. "It wasn't easy for you."

"I thought you weren't going to be sympathetic?" Gracielis was silent. "I'm hardly the first man to quarrel with his wife." Thiercelin sighed. "I turned up, as required. I owe her nothing else, nor she to me . . . Shall we talk about something different?" He did not want to think about it. Yvelliane had barely spoken to him last night. It would drive him to despair if he dwelled on that. He said, "What were you thinking about earlier?"

Gracielis looked at the floor, tracing a knot on a floorboard. He said, "Quenfrida. And you." He looked up again, and his eyes were wicked. "Pain and paradise."

"That," said Thiercelin, "was either excessively insulting, or excessively sentimental. Stop it."

"Monseigneur will break my heart."

"Oh, absolutely. Into twenty-three monogrammed pieces! You're a shocking liar." Gracielis affected graceful injury. Thiercelin ignored him. "And I don't see the connection."

Gracielis gestured at the window. "Her work. You wish it undone." He hesitated. "Kenan's work, also. Did I tell you I met him last night?"

"I think you mentioned it when you came in." Thiercelin considered him. "Am I allowed to ask where you were until dawn?"

"Yes. But I may not answer."

"I see." Thiercelin sighed again. "Meaning you were with Yviane?"

"No." Gracielis rose to his knees and took both of Thiercelin's hands. "That much I swear." Thiercelin gazed at him, caught between depression and disbelief. "By any vow you choose."

"Is there anything you care enough about to hold sacred?"

"Yes." Gracielis smiled. "And I swear by it. I discussed with her the state of your city, and I signed the papers she required. Nothing more."

Thiercelin looked away. A log fell in the hearth, scattering sparks. He watched them, bright in the dim room, and said irrelevantly, "We should light the candles."

"As you wish." Rising, Gracielis obeyed. The new candlelight found hollows along the lines of his fine bones. He set one branched candelabra on the sideboard, another on the table. Then he closed the casement. He said, "Shall I command the evening meal?"

"If you like."

"Not if you aren't hungry." He hesitated, then sat down again at Thiercelin's feet. "Does it matter where I was last night?"

Yes . . . Thiercelin stared at the fire and said, "Of course not. It was Quenfrida, I assume."

"No. She, for one, is done with me. I was with a client. That's all."

"Who?"

Gracielis said, "Shall I tell you why I usually don't drink?"

"Don't change the subject." Gracielis said nothing. Thiercelin studied him. "And don't play discretion. You feed information to Yviane. Why not to me?"

Gracielis said, "That's unkind."

Thiercelin looked away. "You behaved very oddly last night. You made a scene on the dance floor. And you've been edgy all today."

Gracielis hugged his knees. The long hair screened his face. He said, "Oh, Thierry." Then, turning, "I was with Amalie. I feel safe with her."

"I'm sorry." Thiercelin reached down and squeezed Gracielis' shoulder. "I had no right to ask."

Gracielis turned and laid a hand against Thiercelin's cheek. His fingers were cool. He said, "Your wife loves you. She would never betray you with me or any other."

Thiercelin leaned into his fingers, closing his eyes. He said, "It makes no sense . . . I'm with you, thinking of Yviane. I might as well be back where I started, admiring her through Valdin."

Gracielis smiled. Thiercelin heard the amusement catch in the slow tide of his breathing. He said, "I can't tell you. My wares lie in the domains of fever, not of sense."

Thiercelin said, "River drown it," and rubbed a hand across his eyes. Opening them, he looked down at Gracielis and said, "We have this backward, somehow. I can't afford to dwell on it, not now." The rhythm of his heart, under Gracielis' cool hand, was in line with the other's breath. "I don't even understand why I want you."

"You do." Thiercelin looked inquiring. Gracielis circled his own face with a graceful hand then held it out, palm up. "It is as I told you. I'm trained to make others desire me. It's an aspect of *undarios* power." He hesitated. "It's connected to why I don't usually drink."

"How?"

"Drinking heightens certain . . . sensitivities. I'm more aware of some matters. The provenance of a fabric or a wood. The quality of an atmosphere. I've touched Kenan. I have his measure now, and he's more than I. He knows it, too." He looked down. "It might be enough, I don't know."

"Enough for what?" Thiercelin watched the remoteness in that narrow face. This was a more serene Gracielis than he was wont to know.

"You asked me to help you. But I'm not *undarios*. I can't do it easily. Nevertheless . . ." Gracielis shook his head. He gestured at the window. "We'll see."

"You're going to try and stop this?"

"I mean to weaken it, a little, at least."

"How?" Thiercelin asked.

"As best as I can." Gracielis turned away. "Don't worry, monseigneur. It will be well." His tone did not quite support the words.

"You're going to try something dangerous." Thiercelin stood. "Let me help."

"You cannot. To do this . . . You don't have the blood or the training. It could only harm you. If I do this, it has to be alone."

"But . . ."

Gracielis rose in turn, came to stand beside him. "It will help me to know you are here and safe. Go to bed." He smiled. "I'll see you in the morning."

Go to bed. There never was a role for him, not with Yvelliane, not now. Thiercelin stared at his feet. Gracielis stood at his shoulder for a moment longer, then went into the other room, leaving him alone.

Joyain's head was pounding. He leaned on the tavern wall and tried to review how much he'd had to drink since leaving the chapel. The numbers eluded him. His stomach hurt, too. He swallowed bile and wondered if another drink might help.

There was something he needed to remember. Would remember, soon, once he'd had that drink . . . He fumbled for his purse and found it empty. He'd have to ask for credit, then, or else borrow. No problem. Leladrien was always good for a few livres.

Something to remember, connected with Lelien . . . Swallowing again, he tried to decide if he knew where he was. He had to face it; he was a little drunk. It might be better to head back to the mess. Yes, that was it; he'd start back now, and have that drink with his friends. He looked around him, noticing with interest that it seemed to have grown rather dark.

Misty, too. Drown these city autumns. (There was something about that too, which clutched at him—something to do with mist and night and fire.) He was probably somewhere in the old town. He didn't immediately recognize the tavern sign, but that meant nothing. Places changed hands so fast these days. In the old town, yes, and near Leladrien's place, that was it, near that chapel. He'd need to bear left then, and north.

The air was hot and clammy. It tasted unpleasant in his mouth. Ash, or some such. Now that he came to think about it, he felt sick, too. The tavern keeper probably kept bad ale.

Joyain straightened and let go of the wall. His perspective spun. He stumbled, retching. River rot it. He was going to regret this one, he could tell—and where was Lelien, anyway, when he was needed? He vomited into the gutter and stood there gasping. He could feel sweat cold on his skin. He was shaking.

There was something . . . something connected with Leladrien and with the bitter taste of smoke. His inability to remember was beginning to frighten him. He wrapped his arms about himself and fought to clear his head. He felt awful. Even waiting until he'd been sick twice more didn't help much.

He couldn't remember . . . Too much to drink. He cursed himself and tried to recall at least why he'd been drinking in the first place. He'd gone to a temple, to a priest . . . Before that, surely he'd been on duty, down on the waterfront . . . ?

Flame reflected in water, and the smell of decomposition in a narrow room. *Jean, shoot your deserters.*

Jean, shoot me.

Leladrien was dead.

Joyain swayed, gulping. He had put a gun to his best friend's head and pulled the trigger. He had put a torch to what was left.

Oh, river bless.

He was hot with terror. Alone in the streets after dark, alone with the mist and the horror and the vileness of his own actions.

And he didn't even know where he was.

There was a point, on the route down from the aristocrats' quarter, where one might see most of the rest of Merafi spread out between the three arms of the river. Usually, anyway. Looking down at it, Gracielis pulled his cloak tighter about him and sighed, Mist lay everywhere, cut in places by dull hints of fire, painful to his ghost-sight. Even up here, relatively mist-free, the streets were chill and empty. He was conspicuous again, and not solely for his foreignness.

He did not waste long staring at the city: his time was limited. He saw too much, unable to hold up his usual protections.

Well, that, at least, might work for him. He had chosen the long route around, keeping well clear of the river. For all that, his nerves spoke to him of shapes that might almost be pacing him. He would hold clear of them: he must. He could avoid the river almost for the whole of his journey; only at the very last must he approach it, and then only the safer, north arm, its manmade channel.

It had never occurred to Gracielis to view the prospect

of death with anything other than fear. He had not the required strength to disbelieve it, nor the confidence. He had expected to go down, when his time came, screaming and debased. He had not expected that beneath his fear he would find a level of dulled acceptance. He had not conquered fear, but he had, at the last, come to learn to live—to die—unmastered by it.

He was going to fail: he was not apt for these workings, nor did he possess ability sufficient to undo what Quenfrida had done. But for all that, something—some sense of pride—dictated that it would be better to try than simply to concede.

And he had given his word to Thiercelin. Gracielis still was not quite ready to pursue his own motives on that point. His fine brows drew together under his hat brim, and he turned away.

Familiar streets, for all their emptiness. The ground was damp: the still air muffled his steps. He walked quickly, avoiding looking about him. He was beginning to perspire. *Don't think about death . . . Think of what needs to be done, to shift this death of water, to ease it . . .* Blood, to bind, though his own ran chill and thin. It would sear him, pulled in opposition to sky-eyed Quenfrida.

It was going to hurt. Gracielis wrapped his arms around himself. It would rip through him with forest fury and leave him broken. He was going to die . . . He had come after all back around to the magnolia path and the unopened gate. He might, earlier, have chosen otherwise. He might have compounded with Quenfrida and gone into this blessed.

He had elected otherwise. He had chosen death, a death inherent from that first glance in the coffeehouse, and from that raw need he had so wished not to meet in Thiercelin of Sannazar.

It was too late, now. Gracielis inhaled and made himself straighten. He had his grace still: let that stand for

him, to mark what he must do as distinctively his, wistful
as the memory of a perfume, elegant as silk-wrapped
steel, beautiful as . . .

Beautiful as death.

He was well into the west quarter now. To his right,
he could see the tip of the River Temple, high above
the shroud of mist. Lights burned on the leads, as priests
watched over their ailing city. Perhaps they prayed. Perhaps that would help, a little. He came to the end of
Silk Street, near the west quarter watch house. Here,
there were a few people still out; though only a handful,
and those the most desperate. One or two of the whores
glanced at him; no one called his street name.

He had never belonged here, anyway. He belonged
nowhere. He turned onto the quay and swallowed as
mist closed in on him, hazy with half-formed movement.
The moons were invisible. Ghost-sight, poison-enhanced,
defined the shapes for him. The tang of honeysuckle
began to overlay his perfume. The air murmured around
him, too soft to be formed into words. Nothing approached, though the mist kept pace with him and his
skin was electric with awareness. He withheld from himself
too great a recognition of it. Slick gray water-skinned creatures, edged in malice, razor-clawed, sour-toothed. In his
veins and theirs a common bond, a likeness which held
them from him, barely. *Not wholly inhuman.* Human
enough to bleed. Human enough to care. To feel necessary pain—and it was going to hurt, His right hand
rubbed at his left wrist absently, remembering the dragging touch of the knife. A worse pain than that one, or
than any of the beatings he had ever endured. He gained
nothing, dwelling on it. It was appointed. It would not
change. There was a thundering in his head, like water
falling . . . That much comfort, at least: Dead Valdarrien
would not, now, have him. Now, or ever.

He had almost reached the guard post when he heard
the scrape of steel on stone, heard the voice that cried
out in the night, desperate, and bitterly familiar.

He turned and ran back along the quay into the mist's heart.

Thiercelin waited until he heard Gracielis going down-stairs, then buckled on his sword belt. He opened the casement and peered out. The main door of the hotel swung shut. A moment later a muffled figure appeared in the street below and began to walk uphill. He pulled a cloak from the armoire. Boots . . . He could see one under his bed. Finding the other lost him precious mo-ments, before it came to light in a corner. He fastened the cloak; then, boots in hand, he climbed out of the window.

Gracielis had strictly forbidden him to follow. Thier-celin had conceded outwardly, while determining to do the exact opposite. Merafi's streets were no longer safe at night, and Gracielis went everywhere unarmed. It was asking for trouble.

He dropped neatly onto the tiles of the stable roof, and paused to establish balance. Edging to the front, he threw his boots into the road and jumped down after them. It was quiet. He tugged them on and set off uphill.

It was also very dark. Overcast, neither moon gave any light. Thiercelin was not too troubled by that. He knew this part of the city extremely well. And, anyway, there were only two routes from here to the west quar-ter, and both of them passed the square around the King Melian IV pillar. At the top of the street Thiercelin set off on an oblique route under the angle of the house belonging to the queen's Third Councillor. Gracielis would be using the roads. Thiercelin smiled to himself and vaulted over the low wall to the back of the prop-erty. Now for some creative trespassing. How long since he'd last done this? Six years or more. Before Valdar-rien's death, certainly, and probably before the ill-starred *affaire* with Iareth.

From the Third Councillor's garden he cut west through two more gardens, then dropped into a jog along the aisle that a fourth cousin of his wife's had built in the last reign to please a fickle mistress. Emerging from the aisle, he heard the distant sweet sound of a clock chiming the quarter hour. He looked right and left, dashed across the road, and climbed the tall wall into the private orchard of the Verledon family. The pillar lay on the avenue that bordered its west side. Thiercelin jogged through it, hoping that none of the family's collection of dogs was about, and scaled the far wall. He could hear footsteps. He froze, and a figure wrapped in a cloak appeared from his right. Gracielis.

Thiercelin waited for him to pass, then dropped into the street and began to follow. Gracielis led him in a slow loop down into the west quarter, keeping wide of the river, across two squares, and behind the Gran' Théâtre. It was cool and damp. As they finally turned down toward the north channel, it began to grow noticeably foggy. Thiercelin put a hand to his sword hilt. They came to the quay. It was getting harder to follow Gracielis without becoming conspicuous. Thiercelin forced himself to hold a steady pace and tried not to notice how alone he was.

The air smelled strange, a near-familiar sweetness. The fog was oily on his skin. He could see no more than five yards in front of him. He slowed, anxious that he would lose his way even in this familiar territory. He could not see Gracielis at all. They had to be almost there by now. There were no lights. He could be anywhere.

Thiercelin stopped dead. It was too quiet. He might be the only person for miles. He could not even hear the lapping of the river. This mist clung to him, faintly unclean. He rubbed a palm and took a step forward.

The ground was wet. He could not see. Another step. Sweat ran chill down his spine, loosening his grip on his sword. Where was he? Another step. Another. It could not be much farther now. Another step. He'd walked this quay a hundred times. More, perhaps. It was simply a still, dark night. Another step. The air wound round him, sensuous with horror. Another step. The cobbles were still there underfoot. He was not displaced. He was not alone. Another step. Gracielis was somewhere ahead of him. The mist would thin once he was farther from the river. Another step. He'd been in worse situations than this. Remember that time when Valdin . . .

Remember Valdin. The late Lord of the Far Blays would have laughed himself sick at the sight of Thiercelin panicked by a little fog. Another step, then; and another, with his head high and a hand on his sword.

Something struck him hard on the right shoulder. Knocked off-balance, Thiercelin staggered and tripped. He caught himself on his hands, sword wrenched out of his grip. Pain lanced through his side and his right arm buckled under him. He could smell dirty water and some other thing. Honeysuckle? It was cold.

He rolled, reaching for his sword. His right arm refused to obey. Water whipped into his eyes. Sound thundered in his ears. His left hand closed on the sword hilt. He clutched it, gasping. The ground felt rough beneath him, more like rock than cobbles. He shook water from his eyes and tried to rise.

Another blow sent him sprawling forward. He landed badly, hitting his head. The sword was trapped under him. Breathing hurt. Pain made him dizzy. Air beat around him, wing-driven, buffeting. He had to get up. He could still see nothing.

He fought nausea and forced himself to his knees. Gray mist swirled around him. He seemed to be alone. He waited, letting the pain subside, then climbed to his feet. He still had his sword. He had never troubled to learn the trick of fighting with his off hand. Here went nothing, then. He drew, then looked right and left. "Who's there?" No answer. He shifted the sword into a better grip. "I'm armed, you know." Silence. He had lost his orientation, and the mist gave nothing away. Still the taste of honeysuckle and water. He counted to ten and took a tentative step forward.

There was a movement in the mist away to his right. Thiercelin turned and brought up his guard. An indistinct form, bulky, slow-moving. He waited. It did not approach him. He took another step, and something cannoned into him from behind.

This time he had no chance to break his fall. He landed hard, and the sword flew out of his hand. His shoulder was white agony. His face pressed to the ground, abrading. He could not turn over. Fighting panic, he tried to move his head enough to look behind him. There was a weight on him like hands pressing him down. Water poured over him. He could not move. He was choking.

Something laid hold of him, and he shuddered. Not hands. He could feel that through the drenched fabric of his shirt. Still he could not move. He could not reach his sword. Something holding on, closing in . . . something biting . . .

Teeth tore into his flank. Pain far worse than that in his shoulder . . . he could feel his flesh ripping away from the bone. He could not struggle. He tasted blood and coughed, cried out with the pain of it. He was being pulled apart. His sight began to blur with water and fear.

Light cut through the mist like a whip-cut. That same sense of wing beats . . . There was a new smell in the air too, alongside rotting honeysuckle—ozone? Suddenly the weight was gone. He could move. Blood pooled under him. His one functional hand was slippery with it. He managed to drag himself a few feet and looked up into the light. Two, maybe three figures, but their outlines kept shifting. Something misshapen and heavy, armed with too many scything teeth . . . They were everywhere, ending limbs, opening abruptly from the body. The other form was scarcely clearer, moving behind the light that ran and dripped from it. Thiercelin

had the confused impression of a blade trailing flame as
it weaved and leaped. A tall, slim man in black, who
smiled as he dealt violence.

Not possible. He was seeing things. Through cracked
lips, Thiercelin said, "Valdin?" And then, as the mist
broke around them, "Valdin, no!"

Fog rose up about the figures. Thiercelin called out
his friend's name a third time, raw-edged. Then something hit him on the back of the head, and the lights
went out.

Gracielis ran into the darkness, and the mist parted
before him. Sour water and honeysuckle out of season.
He should have been defeated by his own frailties, but
he was not. No time for that, now; for he had heard
Thiercelin's voice cry out.

Thierry, I . . . Gracielis owed willing allegiance to no
one. Possession, victim, it was not allowed him. It was a
defiance of all he had been shaped to be, but he arro-
gated it nevertheless to himself. He was burning up,
turning in on all his qualities, and for no better reason
than a cry in the dark.

The mist fringed his vision, unwilling or unable to
come closer. He slowed, and the light that shattered
from him grew steady. He found Thiercelin lying by the
river's edge, unmoving. Gracielis dropped to his knees
beside him and put back the untidy brown hair. Thiercelin's eyes were shut. Blood ran from his lips and shoulder.
His right arm was folded beneath him at an impossible
angle. Lower . . . Gracielis made himself lift the torn
and soiled cloak. Lower down, Thiercelin's side was a
bloody mess. Something had laid bare part of his rib
cage and worried the vulnerable flesh. Gracielis made
himself think. Thiercelin still lived. No artery had been
severed. Healing was no *undarios* gift. It ran counter to
their nature. He must do something, nevertheless. Thiercelin stirred and moaned. Gracielis touched his good
shoulder and murmured reassurance. He was wasting

time. He used his own cloak to staunch the large wound. He needed to summon help somehow. Thiercelin, left alone, would be too easy a prey for whatever lay hidden in the covering mist. They could be no more than a few hundred yards from the nearest building. Gracielis undid his doublet and began to tear strips from his shirt. He might just be able to drag Thiercelin to the nearest shelter, although his abused wrists would protest. Thiercelin groaned again and Gracielis paused to lay a hand on his face, whispering love words.

He could hear water falling somewhere. Water and the slow beat of wings. Under his hands Thiercelin cried out, and Gracielis shivered.

His light was dying. He was burning up too fast; the reaction would, unavoidably, kill him. He did not have enough time. There was movement in the mist: the shadow closing in. His hand tightened on Thiercelin's shoulder. He forced himself to be still, to be calm. He was unprepared. He was all there was. He looked up. Into half-seen eyes he said, "You shall not have him."

The air was thick with wings. His voice was unsteady. Beneath his hand Thiercelin shifted and moaned. It was too dark. Gracielis' palms were damp. He straightened and stared into the shadows. This was not his domain. All about him water tugged and swirled. Into it, into the battering, he spoke the words of dismissal and watched them snatched away. His hair fell into his eyes. He dared not raise a hand to push it back. A dark head tilted, observing him, and there was a gleam of amusement in water-gray eyes. Through dry lips Gracielis whispered, "You should not . . ." and fell silent.

There was a thin smile on the lips of the erstwhile Lord of the Far Blays. Beneath the reddened shreds of his shirt, his shattered breast rose and fell. His right hand was on his sword hilt. The other rested by his side. His black hair hung soaked around his neck. Raising one dark brow, he looked at Gracielis with disdain and said, "I do not need your opinion."

Thiercelin was fading. Gracielis could feel the blood pooling under his fingers. He said, "You will kill him."

"I think not."

"You don't know. You don't understand what you're doing."

"Indeed?" Sarcasm traced the edge of Valdarrien's voice. He paused and drew his sword a little way from its sheath. "You question me?" Pale light ran down the sides of the blade.

Gracielis let his hands clench into Thiercelin's blood and shook his head. "No. I contradict you."

"Novel." Valdarrien considered. "You're nobody, of course."

"As you will." Touching charm, Gracielis let his gaze drop briefly. Thiercelin was pale in his arms, and still. Blood drew shadows along his shoulder and throat. "But this one isn't."

"Thierry," Valdarrien said. "Yes, I think you may be right."

"And you're harming him."

"I doubt it."

"Blood calls to blood. You'll drink his strength, sustaining yourself."

"The image isn't pretty. One might almost feel insulted."

Thiercelin might die. Gracielis said, "You can't feel. You're dead." Caught himself up, sharp on the end word. Swan wings rose and fell in Valdarrien's eyes, snatching at Gracielis' breath. He was trembling, he was cold. He would fail Thiercelin, as he had always failed. *Chai ela,* Quenfrida.

I am yours, Quenfrida. She had no compunction, no compassion. She traded life and death for knowledge. He could not. He was warped under it, too frail to sustain his dual role. Thiercelin's skin was cooling. Gracielis drew one hand up along his shoulder to his throat, where the faint pulse beat. And let himself finally face his own truth.

Thierry, I love you.

The price was too high. Gracielis put memory away from him and raised his eyes to Valdarrien's. "No insult," he said, soft, trembling. "Truth." And then, too quick for an answer, "Your life is no life, unless sustained and bound by blood." Valdarrien's mouth quirked. "I deny you by stone and flame, wind and wave and darkness. You shall not have Thiercelin." Valdarrien took a step toward him. Gracielis fought panic. "You will kill him, if you take anything from him." His hands were wet with Thiercelin's blood. He wiped them on his thighs and stood. Valdarrien was a full head taller than he. Fear washed through him. He said. "You want a life, Lord Valdarrien?" The gray eyes flickered assent. "So. Take mine."

Silence lies on the city, like a hand holding back a pendulum. A stillness, between waking and sleeping. A breath, a waiting, a moment outside. Then time moves on, and the darkness rushes in. To Gracielis, on the quay, it is a soundless thunderclap that knocks him to his knees, opening him to everything. He has no boundaries. He has no control. He feels Thiercelin's touch, and the bitter weight of Quenfrida's ownership. Her lips trace the veins in his throat and drink the blood that gathers there in the sweetest of his hollows. His heart beats with the ringing of the bells. The air bears memories, magnolia and amber and musk. Thiercelin's pain channels through him, then Valdarrien's, until he is breaking with it, and their needs spin out from him into chaos. He is the channel and the flow. The touch on his skin is soft rain, water spray. He feels Valdarrien's longings strip through him, and swan wings drive them home. The feel in his hand of living steel. The wicked joy of anger. The still, cool space that is Iareth Yscoithi. Gracielis clutches at it, feeling his solitude unraveling, and need sets the threads spinning anew. Blood binds . . . There is death in him, around him, he can see it coming.

He touches stone and realizes that it too is within him, legacy of his inhuman ancestry. Aspected in stone, grounded in stone. Water buffets him and breaks. His hands are tangled in Thiercelin's hair. Fire flashes down to burn him. He opens before it and feels it move him without destroying. His body remembers the soft comfort that is Amalie. Winds lay hold of him and tear, accented with Quenfrida's perfume. He puts from him his need for her, and feels the air pour through him. Stolen memory holds him beneath the level grasp of Iareth. He is still, he is stone. He gives no resistance to Valdarrien's exploration of him and feels that strong soul grow stronger. Gracielis draws the touch closer and tastes water and blood. It neither helps nor hinders; it is without will, without consciousness. He slips, silken-graceful, through chains that bespeak Quenfrida's weaving, and pulls Valdarrien with him. He can feel his body beginning to change. He is deafened by a thousand silver bells. He draws his last breath and welcomes ending. It embraces him, fills him, and finds its place. He draws his first breath and knows himself whole.

Gracielis *undarios.*

In the Tarnaroqui embassy Quenfrida lets her goblet fall, and clouds dance in her sky-blue eyes. In his rooms, Kenan starts awake and stares into the darkness, heart pounding. In an inn on East Gold Street, Urien Armenwy throws wide a window and dives swan-form into the night.

Gracielis *undarios.*

17

"**M**AL, STOP THAT." Miraude pushed playfully at her companion's hands.

Maldurel of South Marr looked at her in reproach and leaned back into a corner of the coach. "You're very proper tonight."

She dimpled at him. "Don't rush me."

"Thought you liked to be rushed."

"Well, sometimes I do . . ." Her expression grew wicked. "But tonight I feel like keeping something for later."

"Oh oh!" Maldurel stared at her. "Think I'm not capable, then? Not up to both occasions?" She giggled. He took her hand and kissed the palm. Then the wrist and the inside of her elbow. "Well?"

She stopped giggling long enough to kiss him. Then she pulled away and said primly, "The driver."

"Paid to keep quiet, like all your people." He peered at her. "Trying to tell me something, Mimi?" Miraude stroked his hand. He considered her for a moment, then continued, "Don't tell me you've fallen for Prince Kenan. You've been seen with him a lot lately."

She shrugged, "He's interesting. He knows a lot of history."

"Don't call that interesting," Maldurel said. "Sure you're not turning into a scholar, Mimi?"

"Completely." She smiled at him. One might not trust him with any secret: he had all the discretion of a magpie. Yet she remained fond of him for all that. He had been her first lover; he remained a kind friend. She said, "Have you seen Thierry? He was at the soirée, but I didn't really get to talk to him."

"Not for days. He's holed himself up somewhere and won't come out or answer my notes."

"Yviane's hardly ever home now, either. She practically lives at the palace. And with Thierry having moved out . . ." She turned to him. "It's like when Valdin died. Too quiet. And with all this trouble in the low city . . ."

"Won't touch us here." Maldurel squeezed her fingers. "Thierry always was stubborn. He'll come round."

"I hope so." Miraude put her head on his shoulder. "Thanks, Mal."

"Welcome." He grinned. "I get a reward, then?"

"Oh, you!" She kissed his cheek.

The coach came to a sudden halt, throwing them both forward. Maldurel caught her shoulders and steadied her. She hung onto him, gasping. "What happened?"

"Don't know. Stay here. I'll ask." He opened the door on his side and peered out. "Well?" he called up to the driver.

Miraude opened her window and peered out in turn. By the light of the carriage lamps, she could see the driver standing in the road, bending over something. She could not quite make out what. She called, "What is it?"

The coachman turned and bowed. "I beg your pardon, mademoiselle, monseigneur. There's been an incident. A person . . ."

"We hit someone?" Miraude opened the door and prepared to climb out. "Are they hurt?"

"I'm not sure, mademoiselle." The driver was uncomfortable. "We were driving slowly. This person just seemed to fall into our path, and I had trouble stopping."

Miraude jumped down into the road. The victim was a man of about her own age. He wore a stained and torn cavalry cassock. His face was dirty. He was uncon-

scious. The driver stood to one side, twisting his hands.
He said, "I don't think we hit him."

She waved him into silence. "We can't leave him
here." She called, "Mal, come here, will you?" Maldurel,
grumbling, climbed down from the carriage. "We'll take
him home."

"Can't do that," Maldurel said reasonably. "Don't
know his address."

"Home with *us*, stupid," Miraude said. Maldurel
looked affronted. "You'll have to help lift him into the
coach. We can fetch a doctor later."

Maldurel and the driver exchanged glances. "Now,
Mimi, wait a moment," Maldurel said. "That might not
be for the best. After all, the fellow's a stranger. Could
be anyone. Could be drunk. An inn, that's the answer."

"Oh, Mal! It may be our fault he's hurt." Maldurel
looked unconvinced. She went on, "Yviane would. So
would Thierry."

"Valdin wouldn't."

"Valdin had no manners. Everyone says so."

He shook his head, then sighed. "Yours to command.
As usual."

"Thank you." Miraude hesitated, then stood on tiptoe
and kissed his cheek. "You're very dear, Mal."

"No, I'm not. I'm soft, that's what. Well, let's do it."
Maldurel pulled on his gloves and leaned over to lift the
shoulders of the injured man. "River bless!"

"What is it?"

"I know this fellow. That lantern; bring it here." The
driver brought it. "Yes, I thought so. Cavalry chap.
Thierry wanted to fight him. Can't remember why."
Maldurel hauled at the unconscious figure. "Your house,
you said?" Miraude took the lamp from the driver and
the latter lifted the man's feet.

She said, "Do you remember his name?"

"Not sure." Maldurel panted as he helped with the
carrying. "It'll . . . come back to me." They hoisted the

limp form into the coach and settled it on a seat. "Fellow's a mess. Best not get too close."

"Is he injured?"

Maldurel peered. "Don't think so. But he *is* drunk. Take him to barracks."

"Oh, but . . ." She hesitated. "I still think a doctor . . ."

"Army has doctors, doesn't it?"

"Yes, but . . ."

The man stirred, and his eyes flickered open. He looked at Maldurel without recognition and said, indistinctly, "Iareth?"

"What?" Maldurel said.

Miraude frowned. Then she motioned the driver back to his box and climbed into the coach. Maldurel was right, the man was a mess. His clothing was filthy, and he smelled of ale and vomit. But the expression in his deep-set eyes was pleading. Maldurel opened his mouth. She held up a hand to silence him and said, "We're taking him home. Drive on."

He had black hair to his shoulders and well-shaped gray eyes. His bones were good, but he wore a beard and mustache along the straight jaw and round the thin lips. His skin tone was the warm honey common to Merafiens. He stood medium tall, with a fencer's long muscles beneath the shredded remains of his shirt. A gold stud pierced his left ear. Attractive, in the feral mode.

He was holding his left hand in front of his face and looking at it, turning it slowly, flexing the fingers. Then he put it to his heart. The bloodied shirt parted, but the chest below was whole. His straight black brows lifted, questioning. He was Valdarrien d'Illandre, once Lord of the Far Blays, and he was dead.

Had been dead. Gracielis, on his knees before him, looked up and pushed his soaking hair back. His own hands were filthy with blood and earth; his clothing was ruined. Thiercelin lay between them; the wound torn in his side was no longer bleeding. His breathing was slow and regular. Gracielis felt for a pulse. It was steady. Gracielis whispered thanks into the night. Then he stood and looked again at Valdarrien. There was no weakness in him, no backlash. He could feel his blood pumping clean through him. The long cuts in his abused wrists were healed, marked out only by fading scars. He had never known such a sense of certainty.

He felt like laughing. Mist yet clung to their perimeters. Thiercelin needed help. Gracielis drew in a breath, savoring the movement, and smiled to see Valdarrien doing likewise. Then he said, "This isn't possible."

Valdarrien's straight brows lifted anew. "I have not," said his former lordship, "made any great study of superstitions."

One of them should be dead. Gracielis had passed through his final gate and faced the seventh test through necessity rather than desire. Faced and survived; but the price should have been a life taken, not a life given. At their feet, Thiercelin groaned, and Gracielis put the mystery from him. The fog had thinned a little. He could see the houses along the quay and on the corner of Silk Street. "Thierry needs help," he said. "I have a friend who lives nearby." Pray Amalie was at home tonight. "But I can't carry him alone."

Valdarrien looked down. "What happened to him?"

"He was attacked. Ambushed."

Gray eyes watched him, shaded with suspicion. Mist coiled within them and Gracielis shivered. He said, "You can touch him, can't you?"

Valdarrien looked puzzled. He reached a hand out, questioning. Gracielis held out one of his own. Met warm flesh, solid, real. Not possible . . . Valdarrien said, "What is it? What's happened to me?"

"I don't know," Gracielis said. "Forgive me."

There was a silence; then Valdarrien bent over Thiercelin and lifted him with care. "Is it far?"

"Two streets or so."

Valdarrien shrugged. "Let's do it, then."

They met no one en route. The mist fell back, away from the river. For all that, Gracielis could feel it along his spine. What he had done must have blazed like a beacon, for those who might see. There would be consequences.

Amalie's house was dark. Gracielis suppressed uncertainty and knocked as loudly as he could.

There was a long silence. Amalie *was* out. They would have to go elsewhere, to his old lodgings or some other inn . . . Gracielis conjured Amalie's image beneath his long lashes and prayed. It could not end like this.

The door opened fractionally, and a familiar voice said, "We're closed."

Gracielis said, "It's me, Madame Herlève. Forgive me but I need your help. There's been an . . . accident."

"Another one?"

"To Monseigneur de Sannazar."

There was a pause. Then Herlève said, "You take advantage of Madame Viron."

"I know."

She had liked Thiercelin despite everything. Gracielis heard her sigh; then the door opened wider. She wore her oldest garments, and her hair was covered. The shop behind her was more than half-empty, contents packed into chests. She sniffed and said, "Dueling, I take it?" She stared at them disapprovingly. "There's almost no one here. The boys have been sent ahead, and Madame and I are leaving tomorrow, like you wanted. You'll have to fetch your own doctor. If you can find one willing to come out at this hour, which I doubt." She spoke briskly but, for all that, she helped them take Thiercelin upstairs and set about cleaning and binding his side. She also found some clothing for Valdarrien. Then she ordered them both back to the kitchen, with instructions not to disturb Amalie.

The kitchen was warm and empty. Gracielis, almost

absently, began to make tea. Valdarrien watched him for a few moments, then said, "Thierry needs a doctor."

"Doubtless," Gracielis said. "But you heard Madame Herlève, monseigneur. We'll have to wait until dawn."

Valdarrien put a hand to his sword hilt. "Not necessarily."

Gracielis drew a hand through his disordered hair and suppressed a sigh. As mildly as he could, he said, "That would be inadvisable, I think," and then, as Valdarrien looked disbelieving, "Consider, monseigneur. We're dependent on the good will of Madame Herlève and her mistress. It would be discourteous to make difficulties for them."

"Really?" Valdarrien's tone held all the dismissive arrogance of the born aristocrat.

Gracielis rubbed his eyes. He had washed his face and hands, but he still felt soiled. "Monseigneur, forgive me, but it can't be done. We don't have any money. Dead men don't commonly own property." Valdarrien frowned. Gracielis added, "Monseigneur de Sannazar is in good hands. In the morning I'll petition Madame Viron."

He was very tired. He sat down on a stool and rested his head on his arms. He seemed to be fated to dealings with ghosts.

To living with ghosts. He made himself look up at Valdarrien, into Valdarrien, and heard water falling. Not wholly inhuman . . . Even now, even after what he had done tonight, Gracielis was more human than this creature opposite him. Bound into the present by some past vow, made to the sound of falling water and the beating of swan wings. His skin would be cool, created as he was from mist and pure strength of will. He should not exist.

Instead . . . Gracielis was more than he had ever meant to be; and Valdarrien d'Illandre was back from the dead. He could not understand it. In becoming *undarios*, he should have faced death and driven it away by slaying another. Or else have died himself. He had

never heard of an outcome such as this. He watched the
swan wings rising in the depths of Valdarrien and looked
away. For so long he had been shadowed by this man's
life. He was free now. He did not know if the same was
true of Valdarrien.

It should not have happened. It should never have
happened. Not in Tarnaroq's Bell Temple; not in the
wild places of Lunedith; not—oh, how assuredly—not
and never here in Merafi, where the old powers should
not run. It was part of Quenfrida's weaving, cast up
under the stress of her and Kenan's tampering with what
could, and should, not be. He should go to her and tax
her with it. He should read her, as he had Valdarrien,
and fight to untie whatever bonds she had fabricated.

Except that he was alone and tired and afraid. He put
from him her temptations and said to Valdarrien,
"What's your intention now?"

Valdarrien blinked and looked away. "Does that concern you?"

"Certainly. You know who I am."

"No." Valdarrien's thin lips quirked. "I know what
you are. I owe you nothing."

"As you wish." Gracielis rose and went to the dresser.
He took out bread for himself, hesitated, added a por-
tion for Valdarrien. "You are of course under no obligation." He had had his fill of chains. He had no wish to
shape new ones. "But consequences are usually worth a
little consideration. What do you remember, monseigneur?"

"Thierry," Valdarrien said, and stopped. His brows
drew together. "It's confused. I remember an inn, a
duel . . . Then he talked to me, at home." Again he
paused and frowned. "There's a lot missing. As if I've
been asleep."

You have been dead. But Gracielis could not bring
himself to say that. After a moment Valdarrien said,
"And I know you. You were with Thierry at my duel
and again, somewhere . . ."

"You know me."

"Thierry cried." Valdarrien's hand went to his breast, over his heart. "There was pain."

"Yes."

"But I shouldn't have fought there . . . I'd promised Urien . . ." Valdarrien halted and shivered.

Gracielis put plates onto the table and forced himself to decide. It could be no worse than anything else he had already done.

He said, "You died. You fought a duel with an army officer and were shot. I saw it. So did Thierry." Valdarrien's face gave nothing away. Gracielis continued. "Afterward—six years afterward—you've come back. A shadow. A haunt."

Valdarrien said, "Iareth . . . a warning. I don't understand you."

"No? No matter. I scarcely understand myself." Gracielis sat down, and cut the bread.

Valdarrien said, "I saw her, here in Merafi. My Iareth *kai-reth*."

"She's here." Valdarrien half-rose. Gracielis put out a hand. "You can't go now. Merafi is unsafe at night, even for you." Valdarrien hesitated. "And Thierry may need you."

"You," said Valdarrien, "are very free with that name. For a foreigner."

"Indubitably. But that's between me and him. And you," and Gracielis smiled, "have made free with more than his name. You came close to killing him."

"I think not."

"You'd have helped yourself to his life, as you had tried formerly to steal mine. You aren't what you think you are, monseigneur."

"Indeed not?" The tone was dangerous. "And you're expert on this?"

Wind buffeted at the shutters, sudden, harsh. Gracielis dropped the bread knife and turned. There was a chill in the air and some other thing. Again a buffet. Valdarrien rose and went to the window. Before Gracielis could stop him, he threw it open. The wind poured in. No, not wind, but some other thing, driving cold air before it on great white wings. A swan. A vast swan, raising its head to Valdarrien's, and stretching up and back and out into man-shape, naked against the night. Mist began to form, fringing the window, and Gracielis finally found the power to act. He looked to the window and spoke a soft word. The shutters slammed shut, although he had neither risen nor approached them. Then the bar dropped into its place across them. Party tricks . . . Stone-blessed, for barriers and boundaries. No one looked at him, or noticed what he had done. The man blown out of the night faced the man reborn from it, and said, "You will tell me, Valdin *kai-reth*, by what right you disobeyed my express command that you should live."

"Firomelle's asleep, I'm afraid."

Yvelliane jumped and looked around. She had not heard the door in the paneling open. Papers were strewn across the desk before her; but she would have been hard-pressed to describe the contents of any of them. Her head ached. Nevertheless, she rose and made herself smile.

Laurens returned her smile and shut the door behind him. "You look busy."

"There's trouble in the low city."

"Quite." He went to the window and stared out into the darkness. Yvelliane remained standing. He said, "The footman brought your message to me. Fielle sleeps so little these days."

"Yes." He looked as tired as she felt, his skin sallow. She doubted he had had any sleep since before the soirée. She suppressed an urge to go to him. There was nothing either of them could say or do that would ease Firomelle's illness.

Laurens took a final look out at the night and turned.

"Such weather." He sat. "Sit down, Yviane. I need to talk to you."

She sat and he drew a chair up to the side of her desk and joined her. He said, "This is difficult . . . Regarding Quenfrida d'Ivrinez . . . I've seen the documentation you've prepared. It's very thorough. But we can't go through with it."

"What? We agreed . . ."

"Yes, I know that. But now isn't the time to antagonize the Tarnaroqui. We have enough troubles at home."

"There are always disputes in the low city or the docks." She leaned forward. "Please . . ."

"Disease," he said. "Flooding. A quarter of the watch have deserted, and there are two full patrols missing. Parts of the city are abandoned after dark."

Gracielis had spoken to her of danger. He had warned of deliberate, determined, malicious attack, fueled by his Tarnaroqui mistress. She had taken steps to remove that mistress, to expose her for what she was. Yvelliane said, "I'm aware of Tarnaroqui complicity in our problems. The public exposure of Quenfrida . . ."

Laurens sighed and rubbed his eyes. "Fielle had another hemorrhage this morning. She isn't strong enough to deal with a diplomatic incident. She probably doesn't have much longer."

No. But she did not say it. Laurens' face was bleak: he had enough to deal with. She must bear this alone, as she bore the trouble in her marriage. Reaching out, she took his hand. His fingers wrapped about hers tightly. She said, "Is there . . . ?"

He shook his head. "The doctors are just waiting now. There's nothing left to try. And," and he released her hand, "that means we must have stability right now. If we offend Tarnaroq, and she dies . . . It'd be just the excuse they'd need to make trouble. They'd see a regency as the ideal opportunity to move in on our borders and interest."

He was right. That much was undeniable. She had

been too slow to act and now it was too late. She longed for Thiercelin, suddenly, calm and kind and always there for her. Always there, until now. She had driven him away with her intransigence. She said, "What can we do, then?"

"I don't know." There were tears in his eyes. She looked away. One them must stay calm.

She said "I can keep watching Quenfrida. Kenan, too. If one of them does something overt . . ."

"It won't save Fielle."

"It might help Merafi." She made her voice brisk. "We have to look after the country for her now." All her adult life, she had served Firomelle. All her life, she had sought to benefit and protect her country, her city, her people. And it had all come down to this . . . Gracielis would ascribe it to Merafien blindness and arrogance in the face of the irrational, no doubt. Yvelliane did not know what to think. Perhaps there was nothing left to do save wait and hope. Perhaps she should be laying plans to spirit the heir away from Merafi to some distant place of safety. If any such place existed.

Perhaps, if she wrote to him now, at the bottom of her strength, Thiercelin would take pity on her and come.

Perhaps he would not. She said, "I'll start putting together an emergency strategy."

"Dear Yviane." Laurens rested a hand on her shoulder. "We have to support one another now. Firomelle hasn't the strength any longer."

There was a long silence. Gracielis sat motionless. Valdarrien looked at the floor, then the window, then, finally, at the newcomer. His expression was something between surprise and outrage. Speaking, his voice held no small amount of indignation. "Is a man of honor simply to take an insult, Urien *kai-reth*?"

"A man of honor will never be insulted. And even if, through some mischance, insult is forced upon him, he will fight competently, Valdin *kai-reth*."

Valdarrien's gray eyes narrowed. His right hand worked, as if he barely arrested a move to his sword hilt. He said, "An oversight, I grant you."

"Quite so."

Gracielis coughed, and two pairs of eyes turned to look at him. He rose and said, "Good evening."

"And to you also." The newcomer had level green eyes like those of Iareth Yscoithi. He had great dignity despite his nakedness. He studied Gracielis for long moments. "I know what you are, I'm certain of that. But as to who . . . ?"

Swan wings. Swan wings across the sky . . . Gracielis bowed. "I am known as Gracielis de Varnaq. And you are Urien Armenwy, called Urien Swanhame, leader of the guard of Prince Keris Orcandros."

Urien smiled. "You are well informed."

"I'm clear-sighted."

"That isn't a unique ability." The level gaze lay weighty on Gracielis. He stood firm beneath it. Hours before, it would have made him shiver. Urien said, "*Chai ela*, Gracielis *undarios istin-shae* Quenfrida." He glanced at Valdarrien. "Your doing, I think?"

Swan wings and a binding. A promise, it seemed, to live. Gracielis smiled and said, "Not solely mine." And then, in Lunedithin, "He is what he seems to be. More or less."

"So I had surmised." Urien said, in the same tongue. Valdarrien frowned. To him, Urien continued, "I have come in good time, I see. There is a great disturbance in this city."

"Too great," said Gracielis, thinking of Thiercelin.

Defensively Valdarrien said, "It's nothing to do with me." And then, "She's here, also. My Iareth *kai-reth*."

"It was Iareth Yscoithi summoned me." Urien stared him down. To Gracielis he said, "I beg your pardon, but have you anything in which I might clothe myself?"

"I'll see." Gracielis bowed and let himself out of the kitchen. The house was dark. He made his way upstairs for clothing, and paused to check on Thiercelin. Herlève met him in the door. She said, "He's asleep."

"I'm glad." He hesitated. "There's someone here who may be able to treat him further."

"Another of your street friends?"

"No." Gracielis looked down. "I can't explain all this."

"So I've noticed."

"Madame Herlève . . ." He drew in a long breath and looked up. "I'm at your mercy."

"It won't wash, Gracieux." She met his eyes. He would have preferred to face down Kenan.

He said, "I beg you . . ."

"Madame doesn't need the trouble you cause."

"I know. But . . ."

In the corridor a door opened. Then Amalie's voice, misty with sleep, called, "Herlève?"

"Coming, madame." Herlève shot Gracielis another poisoned glance and bustled out.

Thiercelin moved a little and groaned. Gracielis turned and went to the bed. He lifted one of the pale hands carefully. He said in Tarnaroqui, "Oh, my dear one." And then, "Forgive me."

There was no response. Gracielis rested his brow on the back of Thiercelin's hand. He could no longer afford to rely on others. He was alone, he must act. He dropped a kiss on the hand, and raised his head. He could hear Amalie's voice, and Herlève's. Rising, he went out into the corridor and knocked.

He did not wait for an answer. Both women turned to look at him, Amalie in surprise, Herlève in disapproval. He bowed and said, "Madame, I need your help."

"You," said Herlève, "need to recall your famous manners."

"Forgive me, madame." Gracielis did not look at her. "Ladyheart, I've brought you an injured man and two strangers in addition to myself. We need shelter. I throw myself on your protection because I have no one else to trust and nowhere else to go." He hesitated. "Madame Herlève says you're leaving Merafi tomorrow. I don't want to delay you. But I crave your leave to remain here in your absence."

"Well!" Herlève said.

Amalie shushed her, sitting down on the end of her bed and frowning. "You're in trouble." It was not a question. Gracielis said nothing.

She picked at the bedcover. "Joyain sent me a warning today. The unrest is spreading . . . Is it that?"

There was only so much he could tell her. He hesitated, then said, "Yes . . . We were set on. Lord Thiercelin is hurt."

"Herlève told me." Amalie rose and came to stand in front of him. She wore only her nightgown, and her hair was loose. He could see the gray in it. She said, "You know you're always welcome here, love. I'll do whatever I can to help you." Her hand sketched the contours of his face. "I owe you, after all."

He caught the hand and kissed it, back and palm. Then he said, "It is I that owe you. But you must leave as planned tomorrow."

"Come with me?"

"I can't."

She studied him. "You mean that, don't you?"

"Yes. Forgive me?"

"Anything, love."

"Thank you," Gracielis said, and meant it.

Thiercelin was woken by the sound of a clock chiming. His head felt heavy. There was a nagging pain in his side. He could not quite move; the attempt hurt. From somewhere beside him a soft voice said, "Monseigneur?"

Thiercelin opened his eyes. Gracielis was leaning over him, looking concerned. Thiercelin smiled at him and remembered.

Mist and violence and a form that could not be
Valdarrien . . . He said faintly, "Graelis?"

"Here, monseigneur. How are you?"

"Terrible," Thiercelin said, and gasped, because
speaking was painful. He struggled to sit up and the
world went awry. Somewhere in the midst of it, hands
came to help him. He clung to them and hung there. He
felt reassuring warmth behind him and smelled jasmine.
He said, "Debt paid, Graelis." And then, "What time
is it?"

"A little after midnight. We're staying with Madame
Viron. Quite safe."

"Good," Thiercelin said. Gracielis' presence was comforting, but he wanted Yvelliane. He must have spoken
her name, for Gracielis said, "Soon, monseigneur," and
his voice was worried.

"She won't come," Thiercelin said.

"She will. But we must wait for dawn. You should
rest. The Armenwy advises it."

"The Armenwy?" Thiercelin was finding it hard to
think. They must have drugged him with something.

"Urien Swanhame, of whom Iareth spoke. He's here."
Gracielis shifted slightly. "Are you thirsty?"

"A little." The liquid raised to his lips tasted bitter.
He swallowed some of it and dropped his head.

Gracielis said, "It'll ease the pain. But you should
sleep."

"Not yet . . . Are you all right, Graelis?"

"Of course." Thiercelin could picture the smile that
accompanied that remark, beautiful and faintly mocking.
Gracielis added, "Why shouldn't I be?"

"I remember what happened. I was attacked . . . You
didn't get to do what you intended . . ." There was no
answer. Thiercelin finished, "And I saw Valdin, again. I
think he saved me."

"Yes," Gracielis said. And then, "I saw him also. He's
here." Another pause. "Do you want to see him?"

Not possible . . . But Thiercelin was losing his sense

of the rational. He said, "Yes," and waited while Gracielis settled him against a pillow, and went to open the door. Voices, and then . . .

Dark brows that lifted over gray eyes. A half-smile edging thin, bearded lips, Thiercelin said unsurely, "Valdarrien." And then, "Oh, Valdin."

Valdarrien drew up a chair and sat down astride it, resting his arms along the back. "In person," he said. "Good evening, Thierry."

"Good evening?" Thiercelin forgot his pain in outrage. "You come back from the dead, and all you can do is say, 'Good evening'?"

"Certainly not." Valdarrien sounded offended. "I have the most distinct recollection of coming between you and a very nasty attack earlier tonight, and I can't say that I'm impressed by the depths of your gratitude. Such as they are."

Gracielis had sat down on the edge of the bed. Thiercelin looked at him, but his face was shuttered, unhelpful. He looked back at Valdarrien and said, "You're real."

"Evidently."

"But . . ." Thiercelin hesitated. "It's confusing."

"For you, anyway," said Valdarrien. "Will you never learn to keep your guard up?"

"A marksman doesn't need to," Thiercelin said, stung.

"Can't block a lunge with an empty pistol," Valdarrien said. But his face was concerned, and after a moment he said, "It hurts?"

"Diabolically."

"Poor Thierry. The fruits of indolence."

Thiercelin glared. "Indolence? Who was it who spent three months flat on his back for underestimating an out-of-towner?"

Valdarrien shrugged. "I concede I may have been a little overconfident once or twice, but that incident happened when I was all of eighteen!"

"Twenty-one."

"Eighteen." Thiercelin refused to be stared down. Valdarrien sighed. "Maybe twenty. But . . ."

It was very tiring. Thiercelin managed to find a smile for his old friend, but his eyes were closing and he could no longer concentrate. He said, "My thanks, Valdin," and felt a familiar hand grip his arm briefly.

Valdarrien said, "What else would I do?"

That was reassuring. Thiercelin murmured, "Do the same for you . . . some time . . ." and let himself settle back against the pillows.

From a long way away he heard Gracielis say "Let him be, now." A hand came to take his, known in its strength, in the line of callus across the palm. A swordsman's hand . . . Thiercelin returned the pressure and let himself slide away into warm darkness.

Leaving Valdarrien with Thiercelin, Gracielis found Amalie awaiting him. He closed the door quietly and smiled at her. She said, "Well?"

"He's sleeping. Lord Val . . . His friend will sit with him."

"I recognize Valdarrien d'Illandre." Amalie looked at him. "No questions, love."

He was grateful for that. He was tired. Urien and Herlève had retired. Thiercelin was weak but not in danger. There was nothing more that needed to be done, this night . . . He sighed and rubbed his eyes, trying not to think about the retribution that surely awaited him at Quenfrida's hands. Amalie touched his arm and said, "Come to bed. You're worn out."

"I'm imposing."

"No." She drew him into her room and shut the door. "I mean sleep only, love. I know you've had a strange night."

He could not help smiling. He sat down on the bed and began to undress. He said, "Have I thanked you yet?"

"Several times."

"Insufficient." Amalie had taken off her robe and climbed into the bed. She reached out to close the hangings on her side. He stripped to his shirt and said, "I will always be your debtor."

He slid into bed beside her, and she extinguished the candle with a snuffer. Lying on his back, hands behind his head, he stared at the canopy and listened to her breathing. She said, "Your wrists are healed."

"Yes."

"I don't want to know what happened to you tonight. Merafi is growing strange."

"Yes. I'm glad you're going. I shall like to know that you are safe somewhere."

"I'll come back, you know."

"Not soon, I beg you." Gracielis rolled on to his side and looked at her indistinct form. "Go safely, Ladyheart."

"And you, love." She reached out and stroked his cheek. "I'm afraid for you, sometimes."

He kissed her fingers. "Don't be." Her touch was soft and oddly pleasant. He leaned into it. "I have my own protections."

"Yes." Amalie sounded sad. He drew her against him. He could feel her warmth, the soft motions of her breath. He closed his eyes, enjoying the sensation, letting his hand slide over her shoulders. After a moment he bent and kissed her. She pressed close to him, returning it. He shivered, and his hands moved to the lacing on her gown. She helped him, shifting so that he could slip it away and undid his shirt. He lay still, savoring the feeling of her hands on him. There was no urgency to it; he awakened to her gently, kindly. She leaned across him, trailing kisses along his jaw, down his throat. Her lips reached the hollow of his collarbone. He gasped, and something ignited.

This should not be happening . . . He lay in Amalie's arms, letting her explore and arouse him, and he was responding not to memory, but to reality. Not to some ghost-Quenfrida, but to the woman beside him. Amalie's hands stroked down his flank. Need blazed within him. He kissed her with unfamiliar hunger, and heard her gasp.

He was remade in one night. He had been property, spirit and body; and now he was not. He opened his eyes and looked up at Amalie. She smiled. He remembered how it was she liked to be touched and let his hands move. She pressed closer to him, and he felt her pleasure like a wave. His own need was almost too intense to be supported. He arched against her, and she opened for him. That was even better. He heard his breath sob as he moved and moved and moved, closer and closer. Amalie shuddered and called his name. He held her tighter, feeling her climax, unable even to pause. There was a roaring within him, a desperate pressured inward intensity; he would fall in pieces, he would break apart . . . Flame lanced through him, sudden and violent, as his head fell back and he rose against her and lost his fears in unguessed pleasure.

He wept afterward, and she held him close and asked no questions.

18

QUENFRIDA UNLOCKED THE ROSEWOOD casket with a smooth click. The box was old, dark with polish and candle smoke, the inlaid geometric pattern almost indistinguishable. It was Lunedithin-made, worked by a craftsman through whose veins the old clan-blood had run thick and strong. Under her fingertips, she could just about hear the remote murmur of his thoughts. She had had Gracielis read the box for her, long ago in Tarnaroq, as an exercise for his ghost-sight. Even now, she remembered his narrow hand lying on the lid, the intent cast to his face, the serious light in his beautiful eyes. Her own abilities did not lie in that direction; no trace of him remained to her sensing, although he had used power over it. Frail even then: she had been more than half-ready for him to faint as the color left his skin. But at the last, he had turned to her and smiled. "His name was Kierian Penedar," he had said. "A true changer: I can feel the second shape of him, made for running . . . He was thinking of someone, a woman of his clan . . . It's a long way back, Quena."

A long way. Old things were better, for some purposes. Their locked-in memories served to shield more recent contents and events from casual detection by others. She returned the key to the locket around her neck and opened the casket.

It held a number of small parchment wallets, layered and sealed, but otherwise undifferentiated. Quenfrida saw no sense in leaving clues to assist her rivals. Besides, she was perfectly acquainted with the contents of each and would not be confused by any casual disordering. She took out the third from the bottom and shut the box. Then she crossed to her small lacquered escritoire.

She had covered the top with a square of raw, undyed silk, cut rough from the bale and neither hemmed nor embroidered. Candles burned to either side of it, one red, one blue, both scented in her own tones, musk and amber and bitter orange. Without turning, she commanded the room's other candles into darkness: she had to look at the fire to extinguish it, but after a moment, it, too, obeyed her.

She opened the wallet and removed the contents, using silver tweezers. No point risking confusion with her own touch. From a drawer, she took a small porcelain bowl and a knife. She set them on the silk, holding the tweezers with her other hand. There was a length of ribbon on the edge of the table. She flicked the end flat and placed the contents of the wallet upon it. Then she closed her eyes, sat motionless, inhaling the scent of her candles.

When she opened them again, their blue had darkened almost to black. A faint light limned her; her face held a complete calm. Dimly, she felt the presence of her compatriots elsewhere in the embassy, distant, feeble, undistinguished. She exhaled slowly and extended herself along the air currents. There was no one near, no one working. The river had begun to subside with approaching dawn. The hour was good.

She lifted the knife with thoughtful fingers. She did not trouble to test it; she knew it was sharp. Her left hand lifted to hover an inch or so over the bowl; she looked at it, briefly, then brought the knife diagonally across her palm.

It did not hurt. She had learned long ago to control her body, so that she felt pain only when it suited her. She watched as the blood dripped into the bowl, long slow drops. After ten, she turned the palm up and stanched it with a cloth. From a compartment within the desk drawer, she drew out a number of small vials, and an eyedropper. She added drops from several to the bowl, careful of the proportions. With the knife tip, she stirred the liquid. It began to take on an oily iridescence. Its mingled odors rose and entwined with the scent of her candles.

She turned back to the item she had removed from the wallet. A long tress of human hair, dark auburn and slightly waved. From it, she drew two strands with the tweezers and placed them on the silk, beside the bowl. The rest, she replaced in the wallet.

She took up one hair, whispered a few words. Old Tarnaroqui, old Lunedithin, mixed into near incomprehensibility; each reinforcing the other by expansion from blindness. She let the strand fall into the bowl and breathed on it.

The candles flickered. She could hear wind gusting in the garden, considering its way about tree limbs, teasing the catch on her shutters. A clock ticked in the room next door. In the hall, someone laughed. Quenfrida waited, spine straight, eyes wide to the dawn. She was no longer breathing.

A faint shimmer began on the surface of the bowl: she felt the answering inner stir of her sympathetic blood. A ghosting, a shadowing, a miasma rising from the mingled liquids, less substantial than smoke. The light around her brightened, white and cold blue. The thread of near-mist held its own colors and they were dark and warm.

A small frown creased the skin between her brows. Within her, discomfort flickered into life, a dis-ease, a reluctance . . . She unwound the cloth from her hand and held the small wound over the flame of the blue candle. Its smoke turned acrid; her palm stung remotely. She held it unmoving for ten heartbeats. Then she withdrew it and thrust it into the misty column rising from the bowl.

The tendons jerked back. Her fingers clawed. Her

wrist shook. Her even white teeth bit into her underlip, drawing blood. The taste startled her: she had not felt the pain. Something had changed . . . Last night, some-one out there had tried a working, and she would have the details. Something had happened. Something had changed, and the taste upon it had spoken to her of Gracielis.

He had not the right . . . She had cautioned him and compelled him and forced him ever to her will. Even his last insubordination, with the lieutenant's ghost, should have served only to bind him closer to her, trapped in the web of fear which she had created for him.

He should be of no account.

And yet . . . A whisper of jasmine; a coolness aspected in stone . . . The steam rising from the bowl seared her, clogging her veins, and she gasped. She could feel him, out there, somewhere in the city, sleeping. The familiar touch of him, silken, uncertain, edged now with some other, sharper thing. His blood bright, clean within him. A sense from him of—almost—contentment. And a touch which was neither her own nor yet the water-thunder of the river. He had drawn himself into that; she could feel it. But there was something more . . . The weight of water falling and the texture of stone and a sound. A regular and solid sound, like wings beating . . .

Quenfrida's eyes narrowed. That aura she had touched before. Not here in Merafi, but years before in Lunedith. It had laid deep, there, mingled into the things that lay tangled and quiescent under the old stones of the north. She had realized even then the power inherent in those forces and worked with the young Kenan to unlock them, culminating in the blood spilled unwillingly along-side the great waterfall; Allandurin blood, and Orcandrin . . . But not only those two. It was in the nature of ambushes that many were hurt. The half-blood renegade Iareth Yscoithi. A handful of clansmen from disparate clans. And another, whose touch even then had made her wary.

Urien Armenwy. Full blood, throwback, shapeshifter, and manipulator of forces no less old than those over which Quenfrida sought dominion. His blood had mingled with the waters, with Valdarrien's and Kenan's, in the midst of that careful initiatory awakening.

His touch lay now on Gracielis, who should belong to herself and no other. Urien must, therefore, be somewhere in Merafi. And Gracielis . . . Quenfrida closed her eyes and made one last attempt to read him, to discover just what he had tried to do last night.

She was windborne, domained in air. She could breathe herself inside of him, and fill him wholly. She was *undaria* and dominatrix and mistress of his physical dreams. He had no strength with which he might withstand her. She smiled to herself and reached out to him. Gracielis *arin-shae* Quenfrida.

He was mantled in stone. He was still, he was closed: she could find no way by which she might enter and walk through him.

It should be easy. He should have no defenses. Gracielis-acolyte, possession, of Quenfrida.

Her eyes snapped open, and she stared into the bowl. He had stepped away from her and done what he had once feared to do. Without her presence, without her permission, he had essayed and overcome the seventh test.

He was no longer of no account. Alone in her room, Quenfrida shook her head and began, very softly, to laugh.

There was a room with painted panels and a green-hung bed. Two large long windows overlooked a garden. Overstuffed chairs, a chest, a commode, a heavy armoire. Several silk rugs on the polished wooden floor. In the hearth a small fire burned. Beside it, on the chest top, stood a stoneware jug and ewer filled with fresh warm water. Even the towels looked new. Beside them lay a folded pile of clothing.

Joyain swayed and admitted to himself that he had no idea where he was. His head ached. His mouth tasted foul. Black spots danced before his eyes. His balance was giving him problems. He felt feverish. Washing and dressing in small stages, he listened to the tides of heat which ran through him, and struggled for control. He remembered an inn and too much ale. The backs of his hands were bruised and grazed. The clothes laid out for him were not his own. He'd been looking for someone, something to do with the warnings he'd received. Looking for someone who could help . . . He wasn't sure. Memory, uncoiling backward, presented him with the image of mutilated Leladrien. His stomach lurched. Luckily for his unknown host's rugs, it seemed to be empty.

There was a mirror on top of a dresser, near a window. A quick glance in it assured him that he looked as bad as he felt. He used one of the brushes provided to put his hair in order and decided that he could not, under any circumstances, face trying to shave. He would have to do.

He was lost and he was abominably late. Always assuming that a warrant wasn't out for him, after yesterday. He straightened, cursed his light-headedness, and let himself out of the room.

A long corridor, lit at both ends by large windows and with a wide stair halfway along it. He could hear distant footsteps; then a door opened and he caught a snatch of voices. Downstairs then. He could make it. He'd had worse hangovers.

He arrived at the head of the stairs by dint of pausing frequently and leaning on walls. He was breathless, perspiring. His eyes kept blurring. He gulped and set a foot on the first step.

His surroundings swayed. He made a frantic grab for the banister and clung to it. After five more steps he had to sit down and try to recover his breath. Sweat slicked his palms. His head pounded.

A door opened in the hall below. Joyain gained a blurred impression of a figure in dark red. Then a female voice exclaimed, "Oh!"

Footsteps, light on the stairs. A tentative hand on his shoulder. "Monsieur?"

He looked up. He struggled to rise, said, "Forgive me, mademoiselle."

She helped him. She was tiny, standing barely to his shoulder. She said, "You're ill, monsieur."

"No, I . . ." He was uneasily aware of a rising wave of nausea. He stopped and swallowed.

She said, "You should be in bed. Come; I'll help you." She was expensively dressed. It couldn't possibly be her place to look after him.

Joyain said, "No, please . . ." and gasped as dizziness swept him. He heard her call names, then a pair of strong male arms were supporting him. He made no protest as he was more or less carried back to his room and lifted onto the bed. The pillows were blessedly cool. Careful hands removed his boots and undid his cassock. He lay still, eyes closed. After a while, the dizziness subsided.

He opened his eyes. The young woman sat next to the bed. She said, "How are you?"

"I'm not sure." Joyain licked dry lips. "Where am I?"

"In my family's townhouse, in the hill quarter."

The aristocrats' quarter. He couldn't recall how he might have come to be here. He said, "You're kind."

"My friend and I found you last night. You couldn't tell us your name, so I brought you here to recover."

"Jean," Joyain said. Then, "No, I mean Joyain. Lieutenant Joyain Lievrier."

"I'm Mimi. Miraude d'Iscoigne l'Aborderie."

The sister-in-law of the queen's First Councillor. The famous widow, Lelien had called her. He was in the house of Yvelliane d'Illandre. He said, "I must go . . . my duty . . ." She frowned, and he tried to sit up and explain. That proved disastrous. He retched uncontrollably, humiliatingly, and painfully. He felt rather like crying. Miraude said, "River bless." And then, "You need a doctor."

He needed to tell her that he should go home. He had duties. He had to find Gracielis de Varnaq and shake out of him what the Tarnaroqui had done to Merafi. But his body was recalcitrant and all he managed to say was, weakly, "But . . ."

Her hands were cool and gentle. She stroked his damp hair back from his brow and said, "Let me worry. Do you have a family I should send for?" .

Only Amalie. And he had warned her to leave. This kindly Miraude should leave too, for her own safety. He had not the time for illness, he had to get help, he had to act . . . He said, "No," and then, "Iareth . . ."

Iareth, who spied on her own leader, and who was together with him witness to the dangers in Merafi. Iareth would help him. Miraude said, "Iareth Yscoithi? You mentioned her name last night." He didn't remember that. "Are you related to her?"

"No." Joyain was finding it hard to think coherently. He said, "A friend."

Miraude had been frowning. At that, her face cleared. "Do you want her? I can send a message. Although . . ." and her brows drew together, "she might not want to come here . . . Well, I can find out."

He said, "Please." And then, "Sorry—so much trouble."

"No." Miraude smiled at him. "You're my guest until you're well again. I'll have the doctor see you, and I'll send for Iareth."

She was so kind. He succeeded in raising a hand to her, although it shook. He said, "Thank you."

"You're very welcome." She patted his hand. Her fingers were cold. She said, "Now, lie still, and I'll sort it out." She rose. "Don't worry. Sleep, if you can. I'll have my maid come and sit with you in case you need anything." She hesitated. "Sleep," she repeated.

Joyain closed his eyes.

*   *   *

Tafarin Morwenedd was talking to someone in the yard, under Kenan's window. His voice disturbed Kenan's concentration, as he tried to force sense from the cards patterned before him. He had cut short the life of his rival; he had twice paid the blood-price necessary for *undarios* power. He should be able to bend it to his will utterly . . . He stared down at the spread and saw nothing. Painted pictures.

It should be easy. An exercise, a task within the ability of any acolyte. It was Tafarin's fault, distracting him. Kenan passed a hand over the cards, disarraying them. New conjunctions formed, silently. Illustrated eyes met. Kenan muttered an imprecation and rose.

He would deal with Tafarin. And then . . . Then, he would see.

He went downstairs and out through the hall. Tafarin stood in the gateway, talking to someone in the street. Kenan could not see who. A guardsman or a street vendor, no doubt. Tafarin had no sense of what was right. No sense of the dignity due to a prince. Merafi had taught Kenan that much, at least. He paused at the foot of the outside steps and called, crossly, "Tafarin *kai-reth!*"

Tafarin looked round, waved, and went back to his conversation. He held something in his left hand; a piece of paper . . . Kenan glared at his back, then stalked across the yard. "Tafarin *kai-reth*, you have disturbed me."

Tafarin turned. "My regrets, Kenan *kai-reth*." He did not sound especially sincere: having made his apology, he again looked away.

It was not to be borne. Kenan drew in a breath and turned to Tafarin's companion, intending to dismiss him. Young, dressed simply, hair drawn off a narrow face in a Lunedithin-style braid . . . It took Kenan several shameful moments to recognize who it was. No paint. No silken artifice. But the devastating eyes were the same and there was a perfume on the air, speaking the syllables of a name. Gracielis de Varnaq looked back at him and bowed, too shallowly for courtesy. He said softly, "Good day, monseigneur."

Kenan gave Gracielis a curt nod, and said nothing. He shivered, a little, and realized that it was cold. That it was not raining, although the ground was damp.

Tafarin said, "Go in, Kenan *kai-reth*. There is no need for you to freeze out here."

"But I know Monsieur de Varnaq." Kenan said. "We met at the palace." Tafarin looked politely blank. "Perhaps he would care to break his fast with us?"

Gracielis looked at Kenan's hands. Then he said, "I thank you, but no. I have errands to run."

"For your mistress?" Kenan asked, nastily.

Gracielis smiled. Gently, he said, "Better, I think, for mine than for yours." He turned to Tafarin. "Good day to you, and my thanks."

"You are most welcome. I will inform Iareth *kai-reth*." Tafarin smiled in turn, and Gracielis bowed to him. Then he walked away down the street.

He looked perfectly healthy. Better, indeed, than he had when Kenan had met him at the palace. And there was something else, something Kenan could not quite identify, some quality . . .

He had been cheated in the creation of his bindings. He had handed power to sly Quenfrida, and still achieved only gleanings for himself. Kenan glared at Tafarin and said, "You will have no further dealings with that individual. I expressly forbid it."

Oh, do you . . . But Tafarin did not say that, for all that it was written over him. He said, quietly, "Good morning, Kenan *kai-reth*," and began to walk away.

Kenan's grandsire, Prince Keris, was too tolerant. It was the influence of foreigners and of the meddler Urien Armenwy. The Armenwy was too deep in the prince's counsel. When Kenan became prince, that would change . . . His grandsire and Urien had saddled him with companions of their choice. Insubordinate Tafarin Morwenedd, too long Urien's deputy. Cold Iareth Yscoithi, twice a traitor to her own kind, by virtue of her half-breed blood and her ill-fated liaison with Valdarrien of the Far Blays.

Valdarrien's Allandurin blood had been shed on Kenan's behalf, to buy his power. He would no longer brook these checks, these spies. He caught up with Tafarin and said, "What did he want?"

"Gracielis?" Tafarin said. Kenan nodded, holding grimly to his patience. "I know not. He brought a letter for Iareth."

Iareth Yscoithi should not be receiving letters from inhabitants of Merafi . . . Kenan swallowed and said, "Where is she?"

"I do not know. She went out."

Nor should she leave without first informing Kenan. He held out his hand and said, "Give it to me." Tafarin was silent, studying him. "I will ensure she receives it."

"It's private," Tafarin said, mildly.

"So she has taken another of these out-clan Merafiens to her bed?" Again, no answer. "That does not accord well with our laws, Tafarin *kai-reth*. Give that letter to me."

"I think not, Kenan *kai-reth*."

"I remind you, then, of clan ranking. I am Orcandrin-born. When my grandsire dies, I will be the Orcandros, ruler not only of my clan, but of our land in its entirety, by the old right of the otter-clan. You are Morweneddin. The fox does not run ahead of the otter. By blood- and birthright, I command you, Tafarin Morwenedd. Do my bidding."

Quenfrida had taught him something of the craft of commanding. Kenan let her dictums settle on him, speaking slowly, calmly; holding his gaze mild and level. Tafarin shuffled and tried to look away. Kenan put out a hand, and looked expectant. There was a pause, then Tafarin put the letter into it.

It was a small triumph. Tafarin was his elder and no respecter of customs which happened not to suit him. An unsuitable person to co-lead the royal *kai-rethin* guard. Kenan would change that when he was prince. He smiled now and said gently, "Thank you, Tafarin *kai-reth*."

Six hundred years of hot clan-blood looked back at him out of Tafarin's eyes. Tafarin snapped, "You are *not* welcome," and turned to go. Kenan went right on smiling.

He opened the letter in the privacy of his suite. Two lines, no more. No address. But it was sufficient. Iareth Yscoithi of Alfial would learn better than to go behind his back. Iareth Yscoithi of Alfial would discover what it meant to cross him.

The handwriting was that of Urien Armenwy. He was here, in Merafi, in defiance of Kenan. It could only be Iareth who had summoned him. It was only the generosity of Kenan's grandsire which had conferred on Iareth the rank and privilege of *kai-reth*. Her bastard breeding should have withheld it from her, out-clan, *elor-reth*.

There were rules, and rules. One set for the clan-bred, the *kai-rethin*. Another, wholly separate, for the bastard *elor-rethin*.

And Iareth *elor-reth*, called Iareth Yscoithi of Alfial, was about to discover the depths of the difference.

A few streets away, Iareth Yscoithi had other things on her mind than what Kenan might think of her. She had been at her morning sword practice when a liveried footman arrived and handed her a letter. She had excused herself to her sparring partner, then opened it, frowning. The writing was unknown to her. The seal was not. The Far Blays.

It was a short note, to the point and frostily polite. Lieutenant Joyain Lievrier had been taken ill. He was under the protection of the d'Illandre family. He had asked for Iareth; the writer would be obliged if she would visit, although equally the writer would understand any reluctance she might feel to enter that house. It was signed "Miraude d'Iscoigne l'Aborderie."

Valdarrien's wife. Valdarrien's widow, whom he once had offered to put aside for Iareth's sake. But Iareth had refused him and returned to her kin, leaving him in turn to this Miraude. And Valdarrien had died.

Iareth had come back to Merafi, but she had had no intention of returning to Valdarrien's home. Not even Urien might compel her so far. But this . . . She could not imagine how Joyain might have come to be under Miraude's protection, but it was there in black and white. Ill, and asking for her . . . She had heard the rumors of sickness in the city, seen the fires. With Joyain, she had fought in the mist. She had not missed the joy that Kenan found in Merafi's misfortunes. She owed Joyain this much at least.

She did not want to enter that house. It was her duty, nevertheless, to do so. Having once decided, she permitted herself no hesitation. It lay within easy walking distance of the embassy and it took a matter of minutes to reach it. She knocked upon its door and stated her name and purpose to the footman. He was strange to her. He ushered her in, took her cloak, and showed her into a room she remembered, to wait for Miraude.

A morning room, neat and bright, facing the garden. She had sat here with Valdarrien. She put the memory from her and sat with her back to the view. When the door opened, she neither started nor rose. It was Miraude who looked nervous, here on her own ground. She did not sit and she said, "You're Iareth Yscoithi. Thank you for coming."

"I understand that Lieutenant Lievrier has asked for me."

"Yes." Miraude began to play with one of her ribbons. "He's ill . . . It's good of you to come, after . . ."

Iareth said, "A house is only stone. I have no reason to fear it."

"No, I suppose not." Miraude sat. "But I thought you mightn't want to come. Because of Valdin." Her voice stumbled on the last word and she looked down.

"I came for Lieutenant Lievrier."

"I saw you the other evening. At the palace." Miraude said. "I wanted to talk to you then, but I couldn't." Her fingers pleated her gown. "Valdin missed you terribly, you know."

It sounded like a reproach. Probably it was a reproach. Miraude had no reason to love her. Iareth said, "That is regrettable." It was her business, how she felt about Valdarrien's death and why she had left him.

Miraude said, "You seem to be rather good at it. Being on the minds of men in pain."

"My connection with Lieutenant Lievrier is purely professional," Iareth said. And then, a little more kindly, "It is good of you to take him in."

"I could hardly leave someone lying in the road." Miraude rose. "Do you want to see him now?"

"Certainly." Iareth also rose.

Miraude went to the door, hesitated. "May I ask you something?"

Iareth made no reply.

"About Valdin . . . Why did you leave him?"

The matter was between Iareth and lost Valdarrien. Except Miraude was Valdarrien's widow. She had the right of any kinsman to show concern. Iareth drew herself up to her full height and said, "Duty."

"Duty?" Miraude frowned. "I don't see . . ."

"I am Lunedithin. I owe the greater part of myself to my kin. They had need of me. I returned to them. Valdin Allandur was my *kai-reth* by courtesy alone. His claim on me was lesser."

"You're very cold," Miraude said. "Someone will conduct you to the lieutenant." She opened the door and beckoned a servant.

Iareth followed the girl in silence, feeling Miraude watching her. *You're very cold*. It was possible. She had made her choices; she had learned to live within them. They went up the wide stair she remembered, into the gallery and into a chamber she did not recall, one floor down from where she had lain with Valdarrien.

Another maid sat beside the bed, watching over Joyain. She rose and curtsyed as Iareth entered; then both servants left the room. Iareth sat on the stool and looked at Joyain. There was a scent in the air that Iareth recognized: honeysuckle and death. The scent she remembered from the fight in the mist. She laid a hand over one of his and said softly, "Jean?"

No answer. He shifted and turned, flesh burning. There was water beside the bed. She touched a little of it to his lips and repeated his name. This time, his lids fluttered and opened.

His voice was indistinct. He said a name she did not know. It sounded like "Lelien,"

"It is Iareth Yscoithi."

Joyain said, "No," and his hand pulled out from hers. He gasped as though the movement pained him. His face contorted. She hesitated, then put her hand against it. His skin was damp. He had, at some point, asked for her, but he did not know her now. He had wanted her for some reason. She bit her lip and said, "Miraude Allandur says that you wanted me." A pause. "I have come."

He repeated, "No." His eyes opened. He looked at her. She sat motionless, although fear at last had her, and waited. He said, on a note of wonder, "Iareth?"

"So."

"I saw . . ." He licked dry lips. "He's dead." Another pause. "Shoot your deserters . . . The city will fall."

It meant nothing to her, but her hand stroked his hair, and she made herself smile. Joyain lifted a hand and tried to reach hers. He lacked the control to complete the motion. Iareth took it in her spare one. She said, "Do you want anything?"

He did not seem to hear her. He was looking past her

now, and his eyes were unfocused. He said, "Too late," and then, "Iareth."

"Yes?"

"Not dead . . . I saw him, with Lord Thiercelin . . . He'll kill me."

"Who?"

He looked back at her, and for a short moment his eyes were clear. His hand clung to hers. He said, "Iareth . . ."

"Yes?"

"I saw your . . . Valdarrien."

He had mentioned it before. He was not the only one. Iareth put that from her. She was in no case to be burdened with the problems of the city. She said, "It was a dream only. A product of the fever."

"No . . . He's not the only thing . . . Lelien saw. And we did."

She was silent. He seemed to forget her, gaze wandering away. Under her hands she could feel the heat that consumed him. And he was young and strong. Shoot your deserters? It made a certain amount of sense to her. He had left the embassy for duties in the low city, where the sickness was. Deserters would carry that same sickness throughout Merafi.

As Joyain himself had done. He was part of Kenan's silent war. He shifted again and looked at her. His hand clenched on hers. "Iareth," he said. "Iareth. The city is drowning."

He did not know her again after that, although he spoke from time to time. Iareth sat with him a further half hour; then she rose and went in search of Miraude.

She found her in a withdrawing room, picking out tunes on a harpsichord. As Iareth entered, Miraude looked up and frowned.

Without gilding, Iareth said, "He might die. You should not have brought him under your roof."

Miraude said, "Not your business, I think."

"No."

"Shouldn't you be leaving?"

"Indubitably," Iareth said, and yearned for Urien's calm good sense. "Where is Yviane Allandur?"

"At the palace. She doesn't spend much time here. Her messages are forwarded every day or so. I very much doubt she'll receive you."

"You are right. I have wronged you." Iareth spoke quickly, cold, hard. The Yscoithi had not, over the years, forgotten their claws. "You have every reason for your disdain. Yet it would go better if you listen to me."

"I'd be surprised," Miraude said, "if your homespun wisdom surpasses the medical knowledge of my doctor." Iareth said nothing. "He has a fever, but . . ."

"Don't you ever leave the hill?" Without meaning to, Iareth took a pace forward. Miraude flinched and looked away. "There is plague in Merafi, Miraude Allandur; and you have carried it under your roof."

Miraude said, "But . . ."

"He spent his last few days in the low city; in the heart of the plague area. He will have contracted it there. And now," Iareth spread her hands out before her, "he will pass it to you, to your household, and to your friends."

"No," Miraude said. "I don't believe you." But her voice was uncertain, and her face gave her the lie.

Iareth said, "I wish it were otherwise. You must burn his bedding and the bed also, if he should die." Miraude made to speak. Iareth held up a hand. "How many people have been in contact with him since you brought him here?"

"I'm not sure. Six. Ten, perhaps."

"And how many of them have left the house?"

Miraude twisted her fingers together. "Most of them, I think."

Iareth cursed. Then she said, "It is too late, then, maybe. Having brought him here, you should have imposed quarantine. You must try and minimize further contacts. And you must issue a warning to those not of your household who have also been in contact with him. If you write to them, I will undertake the delivery."

"You," said Miraude, with a certain satisfaction, "are as much a contact as me, or anyone else here."

"I," said Iareth Yscoithi of Alfial, "am a bastard." Her head came up, proud. "Do you understand clan-blood, Miraude Allandur?" Miraude shook her head. "We breed within our clans, to keep the lines pure and to ensure transmission of the old shapeshifting gifts, where they still survive."

"Shapeshifting," Miraude said, and her eyes were wide. "You mean you . . . ?"

"No Yscoithi has that gift. Our blood has grown too thin." She had said it. It had taken her half her lifetime to recognize it, but she had faced and said it at last. "I am not pure Yscoithi. I am bred across-clan, *elor-reth*. My blood is mixed. Yscoithi and Armenwy."

"So?"

"My sire's Armenwy blood is strong. He has the old abilities, the old defenses. He could not pass to me his shifting power, but he did transmit other things." Probably. But Iareth had no intention of voicing any doubt. She held her hands out before her and looked at them. Long hands, light, like the rest of her. Too tall for a true Yscoithi. Too fair. "The old clan-blood confers certain protections. In particular, strengths against such plagues as this one. It is improbable that I will either catch or transmit it. But there are too few here in your city who can say that." Iareth looked up. "So, Miraude Allandur, command me. You may not have long."

19

THE DAY WORE ON, COLD, OVERCAST. No rain fell, though the air was moist and the ground slippery, as though the dew had never quite risen. The low city lay quiescent, wrapped in mist and the scent of honeysuckle. Intermittent fires burned, but their light was pale and they gave off little heat in comparison with the fever that gripped so many. At army HQ, no questions were asked about the whereabouts of one Joyain Lievrier. There were so many others missing. The river ran high and loud: water began to replace feet on the streets of the new dock and the south Artisans' quarter. In the Rose Palace, Yvelliane d'Illandre fought to make sense of the demands placed on her time and did not look out of the windows. The queen grew worse: there had been an alarm in the night, The doctors spoke only in low voices and rumor hinted at another heamorrhage. Ambassador Sigeris sent up his kindest sympathies: Yvelliane was hard put not to throw that letter into the fire.

Joyain was not aware that he was enjoying her hospitality. Fever-caught, he lay senseless, under the frightened eyes of Miraude d'Iscoigne l'Aborderie. One of the footmen had complained of feeling unwell . . . She was cold with Iareth's warning and unsure what she should do. No word came for her from Maldurel, trying to convince himself that his pounding head and uneasy stomach were merely the result of a disturbed night.

The west quarter felt too quiet. From Amalie's windows few people might be seen; and most of those the poorest. The last of her carts was parked outside the door, ready to take her and her possessions out of Merafi before sunset. Returning from his errands, Gracielis confirmed that a steady stream of inhabitants were leaving by the two north gates. He could bring no news of Yvelliane. He had left his missive and taken time to inform Iareth Yscoithi, whom he had encountered in the street outside the Far Blays town house, of Urien's address. He had hesitated, then told her also of Valdarrien's untimely rebirth. She had said nothing, only smiled and turned away to pursue errands of her own.

He had forced himself to come home via the river. Its dark waters repelled him, but he had made himself study them and refused dominion to the fear which might have seized him. Merafi was sinking. Only around the River Temple did the surface still seem clear. The air tasted to him of Quenfrida. The old city was even quieter than the west quarter, and many of the houses were boarded up. He did not venture farther south. He could smell the death there in the wind, as the pyres grew more common.

He was running out of time. Last night both moons had been close to full. When they met, when they both exerted pull over the river and the estuary . . . He needed Amalie's help for that, used as she was to working out the movements of the tides. He must find his one moment, when salt and sweet waters both rose, to try to sever Quenfrida's bindings. There would be no other chance.

He doubted that this one would be enough. At least Amalie would be away from it. And Thiercelin . . . Gracielis had begun to realize that there were, after all, reasons for which he might kill.

In Amalie's house Thiercelin still slept. Beneath the bandages his wounds healed with a speed that surprised everyone but Urien. The Armenwy kept his own counsel, though his eyes watched Valdarrien, or studied the place where scars should have marred Gracielis' wrists. Healing was no gift of the *undarii*. But Gracielis had enacted his ritual in disorder and brought life where death should have walked. It was not in Urien's nature to make too many rules concerning what was, and was not, possible.

Under the same roof, Valdarrien prowled, restless. Somewhere out in the city, under the same sky, was Iareth Yscoithi.

They had parted once, and she had said they would not meet again. He had defied death to prove her wrong. Thiercelin had spoken of years elapsed, but Valdarrien could account for only a handful of months. About him, familiar faces gave memory the lie, for there was gray in Thierry's hair and new lines in Urien's face. He paid no heed to that, certain that his fate would return Iareth to him, and soon.

She came with the sunset. He was alone in Amalie's salon. Gracielis was outside, making his farewells to his mistress, and Urien was with Thiercelin. She closed the door behind her and came to stand in the center of the room. He cursed himself that he had forgotten that her eyes were that precise shade of cool green. She watched him without surprise, and it was everything. Her head tilted, she said, gentle, familiar, "Valdin *kai-reth*."

He was weeping, he who never wept, Valdarrien the duelist, the killer. He said, "Iareth . . ." and stopped, looking at her, seeing the beauty in her stillness.

Her hand lifted, touched her sword hilt lightly, traveled upward to her heart, passed on, and stretched out toward him, palm up. The Lunedithin salute, given to their prince, and to their guests, and to their kinsmen by blood or vow: *I serve you. I honor you. I am yours.*

I am yours. He said, "You came back." She was silent. "You said you wouldn't, but you did."

Her lips twitched. She said, "I am not alone in that. You have had a longer journey back than I."

He remembered, after the uncertain fashion of dreams, a conversation in a darkened room; a dance. He said, "I told you." And then, "Iareth *kai-reth*, can I— may I—touch you?"

"I do not know. You might try."

Two steps brought him to her. He could feel her warmth. His hands found her shoulders and seized them. His head bowed against her. He closed his eyes. He could feel the soft tide of her breath, hear the murmur that was her heart. He had won her back and he would break in pieces before he lost her again. Her arms came around him, about his waist, and he felt that she did not tremble. Whip-cord and willow; pliant only as it pleased her. Beside her, he was glass. Into her hair, he said, "Not again. Never again."

Another of her qualities, that she always understood him. She raised her head and looked at him. "We will be together while we may."

"Always," he said. "You promised it . . . I shall fight to keep you this time."

"Valdin *kai-reth*." She put a hand under his chin and lifted it. "Look at me." He opened his eyes. "What do you see?"

"You," Valdarrien said.

"So." She smiled at that, and he awoke to her anew. "Look closer." She shook her braid forward over a shoulder. "For you it has been a handful of months only. For me, six years." She hesitated. "I am no longer the same, Valdin *kai-reth*."

"You love me." He was as sure of that as he could be of anything. "We are *kai-rethin*, each to the other. That was our compact. It doesn't change."

"No. But . . ." Again, that pause. He watched in fascination as her brows drew together. He had forgotten that, too. She said, "My duty to my clan is also unchanged."

"So what?" he said. Amusement flickered on her face. "They've had most of your life. It's my turn now."

"And I have no say in this?"

"No. Not unless you agree with me. Agree with me, Iareth *kai-reth*."

She smiled. Then she laughed. Her head dropped to his shoulder. "You do not change."

"No."

"Kenan . . ." She paused and shook her head. "There are troubles of which you know nothing." He shrugged. She said, "By rights, this is impossible."

"I do not," said Valdarrien, "see any reason to conform to 'rights'. All that matters is that I'm here. Say yes."

Iareth gasped. Voice uneven, she said, "You are imperious. As ever."

"Yes." He stood back, and looked into her eyes. "You're all I want. Agree, my Iareth."

Her hand traced the side of his face. She said, "Real . . ." And then, "There are matters to which I must attend for Urien and others. Your wife . . ."

"Whatever you do, I'll do as well."

"So simple? I wonder . . ." She drew in a long breath. "I do not understand, Valdin *kai-reth*."

"Nor do I," he said. "Urien—and that Tarnaroqui, Gracielis—have notions . . . I understand that I need you, Iareth *kai-reth*. The rest can drown."

She looked up at him and shook her head. Amused despite herself, she said, "Merafien!"

"Say yes. I won't stop asking until you do."

She looked down. Her left hand twisted in her braid. Her right still touched him. She said, "This does not happen."

"Only to us."

"Valdin Allandur *kai-reth*," Her tone was formal. He caught at her hand, fighting sudden chill. "We are kin by oath. The bond cannot be broken. You know your answer."

"No. Say it."

"To you?" He nodded. She said, "Urien has ever said I chose wrongly." He waited, trembling. She looked straight at him. "To you, yes. Always and always yes." Her hand knotted in his. "By stone and flame, wind and wave and darkness, I swear it. Always, Valdin *kai-reth*."

He kissed her, then.

"Don't refuse me, love." Amalie closed the lid of the final chest and turned. "I don't understand what you're doing, but I trust you. And I want to help." She had taken a cloth bag out of the chest. Now she held it out. "You almost never let me give you things."

Gracielis looked at the floor. He said, "You know what I am."

"Yes." She was brisk. "But I also know you."

"I'm not . . ." Gracielis stopped, fidgeted with his hair. The shop was bare. He said, "Amalie. Ladyheart. I'm a whore."

"You're my lover." In turn she hesitated. "And you've dealt fairly with me, where others of your profession might not."

He said, "You can't know that."

"Can't I? Look at me, love." He looked up. Her face was calm and serious. "I'm a woman alone, that's true. I have no family here, apart from Jean. But I'm not a court beauty or a sheltered treasure; I'm a guildswoman. I live by commerce. I learned long ago to recognize a good deal." She looked down. "I always knew I couldn't buy your heart." He made to speak at that, but she held up a hand. "You're dear to me and you've been good to me. If it wasn't me that you thought of in bed, then the deception was graceful and well done. I know you've always thought you took from me; but the truth is, you only ever took money. The rest was giving."

He said, "Forgive me."

"For what? For kindness?"

"You deserve better."

"And I've had it." Amalie put the bag down on the chest, then crossed the room and took his hands. "Are we friends, Gracielis?"

He made himself look up, and banished all artifice. He said, "I'm not good at loving . . . If I were, I would've loved you, Ladyheart."

She kissed his cheek. "Listen, love. I want to help, but I'm not sure how. Except . . . What I do have is money, and you can't live on air. Please don't be too proud."

"It isn't pride." He lifted her hand. "Forgive me."

"Always, love."

"It wasn't contempt, I swear. It's simply that I . . ." He could not say it. He could not name Quenfrida to her. "I had a duty to someone at home. I'm ashamed."

"Don't." Amalie squeezed his hand. "We've been good to each other, you and I. Let's leave it at that." There was an odd note of finality in her voice. She smiled at him again and released his hands. She said, "You'll need money, prices are rising. This," and she passed him the bag, "should cover you and your friends for a month or so. Beyond that, I've left instructions with my guild master that you may draw on my funds." Gracielis reached out to her. "I've left details of my forwarding address upstairs in the office. I don't expect you to transact business for me, but I'd be grateful if you could forward any messages. Write to me, if you have time." She stopped and looked down. "Good-bye, love."

The last of her luggage was by the door, a small valise and the cat in a basket. He made to carry it for her. They collided in the doorway. The feel of her was so very familiar. He gasped and turned away. Amalie put her arms around him. He said, "I have nothing to give you . . ."

"It doesn't matter."

He said, "Amalie," and stopped. The truth was, he had nothing to say. She reached up, and kissed him.

She said, "He's a good man, Lord Thiercelin."

"What?"

"Dearest one, I've known you five years . . . there are some things I can tell. I know you're in love with him."

"And he with his wife." Gracielis drew in a breath. "You know you may always call on me?"

"Yes."

He kissed her hand. "Then let me carry your bags, at least." She looked at him and he shook back his cuffs. "Since last night my wrists are healed." She smiled then and acquiesced.

Her carriage waited outside. Herlève was already inside. Gracielis passed the cat up to her, then handed the valise to the driver. He helped Amalie with the step, then bowed over her hand. She settled herself by the window. He began to step back, then halted, holding on to the frame. Herlève clicked her tongue at him.

"What is it?" Amalie asked.

"The river tides." He frowned. "You have tables for them, but the pattern's probably changing. Do you know when the next high winter tide is due?"

She considered. "Mothmoon is at half-phase. Handmoon approaching it, I think. That means double-full this month. The river was last very high four months ago. It's only a guess, but I'd think it'll be in about four days. You could ask the guild master. Or I can try to calculate it properly and have the result couriered to you. I take it it's important?"

"Yes." He kissed her hand again. "I am always thanking you."

"I'll write." Amalie released his hand, and shut the door. "Be safe, love."

"And you, Ladyheart."

She waved to him as the coach turned the street corner, but his sight was too blurred to see it.

"What time is it?"

"A little after sunrise."

The voice that answered Thiercelin's question was not

the one he expected. He turned, hissing as pain caught him in the side, and squinted upward. A man of middle years sat by the bed. He reminded Thiercelin of someone. He met Thiercelin's gaze and said, "How is it with you?"

Thiercelin considered. His dreams had been high-colored and disturbing. He was stiff, and his side ached. His arm, strapped across his chest, pained him, too. He was aware that he probably ought to have felt worse. He said, "I'm not sure," and then, "How long was I asleep?"

"A full day, and half another. Do you recall what befell you?"

"Yes." Thiercelin winced. He did not want to remember that. He looked at his companion. "Forgive me, do I know you?"

"I am Urien Armenwy."

"This is Madame Viron's house . . ." Thiercelin remembered Gracielis telling him that, last night—no, the night before. The night he'd talked again to Valdarrien. But that, surely, had been a dream? He said, "Has Yviane . . . Has my wife been told what's happened to me?"

"Gracielis *undarios* took word to her. I expect she will come shortly."

"Iareth sent for you?"

"So. She is here also with Valdin Allandur." Urien's eyes held Thiercelin's. It was hard to return the gaze without faltering.

Thiercelin said, "It wasn't a dream."

"No." Urien said.

And another voice, dearly familiar, said, "Oh, charming." Valdarrien stood in the door. Iareth was beside him, and Thiercelin had to look away from the expression on her face. Valdarrien favored Thiercelin with a hard stare and added, "I find your perpetual disbelief most hurtful, Thierry."

"Well, what do you expect?" He had no right to his

sudden jealousy. He was being petty. "Valdin, you're . . ."

"Dead. I know." Valdarrien came into the room and sat on the bed. Iareth folded silently cross-legged at his feet. She looked at Urien; some message seemed to pass between them. Valdarrien said, "We just don't seem to be able to get past that one little detail. I'm bored with the topic."

Thiercelin could think of no obvious answer to that. Urien said, "You lack patience, Valdin *kai-reth*." Valdarrien looked at his feet. Iareth reached up and took his hand.

Yvelliane had not yet come. Thiercelin tried again to suppress his envy. Six years of marriage, and she had not come. Whereas Valdarrien . . . Thiercelin sat hard on his self-pity and said, "Where's Graelis?"

Valdarrien said, "I really have no idea. But I must say, Thierry, I question your interest in him. He's a foreigner, to start with—saving your presence, Urien *kai-reth*—and he's a . . ."

"Whore?" The interruption came from Gracielis himself. Leaning on the door frame, he smiled. He was hatless, and his bright hair hung loose. He watched Valdarrien, open-eyed, playing innocence. Then the long lashes swept down. Toying with his lovelock, he said, "I crave your pardon, monseigneur of the Far Blays." He glanced at the two-colored gloves at his belt and shrugged, beautiful to the bone. "Shall I leave you to your privacy?"

Urien said, "Madame Viron has left her home and resources in your hands. It is not for you to seek permission under this roof."

"Perhaps not." Gracielis looked up. "But since Lord Valdarrien disapproves of me . . ."

"He possesses, without doubt, the facility to keep his views to himself." Urien did not frown, he merely looked at Valdarrien, who once again looked at the floor. "As you do yourself, Gracielis *undarios*."

Gracielis looked momentarily blank. Then he smiled and shook his head. Thiercelin knew a sudden desire to ask Urien just how such meekness might be compelled. There was a chair near the door. Gracielis moved it into the circle and sat. He looked once at Thiercelin. Thiercelin smiled back. To Urien, Gracielis said, "I've been to see the master of the Haberdashers' Guild about the tides." He hesitated then added, "However, he wasn't at liberty to make any calculations; and I'm not competent to do so. We must either await word from Amalie—which may take too long—or find someone with a head for figures."

Yvelliane. But Thiercelin did not say it. He shifted and winced as the motion tugged at the bindings on his arm. Gracielis leaned forward, concerned. Thiercelin avoided his gaze.

Urien said, "We will do so."

"Forgive me," Valdarrien said, "but I seem to be missing something here. Tides?"

"I told you," Iareth said gently. "Urien believes that the old powers awaken in your city. We must undo that."

"Superstition," said Valdarrien. Thiercelin, despite himself, snorted. "And I fail to see, Thierry, what you find so amusing."

"Nothing," Thiercelin said. "Only the incongruity of you, of all people, complaining about superstition. Not in a very strong position to do that, Valdin. Under your circumstances."

Valdarrien glared at him. Then he turned to Urien and said, "Iareth told me last night about what's happening. Kenan Orcandros and Quenfrida d'Ivrinez." His voice held a certain satisfaction. Thiercelin looked at him in alarm and caught Iareth doing the same. "The woman might be a problem, I grant you—perhaps we can set my sister Yviane onto that?—but Kenan should be easy enough." He patted his sword hilt. "A fair challenge, and . . ."

"No, Valdin *kai-reth*." Iareth rose to her knees. "There is a risk to it."

"So?"

She looked at Urien. Into the silence, Gracielis said, "It wouldn't work. Killing the principal won't stop or undo the working. And, anyway, you wouldn't be the right person. You're a part of the working."

"If," Valdarrien said, "you are insinuating that I . . ."

"Shut up," Thiercelin said, startling everyone, himself included. "I don't claim to understand how or why you're alive, Valdin, but I for one am not going to stand by and watch you make all the same mistakes again. If Graelis thinks there's another way, then we'll use that. All right?" The long speech left him breathless. He leaned back on his pillows and closed his eyes.

Urien's quiet voice said, "Thierry speaks rightly. We will find out the time of the highest tide, and then act."

"It may not be possible," Gracielis said. "Quenfrida is skilled and experienced."

"We can try," said Urien.

It was an hour or so later that Gracielis found Urien in Amalie's workroom. Thiercelin was asleep again. Valdarrien and Iareth were nowhere in evidence. Going to the window, Gracielis looked out. The day was gray and drizzly. Half the houses in the street were shuttered, and a pall of dirty smoke hung over the low city. He drew in a long breath and let ghost-sight take him. Under the mantle of sickness and mist there was a vast and weighty silence, coiled tightly around the vitals of Merafi, not yet ready to close in. It would take only a breath to set it into motion. He could not see the river, he could not see the bindings linking this curled power to Quenfrida, to Kenan. They lay just beyond him, heavy, half guessed at. He passed a hand over his eyes and exhaled. To Urien he said, "They are too strong for me."

"Mayhap."

"I'm not properly trained." Gracielis turned. "What they've done must be contained and turned. That's hard."

"I know."

"If my control is inadequate—and it will be . . ."

"Peace." Urien lifted a hand. "We have some time to prepare."

"Perhaps."

"What we do not have," Urien said, "is a choice."

"Don't we?" Gracielis looked down. "You're Lunedithin, I'm Tarnaroqui. Perhaps the Merafiens should restore order themselves."

"Perhaps. But should the servant of a guest make trouble for his host, should not the guest rebuke his servant?"

Gracielis smiled. "I doubt Quenfrida would care for the analogy."

Urien said, "The sickness has spread throughout the whole city. Iareth has seen it even under the roof of Valdin's kin, although as yet Yviane Allandur is safe."

There was a silence. Then Gracielis said, "If I do fail . . ."

"There are contingencies."

"Yes. But if the river isn't brought back under control . . ." Gracielis stopped and shook his head. "You're considering a sacrifice."

"It may prove necessary. My ancestor stood beside Yestinn Allandur when he committed the killing that first laid the bonds upon these waters."

"Orcandrin blood, shed unwillingly, and in anger," Gracielis said. "But Kenan revoked that death. If Kenan is your sacrifice, it'll make an uneasy binding."

"I was not considering an unwilling sacrifice." Urien looked straight at him. "Kenan awoke this power by spilling Allandurin blood, not Orcandrin. Valdin's, drawn unwillingly. A descendant of the first sacrifice offering the blood of the descendant of the first sacrificer."

"Valdarrien d'Illandre wouldn't make a fit sacrifice.

He's no longer human, and I doubt he'd be willing." Gracielis hesitated. "The symmetry's pleasing but surely it won't work. You'd need an Orcandrin slayer to kill your Allandurin offering. And I doubt Kenan would play that role either."

"I am aware of that." Gracielis waited for Urien to continue. He did not. Gracielis sat and began to play with a pen that lay upon the table. Urien watched him. After a moment the Armenwy said, "How is Thierry?"

"Sleeping," Gracielis said. Thiercelin would willingly offer up his life for this city, if it would redeem those he loved. If it would protect Yvelliane. Gracielis said, "No."

Urien looked inquiring.

"He's unsuitable. He's only married into that line, he doesn't share its blood."

"Peace. He will come to no more harm."

Gracielis said, "Then who?" And fell silent. He looked at his hands. Once, Quenfrida had asked him to encompass this very death . . . He said, "Does she know?"

"As yet she does not even know that I am in Merafi."

Yvelliane d'Illandre. As purebred as her brother Valdarrien and possessed of many times his courage. Her clear sight would lead her, step by logical step, to agreement with Urien's plan. If it came to a sacrifice, Gracielis could think of no one better. He said, "It will break Thierry. He loves her very much." Gracielis realized he was avoiding the center of the issue and raised his eyes. "I'm helping you because Thierry asked it. And now you're telling me that I may have to shield him from heartbreak."

"That is your part of our burden," Urien said.

"Don't tell him."

Urien rose and said, "You believe we cannot wait for a communication from Madame Viron regarding the tides?"

"Yes."

"So. Then I will follow the suggestion made by Valdin

Allandur and apply to his sister. I will tell her again that
Thierry asks for her."

Gracielis rose also. "The high city may no longer be
safe."

"I will be cautious." Urien smiled. "And I will be
aware. That, after all, is my share in what we do."

Gracielis turned away and went back to the window.

Cold. Cold water. A touch on his lips, which felt
shapeless and old. A passage over skin that burned. Joyain turned into it and felt the heat sear him, roll him
like a wave. He was weightless, adrift on this scorching
sea; tossed and borne, limbs constrained and entangled
as if in some cramping net. Dim light hovered before
his eyes, crossed by a sense of movement, akin to the
passing of a cloud. He made out Leladrien's form, leaning over him, over the leaping heat. Joyain could call
out no warning as the flames spiraled higher. Leladrien
gasped, as they met him, as he writhed within them, skin
peeling back, blown blackened from the bone. His ash
covered Joyain, flakes filling eyes and ears and mouth,
burning through the net. He was drowning in flame . . .
A smile formed on Lelien's lipless mouth, which did not
reach his single eye, and he spoke a word that Joyain
did not know. He lifted a hand to brush away the ash
and felt the fire seize it; watched, then, as his own flesh
turned painlessly to black fragments and whirled away.
He could see through to the bones. They were hollow,
channeling liquid flame, pooling down inside him, consuming, feeding the web. His body knotted within it,
trapped, lingering, listening to the devouring roar. His
breath crisped the air. His smoke curled upward, burning
off the tips of his wings, falling into the sun. It twined
down through his naked bones; it blew through Leladrien and drew him into elongated destruction, stretched
to nothing all along the wind. His single eye watched
Joyain, fading, weeping cinders and reproach. He was
gone in flame, he was turned to ash and air, he would

not hear, now, when Joyain had at last the time to speak his regrets. *Lelien, Lelien, I'm sorry, but the city is drowning, and I've forgotten how to fly . . .* The eye turned to nothing: the black flakes floated down, banking about Joyain. He lay there, bound to the earth, cast up on a burning shore, and he might, after all, be alone. There had been kindness, once, and the touch by night of tender hands. His skin had warmed to passion against another, lying embraced and embracing in that other heat. Her eyes—not like Leladrien's—had been cooler than the river. She had offered no reproaches as she turned away from him to entwine herself with mist. Iareth Yscoithi in the dark arms of lost Valdarrien, who had once come between Joyain and a bullet in the Winter Gardens; and who had come once again, to reclaim his own . . . Joyain had held his hand over another's property and felt the fire. He had been warned, he had been told, and the card bearing her face caught fire beside him, running flame-course, as she burned him, according to the promise.

He had never meant to come to this. He had never known what he could be.

Joyain exhaled and felt his body fall away into flame.

Beside him, Miraude d'Iscoigne l'Aborderie clung to his hand and wept and whispered, over and over again: "Oh, don't die. Oh, please, don't bring death on us here."

20

YVELLIANE LOOKED AT THE CLOCK and sighed. Noon, and there was still no word from the queen's doctors. Firomelle had risen only once since the great soirée, and then only for an hour. No one was quite sure anymore who was in charge. Yvelliane had sat up most of the night before, trying to sort out the business of the low city, and had risen at dawn in an attempt to assimilate all the reports. A sickness, emanating originally from the new dock and the shantytown, now traveling deep into Merafi. No figures available upon its victims—who knew how many people had lived in those debatable parts? The watch was losing its own men too fast to trouble itself with reckoning civilian deaths. Some of the least reputable parts of Merafi were virtually deserted, boarded up and reeking of death. The wide southern arm of the river had flooded the south Artisans' quarter and sections of Low Town. And through it all, violence was spreading. The watch had been reinforced from other regiments, but still the trouble went unchecked. Street fights, ambushes, unexplained bodies . . . One platoon had mutinied the night before last, when their officer had tried to order them to patrol the area between Low Town and the southwest trade district. After dark, almost no one would set foot in that part of Merafi.

The northern city fared only slightly better. The more recent reports spoke of sickness appearing patchily in the west quarter and the more respectable parts of the old city. The wealthier citizens had begun to leave, loading their property onto carts, heading out into the plains and the hinterland. There were almost as many houses boarded up for desertion as there were for plague. At the same time, fewer and fewer traders were making their way into the city as rumors of the troubles spread. The south gate was in disarray, unmanned and uncontrolled. Army HQ disclaimed all responsibility: by day, they struggled to hold their men in position, but by night, order dissolved. An informer from the main old city hinted at army shootings of panicked civilians in the debatable districts. The army reports spoke only of "necessary force."

Plague. Riot. Desertion. That was only the picture painted by the more sensible of the reports. There was more. Accounts of people seeing ghosts or of encounters with impossible, monstrous creatures made out of mist. Descriptions of bodies found mangled and mauled beyond the ability of even the most sadistic street gang. A woman from Little Ash Lane swore that her child, dead of plague, had returned to life and blown away amidst the fog. Some of the tales could doubtlessly be discounted as the products of alcohol or delirium. Others . . . Yvelliane's eyes kept returning to a sober record from a junior priest who had barely escaped alive from an encounter with a creature he described as inhuman. The attached surgical memorandum testified to bites and claw-inflicted wounds upon his body. The surgeon had been confident that the beast involved could not have been anything so mundane as an enraged stray dog. Another record told of a respectable cavalry widow who had simply disappeared into the night, after vowing to her family that she had seen her deceased husband outside her windows.

Yvelliane had been warned. Gracielis had told her that harm was coming upon Merafi. She had had her hand—almost—upon Quenfrida, so certain that simple

expulsion would provide the solution. But circumstances
had forestalled her. She had to resolve this conundrum,
to redeem Merafi in Firomelle's name from the madness
that engulfed it, and her hands were tied.

And even supposing the sickness could be brought
swiftly under control (and *what* had the watch commander been thinking of, not to quarantine the shantytown right at the start?), there was still the river. No
ship had been able to dock for nigh on a month. The
old docks were silted up and partly flooded; the new one
had been half burned. Merafi was losing her grip upon
commerce and without that same commerce, Merafi
might as well embrace the plague and have done.

Yvelliane pushed her hair off her face and sighed. She
was so tired. It had been too long since she had been
home, sleeping here in the palace on an army cot in her
office. She missed the peace of the Far Blays house.
There had been no word from Miraude for two days.
No word at all from Thiercelin. She closed her eyes,
remembering the reassuring strength of his hands on her
overweighted shoulders. He always hated it when she
overworked.

Had hated it. For all she knew, he was gone for good.
She had had her chance to mend that breach and failed.
It might already be too late. Perhaps he no longer loved
her, worn out by her neglect. He was out there, somewhere in the city. She had failed to protect him, just as
she had failed Valdarrien. As she had failed Firomelle.
It seemed she was fated to bring pain upon those she
loved . . .

She straightened her shoulders and opened her eyes.
She could not afford this. There was no time for self-
indulgence. Assuming that the decline in the rate of
entry of comestibles into Merafi continued at the same
pace, how long could the city survive before starvation
became a problem? She stared at her neat columns of
figures. Right. She knew the approximate size of existing
food stocks and the normal rate of consumption. That

did not help; without definite information on the level of deaths from sickness or violence and upon the numbers of those deserting the city, she could not come up with any sensible answer to her question. The more people died or departed, the longer the food stocks would last (less reduction for perishables, of course). But since she had no really good idea of the mortality rate, nor of the way and speed with which the plague and other disruptions were spreading . . .

Her head ached abominably. Ideally, she should go down into the low city herself and observe. Interview officers and reputable witnesses . . . She had suggested doing so yesterday, but the commander of the queen's household guard had refused her an escort. Too dangerous. Yvelliane hesitated at the option of going unaccompanied. It was important, but . . .

A knock at the door interrupted her thoughts. She shook her head to clear it and called, "Come in."

A maid entered. "A man has come with your messages, madame." She held out a handful of papers.

"Thank you. Put them on the desk." The maid obeyed, but hesitantly. Yvelliane said, "Is something wrong?"

"No, madame . . ." The maid paused. "It's just . . . The man was a stranger, madame, and not in your livery. He said your house is closed; the messages were handed out to him through the gate."

Cold shivered through Yvelliane. "Is he still here?"

"No, madame. The porters tried to have him detained, but . . ." The maid's voice tailed off. "I'm sorry, madame."

Wonderful. But Yvelliane made herself smile. It was probably nothing. Perhaps Miraude planned a party. Perhaps all the regular staff were busy with that . . . "Never mind." The maid curtsied and went out. Yvelliane picked up the pile of correspondence.

Most of it was insignificant. Bills from assorted tradespeople. A note from a distant cousin, asking her advice on a business proposition. Another note, from Miraude's uncle, complaining that Yvelliane let her run wild. At the very bottom were a longish letter in Miraude's hand, and another in writing that Yvelliane recognized as that of Gracielis.

She put the latter to one side and opened Miraude's missive, scrawled and expansive on scented paper. Yvelliane smiled as she began to read it, but before her eye had completed the first paragraph, she was frowning.

Dearest Yviane, it began, *Here are all your letters. I'd have sent them sooner, but I've been busy. Really busy— not an excuse to stop you reading whatever it is my uncle wants to moan about (me, I expect).*

I've done something stupid. (No, it's not to do with the early matter: I obeyed you on that and have avoided the gentleman.) I don't know how to tell you. Oh, Yviane! The other night, Mal and I found a man—a cavalry officer (his name's Joyain Lievrier)—lying in the road, and I took him in here. I thought at first he was hurt—that my coach had hit him—but he'd taken the sickness from the low city. By the time I realized, it was too late. Iareth Yscoithi came here (Yvelliane's mouth set), *because he knew her; and she told me to shut up the house and let no one out, or the plague would spread. But the doctor had been in and gone, and half the household, and, of course, Mal had gone to his own lodgings.*

It gets worse. I think the officer is dying; and the cook has taken sick and so did one of the footmen last night— and, Yviane, he died! Mal's valet was here this morning, and Mal is ill, too. Here, the words were blurred, and Yvelliane suspected that Miraude had been crying. *I'm still all right, so far, and I've shut the house, as Iareth told me. But I don't know what to do.*

You mustn't come back till it's over. I'm so sorry, Yviane, and I'm scared for Mal, and the officer. And for Thierry, too, wherever he is. I'd wish you were here, but then you'd only be at risk, too.

I'm sorry, I'm sorry. Don't come home. Forgive me, Yviane.

It was signed: *Your foolish Mimi.*

Plague in the low city and around the new harbor. In the secondary area to the southwest. In the shantytown and the old docks. In Yvelliane's home. She folded the letter and let it drop. Then she rose and went to the sideboard. A decanter stood upon it: she poured herself a drink and swallowed it down in one gulp.

Iareth Yscoithi had come once more under the Far Blays' roof and once more brought death with her. A cavalry officer named Joyain Lievrier . . . Yvelliane was good with names: she had no difficulty placing that one. The tall, fair lieutenant with the deep-set eyes, who had fought a duel with Thiercelin for the sake of Iareth Yscoithi. Now this same Joyain was dying and had gifted his death to Yvelliane's kin.

She would lose everything. She would not weep; she was stronger than that. Besides, she had too much to do. She would arrange something. She had work to attend to. She bit her lip and went back to the desk.

There was another knock. Sighing, Yvelliane said, "Yes?" The same maid came in. "Well?"

"Excuse me, madame. There is a gentleman to see you. A Monsieur Urien Armenwy."

Yvelliane looked up. No word had come to advise her that Urien, Prince Keris' right hand, was expected. A thin film of hope formed about her heart. Urien had abilities beyond the usual. If he had come, now . . . She said, "Show him in," and hastily tidied up her desktop.

She rose, as he entered, and curtsied. He refused refreshment and took a straight-backed chair. Without preamble, he said, "I need your aid, Yviane Allandur."

"I'm at your service, naturally." Yvelliane sat down. "What is it? Kenan didn't tell me you were expected."

"Kenan is not aware of my presence."

Now, that was interesting. Yvelliane concealed a smile

at Urien noticing her noticing, and waited. He said, "You are acquainted with one Gracielis de Varnaq, a Tarnaroqui?" She nodded. "And he has spoken to you, regarding an association between the heir of my liege, Kenan Orcandros, and the woman Quenfrida d'Ivrinez?"

"Gracielis has a conspiracy theory," Yvelliane was brisk; whatever her feeling about Quenfrida and Kenan, she was bound by her promise to Laurens. "I can't tell you how correct it is."

"You can, I think." Urien looked at her squarely. She was silent. "Yviane Allandur, I have a thing to say unto you. Your city is sinking." Yvelliane looked at the pile of depressing reports. Urien said, "I would work to alter that. But I cannot do so without your help."

"Any direct political support must be ratified with the council . . ."

Urien cut her short. "I do not require the countenance of the council. Nor do I require anything that can compromise you. It is a matter simply of some calculations. You have the skill to perform them. I do not."

More arithmetic. Yvelliane put her head in her hands and said, "Of course."

"It concerns the tidal pattern of the river and the moons." Rising, Urien came to stand beside her. He placed several sheets before her. She stared at them blankly. "I regret the imposition, but the matter is of some urgency."

"They always are," she said, wearily. "When do you need this by?"

"As soon as possible." Urien put his hand on her shoulder. "There is a second thing."

"More sums?"

"No. You have received a letter from Gracielis *undarios*?"

"Yes. It's here somewhere . . . I haven't had time to read it yet." She stopped, and looked up at him. "Gracielis *undarios*?" Urien was silent. "You're not going to tell me, are you?"

"It is not my affair."

Yvelliane shrugged, and began to hunt for Gracielis' letter. "So, what's the second matter?" She located the note under a pile of other papers,she fished it out and broke the seal.

"It concerns Thierry."

She was still looking at the desk. Alarm caught at her. Swallowing, she found she did, after all, still have her voice. Flatly, she said, "Is he dead?" And kept her eyes downcast.

"No," Urien said. Yvelliane shut her eyes. "But he is unwell. He has asked for you."

"If it's the plague, I can't come." She spoke harshly. She could not afford to think about this. "Given Firomelle's current condition, the possibility of infection . . ."

"It is not the plague." In spite of herself, Yvelliane gasped. Urien continued. "He has been injured in an attack."

She had to retain her self-control. "Is it bad?" She made herself open her eyes and look up.

"Moderately. Gracielis *undarios* believes your presence would help."

"What happened?"

Urien said, "He was attacked. Fey things walk by night here."

Monsters in the mist . . . If she had been kinder, if she had been more careful, Thiercelin would never have been in the lower part of the city. He would have been at the town house, with Miraude and the plague. She rose and went to the window. She said, "Where is he?"

"At the house of Madame Viron, a spice merchant known to Gracielis."

Gracielis . . . She could not feel jealousy through her fear. He was Tarnaroqui, he was perhaps *undarios*. He might have skills, knowledge that could save Thiercelin. She turned. "Let me get my cloak. We can take one of the palace carraiges." She could bring him back here: he did not have the sickness. He would be safe here, and

she could watch over him. Gracielis could help her . . .
She was losing Firomelle, she had almost lost Thiercelin.
If she acted now . . .

Urien said, "Wait." His voice was solemn. Looking at
him, she felt her hopes grow chill. He said. "Thierry will
doubtless be pleased to see you. But there is a thing I
must ask you first."

"Can't we talk on the way?"

"No."

She sat, watching him. His face was kind, but there
was sorrow underlying the kindness. Very quietly, he
said, "Yviane Allandur, I must ask you a thing. Just how
far would you go to ensure the safety of your city?"

The Lunedithin residence was quiet when Iareth returned. A handful of the staff were busy in the kitchens,
but no one else was in evidence. Iareth checked the
salon for Tafarin, then went upstairs. It was early afternoon: it was likely that most of the residents were out
at various engagements. She was doubtless meant to be
with them somewhere. She did not heed that, quiet in
her inner jubilation. She had all in one moment gone
back upon her choice of six years past and cleaved to
the impossibility that was reborn Valdarrien.

Her blood was not pure. She had given twenty-eight
years to the half of her that was Yscoithi; at last Armenwy patience had won through. It is one thing to be
loved by a dashing stranger. Another entirely, when the
same stranger loves you enough to defy death itself to
claim you. She had against all likelihood been granted
the chance to remake her choice.

She was not foolish enough to risk loss a second time.

She finished changing. The house was too quiet. Someone should be about by now. She went out into the hall
and listened. Distantly, she heard the voices of the staff
on the ground floor. A door closing. Footsteps. She was
jumping at shadows. She shook her head and ran downstairs to see if anyone had left her a message. The library

was empty; so, too, was the office that had once been Joyain's. Paperwork was piled high on the desk. That might perhaps bear investigation, given Urien's concern over the state of the city. Her hand lingered on the chair back. If Joyain's sense of duty had not led him to transfer to the low city, he might well have been here now, frowning over his accounts. Here, and not as she had last seen him, fever-wracked in the Far Blays town house. *The city is drowning* . . . She shivered as memory cast a shadow over her. Joyain had done nothing to merit his suffering, and she could offer no help.

They had shared a little comfort, a little kindness. It was no fault of hers that had led him to expose himself to the sickness. Another woman might have looked for guilt, for symmetry in the injuries endured by her lovers, but Iareth did not rate her own importance so highly.

Except to Valdarrien, who was no longer outside her reach.

There were no messages for her. Shrugging, she went back upstairs and knocked on Kenan's door. There was a faint, sweet smell on the landing outside. Familiar, although she could not quite place it. She began to feel uncomfortable. There was a long silence then Kenan's voice called, in Lunedithin, "Enter."

She went in. The room was dark, casements closed. It was stiflingly hot; the air was heavily scented. She forced herself to ignore it. She said briskly, "Good even, Kenan *kai-reth*."

Sparks spluttered as Kenan struck a flint and lit a candle. She was aware of the beginnings of a headache. She rubbed her temple and turned to him. He stood next to a high-backed chair between the hearth and the door. He wore Tarnaroqui-style robes. There was something odd about his face. He said, "Sit, Iareth *kai-reth*. I would speak with you."

The nearest chair would put him between her and the door. For some reason that worried her. Her hand went to her belt and she realized that she was unarmed. She inhaled, counting her heartbeats. This was foolish. One did not need to go armed in the presence of one's *kai-rethin*.

She schooled herself to composure and said, "Certainly. I will return when you are dressed."

"You will remain here." Kenan went to a dresser and lit further candles. The movement took him closer to the door. Iareth refused to let herself frown. He passed between her and the door, and set a final candle upon a side table. Then he halted and smiled, "You did not return here last night."

"No."

"You did not think that your absence might provoke concern?"

"No. It has not been our custom to be overly involved in each other's business."

"Indeed not." Kenan moved so that he stood directly in front of the door. "Sit, Iareth."

She remained standing.

He looked amused. He said, "Given the current trouble that our hosts are experiencing, do you not concede it possible that I might have been concerned?"

No. But one did not say that to the heir to Lunedith. Not even when he was known to be involved in treachery. Quietly Iareth said, "An oversight. I ask your pardon, Kenan *kai-reth*."

"Granted, of course."

It was far too warm. Iareth began to feel breathless. She made herself ignore it and said, "I thank you."

"You are welcome."

There was silence. Iareth refused to lower her gaze. Kenan leaned back against the door. Softly, he said, "You are disloyal."

She raised her brows. "Because I spent a night away from this house?"

"That is a symptom." Kenan folded his arms. There was a cloth knotted about his right hand. "But the canker lies deeper. You're conspiring against me, my Iareth."

She was not his. The sweet smoke wound about her. She summoned calm and said, "I think not. I am here at your grandsire's request. I have performed the duties laid out for me by him. You are mistaken, Kenan *kai-reth*."

"I am not your *kai-reth*." Kenan said. "Where did you pass last night?"

"In the city." She swallowed, trying not to cough. Her hands felt slick.

He said, "Indubitably. But the answer lacks precision."

"Mayhap."

"What connection have you with a Tarnaroqui called Gracielis de Varnaq?"

Iareth put her hands behind her, to prevent herself from knotting them. She must be calm. The Orcandrin rages were renowned. She had only to weather this. If only it were cooler in here. She said, "Who?"

There was a silence. Then Kenan nodded to himself and said, "And you also do not know Yviane Allandur, I take it?"

"Yviane Allandur is the queen's First Councillor."

"And you intrigue with her."

Despite her growing discomfort, Iareth smiled. "No, Kenan *kai-reth*. She will have no truck with me. There is the matter of her brother's death between us."

He laughed, and she could not repress a shiver. The air was thick with perfume. He said, "Yviane Allandur corresponds with Urien Armenwy. And Urien corresponds with you."

"Urien is my . . ." Iareth began and stopped, there on the brink. A trap, and she had come readily within its confines. The smoke was making her careless. Everyone knew, no doubt, that Urien had sired her; but among her countrymen such things were not spoken of. To speak of it now would be to admit to Kenan that her blood was impure. She looked down.

"Urien is your . . . ?" Kenan prompted. "There is that which I should know?" She was silent. "You invited Urien Armenwy here to Merafi specifically to interfere with my embassy."

"No."

"The Armenwy persuaded my grandsire to place you in my guard. His sole purpose in so doing was to provide himself with a spy."

She had looked down, and now she could not raise her eyes. The candle smoke clogged her thoughts. She could think of no easy answer. She said, again, "No," and knew it to be insufficient.

She had laid herself open to this. Distracted by her concern over Valdarrien, she had underestimated Kenan. He was between her and the door. She was unarmed. She could feel his eyes on her. She had yet enough control to stand firm under that.

He said, "Look at me."

Despite herself, she obeyed. She looked up. He smiled, watching her. He held another paper in his hand. "This letter carries the seal of the house of the Far Blays. Do you still deny your connection to that line?"

That, at least, was solid ground. She said, "I do," and kept her head high.

"Visits to the Allandurin. Letters to the Armenwy. Investigations of my rooms—that, you need not trouble to deny, my Iareth, for I have observed your attempts to follow me and spy upon me." He hesitated. Iareth was losing the courage to hold his gaze. He said, "You displease me, Iareth called Yscoithi."

"So I gather." Iareth tried to think. If she could only get out of this heat . . . He was one man, and she was easily his better in a trial of arms.

She was unarmed. Kenan watched her with satisfied eyes, and she knew he understood what was on her mind. He turned and she heard the lock of the door snap shut. He held up the key and said, "Tell me where in Merafi I may find Urien Armenwy, and I will release you."

She lifted her chin, though her head swam, and said, "I will not." Her hands knotted at her sides. She was alone. She had nothing beyond her old, stern loyalty. But that would not desert her, however much she feared.

And she was afraid, although her bastard Yscoithi pride would hide it. Kenan smiled again and said, "Be wise."

"No," she said, and licked dry lips. For dead Valdarrien, she was come to this, and she would fail neither him nor Urien. Kenan, for all his dealings with Tarnaroqui witcheries, was still only a man. He could only hurt her.

"So," he said. He stepped away from the door and lifted a saddlebag from the dresser. "Do you recall this, my Iareth? I'm certain you have encountered it while snooping through my property." She was silent, watching his hands unraveling the knots. He removed the contents slowly one by one, laying them atop the dresser. His Orcandrin clan-brooch. His ring. A small blue box. A leather bottle. A scarf. A deck of cards. A knife, small, and wickedly sharp, sheathed in padded silk and hafted in ivory. Kenan stopped, holding the latter, and looked at her. Then he unwrapped the cloth from his right hand and closed his fingers about the blade. Blood ran between them, dripped on the floor. Against all her desire, she shivered. He raised his brows and said, quietly "Blood binds, Iareth called Yscoithi. Before and after death, strongest of all bonds."

She had sworn to Valdarrien in five domains, five domains ruled by sun and moons. Neither by her clanblood, nor by the the hybrid power in Tarnaroqui blood. They had fought side by side at the ancient waterfall, and Valdarrien's blood had been shed. Hers also, each protecting the other. Blood binds. Fighting alongside each other had surely been sufficient, needing no further

vow. She watched Kenan's blood spread on the floor
and fought nausea. Kenan too had bled in that place of
old power, where the Allandurin kings had enforced
peace on the old ways by binding them with human
blood. Clan-blood.

Orcandrin blood.

She took a step back and said, "No." Urien—she was
bound in her blood to Urien—had spoken of Kenan's
meddling with those old powers, and set her as a guard.
She had witnessed the effects of that meddling upon
Merafi. Yet she had somehow always thought herself to
be safe. She took another step and found herself somehow backed against the casement.

Smoke wove from the blood on the floor, mixing with
the candles. Iron and foxglove and something other.

Honeysuckle. She remembered now where she had
smelled it before. Clinging to the streets, the night she
and Joyain fought the mist creatures. She was afraid,
and her composure was beginning to desert her.

Kenan smiled. He walked across the room and took
her face in his hands, smearing it with his blood. She
could not raise her hands to prevent him; her lungs were
choked with perfumed smoke. He said, "I need a life,
Iareth." His palms were warm; his eyes dark, pupils di-
lated. "The law of our homeland forbids me to shed
clan-blood." She watched him, impotent. "Who sired
you, Iareth called Yscoithi?"

She was silent. He stared at her for long moments.
Then he said, "Shall I tell you? I can see it, Iareth. I
can look into your eyes and read your parentage. Your
blood is not pure."

"Your grandsire adjudged me Yscoithi." Iareth somehow found she might yet speak, although her voice was
faint. Her hands hung useless at her sides. "My Yscoithi
kai-rethin have never questioned it."

He shrugged. "The Armenwy sired you. The Yscoithi
raised you. But you belong to neither. You are out-clan,
Iareth. You are *elor-reth*."

She forced herself to be proud. "You have no right to make that judgment, Kenan *kai-reth*."

His bloody right hand coiled itself about her throat, knotting in her collar. His left hand came up to hold the knife before her face. "*Elor-reth*," he repeated. "And *elor-rethin* have no protection in law. There is no penalty for slaying them." The knife drifted closer, too close. She could not breathe. The scented air was emptying from her lungs. She looked at the knife and saw Kenan's blood still staining it.

He had not the right. Urien would uphold her. From somewhere, her old calm determination rose up and she twisted in his grip. She drove her right hand in under his ribs. With the left, she snatched at the knife.

He doubled up, gasping, and the force of it knocked her to her knees. His grasp slackened. She used her elbows to hold him from her, and sank her teeth into his imprisoning arm. He let go. She did not try to rise. Ducking out from under him, she grabbed again at the knife. He started to straighten up. She stamped on his bare foot and watched him curl. She had to relieve him of knife and key and incapacitate him enough to let her escape. His grip on the knife was tenacious, and his other hand was still free. She hooked her left arm around his neck and wrapped her right hand about his left wrist. She was still behind him. A short jerk raised his head and trapped him against her, her forearm cutting across his windpipe.

She said, "Drop it." He struggled. She tightened her grip and repeated the command.

He coughed and tugged at her arm. She resisted. "I said drop it."

He dropped it. Iareth hesitated, then released his wrist and picked up the knife. The handle felt unpleasantly warm. She tucked the tip under his ribs. "Now the key." Again he was still. She dug the knife in and heard him moan as she drew blood. His unwounded hand clawed at a pocket and the key fell out onto the floor.

She brought the knife to rest at the fragile point where his spine joined his skull, then cautiously released the neck-lock. He fell forward, panting. She snatched up the key and ran for the door. The smoke was sickening.

Her hand shook. She fumbled with the lock. It was stiff. She could spare only half her attention for it, needing to watch Kenan. He lay still, face averted, cursing softly. The air tasted bad.

She had mishandled it somehow. That was her only clear thought, apart from the driving need to escape. The key would not turn. Smoke choked her. She coughed and found her vision beginning to blur. Her head hurt so . . . the perfume confused everything . . . She raised a hand to rub her eyes, and the key dropped from her damp fingers.

Smoke wrapped about her, clinging as river-mist. She could not see. The door was her only reference, solid, impassable. She coughed and pain doubled her to her knees. Nerveless, her hands brushed the floor. Somewhere she could hear Kenan speaking. The words made no sense. She could see nothing. His knife was still in one hand. The handle seared her. There were creatures somewhere in this mist, and she had no fire with which to banish them. They would find her, misbegotten creatures, and trap and tear and rend. She had lost Joyain in the cloying fog and she must—she *must*—find him. She must act.

Hands laid hold of her and dragged her upright. She fell into them, limbs too drugged to resist. Warm flesh against hers, and a touch on her face, quiet, possessive. She coughed again and said, "Valdin *kai-reth*?" That was wrong, she knew it as soon as she spoke, but she had forgotten the correct name. The hands drew her ungently from the door and dropped her in some boundless, misted limbo. Her hair was in her face; she could not make her hands move to push it back.

"Iareth *elor-reth*," a voice said out of the mist. Fingers

seized her chin so that her head fell back. His form was only barely distinct; pale eyes in a pale face beside her. He bent over her, and his breath carried that same cling of honeysuckle. He said, "Valdin Allandur's whore. No fit companion for a clansman, I think." She could not think; she could not speak. A point of red heat ran across her cheek, and she realized that it was the tip of a knife. Her blood, running down her face, felt cool, cold as her public persona. She could see herself flowing out with it, fragments of Iareth Yscoithi. Her eyes were filled with feathers, her ears with the sound of water falling. The knife touched her again, drawn along the outside of her right forearm. The fabric of her tunic dropped before it. No more *kai-rethin* uniform. The edges that defined her were breaking, pouring away with the dripping of her blood. There was no pain. There was only the knowledge of her dissolution.

She could not move. The knife stole her in pieces and she had no defense against it, bound by scented smoke. There were tears in her blind eyes, but she would not let them fall. Her hands were wet with her blood, touching memory, seeing at last the contradiction of her nature, half-blood, half-caste, half-committed, in deed and word and vow. By stone and flame, wind and wave and darkness . . . But not by blood, and blood is the last of all bindings.

She could find time, caught in this vague peaceful destruction, to wonder if Urien would forgive her failure. If Valdarrien would comprehend and remember. The knife was at her throat now, and it seared her. She raised her eyes and found that at the last they cleared. Kenan knelt over her and his face was blank. He said, "There is always a cost, dearest Iareth. And for me it is blood. To have what I most want, I require a life." His free hand reached out to her and stroked her face. "You understand that this is not personal?" She was beyond speech. She could only look, and she knew that her eyes—her green Armenwy eyes—were mute. "A harsh punishment even for your treachery. But you may take comfort in knowing that your death will serve me."

She had no words. The flow of her blood had taken with it the strength to hate. She was thinking of Valdarrien, who had surrendered his own life to a duelist's bullet and cheated death to come back to her. She was failing him; she was abandoning him once again. If she could, she would have spoken his name and taken the taste of it with her into oblivion.

She could not. She could only hold to it, last of her memories, as her throat went under the knife.

In the salon of Amalie's house, all the candles went out. Valdarrien d'Illandre let the glass he held drop to the floor, eyes wide, heart racing, hand already tightening on the grip of his sword.

Kai-rethin, and one.

21

Ꭰ

JARETH YSCOITHI.

Valdarrien could feel her: she was everywhere in the air. The scent of her clung to the air crowding in on him; the low breeze brushed his skin with her fingers. Everywhere and nowhere, wrapping him in alarm. It was still early; the streets of Merafi were unnaturally quiet. Shops remained shuttered, few carts rattled over the cobbled streets. The market squares were empty. Here and there, a prostitute hovered on a street corner or an anxious underservant scurried to work or a beggar poked through the gutters. It seemed that no one wished to be abroad unless they had no other choice. The city was being surrendered to shadows and unnatural things.

Like him. The light mist coiled toward him, lapped his boots and retreated. He paid it no heed, drawn on by that sense, that calling that told him all was not well. He should have forbidden her from leaving Amalie's, he should have barred her way and forced her to remain. Her Lunedithin masters had no claim on her, no rights by comparison to his. He should have known danger lay ahead from the moment that word had fallen from her lips.

"I must return at least once to the residence, Valdin *kai-reth*. It is my duty."

An ill omen trailed it, that duty of hers. He should have appealed to Urien to repeal it. But Urien had gone out in search of some irrelevance concerned with tides, and Thiercelin was asleep, and Gracielis . . .

Valdarrien had nothing to say to Gracielis. Merafi in peril, Tarnaroqui plots: none of that mattered in the least. She was in danger, his Iareth, and he must find her and win her back from whatever—whoever—it was that dared to threaten her. He climbed the cobbled road up from the low city to the hill, crossing the river at the Dancing Bridge. On higher ground, there were more signs of life. Here lights showed behind casements, there a faint strain of music drifted out. The low beat of bells spoke from the precincts of the Old Temple. The gates to the Lunedithin residence stood open: the guardhouse was lit but its doors were closed. No one challenged him as he entered and crossed the courtyard to the front door. He banged on it with his fist, once, thrice, five times, the sound bouncing round the walls. No one answered; he banged again, louder, and the door swung open. A young maidservant gawped at him as he pushed past her into the hall. "Monsieur . . . monsieur, please . . ." The taste of Iareth was stronger here, stronger and bloodier. Ignoring the girl, Valdarrien strode toward the stairs. Behind him, she called out to the household for help. His hand settled onto the hilt of his sword, cool and comforting. About him, doors slammed and feet hurried over wooden or tiled floors. His eyes narrowed.

A man stood at the head of the stairs, blocking his path. Red hair and a gray uniform, one of the royal *kai-rethin*. Valdarrien stopped, tightening his grip on the sword. He knew that face from somewhere . . . The man began to draw his own blade, stopped, gasped.

"Valdin Allandur?" The voice was light and accented, the thin face edgy and afraid. Valdarrien stared at him. The man—Tafarin Morwenedd, that was it—swallowed, said quietly, "Not possible . . ."

"Iareth Yscoithi," Valdarrien said. "Where is she?"

"I . . . No one's seen her today. She went out . . ."

"She came here. I can feel her."

Tafarin fell back a step. "I don't know . . . maybe Kenan . . ."

"I will find her." Valdarrien closed the distance between them.

"Of course." Tafarin dropped back another pace. "I mean, if you want to look . . ."

"I do not require your permission."

"No . . ." Tafarin's voice was faint. Valdarrien considered him in silence for a long moment. Then Tafarin stepped aside to let him pass. *Iareth Yscoithi* . . . She was here, he was certain of it, and yet . . . Her scent tugged at him, drew him on down the hallway. He heard Tafarin behind him issue orders that he was to be left alone.

There were, it seemed, certain advantages to being dead, after all.

Her calling, that sense of her, drew him up another flight of stairs, along several passages and, at the last, to a door in the west wing of the residence. It stood ajar. At his touch, it swung open before him. The room beyond was gloomy, shaded from the weak light by a dense row of pines outside its windows. The casements stood open, framing those dour trees. The air tasted sour, spiced with iron and blood. The remains of several candles stood on various tables. A number of them had overflowed, trailing wax across the polished wood. There was a dirty-looking stain on one rug. The feel of Iareth Yscoithi was everywhere.

It was not her room. A pair of men's gloves lay atop a chair; on the largest table a scatter of letters with aristocratic seals tangled with the candle wax. A line of invitation cards studded the mantelpiece. *His Lordship requests the pleasure of the company of Prince Kenan Orcandros.*

Kenan Orcandros. The sneering boy of fourteen who thought himself fit to rule an independent Lunedith and who had ambushed Valdarrien at Saefoss. Who had laid

hands, now, upon Valdarrien's Iareth. He could see her,
now, on the fringes of his sight, straight and slim and
trembling. Here, her hand had rested; here, where the
floorboards were scuffed, she had struggled. Strands of
her fine light hair were caught in the wood of the door,
dusted the weave of the rugs. He was walking through
her, lapped and drawn by her fear and her devotion.
Entwined, entranced, he followed her from the salon to
the bedroom beyond. Flakes of blood, flakes of skin
shifted about him. Kenan's spoor overlaid her, bitter,
cruel. She had redeemed Valdarrien's life at Saefoss
from this same Kenan. Yet now . . .

Now . . . On the bed lay a blanket-wrapped bundle,
dark and seeping. Valdarrien's hand dropped from his
sword. Blood on that blanket, on the floor about him,
in the air . . . He reached out and pulled the blanket
aside. Her face was as still as marble, calm and cool as
he had always known her. Her throat was a bloody
wreck. His fingers tightened on her shoulders, dug in,
clutched at her, and she gave him no response. He
dropped to his knees, brow resting against hers, each
now as cold as the other. Nothing he did, it seemed,
could hold her. He had fought back to her, and she had
fled him once again.

Kenan would not escape. Her limp hand in his, her
blood on his lips, Valdarrien swore it and lifted his head.
The room was cold. Somewhere, out in the city, in the
mist, Kenan still lived.

He would not live for much longer.

The river stirred, shifted, thickened. Across Merafi,
windows were being locked, fires built up as fear pressed
in. The mist lay dense and heavy over the low city,
reaching its killing hands upslope toward the homes of
the rich and the privileged and blanking out the thin
autumn daylight. In her rooms at the Tarnaroqui embassy, Quenfrida shivered. Changes in the air, a wrong-
ness, a sourness that should not be there. Something had

been added, something had been done, scratching and straining at the fine bonds of her working. *Kenan*. He was a fool, always wanting too much, wanting more. If he overreached himself now . . .

Deeper into the city, Gracielis paced the length of Amalie's kitchen. His feet were bare: under them, the flagstones spoke of old power, of enmity, of a violence without boundaries. Something building, something shifting out of kilter. He could not find it, could not sense if it was for good or for ill. Frown lines traced themselves across his brow. Urien had yet to return from the Rose Palace. There was no one else he could ask.

It did not taste like Quenfrida, not this time. This was both older and less controlled, as if the city itself was beginning to awaken, to remember. *Stone memory is the oldest*. That was written in the *First Book of Marcellan*. Stone memory and the blood of beginnings.

The river and the city were pulling apart.

Cold hands had hold of Valdarrien, drawing him through the streets. His face was dark. No one who looked on it once looked again. No one remained for long in his path. His hand was clenched and sore about the hilt of his sword. He had died in her name and transcended death to find her again.

For this. To be cheated of her by Kenan Orcandros. He had never known he could burn so deeply. He let it lead him, feeling Kenan ahead of him, like a candle, a pale bright point amid the shadows populating Merafi. Kenan had bound power into him, along with the river. Kenan would learn to regret that. Valdarrien's path took him across the river, heedless of the poor state of the bridges, of the refuse and decay in the streets; then down through the old city into the deserted area around the old docks, past husked-out buildings. Perhaps there were bodies in the alleys and covered passages. He did not choose to notice them, any more than he registered shuttered windows and sealed doors, the odor of burning and sickness. He was drawn, he was certain . . . Through the old docks, to the remains of the bridge that had once led to the submerged shantytown. The river lay vast and swollen, sluggish with filth and debris. It smelled foul. The floating dock was gone. Away to the east flames burned over the estuary. Valdarrien stopped on the very edge of the river and spoke a name.

"Kenan Orcandros."

No reply. He waited, then spoke it again. He seemed to be wholly alone in this rotted part of the city; even the garrison had withdrawn. He hesitated and spoke the name a third time. This time there was a response. Below him the waters stirred and shivered, beginning to mist. From behind him came a footfall.

Valdarrien turned. Kenan, clad in bloody clothing, stood some twenty feet away, on the steps of what had once been a sugar merchant's store. His face showed no surprise. He was older than Valdarrien remembered, taller, broader. That did not matter in the slightest. He said, "Valdin Allandur. Ill met."

Valdarrien bowed. "For you, perhaps."

"I thank you. You have some cause for troubling me?"

"You know that I do." Valdarrien took a step toward him. The blood on that tunic might be hers. He longed to strike Kenan down with a word.

He longed to kill him by slow inches and make mockery of his pleas for mercy. He drew his sword and said, shaking, "I shall kill you."

"For Iareth *elor-reth*? I doubt it." Kenan stood motionless, hands on his hips. "You are illusion, Valdin Allandur. You have no power over me. Not now. Neither you nor the Armenwy can harm me. I have taken her blood to ensure that."

"Don't bet on it." Valdarrien took another step. "Defend yourself."

Kenan shrugged. "As you wish." His voice was

amused. He gestured at the river and spoke a word in some foreign tongue.

Mist rose. Valdarrien felt it as a chill in his veins. Water thundered in his ears. He drew before him the image of Iareth and took another step forward. Kenan spoke again. Another step. Perplexity began to show on Kenan's face. Valdarrien smiled and quickened his pace. The mist was all about him. He moved through it and felt it slide in turn through him. No longer quite human, no longer quite real. Gracielis de Varnaq had diagnosed him and shivered. Now Kenan shivered in his turn, and Valdarrien laughed. Creature of water, he could take no harm from the water Kenan sought to use against him.

He came to the foot of the steps. He looked up at Kenan, and said, *"En garde."*

Kenan drew.

They were much of a height, although the steps gave Kenan an advantage. Valdarrien studied him in silence for a few moments. A little broader than himself, perhaps overconfident. To stack against that, Kenan was armed Lunedithin style, hand-and-a-half sword, weighted to cut and slash, slower than Valdarrien's rapier, but heavier, heavier. Then, too, Kenan had known a lifetime of drill under the calm eye and expert counsel of Urien Armenwy. Not easy. Not very easy.

Valdarrien lunged, aiming for the thigh. Kenan's blade shifted sideways from his low guard, deflecting. Valdarrien stepped back and waited.

Kenan smiled, holding position. His eyes were measuring. He could simply go on standing there. Valdarrien exhaled and attacked again; a beat, a beat, then a disengage under Kenan's blade, striking upward.

Cloth tore. Kenan twisted and jumped off the step, landing on the other side. He still smiled. Valdarrien circled toward him, and Kenan switched guard, using both hands. Mist drifted and swirled between them.

Broader, and probably slower . . . The long pauses

were a feint, that was all, designed to wear down Valdarrien's nerves and play upon his frustrated anger. Valdarrien continued to circle, hand tight on his sword hilt, courting calm. *Don't think about Iareth, now; don't dwell on the loss of her.* Think now only of the moment, of the man before him.

Kenan cut at him in *quarte*. Valdarrien remembered in time not to block the blow and ducked away from it, coming up a little to one side. The tip of his blade circled under Kenan's arm, probing for the flank. Kenan had to step back to avoid it. Valdarrien pursued the advantage, feinting right, then flicking in under Kenan's guard. Kenan drew back with a curse. Blood dripped from his forearm. This time, Valdarrien smiled.

That proved to be a mistake. Kenan broke rhythm and cut to his side. Valdarrien, wasting time gloating, tried to twist away and had to step back, losing ground. He cursed and struck back.

Kenan parried, struck in turn, was parried. His face was intent, passionless. His breathing was quite regular. Valdarrien caught himself starting to hyperventilate; controlled it. So Kenan was good. So what. Valdarrien had fought better and won. He risked a head cut, trying to get Kenan to raise his guard, and succeeded in tearing another hole in his opponent's tunic with the follow-through. Kenan dropped back and looked at him.

"I was wondering, Valdin Allandur," he said pleasantly, "if we play or fight?"

"Iareth Yscoithi," Valdarrien said.

Kenan shrugged. "I regret I do not see the cause. By the law of my people there is no vengeance due for her kind."

"I'm not subject to your laws."

"Indeed? Nor to those of your homeland, I think. Is it not forbidden to fight in the public street in Merafi?"

"I'm dead," Valdarrien said and enjoyed it. "Dead men have no laws." He looked at Kenan. "You'll no doubt discover that when I've killed you."

"If," said Kenan, reprovingly. "I dislike finding myself dismissed so certainly."

"My heart bleeds."

"Pray that you do not have the gift of prophecy."

Valdarrien attacked in *seconde*, evaded Kenan's block, and slashed upward. Kenan twisted free and struck. Valdarrien longed for an off-hand weapon, as he parried and sidestepped. The air was still and a little sticky; the mist wrapped them in the odors of burning and decay. Perhaps it troubled Kenan. Valdarrien paid it no heed.

He feinted, drew back, feinted again on the other side, and succeeded in wrong-footing Kenan. The mistake left his opponent off-balance and with his right side open. Valdarrien lunged straight into the gap and felt the impact jar down his arm as his sword tip met bone. Kenan gasped and pulled away. Valdarrien pressed the advantage, driving blows against the other's guard. That cut on the forearm must be beginning to tell on Kenan by now. Valdarrien dropped his own guard momentarily, then leaped aside and used Kenan's attempt at a hit to bring in a blow to the same forearm.

Kenan shifted his sword to a single-hand grip. He was beginning to pant a little, and his look of concentration was sliding. His injured arm hung by his side. Valdarrien paused to check his own footing, then advanced and struck.

A high blow, a *flêche*, blade snake-sudden. Kenan was still recovering. His guard was not solid. He tried to parry, fumbling, and left himself open. The tip of Valdarrien's sword slid past his wavering blade and came in at the base of his throat between the bones, where the veins lay. Kenan looked up into Valdarrien's eyes, and his face spoke disbelief.

The late Lord of the Far Blays smiled at him, and drove the sword home.

22

HIS HEAD DIDN'T HURT.

This was so unexpected that it took Joyain a minute or so to register the fact. He opened a very cautious eye, swallowed (his mouth tasted foul), and waited for reaction to set in. Nothing. He felt weak, yes, and tired, but beyond that . . . no headache, no nausea, and blessedly no fever. He was alone in a wide bed in a room he dimly remembered as belonging to the young noblewoman with the pretty smile. Miraude, that was it. The one Leladrien had called the famous widow.

He'd dreamed about Lelien, bitter-colored dreams. He didn't want to think about that or about the realities preceding them. He tried to sit up and discovered that he could do so without anything beyond a mild dizziness. He was very thirsty. The pitcher by the bed contained a liquid he identified as watered milk. He drank, pulling a face at the taste. Then he looked around him. It was day. Light filtered through the half-closed casements. The fire in the grate had gone out. There were no candles. The house was quiet. He hesitated, then decided to risk getting out of bed.

The process proved slow, but far less distressing than the last occasion. He couldn't find a robe. He wrapped a sheet around himself and, in careful stages, went out into the corridor.

The house was in semidarkness. It smelled musty, untended, and beneath that there was the sour stench of illness, the bitterness of ash. How contagious was this plague? Joyain pushed the thought away. Kindness deserved a better reparation than this. He wondered how many days had elapsed since he first woke up here. Room after room was deserted. The hearths were cold. None of the clocks seemed to be running. Several of the beds had been used, but all were empty now.

At the bottom of the back stairs he finally heard a sound. He hesitated, then climbed in cautious stages. His breath caught. He needed to use both hands on the banister. At the head he stopped and listened again. Then he called out, "Hello?"

There was a gasp, a silence. From a room to his right he heard a chair scrape over floorboards. He hesitated again, then tapped lightly on the door, and went in.

A small room under the eaves. The casement was shut tight, the fire was out. The air smelled vile. A still form lay in the bed, another stood in the middle of the room, blinking in the low light from the hall. The beautiful Miraude d'Iscoigne l'Aborderie. Her skin was gray with fatigue, her hair uncombed and lifeless. Her bright gown was torn and stained. She looked at Joyain with dulled eyes and swayed as she stood. She was silent.

He said awkwardly, "Mademoiselle?"

She gulped, not really looking at him. Then she said, "She's dead. Coralie. And the others have died or run away."

Joyain remembered what he had seen in the cellar of Leladrien's garrison. He did not want to look too closely at the woman on the bed. He could smell gathering decomposition. To Miraude he said, "You should come downstairs," and then, when she did not move, "Here."

He held out his arm. She rubbed her eyes, then looked at him properly. She said, "I thought you were dead, too." Her voice was uncertain. He could hear panic awakening within it. "You can't be alive . . . you brought it here."

"I'm sorry," Joyain said, and stopped.

A little unsteadily she said, "This is too absurd." Her hand knotted in her disordered hair. "You're apologizing for living?" He was silent. She began to laugh unevenly. After a moment, this turned into sobbing.

"Oh, don't," Joyain said, horrified. He felt so tired. He wasn't up to this. She stood there with her hand pressed to her mouth. He had to do something. She couldn't stay here. "Please don't." She didn't seem to hear him. He took hold of her arm and led her out of the room. The one next to it was clean and empty. He virtually pulled her into it. There was a chair and an unmade bed. He sank onto the latter, exhausted, and looked at her. She stood a moment, shivering, then she sat down beside him. She was still crying. He hesitated, then put an arm about her. She turned her head into his shoulder. He said again, "I'm sorry."

"Not . . . your fault," she said. She paused, then seemed to gather her energy, lifting her head and wiping her eyes. "I don't know what to do. I've tried to keep a quarantine, but . . ."

He said, "How long have I been here?"

"Three days . . . People got ill so quickly. Iareth told me to shut the house and wait till the plague burned itself out, but I don't know how long that is . . ." She seemed to be fighting further tears. Joyain tightened his hold on her. He felt horribly guilty.

He said, "How do you feel?"

"Oh, I'm fine." Miraude was bitter. "Everyone else was taken ill, but I'm just tired . . . The doctor took the bodies yesterday, but today he didn't come, and Coralie . . ."

"Don't think about it," Joyain said.

She said, "*You* recovered."

"Yes." He couldn't explain that. He said, "It'll be all right," unsure whether or not he believed it. And then: "Iareth told you?"

"You asked for her."

"Oh." He didn't remember. He said, "You've been very kind to me . . . I've repaid you poorly."

She ignored that. Instead she said, "But what do we do now?"

"I don't know." Joyain looked at her. "We wait, I suppose."

"I heard voices," Thiercelin said. "Is Urien back?"

"Not yet." Gracielis finished rearranging the pillows and began to fidget with the objects on the occasional table. "Do you have any pain?"

"I don't think so." Thiercelin leaned back and tried to analyze his physical condition. His side ached but his head was clear. "I think it's healing."

"So Urien says."

"Yes. I owe him for that. And you, Graelis."

Gracielis glanced at him sidelong. "I am, of course, wholly at your service."

"Of course." Thiercelin pulled a face. To his surprise, Gracielis neither smiled nor played up to him. "Is something wrong?"

"What would be wrong?"

"Plenty, on current progress. Has the river risen?"

"Probably."

Gracielis turned his back and went to the fireplace. Thiercelin said, "Talk to me, Graelis. Is it Yviane?"

"No." Gracielis stared into the mirror over the mantelpiece. The angle was too steep to permit Thiercelin to see his reflection. "Urien went to see her. You'll have news of her later."

"There's something to look forward to." Thiercelin said. Gracielis turned to look at him. Thiercelin hesitated, then raised a cautious hand. "Come over here."

"If you wish." Gracielis came and sat on the bed.

Thiercelin possessed himself of one of his companion's hands and turned it palm up. The wrists were unmarked. Thiercelin ran a finger along the line of a tendon. "Even the scar has gone."

"Yes. The *undarii* heal quickly."

"So, how's the plan for world domination?"

Gracielis looked startled. "Urien's or Quenfrida's?"

"Urien's, of course."

Gracielis started to play with the ends of his hair. "We should be able to act shortly . . ."

"I'm sorry," Thiercelin said. "You don't need me to remind you of that."

Gracielis looked up. "I shall always need you, monseigneur. Even in that capacity."

"Thierry," said Thiercelin. And then, "Liar."

Gracielis sighed extravagantly. "My heart will surely shatter."

"I doubt it."

"Without you . . ." Gracielis stopped and looked away. After a moment he turned back and said, "Thierry?"

"Yes?"

"Something's happening, something I can't quite recognize. Something's out of balance." Gracielis took his hand away from Thiercelin. "I don't know if I can do this at all, and now . . ."

"What?" Thiercelin stared. "I'm not following you. I can understand if you're concerned about Quenfrida . . ."

Gracielis cut him short. "I fear that something has happened to Iareth Yscoithi. There was a . . . a disturbance, something like that. And then Lord Valdarrien rushed out, and since then . . ."

"River bless." Thiercelin hesitated. "Was she attacked by those mist creatures?"

"I don't know. It felt different, as if someone was raising power. Not Quenfrida. Kenan."

Thiercelin forgot himself and sat up. "And if Valdin finds that out . . . He'll go looking for Kenan." It was not a question. Thiercelin knew Valdarrien too well to have any doubt on that. "Well, there's nothing we can do about it now, I suppose."

Gracielis turned to him. "You aren't angry?"

"Why should I be?"

"I failed to prevent Lord Valdarrien . . ."

"No one," said Thiercelin, "has ever been able to stop Valdin, that I recall. It's one of his least endearing features." He stopped and looked at Gracielis. "No one except maybe Iareth. He doesn't change. And neither do our responses to him. If he does kill Kenan, the diplomatic consequences are going to drive Yviane to distraction." He sighed, shook his head. Yvelliane still had not come.

Gracielis laid a hand on his shoulder. "Diplomacy may not matter."

"How so?"

"What troubles me . . ." Gracielis halted, and rose. "I should leave this. Your injuries . . ."

"Don't hedge," Thiercelin said. Gracielis glanced round, looking resigned. "If you don't tell me, I promise I'll lie awake worrying."

"Blackmail. Very well, then. It is simply that if Kenan dies . . ." Gracielis hesitated, apparently seeking words. "There were two, who raised this old power against Merafi. To remove one like this is highly dangerous."

"You said something to that effect yesterday."

"Yes." Gracielis came back to the bed, and sat down. "There're two reasons why. The first—the simplest—is that the *undarii* are sometimes hard to kill. The second . . ." He began to pleat a corner of the sheet between his fingers. "If you kill the controller without first breaking the powers bound to them, then those powers may go out of control. And Kenan has already done something that tends that way."

Thiercelin sighed, caught once again by the paradox between the rational and the unnatural. Gracielis looked at him with eyes that were both candid and pleading. "Go on."

"There's a further strangeness . . ."

"There would be. All right, Graelis, I believe you."

"Valdarrien d'Illandre is in some sense a side creation of the forces awoken by Kenan and Quenfrida. That

night by the quay . . ." Gracielis hesitated. "I was afraid
for you."

"Well, I still seem to be here," Thiercelin said. "Along
with one or two other people." Gracielis would not meet
his eyes. "Tell me?"

"Lord Valdarrien . . . He wasn't what I meant to do.
I wasn't *undarios*. That night . . . I had hoped at best to
weaken the effects of Quenfrida's working a little. But
when you called out, I was afraid. For you rather than
myself." He shrugged. "A new experience. I used what
power was to hand to defend you, and . . . Well, you've
seen the consequences."

"Valdin."

"He was dead. Now he lives, after a fashion." Gracielis looked at Thiercelin. "To become *undarios* . . .
There is a series of rituals, tests, designed to awaken
ability. The last, the seventh, involves a death. The acolyte must kill or be killed. I could never face it." He
paused, looked away. "The killing is used as the key to
unlock power in the blood. That night on the quay I let
the power in the river into me, trying to help you. I
meant to kill myself. But Valdarrien d'Illandre was
there. He was already bound to that power, since his
was the blood shed to awaken it. I went through him
and into the forces behind him. It should have finished
both of us. It didn't. I still don't know why." Gracielis
shook his head. "However, it happened, he's still in part
a creation of the power in that river. For Kenan to die
at his hand . . . It's equivalent, almost, to Kenan being
killed by his own power."

"That doesn't sound good," Thiercelin said.

"It isn't. It's virtually a guarantee of full loss of control
over the old power. It probably means an almost immediate deterioration in the state of Merafi. The only posi-
tive side effect is that Quenfrida may have to
overextend herself."

Thiercelin said, "I see." It was, he recognized, an inadequate response, but it was the best he could come up with.

Gracielis said, "I'm sorry."

There was a silence. Thiercelin frowned. Then he said, "Poor Valdin." Another remark without apparent relevance. He added, "Even now, I don't know quite how to react to him. I suppose I must have grown more used to his having died than I thought." Gracielis said nothing. "But to lose Iareth again . . ." Thiercelin paused and shivered. "You can't know what he was like when she left him Even Yviane could do nothing with him. And I'm stuck here, worse than useless."

"Above all else," Gracielis said, "you are not responsible for what's just happened."

"I'm not? If I hadn't asked you to go looking for him in the first place . . . If I'd told Yvelliane, instead of trying to do everything myself . . ."

"Things would probably have turned out much the same. And," and Gracielis looked wicked, "you wouldn't have had the privilege and experience of my company." He looked at Thiercelin sidelong.

Thiercelin was not going to be provoked. He raised his brows. "Oh, now that would've been a real tragedy."

"Naturally." But the amusement was already gone from Gracielis' face. He put out a hand and said, "Thierry, I . . ."

There was a brisk tap on the door. Gracielis broke off, and went to answer it.

It was Yvelliane.

There is a stillness in the air, a quality of waiting that is, in some oblique way, new. The rain holds back, uncertain, immanent. Deep down, below the river, through the water table, west to the great lake, north through the arterial tributaries, something is awakening.

It has no memory. How can it, lacking any sense of self? It has no consciousness. It does not notice the hiatus in its existence, since it can feel nothing, neither imprisonment nor cessation. It can simply be and move and grow.

The city of Merafi, built at the mingling of two waters, salt and sweet, lies like a weight upon it, half felt, half ignored. It is blind to the remaining life within that city, aware only of the compression wrought by stone and brick and timber. Two moons tug at it, subtly out of alignment, hinting at force to come. High in the distant lake a head begins to build.

The river is rising. Thick, dirty water laves the edges of the old docks, the remains of the city wall, the fringes of the central city. To the south the water runs insistent, dominating its surroundings. The canalized north channel chafes at its bindings, beginning to test its boundaries, tugging on the pylons of the bridges, washing debris from the face of the lower cliff. Water tastes the high wall along the west quarter quayside.

Yvelliane hovered in the doorway, eyes on Thiercelin. They were dark-circled, and the lines of worry had settled even more deeply into her face. He longed to go to her, gather her to him. He could do no more than hold out his hands. "Yviane . . ." He was used to her being tired, but this was something more, something darker. He said, "The queen . . . She hasn't . . . I mean, she isn't . . . ?"

"Firomelle is no worse."

"I'm glad."

There was a silence. Into it, Gracielis said, "I have things I should be doing." He bowed. "If you would excuse me, madame."

Yvelliane was still staring at Thiercelin. She said, "Of course," and stepped aside as he passed her.

She would not come closer. Thiercelin dropped his hands. He said, "And you? How are you? You look tired."

"As ever." Something—not a smile—tugged at the

corners of her mouth. She moved a little closer, came to a halt just before the foot of his bed. She said, "You were hurt . . . How are you?"

"Recovering." He smiled at her. Was she worrying over him? Hope awoke within him, faint, enduring. He said, "It's not as bad as it looks. Urien's a good doctor."

"I'm glad." But her face was not glad. She fidgeted with the edge of her cloak. "I'm sorry, Thierry. I'm such a bad wife to you."

"What?" He started toward her, came up short with an exclamation of pain. She dropped her cloak to the floor and came round the bed to support him. Her hands were cold, her fingers tight on his forearm.

She said, "I'm sorry, I'm so sorry." Her voice shook.

"I must try not to do that." He put his free hand over hers. "It's all right, I'm all right, Yviane."

"Yes, but . . ." She would not look at him. "This is all my fault. I ignored you and hurt you and pushed you away, and now . . ."

"It's not your fault. It was an accident. Sort of. Or it was my fault, for trying to do something that was too difficult for me."

"You couldn't trust me." There were tears in Yvelli-ane's voice. "Urien told me what you've been doing, you and Gracielis. I made you afraid to tell me."

"No." He did not know what to say. He could barely recall the last time he had seen her this visibly distressed, this close to broken. Those first days after Valdarrien died, perhaps. He inhaled, slowly and said, "Sit down." She sat on the edge of the bed. He tightened his grip on her hand. "I wanted to help. You're always so over-worked, and it sounded crazy."

"And you thought I wouldn't listen." Finally, she looked at him. "You'd have been right. I don't listen."

"It doesn't matter. You're here now."

"Yes." But her eyes evaded his.

He said, "What's wrong?"

She sat without speaking for several moments. Then

she lifted her head and smiled at him. It was a little
crooked and her eyes were damp, but for all that it was
real. She said, "I do love you, Thierry."

She had never said it, not once in the six years of
their marriage. His breath had gone awry. He knew he
was clutching her hand too tightly. She said, "I wanted
you to know . . . to be sure." He swallowed, mouth dry.
She went on, "And I realized . . . You could have died.
Everything's out of control, in the city, at home. And
now . . ." She stopped, rested her face against his shoulder. "The sickness has reached our house. I've been living at the palace."

"Is Mimi all right?"

"I had a letter this morning. I think so. But your
friend Maldurel . . . I'm sorry, Thierry."

He had not seen Maldurel since the aborted duel.
Now, it seemed, he never would again. It had not been
much of a good-bye. The Merafi he had known for so
long was changing, and he was complicit in that. He said,
"It'll get better. Urien and Gracielis . . ."

"Urien told me," Yvelliane said. "I tried to have
Quenfrida sent away, but the council blocked me. While
you . . ." She kissed his cheek. "You did the right thing
straight away. And I suspected you for it."

He had waited so long for this, for her to trust him.
He was not sure he wanted it at this price, for Yvelliane
to be so broken. He said, "That doesn't matter."

"It ought to." She raised her head. "Thierry, I . . ."

"But it doesn't, not so long as you love me." He could
not find the words. "That's the important bit. The rest
is just trappings. I love you. That's what it comes
down to."

"I don't deserve you." There was something in her
face he did not understand. She kissed him again, this
time on the lips, and then stood. "I have to go. It's
nearly dusk. I'm sorry. There's so much I have to do by
tomorrow evening."

"You will come back?"

"Of course I will." But this time, her smile did not reach her eyes. "Sleep well, love." And, gathering her cloak from the floor, she was gone.

He stared after her for long, quiet minutes, caught between joy and fear. Something was wrong, and he had no way at all of discovering what.

"Your city will fall," Urien had said, calm eyes on her. "We may be able to protect it somewhat, but the forces you must deflect are not trivial. And protection is not cure." She had held silent, watching him. His expression had given nothing away; he had too long studied pragmatic control.

That should have been something they held in common. But Yvelliane had begun finally to question her own pragmatism. There are other fanaticisms than those of flame and thunder.

"Gracielis de Varnaq," Urien had said, "is no match for the woman Quenfrida. And she has the additional aid of Prince Kenan. It is likely that in a trial between them, Gracielis *undarios* will go under."

"So he's told me." Yvelliane had sighed. "I tried to have her removed, but the times aren't right. To offer such an insult to Tarnaroq . . ."

"Peace." Urien had raised a hand. "Granted our present strengths, no gain will be made by expelling her from Merafi. The time for that is long past." Yvelliane had looked down. "Her working must be undone, Yviane Allandur, and the old bonds remade."

Her mouth had been dry, asking, "How?" His answer had been to repeat to her the old tale of Yestinn Allandur, who had enacted a sacrifice to bind the old powers. Orcandrin blood to seal Allandurin rule; and the overthrow of the old clan ways had followed. He had moved his capital from remote Skarholm, too close to the places of greatest power, and come south to found Merafi. The great city built where the old powers were weakest, where stone met wave, where two waters, salt and fresh, mingled. And the old power had slept, until ambitious Kenan disturbed it and found in Quenfrida a tutor to learn to use it.

Kenan, of course, had probably wanted no more than to free Lunedith from dependence upon Gran' Romagne. It would be Quenfrida who had initiated the attempt to destroy Gran' Romagne's heart-city totally.

Now Urien—the Lunedithin—and Gracielis—the Tarnaroqui—seemed to wish to lay this force again to sleep. Yvelliane had listened without comment. But in the back of her mind, a suspicion had begun to rise.

To impose that ancient pact, Yestinn had made a blood sacrifice. Kenan in turn had shed blood— Allandurin and his own—to create this disturbance. To reimpose quiescence . . .

Urien had perhaps detected where her thoughts had led her. He had paused and said, "The first compact— Yestinn's—was made in Lunedith. But it is for Merafi that we now work. It is thus better that we make our new compact here, sealing Merafi once again against that which has entered it unwholesomely."

Yvelliane had made no great study of the old beliefs regarding powers and balances. The river priests pursued such matters; and to the south the Tarnaroqui struggled to use what arcane fragments they possessed to their own aggrandizement. She had frowned and said, "Simplicity suggests Kenan must die—at Allandurin hands?— to reimpose calm. But that option doesn't seem to take care of Quenfrida. And Kenan's hardly likely to cooperate."

"Gaverne Orcandros—the first sacrifice—was unwilling." Urien said, levelly.

"Hmm." Yvelliane steepled her fingers. "But Kenan is linked to this whatever-it-is in a way Gaverne wasn't. He's on its side . . . I wonder if killing him might not tend to feed, rather than pacify it?"

"Indeed."

"In which case, you need a different victim . . . Merafi

isn't Orcandrin territory, anyway. It belongs to my family, if anyone . . ." She raised her eyes to meet his. "Not Firomelle. You can't ask this of her."

"No." Urien was not, in general, demonstrative, but he had risen and laid his hands over hers. "Yviane Allandur, do you know what I must now ask you?"

She had run cold. She swallowed, forcing herself to think logically. If all this superstition was true—and Urien certainly was not given to irrationalities—then the situation was desperate. Urien would not—ever—make such a suggestion to her otherwise.

And Firomelle was dying, and Yvelliane had already surrendered her brother, her marriage, her private self, to Firomelle's service.

Firomelle's, not Merafi's. Viewed too clearly in this moment, she could see how much her devotion to duty had derived from her love for the queen. Yvelliane had looked at Urien and said, "Will it work?"

"An Allandurin sacrifice?"

She nodded.

"Granted the necessary conditions, I believe so."

"And Firomelle?"

"I know not if her illness is a part of this. Her city may be redeemed, but the sacrifice may not renew her. Forgive me."

"I just wondered." Firomelle's greatest concern was the survival of her city against internal and external threat. Yvelliane had always supported her in that. She could not fail her now, however much she might want to retreat, to hide, to go to Thiercelin and beg his forgiveness. She was calm, suddenly. Her duty was clear. She had looked at Urien, and said, "My blood is Allandurin. You're asking me to die to save Merafi."

"Yes."

"Well," and she straightened. "I won't do it just for Merafi. But for Merafi and Firomelle . . . Yes, Urien, I will lay down life to that end." Her words had been formal, but her sense of relief had not been.

Urien had risen and offered her a salute, Lunedithin fashion. Service, honor, reverence. She had looked down, suddenly awkward, and busied herself with the tidal calculations. She had let Urien draw her, finally, out from her world of calm rationality, and into the twilight of her city's past.

Valdarrien came back around an hour after dark, more like a ghost of himself than he had ever been. Gracielis met him on the stairwell and stepped back. Valdarrien passed him without a word and went into Thiercelin's room. Gracielis trailed him, wary, uncertain. Thiercelin was still awake and reading. Yvelliane's visit had reawakened something, some strength within him. Gracielis did not know whether to be glad or to weep at that. He could not bear to spoil the hope he saw in Thiercelin's face, yet he shivered from the pain that was to come.

Valdarrien sat down on the end of the bed and put his face in his hands. They were bloody. He said, "She's dead, Thierry. I went to her embassy. I saw her . . . Does Urien know?"

"Yes," Gracielis said.

"Her hair still smells the same," Valdarrien said. "She promised to stay with me, but she broke her word." He looked across at Thiercelin. "Is this all we'll ever have?"

Thiercelin said, "I don't know. I'm sorry, Valdin."

"Yes . . ." Valdarrien rose and went to the window. "Perhaps being dead was better, after all . . . She didn't deserve what Kenan did to her." He stared out into the fading light, then shut the casement with a bang. "I told him. I doubt he understood."

"Monseigneur," said Gracielis, "what has befallen Kenan?"

"Is it your business?" But there was no real defiance in Valdarrien's voice. "He's not important."

Thiercelin said, "He's a member of a foreign royal house, Valdin. The consequences . . ."

"May go drown!" Valdarrien turned. "Dead men can't be punished, Thierry. And with Merafi in this state, who's to say how he died. There are so many dangers in the streets."

"So you killed him," Gracielis said.

"Yes." Valdarrien wandered around the room. "And I told Urien so on my way upstairs, so honor is satisfied." Gracielis said nothing. "I've already had the lecture regarding my conduct. I don't choose to submit to another." He paused by the hearth, drumming his fingers on the mantel. "It was necessary, killing him. I enjoyed it."

Gracielis looked at his own hands. He could hear the strain in Valdarrien's voice, underneath the bravado. The dead could feel. Feelings, above all else, are what held them close to the living. He wondered if Kenan's ghost would rise tonight, amid the myriad shadows, to continue his work against Merafi. Perhaps this time it would be Quenfrida who would be haunted.

The room was quiet save for Valdarrien's tapping fingers. Kenan was dead. His powers had been neither blocked nor bound; his sudden absence would leave space for worse things. Gracielis rose and bowed to Thiercelin. "Excuse me, monseigneur, but I should talk to Urien."

"Of course." Thiercelin hesitated then added, "Graelis?"

"Yes?"

"What we were talking about earlier—before Yviane visited—will that happen now?"

"I don't know," Gracielis said. He looked across at Valdarrien, then back to Thiercelin. "I hope not."

"Yes." Thiercelin looked down.

Gracielis went out, closing the door. From behind it, he heard Valdarrien start to speak.

Urien was in the kitchen. Gracielis hesitated on the threshold. Urien turned, and his face held no emotion. Controlled calm, akin to Iareth's calm, which Kenan had shattered . . . Gracielis came into the room and said, in Lunedithin, "I grieve for you."

"I thank you." The tone did not invite further comment. Gracielis sat. Urien finished what he was doing and came back to the table, wiping his hands. "I have the calculations from Yviane Allandur. We have a day." There was a sheaf of papers on the clean end of the board, made out in Yvelliane's precise hand. Gracielis skimmed them. One day. Tomorrow night, both moons would be full and their cycles would be in alignment. The pull upon the river would be at its strongest. High tide. Highest tide, and Quenfrida's control over what she had awakened would be at its weakest.

Gracielis frowned. Urien planned to use force against force, turning the waters back upon their awakener, and sever their bindings to her, simultaneously laying down new bindings of his own. Hard enough with both Kenan and Quenfrida to face. But with Kenan gone, the powers were already half out of control. Gracielis shivered, seeing his death plainly in the neat script before him. He was not Quenfrida's equal and he must turn this tide upon her. He looked up at Urien and said, in his native Tarnaroqui, "I can't." And then, in Lunedithin, "Forgive me."

"There's to be a sacrifice," Urien said. "Perhaps you will only have to create a delay." He paused. "You have your own strengths and your own tie to the river."

"None of my seeking." Gracielis twisted his hair between his fingers. "You mean Valdarrien d'Illandre?" Urien nodded. "His presence isn't my doing."

"I wonder." Urien sat down opposite, and studied him. "I understand that to become *undarios*, you must sacrifice a life? Yet you did not do so, and are *undarios* having instead returned a life that was lost."

"Not properly." Gracielis shivered again at the memory of what he had glimpsed behind Valdarrien.

"Whatever his nature, you called upon the river force to shape him. It may yet serve you." Urien hesitated.

"And I possess resources of my own, which I lay at your disposal."

"Thank you," Gracielis said. It had come to this, after all. Until now he had not quite believed that he would go through with it. For the first time since the night of Valdarrien's rebirth, he felt a sudden, desperate longing for Quenfrida.

Take this from me . . . Chai ela, *Quenfrida, I am much in need of you.* She had promised him death and turned from him. But she alone in all Merafi would understand this fear that gripped him. He was dimly aware of her, a watchful presence amidst the wilder weight of the river. What would she say if he went to her now and demanded her aid? Would she hold out her killing hands and offer temptation? Without Kenan there would be space beside her. He reached out to her in thought.

It was cold . . . He swam against a current, heavy water drenching him, and catching, clawing. He shivered, contracting down within himself. Wave, wind, flame, stone, darkness. It was different this time; the waters were unaware of him. He was small enough to pass, gravel in the undertow. Shapes flickered past him, half-drawn. He could feel the city's walls about him, neither a prison nor a guide. The stones softened, the earth gave way. He gasped, afraid to be pulled into the dark places where the river probed. He surfaced and the air was bright around him, snatching at the water with tiny hands. Quenfrida's domain, this, sky-hallowed, just as his own blood bound him to stone. She was a wind above the dark waters, turning in on herself to enforce and command. Her daily mind was beyond him. She was withdrawn, entranced in her own necessities. All about her, black clouds formed.

He might join her and face them down. He might bind himself into the weight of water rising and watch Merafi drown. He would be redeemed in the eyes of his own kind. He had nothing to lose.

He had promised Thiercelin. Across the light, across

the waves, he remembered their hands, which touched, which held. This city was dear to Thiercelin. He had sought to do the best he could to save it. He loved Yvelliane, whom he must lose, and Valdarrien, whom he had tracked beyond death. He had fought to bring Gracielis to this moment. Thiercelin would lose everything.

There were already too many deaths. Gracielis looked once more into the vortices of Quenfrida's work, and withdrew.

Yvelliane would die for Merafi and for the queen she loved.

Gracielis de Varnaq could not, after all, betray Thiercelin, who stood to lose so very much of what he loved.

His eyes snapped open. From the other side of the table, Urien watched him. Gracielis lowered his head into his hands. He said, "Two days?"

"So. The second night from this one."

"And the sacrifice?"

"Is in hand. I have only to arrange for the means."

"I see, " Gracielis said. And then, "Poor Thierry."

"If we do not try this, his case is no better," Urien said.

"No," said Gracielis. "But I don't suppose that knowledge is likely to be much comfort to him."

23

ONE MORE DAY. At dawn, most of southern Merafi was awash in three feet of dirty water. Fog hovered over it, obscuring the view of onlookers in higher places. The old city was being abandoned. Only the river priests hung on in their island tower as the river they had vowed to serve devoured the city. The air was thick and sour tasting. The crack of falling masonry punctuated the sound of rising water. The surface of the water was nearly opaque, filthy with debris. No one knew the death toll. The water had invaded the headquarters of the city watch. Its skeleton staff had fled without their papers. The guard regiments held clear of the city's core, clinging to the high northern and eastern areas. Between the middle and north channels, fires burned intermittently in the streets. Few people ventured into those streets. The mist creatures grew bolder. Some walked and tore by day. In odd places shattered glass bore testimony to the activities of looters. A handful of residents remained, mainly in the taller buildings, held by stubbornness or plague.

The west quarter lay still, though the north channel lapped hungrily at the verges of the quay. All those who could had already fled. The remainder moved with caution and avoided their fellows, waiting for sickness. There was less mist here, but the wind smelled bad and the rain was dark with ash.

In the aristocrats' quarter seals began to appear on

the high gates of residences. Plague within, do not enter. In the grounds of several, fires blazed, disposing of bodies. One or two stood hollow-windowed and silent.

By noon Tafarin Morwenedd and his remaining compatriots rode north with their burden of ill tidings. Iareth Yscoithi was ash. Sodden, Kenan's body mixed with the sand and silt of the estuary.

In the Far Blays town house, Joyain watched the emptying streets and fought weakness. He could do nothing else now; only wait and try uncertainly to bring comfort to Miraude. Afterward . . . Already in his head he was trying to imagine life in this ghost city.

The Tarnaroqui embassy remained open, its closed windows shedding light and voices and music. Quenfrida's protections held it safe, withdrawn from chaos, as she herself was withdrawn from her companions, into the sanctuary of her rooms. Demons woke in her mind. She looked inward, fighting to control and hold them. She pursued Kenan's failure down avenues of power and wove her own substance into her bindings.

Valdarrien ventured into the old city and found no consolation in fighting mist creatures. They could not touch him. He could carve them into fragments, but they simply re-formed. He had found Iareth and lost her, and he had forgotten purpose.

Thiercelin insisted on rising. Urien said nothing. Gracielis implored, sighed, and offered his shoulder. "If all I can do is wait, at least I can do it sitting up," Thiercelin said. He was waiting for Yvelliane. Gracielis could not bear to watch him, to see his new joy, knowing that it must be transitory. For himself, he did not believe Yvelliane would call again. He could not blame her for that. She would need to cling to what courage she had against what she must face this night.

Viewed from the west quarter, Merafi was a sunken city, drowned in mist. Only the cliff and the tower of the island temple pierced it. The air was heavy with death and fire and decay. Distorted shapes poked and pulled at shutters, shredding the resolve of those who cowered within. Few dared to walk the streets, and fewer returned with a description.

The river was everywhere. No place was secure from the sound of it, run thick and whispering into every corner. Its voice bespoke triumph. On the hill Miraude woke weeping. Joyain held her hands but found no words to comfort her. He should return to his unit in the low city. If he had a unit left at all. He did not know what to do, did not want to leave her alone her in this house of death.

The fires were going out, the air too damp finally to sustain them. Gracielis threw open the windows of the top story of Amalie's house and reached out into the mist. After a moment he said, "She has overreached. Can you feel her?"

"Quenfrida?" said Thiercelin, sitting grimly in a chair and pretending to feel better than he did. "No. Not even slightly."

Gracielis turned and smiled. His eyes were unusually bright, but the fair skin was cool and pale. His movements were remote, as though through water. Thiercelin knew him to have fasted both this day and the one prior. Gracielis closed the window again and said, "The Tarnaroqui embassy sustains her, I think." Thiercelin looked inquiring. "They haven't let the river affect them. That strengthens her. But she's withdrawn into herself."

"Hmmm," Thiercelin said. "It's a pity we can't contaminate it somehow. Open its windows. Not that I'm much use as part of a 'we' right now." He shook his head. "If I hadn't been stupid enough to follow you, I could be some use to someone." He fell silent, aware that Gracielis appeared to be repressing laughter. "All right, so that's funny, Graelis. But . . ."

"Peace." Gracielis held up a hand in Urien's fashion. "Dear monseigneur—dear Thierry—you are more use than you imagine, and I'm blind. Thank you."

"You're welcome," Thiercelin said. And then, "What have I done, exactly?"

"Contamination. Bringing the river to Quenfrida's sanctuary." For the first time in days there was real joy in Gracielis' smile. "It's simple, too. All I have to do is get them to admit Valdarrien d'Illandre. In a certain sense, he's part of the river." Gracielis paused, leaned down, and kissed Thiercelin. "Thank you, my heart. And the very best of it is that he's an embodiment of the power over which Kenan lost control . . . Have you your signet, monseigneur?"

"What?" Thiercelin was starting to feel rather lost. "Which one, Sannazar or the Far Blays?"

"The latter."

"Yes, but . . ."

"May I borrow it? It should provide the passport to Ambassador Sigeris."

"Go on, then." And Thiercelin tugged off the ring he had worn since his marriage to Yvelliane.

Valdarrien smiled when asked to enact the role of courier, and told why. Thiercelin had rapidly lost sight of him as he made his way out into the misted streets, but Gracielis had found from somewhere a fine china bowl in which he mingled scented oils with water, and into which he gazed, while the street grew colder.

Wind began to catch and tangle at the mist. Even Thiercelin saw the flash of blue light in Gracielis' bowl. The latter looked up, and for a moment it seemed to Thiercelin that there were fires alight in his eyes. Then Gracielis smiled and said, "It is done."

High on the hill, Yvelliane d'Illandre threw a note into a fire and straightened her spine. Then she glanced into a glass, nodded to her reflection, and knocked upon the door to the prince consort's study. Firomelle was too ill to receive her. Yvelliane had looked in on the sleeping queen and felt no regret that her farewell must, after all, be silent. She could not have explained to Firomelle what it was she must do; and any other leave-taking would have seemed ill-omened.

Tonight . . . She had written to Miraude a short note

speaking of duty. She had tried to write to Thiercelin, but found herself almost wordless. *Thierry, I love you. I'm sorry* . . . She could bear no more. If she let herself feel too much now, her thin courage would fracture. She had written a simple account for the council archives, although she thought it probable that her colleagues would conclude that she had run mad. She could not afford to care about that either. Now she straightened her spine and lifted her chin, preparing to persuade Laurens to take the action Urien had requested, and readying herself, for the last time, to do her duty.

There is a thrumming in the waters. In the head lake to the west, a bore begins to swell. Ripples play grace notes with the debris of the old city. Wind and wave tug at the pylons of the bridges. From the island temple, the bells begin to ring.

Across Merafi the fires are failing. Joyain paces the length of Miraude's room, nervous amid banked candles. A torchlit procession riding from the Rose Palace falters and stumbles in the rising wind. Some of the riders are turning back.

Overhead, two full moons rise. Their light is colder than any blade.

Quenfrida's eyes snap open, and they are blue like water now, not like the sky. About her, the Tarnaroqui embassy is too quiet. Her silk gown makes the only sound as she goes from room to room, seeking those who should have stood as her guardians. All the windows stand open to the night. The air is misted. Sigeris rides in procession from the palace, seeking advantage even now from his hosts' sudden superstition.

Beneath two moons' light Gracielis waits on the Dancing Bridge. His hair blows back from his painted face. His hands are empty but his eyes see down many aisles. He hears the whisper of Quenfrida's silken skirts and turns his face from the wind.

Valdarrien stands in the River Temple, where Urien

has commanded him. Restless needs rip at him, half-comprehended; and the mist mocks him with Iareth's form. His hand plays with his sword hilt. The priests frown upon him. Thiercelin stands beside him, feverish, pale, risking relapse. But he will not remain alone in Amalie's house. He has entrusted himself to Valdarrien's aid, and to waiting.

He does not know for what exactly it is that he waits.

The moons' light turns the dirty waters to liquid steel, reflecting the broken buildings and other darker things.

There are swan wings over Merafi.

No rain is falling.

From the upper windows of the Far Blays town house, Joyain watched the parade of torches wind their way from the Rose Palace. The flames burned pale and weak, diffused by mist. He could see no point to it. Whoever they were, the torchbearers traveled into nothingness. Beside him, Miraude said, "It's the royal household. It must be some kind of ceremony." He made no answer. She continued, "We could join them."

"Why? Outside isn't safe."

"They're people. Living people." She turned to look at him, and her face was strained.

He could see no safety in numbers. There was no way of knowing if the sickness was over. He could not say it. She had faced enough, alone in this house. His fault, for bringing the plague to her doors. She said, "I'll need my cloak and practical shoes."

To join the procession they would have to reach it. And all the time they followed, the procession too would be moving. Two people would be far easier prey for the things that inhabited the mist. He did not know if he was strong enough to hold off attackers for long.

He could not allow her to go out alone. He said, "We'll need torches, good ones."

"There's plenty of wood in the fire baskets."

A torch was more than a flaming brand. You needed

pitch and . . . and other things. If they must go out
into the night, he would have them as well protected
as possible. She went on, "And there are some torches
somewhere. We used them in a masque this summer.
They're probably in the stableyard store."

Even to reach the store, they would have to go outside. He sighed. The longer he delayed, the greater the
distance they would have to cover. "Get your things."

His uniform was long gone, burned with the bedding.
Everything he wore was the property of the absent Thiercelin duLaurier. That almost certainly contravened some
army regulation or other. Between that and his unexplained absence, he would have nine kinds of trouble to
face when he finally made it back to army headquarters.

Assuming, of course, that there remained an army to
which he might return.

At least he still had his sword, for all the good it
would do. They gathered garments and torches and lamp
oil in silence, and slipped out through a side entrance
into the street. It was chill; the air tasted dank and sour.
Mist curled in thin tendrils about the bases of walls and
muted vision. All around, the houses of the wealthy
stood dark and silent. He forced his fingers away from
the hilt of his sword and took her hand. He could hear
nothing save their hurried footsteps and the raw edge of
his own breath. In his, her fingers were cool and soft.
He hurried them down the slope to where the side road
met the main route down from the palace. Here, there
were traces of the passage of the torchbearers—torn
straw underfoot, fragments of ash, a dropped plume
from a hat. They would be making for the Kings' Bridge,
but beyond that . . . He could see the edges of the mist
up ahead, creeping upslope toward them. Once they
were in amongst that . . . Although there was no rain,
the night was damp, fragments of moisture clinging to
the fringes of garments, to the shafts of the torches. They
burned with a limp, bluish fire, throwing only limited
light. The wood was probably damp to begin with, after

months in the stables. He hoped they would prove
strong enough. They had to. The alternative . . .

He pushed the thought away. Worrying would do him
no good now. He had to get them as far as he could.
He had brought death to Miraude's house. He would
shed his own blood to protect her life now.

They reached a corner. The mist lay thicker here,
shawling the traces of the parade in gray. With horses
and carriages, the court would most likely have taken
the main road, winding in slow loops down the hillside
toward the river. If they followed directly . . . That road
would take them above the mist for a little longer, but
once they were into it, they would have to travel almost
a mile. He could not like their chances, and it was unlikely that any of the households lining the route would
open a door to them, however they begged. The
alternative . . . A steep alleyway led downward between
the rear entrances of a number of houses. It was used
mainly by servants and porters: it was likely to be noisome and slippery, but it was considerably shorter. He
glanced across at Miraude. Her face was set. He said,
"Can you run?"

"Yes." She returned his glance. "What about you?
You've been ill."

"If I have to." He had not been out into these streets
since the day of Leladrien's death. He had no sure idea
of how bad things had become. Well, he was about to
find out. He said, "There are creatures, mist-things.
They'll try to get to us. It does no good to fight them.
Swords and knives go right through them. Fire keeps
them back, but if the torches fail . . ." Bodies, torn and
ripped into bloody rags; teeth out of nowhere to bite
and rend . . . It did no good to think about it. He said,
"We just have to keep going."

"Of course." She smiled at him. "Let's start, then."

"*Chai ela*, Quenfrida."
"You forget yourself, my Gracielis."

In the wake of the torch procession Quenfrida had come to the bridge. Gracielis watched her from under his gilded lids and found himself unmoved. Her hair spilled over her shoulders; her gown hung loose and simple. Her feet were bare. She halted on the threshold of the bridge and smiled at him. "You can't prevent me."

"Perhaps." Gracielis bowed to her, silken precision. Wind tugged at him, whipping his hair into his eyes. He put up a hand to push it aside. "But I've a promise to fulfill."

Something about her had changed. She came toward him, and her movements seemed only half-awake. He said, "Help me. Let's stop this thing together."

"Not with you," she said, and smiled. The smile was feral. She raised her hands, and moonlight found them long and clawed. He fought an impulse to step back. "Never with you. You betrayed me."

"I chose," he said, "as you bade me." His own hands were unchanged. He looked from them back to her and shivered. He could feel the weight of it about him, the mindless urgency of water wanting to break free. From behind him rose the voices of the priests at their evening rite, soft under the bell. He exhaled and said, "You're losing yourself, Quena. You're changing."

"Kenan," said Quenfrida, "failed me." Water hissed under her words, under their feet. Her eyes were blind. "As you failed me."

"You're losing control," he said, willing truth into the words. "You can't contain what you've awakened. It'll kill you."

"I think not." She was only feet away now. In the moons' light he could see what he had never seen before, how old she was. There were disguised lines in her creamy skin, and her rich hair owed its gold to artifice.

He had loved and resented and desired her all his life. Now he felt nothing, not fear, not even pity. He said, "It's you who's failing. You make such bad choices."

Her blind eyes snapped to him, and for an instant she

was herself. He stepped back. She laughed and spoke a word of power.

The bridge buckled underfoot. Hands seized him, dragging him into the heart of the water. He struggled, feeling eyes and ears fill. Thunder. The river was all about him. Its strength was beyond him, beyond any man, mindless, relentless.

He bit his lip, tasting blood, tasting himself. He cried out as his own bonds wove about him, jerking him to a halt. Think of Thiercelin, grim on his determined, half-comprehended path. *Think of Amalie and Urien and stern Yvelliane. Think even of Valdarrien, whose very life was twined round Gracielis' own, through the pounding of the river.* Gracielis reached out and found iron beneath his hands. The rail of the bridge . . . He struggled to breathe, gasping out a word in turn.

He stood on the bridge, under two moons. Water ran down his face, soaking hair and clothing. From upstream he could hear the river gathering force.

He clutched at the rail, letting his hand find for him its nature. Iron from the earth, aspected like himself in stone. He raised his head to look at Quenfrida, bathed in moons' light. Chains surrounded her, woven of mist, stretching into the night. He could see where they chafed, where they strained and tugged and had been repaired. He could see the space where Kenan should have stood. She held proud beneath the burden, and his heart turned cold.

He had never seen such power. Her control was flawed, but it was better than he had hoped. She had tied herself in blood and soul to the river, and she would have her way.

She returned his gaze. She said, "Will I show you again what I can do?"

His hand tightened on the rail. "No, Quena."

"Then let me pass."

"No, Quena." Gracielis pushed down sharp fear and reached along the rail. It grew hot under his hand. He trembled as the bridge stirred, as lightning ran through it. Sparks struck off around him. He shuddered and drew them to him, forcing himself to open. Quenfrida did not stir. He was burning up. He set his teeth against a cry and flung his hands out before him.

White light flashed, carried through the moisture on the bridge. She cried out and her hair became a wild aura about her. Power of iron, most inimical to water . . . His palms were seared and blackened; he was dizzy with pain. He stumbled backward.

The light died. Quenfrida still stood there, shaking. She stepped toward him and said, "I promised you death, did I not? Try this." She spoke a word he had never heard, and stepped back.

A force like dissolution ripped through him, binding the water from his veins. Blood dripped from his eyes, from his burned palms. He could feel the wind beginning to take him, to pull him apart into dust and oblivion. He reached out to her in terror and heard her start to laugh. He was crumbling away. He fought panic, clinging to what time he had left. Beneath his feet, water clutched at the bridge. He caught again at the rail, and mantled down into stone. Stone against air, calm, unyielding. He clung, gasping, forcing himself to be one thing only, to be whole.

When he opened his eyes, he was kneeling, arms locked about the rail. Quenfrida stood over him. He could feel the water gathering force with every second. He said, "Don't," and his voice was all but gone.

She reached a hand out to him. It was empty. She would not risk a blade here. She said, "You're stronger than I thought. Perhaps I didn't choose so badly after all, those years ago."

"I failed you," Gracielis said. Death stood before him in her flesh, and he could hope only to buy time. Pray Urien was watching. "Forgive me."

"It seems unnecessary." But her hand did not move to touch him, not yet.

"I love you," he said, since she seemed to expect it. "I beg you."

"We've been here before. And you lie; you're *undarios* now. The bonds between us are broken."

"Not those of memory," he said. "Please."

"Please what? Don't hurt you?"

"No." Where was Urien? "Say you forgive me."

She was smiling; she was amused. She said, "For what? To make you happy?"

"Yes."

"Why should I want to do that?"

"Because I'm yours." Gracielis closed his eyes.

She was silent a few moments. Then she said very softly, "Look at me, my Gracielis." He looked. Her face was pitiless. "No, I won't forgive you."

By rights he should have wept; that, too, she would expect. But the world had turned inverse, and he was beyond caring for appearances. He sent a thought, pain-winged, to Thiercelin and lowered his head. He felt the bridge under him, good iron. He relaxed into it and hoped it would sustain him. He said, "Then finish me."

"Certainly." He heard the creamy smile in her voice, as her hands came down. His own knotted in the structure of the bridge as he extended himself as far as he could. Think of polished steel, of obsidian. He bowed under the impact, fighting to be glass beneath her, fragile, fine, reflective . . .

Reflective. Talking had left him time to gather what energy remained to him. He blanked his mind as she touched him, emptying so that she should find only herself.

She filled him. Her touch was bitter. She was chaos, fierce drives, fierce needs, all tangled and demanding. The power of the river ran through her, but it was blind to her desires. She clawed and scratched at it, consuming herself in the attempt to bind it into subservience to her will. She bore down on him, and he was glass. Her hands shook, and he felt himself again begin to crumble. Killing force ran through him; some small remaining conscious part of him recollected Valdarrien. Life from death. Death averted. Death reflected . . .

Quenfrida cried out. Gracielis twisted from under her grasp and crawled free. She did not seem to see him. Water poured off her, thunderous, continuous. Behind her the river still rose. She was even yet a part of it, and he had done nothing save strain her a little. The bonds were cool in the moons' light. Only a handful betrayed stress.

Light bathed them. The water poured down. And behind Quenfrida, the river bore went on sweeping downstream.

Every step took them deeper into the mist: ankles, knees, waist. At the end of two hundred yards, Joyain could see no farther than the end of his arms. Beside him, Miraude was no more than a hint, a darker patch in the omnipresent gray. He could barely hear their footsteps; his breath was a faint tide within him. The air tasted bitter, filled with blood and dirt. Their torches guttered and flickered, more ghost than flame. His fear wrapped him, prickling through every inch of skin, tensing each fiber.

They were perhaps a third of the way along the alley when the attack came. A slithering, a slipping, slurping noise and then . . . Something—not human, not fleshy, something rubbery and icy—squelched and oozed against his legs. He leaped aside with a cry and lost hold of Miraude's hand. He felt fabric tear away where he had been touched. Somewhere—it must be close, yet it came as from a distance—he heard Miraude gasp. He waved his torch around him wildly, yelled in alarm as it struck something solid. A wall, a gate . . . From his left, Miraude said, "Jean?" And then, "Someone?" She sounded terrified.

He narrowed his eyes, tried to make sense out of the boiling fog while keeping the torch moving. Maybe over there . . . Yes, to his left and a little ahead of him there was a paler patch. He called back, "I'm here. I'm all right." He reached out to whatever it was he had struck and found it was a wall. Back to it, he inched forward toward her. "I'm coming." A step, another and another and then there she was, huddled against a doorway. He reached out for her, found her arm and gripped it.

She said, "What . . . ?"

"Keep moving."

They inched forward into the mist, backs to the wall. Tendrils and tongues of it lapped at them, tearing clothing, grazing skin. Joyain lost track of how far they had come. The alley sloped down toward the streets behind the Flower Market, he remembered that much, although it took several turnings and was intersected by a number of mews. He could not imagine how they would survive once their route widened out. When the wall at his back gave out, he stopped in a gateway shaking. Miraude said, "What is it?"

"Nothing. I'm just trying to work out where we go next." But his voice shook, and he knew she heard it. "Once it gets wider, we'll need to run."

Easy to go astray in the mist. Even easier, while running. One or both of them could too easily trip or fall, drop a torch . . .

She said, "We're near the Old Temple, I think."

That put them less than halfway down the alley. They must go twelve or fifteen times farther to reach the Island Temple, and in wider streets . . . Something snagged at his arm, and he pulled back. A thin cut traced along it in red. The longer they stood here . . . He said, "We need to find shelter. We can't last out here."

"But . . ." Miraude's sentence ended in a yelp. Something had hold of her, shaking and tugging. Even as he turned, her hand was dragged from his. She cried out again and dropped her torch.

Inside Joyain something snapped. He had seen enough death, enough loss. He had been unable to save anyone.

Perhaps that was still true. But he would fight back while he might. He dived for her torch, rolled upright, holding both of them before him. Together, their light was enough to push the mist back from him a little farther. The mist creatures still feared fire. Well, fire they should have. The wall might be stone, but the gate was wood. Gripping both torches in his left hand, he tugged his flask of lamp oil out of his pocket and flung it at the gate with all his might. With luck, it gave onto a stableyard, where there would be straw and more wood. The torches seemed to take strength from proximity to one another, flames brightening. He did not have long; he could hear Miraude struggling and gasping. This had to work . . . He thrust the torches against the oiled wood and closed his eyes. River bless, by stone and flame, wind and wave and darkness . . . There was nothing more left to him, to his city. One hand on the wall, one on the torches, he waited and hoped.

The gate rocked, rattled, and caught light, a slight fringe at first, growing and winding upward, outward, warming and brightening and reigniting the torches. With a yell, Joyain charged, swinging the torch about him in a great arc. Mist reached for him from behind, and he cursed and kept running. Teeth rasped one ankle; he felt his boot begin to give. Clinging onto the torches, he cannoned into Miraude, knocking them both to the ground. She clutched at him, sobbing. He said, "All right?"

"They bit me . . ." She gulped, wound her fingers into his jacket. He pulled himself to his knees. In the renewed light, her face was dirty. She bled from a jagged gap in her left shoulder. Her cloak was gone and her outer garments shredded to rags. He handed her one torch as she climbed to her feet. He said, "We have to get indoors." The gate was solidly ablaze, its glow clearing a substantial arc through the fog. Miraude leaned against him as he looked around. Perhaps they could take refuge in a stable somewhere . . .

She said, "The Old Temple!"

"What?" He looked at her. She pointed toward the wall opposite.

"It's the back of the Old Temple, where the excavation is." Her words made no sense at all to him. She pulled at him. "There's a tunnel, it goes down to the river. We can use that."

Yvelliane stood on the roof of the temple tower, and looked west. All about her, the priests went about their ritual. Her companions moved amongst them, baffled, resentful. By the light of the two moons, Merafi looked peaceful; more a lake now than a city. She looked up and glimpsed wings high overhead. She felt very calm.

There was little mist. She could see a long way upriver, to the old wall and beyond. The three channels braided the plain, spreading toward each other. There was movement in the silvered distance. She watched it, and almost smiled.

A priest summoned her back to the rite. She followed obediently for the prayer, and the first of the prescribed bathings of hands. Then she withdrew again to her vantage point. Two figures stood below her on the Dancing Bridge. She watched them, feeling the wind on her face.

Two cloaked forms made their way across the roof toward her, one leaning on the other. She frowned a little, unwilling to be disturbed. She had fielded enough questions from the courtiers. She needed these last few minutes alone. The figures halted a few feet away and one sank down, back against the parapet. She could hear his breathing even over the chanting.

After a few minutes he pushed back his hood and looked up at her. Thiercelin. There was a lump in her throat, closing it, impeding her breathing. She had thought . . . She had expected that his injury would keep him safely away. She should have known better. She should have expected this. She wound her hands in the folds of her cloak. She could not bear this, not now . . .

He said, "Yviane."

"Thierry," she said. "Why are you here? You should be resting."

"I wanted to come."

She wanted to bury her face in his shoulder and have him banish all her pain and fear. She wanted to run away. She could afford to do neither. She said, softly, "Oh, Thierry . . ." and felt tears form in her eyes.

"What's wrong?" He held out a hand to her, wincing as it pulled at his injury. "It's all right. Gracielis and Urien . . ."

He did not know. She had begged that of Urien. If she had only known she would meet him here and now . . . She said, "I'm tired, I . . ."

"You're lying." He frowned. "Something's going to happen. What is it?"

"It's all right."

She watched fear and puzzlement battle each other across his face. He said, "Is it Graelis? Will he . . ."

"What he's doing is dangerous." Perhaps this was her way out, his concern for his friend. She felt no jealousy, she was beyond that. Perhaps, if Gracielis survived, he could bring Thiercelin some measure of comfort. She said, "You're fond of him, aren't you?"

"Not like that," Thiercelin said. "I love *you*, Yviane. He's a friend, that's all."

She reached out and touched his shoulder. "I'm glad."

"What?" Fear was winning out in Thiercelin's face. "What is it? Tell me?"

She could not. It would break her and, with that, condemn Merafi. Standing on tiptoe, she kissed him once, gently, on the mouth. "It's all right, Thierry. Everything's going to be all right."

There was a silence. She had to escape, or she would give way. She said, "I have to go. I'm so sorry, Thierry," and walked away along the parapet, to the gate onto the leads, moving quickly lest he suspect her weakness.

A hand touched her arm. She turned, expecting Urien.

Another robed figure . . . His hood was back, and his face was dearly familiar. He said, softly, "Hello, Yviane."

"Valdin . . ." Her hand reached out to him. His skin was cool. It did not seem so strange to her to meet him here now. She clutched at him. Perhaps she was already dead. Perhaps the boundary between the living and the dead was breaking, welcoming her in. "Oh, Valdin." As his arms drew her to him, for a moment she allowed herself to feel the terror of what she must do. He was warm against her, breast moving with the slow tide of breath. She made herself look up. "Did Urien send you?"

"Yes." There was a glitter in his spare hand, light on a blade. He said, "She's dead, my Iareth *kai-reth*. Did you know?"

So are you . . . But that had no meaning now. She said, "No. I'm sorry."

"I just go on losing her . . ." He stopped. They clung together for another long moment, her face against his shoulder, his buried in her hair. She was safe at long last, she was safe, and it was over save for one last little step.

She said, "Is it time?"

"Yes . . . I'm coming with you. I thought I wanted to live, but . . ."

"Hush," Yvelliane said, reaching out to him. "We'll go together, love. I'm ready."

His blade flashed up between them. He said, "There must be blood shed, then the river. It will hurt. I'm sorry."

"Don't be." She leaned forward and kissed his cheek. Then she took her arm from his hand and walked to the very edge of the roof. "Will this do?"

"Yes." Valdarrien came to her, his dark face gentle in the moons' light. The sword tip touched the base of her throat, cool, forgiving. With his spare hand he reached out and took a firm grasp on one of hers. She could hear the river thundering a hundred or more feet below. "For Merafi," he said, "blood binds."

He was right. There was pain for one bitter moment, and fear, too, and the sour taste of blood. Then the darkness flashed about her and her head fell back, and her body with it, all the way down to the water.

His hand was still tangled in hers. The weight of her falling dragged him unresisting after her.

Alone, Thiercelin sat with his back to the parapet and tried not to close his eyes. His side pounded. Pressing a hand to it, he found the bandages damp. He should not be here; he had barely the strength to stand. Valdarrien had virtually dragged him up the long flights of stairs to the tower. He had no idea how he was going to get back down.

It didn't matter, anyway.

He was a little to one side of the ritual area, near the priests. He had only a partial view of the ceremony, but that did not trouble him. He had little interest in the proceedings. Craning his neck, he could just about make out Yvelliane and Valdarrien on the leads. Yvelliane's face was serious. Valdarrien looked tired, if the dead could tire.

The latter had spent a long time closeted with Urien, and had been unwontedly quiet ever since. Thiercelin, long accustomed to his moods, had asked no questions. But he was troubled. Both Valdarrien and Gracielis had been unusually gentle toward him. As if they protected him from something. Even Urien had shown signs of it. High on the tower, Thiercelin watched his wife and shivered.

There was something hidden. Something wrong. He could hear the river roaring even through the priests' chanting, and he looked up at the moons. Swan wings lifted and circled. Whatever happened, Thiercelin was sure to lose tonight. He looked again at Yvelliane and felt cold. She should not be here. It was too dangerous.

Wind gusted, setting the pennants flying, making the torches gutter. He wrapped his cloak more closely and looked back at the priests. They were moving into the second part of the rite. The congregation had drawn back. The wind was definitely growing stronger.

The torches went out. Wind clutched and tugged, hats went flying, robes flapped. Thiercelin crouched against his sheltering wall. One priest cried out as water from the bowl he held blew out over his hands and arms, burning.

There was a pounding all around, like wings, like water falling. The senior priest stepped back as the air before him filled with feathers. Over the sanctuary came a thunder of wings. White feathers shredded and fell. For a moment it seemed that the moons fell, swan-wise. Then the form coalesced to hang over the sanctuary, neither bird nor man, feral eyes, strong bones, great white wings.

The Armenwy. Thiercelin struggled to his feet, clutching at his side. His blood trickled through his fingers and splashed onto the stone of the parapet. Some of the priests had fallen to their knees. Beyond them the prince consort stood, looking upward.

Urien spoke. The tongue was one Thiercelin had never heard, smooth cadences like wings rising over a wind. There was something permanent to it, solid as the stone under his hand. The water went quiet. From somewhere below, light flashed. Urien threw back his head and cried out to the moons. The tower began, very slightly, to shake. Urien hung silver in the moons' light, mist rising about him, deep, luminescent. The great wings beat and struggled, and bonds sought to form about them. Forgetful of his own weakness, Thiercelin took a step forward, reaching for a sword he was not carrying. Urien spoke again, and the mist crouched back. The top of the tower went silent save for the beating of wings.

Thiercelin looked at the consort and saw he was not watching Urien. Thiercelin turned his own head and bit back a cry. Yvelliane stood on the very edge of the roof, head flung up to the night. Valdarrien was beside her, dark, forbidding. To her throat, he held a sword.

Blood binds . . . Gracielis had told him and Urien over and over again that old tale of Yestinn Allandur, and a sacrifice. Thiercelin stumbled forward, almost blind, unable to call out. Light ran like oil down Valdarrien's blade as it twisted and turned black under his hands. Yvelliane's neck turned dark, and her body jerked backward. Thiercelin was too far away even to hear if she cried out. He reached out to her anyway, and fell to his knees on the stone, jarring the breath from him. Behind him Urien's voice rose again.

There was a crack like thunder. Suddenly all the torches sprang back to life.

The precincts of the Old Temple were silent. From within the buildings came the low glow of candlelight, the susurration of voices at prayer. In this holy space, the mist lay thinner, yet its fronds still swirled and licked at lintels and sills. Miraude hurried them across the courtyard and along a cloister to a door behind the main temple. She tried the handle, found it locked. From behind her, Joyain said, "Maybe we should just go into the shrine. The priests would shelter us."

Kenan had come here, and it had been in some way important to him. She was certain of that. Kenan was involved, somehow, in the disasters that threatened her city. Miraude said, firmly, "We have to go on."

"But a tunnel . . ." Joyain sounded uncertain. "It could easily be damp, after all this rain. It could be as dangerous as the streets."

"But narrower. Hold my torch for a moment." Miraude tried the door again. Its frame was old and soft. If she leaned a little and lifted . . . There. Wood creaked and splintered close to the edge of the lock. She lifted up on the lock itself and pushed: the tongue eased free of its socket and the door swung open. Valdarrien had shown her the trick years ago, during one of his rare visits to her during their engagement. She had been a child, back then, no more than ten and not strong enough, but she had remembered. "It only works on old locks, mind you," he had said, tugging on one of her plaits, "but it's good for stables and old gates and suchlike." She took her torch back from Joyain.

He said, "Should we . . . ?"

"Yes. Come on." She thought she could retrace the route down to the undercroft. It was cold, in here. Somewhere, she could hear water running. Their footsteps were loud in the darkness. The air tasted acrid. She led them through corridors, into the cellars, picking her way between wine racks and rice vats into the broken undercroft. The stairs down into the oldest remains were slippery. The closer they came to the clan hall, the older and sourer the air became. The torches were once again growing blue. Joyain coughed, making her jump. The darkness clung to them, sticky and hindering.

A chill pinkish light played around the entrance to the clan hall: the water sound was thunderous. She had been right: this place mattered. Joyain's hand closed on her arm. She looked up at him. His face was gray. She said, "We have to . . . Kenan came here." His fingers tightened for an instant, and then he released her. She inhaled slowly and stepped through. She had to see this through. She had been complicit, after all, in bringing Kenan here in the first place.

Yvelliane would have counseled caution. Yvelliane was not here. There was no one here, save her and Joyain. She had no special skills, neither the ancient knowledge that Kenan chased nor the erudition of the missing scholar. She was all there was. Torch held high, she followed the pink glow along the rock passage and out into the main cavern. Joyain followed her, his breath warm and reassuring on her nape. The light wavered, ebbing and flowing with the water-beat from behind the walls. All across the cavern floor extended a fine network of channels, running red. She stepped back into Joyain, felt

his hand close over her shoulder. Blood . . . It could not
be blood, that made no sense. Although the scholar was
missing and Kenan . . . She could believe that Kenan
would kill, if it served him. Joyain said softly, "A net of
fire . . . I saw this, I saw Lelien."

It was not fire; it was tainted water. She turned to
tell him, but he was already striding past her. She said,
"I don't . . ."

"Fire and water . . ." Joyain stopped at the edge of
the pattern and looked back at her. "We have to break
it. Fire and earth and water . . ." He switched his torch
to his left hand and drew his sword. "We have to burn
it. Do you still have your lamp oil?"

"Yes." She came to stand beside him.

"I'm going to cut the sides of the channels. I want
you to throw the lamp oil over the edge and set fire to
them." He smiled at her. "On the count of three."

Gracielis was stone. All around him water clutched
and dragged. He closed himself against it, falling through
the chains. They tangled, weaving to catch him, but he
was not there, he was below them, under their moving
weight, still, unyielding, stone. He had lost all sense of
Quenfrida. He could feel only himself and the water. No
anger there, no need for revenge (unless in Quenfrida
herself, wherever she might be). He reached out under
it and found the bore, moon-drawn to the sea. Too fast,
too hard. It would rock Merafi to her knees. Gracielis
paused, then reached out into the heart of it, for the
bindings that turned the natural into the monstrous.

About him the water changed its color. He could see
nothing, yet he felt it. As blind as he was, the river
neither assisted nor resisted while Merafi's life bled into
it. He followed the change, found more stone and a great
cacophony of wings.

The bindings were dissolving. Hallowed under two
moons, the river began to pull free of living control.
Quenfrida had woken it; now it evaded her. He felt out

into that winged thunder and tasted blood. Not the blood that pooled in the water, but something more familiar. He had knelt on the quay, hands slick with blood, and defended Thiercelin . . . Slick with Thiercelin's blood . . .

A promise. And Thiercelin was with him. Stone-careful, Gracielis opened his eyes to the river-world and reached for the first of the bindings.

The water was dark with blood. It resisted as he wove into it the new covenant, but the will behind its resistance was alien. Gracielis held to his bonds, reached into the stillness that was Urien. Resistance warped and melted; briefly, he was aware of Quenfrida. Her face was covered but her hands were turning translucent. Strengthened by Urien, Gracielis cut her from her working, using the knife edge of Allandurin blood. The river began to turn back where it belonged, sleep renewed by the willing sacrifice.

The clans had fought for identity against their changing, dreaming land, and found the power to achieve it latent in their own blood. Yvelliane's was as mixed as Gracielis' own, Allandurin at heart, but mingled through the generations with many other lines. They were all there, all the people of Merafi, working through his weaving to lay their river to rest. He could hear them, light and serious, weak and strong, brave and lost, and clinging. Coiled amid them was a part of the river-force itself, once briefly manifest as Valdarrien, brought by choice to desire quiescence.

Gracielis held his hands out over the waters and felt them subside. He found Quenfrida, then, caught in the ebb, and reached out for her. Her blue eyes were gone to water. His hands passed through her as the power lashed back upon her and drained her away. Upriver, the bore contracted into its proper path.

Across Merafi the waters began to subside, leaving streets chaotic with mud and debris. The bore reached the place where the channels split, and poured along its accustomed course, washing away the last of shantytown.

In the ancient hall, Miraude cried out in surprise as the channels on the floor flamed, crisped, and faded. Beside her, Joyain leaned on his sword, gasping. On the temple roof the torches flickered and danced. In the sanctuary crouched a naked man, his gray hair drenched. The floor beneath his feet was carpeted with swan feathers. Another man lay unconscious on the iron of the Dancing Bridge.

Crouched against the parapet, Thiercelin of Sannazar covered his face with his dirty hands and wept.

24

THE WATERS PULLED AWAY from the city, drawing the mist after them. For a day or two Merafi was still, holding its breath against a new catastrophe. Two nights passed, clear and calm. No new cases of sickness were reported. Cautiously the remaining inhabitants stepped out to assess the damage. Small groups formed on street corners to exchange tales. Here, a woman scrubbed mud from her floors. There, a bakery relit its ovens. There was very little looting. Perhaps the Merafiens were too pleased to meet others to want to take advantage. Perhaps they were simply relieved to have survived. Distant acquaintances helped one another with repairs; strangers housed the displaced as guests and friends. Venturing down to army headquarters, Joyain found it staffed by a motley assortment of city watch, royal infantry, and fragments of other companies. The ranking officer was a major of dragoons whom he had never seen before. Presenting the letter he had brought with him from the palace, he waited for the major's reaction. He had abandoned his post and lost his uniform.

He had somehow helped to redeem Merafi. It might just balance out. The dragoon major looked up at him and said, "Glad to see you alive, Lieutenant. Not many left from your company." Joyain did not know what to say. The major continued, "You probably should hand in a report at some point, but not right now. Take a unit of men down to the docks and see if you can help with the cleanup.''

In the merchants' district, Gracielis sat at Amalie's kitchen table and composed a letter to her. Around him the house was quiet. Upstairs, Urien sat with Thiercelin, but if they talked, no word of it could be heard. Not that Gracielis had tried to overhear. What Thiercelin wished of him now—if anything—he did not know, and for once he did not know how to ask. He could neither restore nor replace Yvelliane. In the face of Thiercelin's mourning he could offer up only silence and trust that he did so gracefully.

He did not mourn Quenfrida. She had owned him. Now, she did not. It seemed that in the end that was all there had been between them. Perhaps that was the price of becoming *undarios*, that one became ever more detached. Urien might know. Gracielis did not think he would ask. He had known Quenfrida; he had craved her almost beyond bearing. He had destroyed her. His need of her had been very far from love.

If he might, he would choose to go on loving. He suspected that *undarii* set little store by love.

If he had not become *undarios*, he would in the end have been of little use to Thiercelin. As it was, such help as he had rendered had come at a bitter price. It might yet become more bitter still, at least where he was concerned.

He wanted to go upstairs to Thiercelin to offer comfort and himself. That was not what was needed, not now, perhaps not ever. Yvelliane was dead and he was complicit in that. Such things were not easily forgiven.

He turned back to his letter. *Although it is only a handful of days since you left, I write to tell you that the city is once again safe. It is not as it was, and will need much rebuilding, but you may return without danger. I think those who come back soon will be particularly welcome. Your home is undamaged. I remain here against your return.* He stared at the words. So neat, so formal. Slowly, he added, *Please come. I miss you.* He closed his eyes. The kitchen smelled of soot and beeswax and spices. Under his elbows the table was smooth and cool. All about him, Merafi settled. He felt it weigh back down into its former solidity, hazy and thick to his senses. It was not easy to be a foreigner in Merafi. There would be no rewards for his struggle on the bridge. He opened his eyes and tilted his head back, stretching his neck. He was between one thing and another, not his old self, not yet someone new. He had no idea what he would do next.

Well, in the here and now, he must finish the letter and then produce a meal and perhaps even win a response of some kind from Thiercelin in honor of his bad cooking. And then, and then . . . He shrugged and signed his name at the base of the letter.

Shops and booths and houses were repaired. All across the city hung the smells of sawdust and mud plaster. Boats and barges began once again to make their way into the docks, unloading building materials and foodstuffs. Day after day refugees returned to reopen homes and businesses. At the government offices in the Old Palace, clerks sifted through records, questioned survivors, pestered the watch for reports, and posted requests for information. Lists of what was known began to appear in its portico, giving numbers of bodies recovered, names of those known dead, or of those still missing. Day after day the lists grew, but they were unlikely ever to be complete. No one knew exactly how many had lived and died in the margins of the city, in shanties and docks and back streets. A few of the wealthier merchants had begun to stake out new building plots atop the cliff, high out of reach of the river.

"But how can people just not count?" Miraude said, standing on the steps of the Old Palace about a fortnight after the sacrifice. "Someone must have known them. Someone must've cared."

"Perhaps those people are dead, too," Gracielis said. "Or perhaps they want to go on not being counted." He had met her near the Gran' Théâtre, and walked with her. Like many others, he made almost daily visits to consult the lists, looking for names he knew. He had gone himself to report the deaths of Sylvine and Chirielle. He had said nothing of Quenfrida, nor had her name yet appeared on any list.

Miraude said, "I don't understand. Why would someone not want to count?"

There were tears in her eyes. Taking her elbow, he steered her to a nearby booth selling hot wine. He found them a table at the back and ordered for them both. Then he said, "There can be many reasons. People run away. They hide."

"It seems so unfair."

He made no reply, looking out into the street. A waiter brought their drinks, and they sat for a time in silence. Then Miraude said, "You look different."

He looked like himself, the kernel beneath the shell of artifice. His hair was beginning to show brown at the roots. Amalie liked it. She had been one of the first to return. She said that he was finally turning into someone real.

Miraude continued, "You look more . . ."

"Ordinary?"

"No. More relaxed. You're not acting."

He smiled. He was always acting. So many things to hide, so many to elide. It was not legal, to be *undarios* in Merafi. He could say none of that to her. He could not even say it to Amalie. He said, "I'm changing my profession."

There was another silence. She said, "Thierry's all right. I mean . . . He's miserable, but his injury is healing well."

"That's good." Thiercelin had left Amalie's house the week before, to return to the Far Blays town house. Gracielis tried not to think about that. "Please try to understand," Thiercelin had said, "I need to be quiet. I need for things not to be complicated." And Gracielis had nodded and smiled and said, "Of course."

Now Miraude said, "Can I take him a message from you?"

"No. I don't think it would be wise." He drained his cup. "Can I escort you back to your carriage?"

"I don't have one. I walked down here. It isn't very far." Her chin rose. "Iar . . . Iareth Yscoithi did it all the time."

He considered her. It was not done for a woman of her rank to wander the city alone. He should offer to see her home. Her gaze was defiant. He smiled. She said, "What?"

"I was thinking that Lord Valdarrien was surrounded by women of very strong character."

"Thierry, I want something from you." Firomelle sat in her high-backed chair beside the fireplace in the small library at the Rose Palace. Winter light filtered in through the windows onto a face that was still thin, but no longer drawn or pale. Standing on the rug before her, Thiercelin did not know how to respond. He fixed his gaze on the floor. He did not want to be here. He did not want to be anywhere in this world, which lacked Yvelliane. Had it not been for Miraude, mercilessly bullying him out of bed, he would still be at home now.

"Sit down. I'm not going to eat you." There was a chair behind him, opposite Firomelle's. He sat. The fire was warm on hands and face, softening the chill light. This must have been Yvelliane's chair. He closed a hand on its arm, seeking a memory of her touch. Nothing. There were no more ghosts haunting him. Did Yvelliane's ghost walk the corridors of this place she had saved? Gracielis, doubtless, could tell him. He was not ready, not yet, to face Gracielis.

Firomelle said, "I'm so sorry about Yviane. You know

that. There aren't words big enough . . . But I didn't summon you to talk about her."

He had been silent too long. To the floor, he murmured, "Madame."

"Before he returned to Lunedith, Urien Armenwy came to see me. He told me what had happened." She rose and went to the window, back straight. "Yviane gave me back my city and helped save my life. But the gift began with you and Monsieur de Varnaq." She was silent a moment. Then, "Come here."

He joined her. Outside, the trees stood bare against the gray sky. The lawns were empty. She said, "You can't see the city from anywhere in this palace, did you know? It was built like that on purpose. I'm beginning to wonder if that was a mistake." She did not seem to require an answer. "I've let things slide. Yviane tried to warn me."

"You were ill, madame."

"That's no excuse, not for a queen." She shook her head. "Look at me, Thierry."

That was hard, almost as hard as rising, as thinking. The lines of her face, the shape of her, bespoke Yvelliane. He turned. She said, "I have to make Merafi strong again. I want you to help me."

"I'm not political."

"You're intelligent and sensible. You know how to think." She smiled. "You are also, I admit, lazy and wary of responsibility." He blushed. She went on, "Miraude d'Iscoigne l'Aborderie tells me you spend your days locked away in your room." She reached out, took his hand. "I know it's been no more than a few weeks. But you must stop. I command it."

"Madame, I . . ."

"The fact is we don't have time to mourn. We have to go on. Yviane would agree with me. And you . . . You know what happened. You were there. I need you."

There was no retreat from this. He was not ready.

He'd never wanted anything like this. She said, "Don't waste what Yviane did."

It was not fair. He might not say so. He said, "I doubt I'll be very good."

"You'll learn." She took his hand. "Now, come back to the fire and advise me about one of my problems. You know Gracielis de Varnaq. Tell me about him."

Ten days later, Thiercelin called at Amalie's. The house was in disarray. Several wicker trunks occupied part of the hallway, and in the parlor a travel case stood open. Standing before the hearth, he kept his head high, but behind his back his hands were tense. He was here because it was right, and because it was due, and because . . .

He could wish he had made himself come earlier, or not at all. Not, he knew, that that would have meant he was any clearer as to what he wanted to say. He was here because he owed it to Gracielis.

The door opened to admit a brown-haired young man in shirtsleeves. For an instant Thiercelin stared, and then: "Graelis?"

Gracielis bowed. "Monseigneur."

"What happened to your hair?" That was not what Thiercelin had intended to say. As ever, with Gracielis nothing would go as he had planned it.

"This is, I regret, its real color. I've grown sadly lax lately." Gracielis shrugged. "My apologies. You are well, monseigneur?"

"Physically, yes." And that was sharper than Thiercelin had intended. He looked down. He had had it all prepared, what he would say and how. He had forgotten that Gracielis would speak. He had forgotten that this man was his friend. He said, "I have a message for you, from Firo . . . from the queen. I could have sent it, but I thought . . ."

"Her Majesty thanks me for my services, but requests that I leave her city?"

"Not just that." Thiercelin looked up. "There are options. How did you know what I was going to say?"

"As far as I know, it's still illegal to be *undarios* here."

"Yes." There was a small silence.

Gracielis said "What happened at the River Temple . . . If there had been another way . . ."

"I am not," said Thiercelin, "so foolish as to hold you responsible for what Yvelliane chose to do."

"I know. But you are angry, monseigneur."

"Not with you." But it was untrue, and, watching Gracielis' face, Thiercelin was aware he knew it. He had never asked Gracielis to love him. He had asked for help. He had asked Gracielis to use those same abilities that might now drive him from Merafi. He had not thought that his request could have such consequences. He should have known. Nothing to do with Valdarrien had ever been simple.

Gracielis said, "She loved you, monseigneur."

"Don't." Thiercelin could not talk about this, not now. He gestured at the travel case. "Has Madame Viron just returned?"

"She returned some weeks ago. But she's preparing for a new journey."

"I see." Thiercelin inhaled slowly. "You don't have to leave. If you choose to swear allegiance to the queen, you can stay." He looked again at the travel case. "But you're going, aren't you?" Gracielis did not answer. "Why?"

"I could offer you a variety of reasons. I am Tarnaroqui and *undarios*. I need to seek a new job."

"But?"

Gracielis looked down. When he spoke, his voice was low. "I think . . . I think it will be better if I go away, for now at least."

"Because of me?" Again, there was no answer. Thiercelin said, "Have you seen her? Yviane, I mean?"

"No, monseigneur. Nor do I expect to." Gracielis

looked up. "Such deaths . . . They don't tend to leave ghosts."

"I see." Thiercelin counted his breaths. "If I asked, would you stay?" Gracielis shook his head. "Why not?"

"Because you don't really want me to."

It was true. Thiercelin sighed. "Then, will you write to me?"

"With pleasure, monseigneur."

"Thierry."

Gracielis smiled. "Thierry, then."

"Thank you." The clock struck the hour, quarter past two. "I should go, I suppose," Thiercelin said. "I'm interrupting your packing." He headed to the door, began to open it. Then he turned. "Thank you, Graelis. For everything."

There was no reply. Thiercelin left the room and closed the door softly behind him.

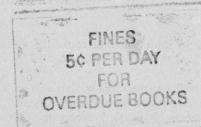

Tanya Huff's
Blood Books

*Private eye, vampire, and cop: supernatural crime
solvers—and the most unusual love triangle in town.*
Now a Lifetime original series.

"Smashing entertainment for a wide audience"
—*Romantic Times*

BLOOD PRICE
978-0-7564-0501-4
BLOOD TRAIL
978-0-7564-0502-1
BLOOD LINES
978-0-7564-0503-8
BLOOD PACT
978-0-7564-0504-5
BLOOD DEBT
978-0-7564-0505-2
BLOOD BANK
978-0-7564-0507-6

To Order Call: 1-800-788-6262

DAW 75

Tanya Huff

Tony Foster—familiar to Tanya Huff fans from her *Blood* series—has relocated to Vancouver with Henry Fitzroy, vampire son of Henry VIII. Tony landed a job as a production assistant at CB Productions, ironically working on a syndicated TV series, "Darkest Night," about a vampire detective. Tony was pretty content with his new life—until wizards, demons, and haunted houses became more than just episodes on his TV series...

"An exciting, creepy adventure"—*Booklist*

SMOKE AND SHADOWS
0-7564-0263-8 $6.99
SMOKE AND MIRRORS
0-7564-0348-0 $7.99
SMOKE AND ASHES
0-7564-0415-4 $7.99

To Order Call: 1-800-788-6262
www.dawbooks.com